*The Daughters
of Danaus*

The Daughters
of Danaus

Mona Caird
Afterword by Margaret Morganroth Gullette

THE FEMINIST PRESS
at The City University of New York
New York

Afterword © 1989 by Margaret Morganroth Gullette
All rights reserved
Published 1989 by The Feminist Press at The City University
of New York, 311 East 94 Street, New York, N.Y. 10128
Distributed by The Talman Company, 150 Fifth Avenue, New York,
N.Y. 10011

93 92 91 90 89 5 4 3 2 1

The Daughters of Danaus was first published in 1894 in London by
Bliss, Sands, and Foster.

Library of Congress Cataloging-in-Publication Data

The daughters of Danaus / Mona Caird; afterword by Margaret
Morganroth Gullette.
   p. cm.
   "First published in 1894 in London by Bliss, Sands, and Foster"—
T.p. verso
   Bibliography: p.
   ISBN 1-55861-014-6: $29.95. — ISBN 1-55861-015-4: $11.95 (pbk.)
   I. Gullette, Margaret Morganroth. II. Title.
PR6005.A245D38   1989
823'.912—dc20   89-11627
                                                              CIP

This publication is made possible, in part, by a grant from the New
York State Council on the Arts.

The Feminist Press at The City University of New York gratefully
acknowledges the assistance of Johnnetta B. Cole, James T. Laney,
Ann Matheson, the Emory University Library, and the National
Library of Scotland in the publication of this book.

Front cover art: *Miss Berthe* (1901), oil on canvas, by Cecilia Beaux.
Reproduced by permission of Radcliffe College
Back cover photo: Mona Caird, c. 1899

Printed in the United States on acid-free paper by McNaughton &
Gunn, Inc.

CONTENTS

THE DAUGHTERS OF DANAUS

CHAPTER I.

I T was only just light enough to discern the five human
forms in the dimness of the garret; the rays of the moon
having to find their way through the deep window-embrasures
of the keep. Less illumination would have sufficed to disclose
the ancient character of the garret, with its low ceiling, and
the graduated mouldings of the cornice, giving the effect of a
shallow dome. The house stood obviously very high, for one
could see from the windows for miles over a bleak country,
coldly lit by the rays of the moon, which was almost at the
full. Into the half light stole presently the sound of some
lively instrument : a reel tune played, as it were, beneath one's
breath, but with all the revel and rollicking emphasis of that
intoxicating primitive music. And then in correspondingly
low relief, but with no less emphasis, the occupants of this
singular ball-room began to dance. One might have fancied
them some midnight company of the dead, risen from their
graves for this secret revelry, so strange was the appearance of
the moving figures, with the moonlight catching, as they passed,
the faces or the hands. They danced excellently well, as to the
manner born, tripping in and out among the shadows, with
occasional stamping, in time to the music, and now and again
that wild Celtic shout or cry that sets the nerves athrill. In
spite of the whole scene's being enacted in a low key, it seemed

5

only to gain in intensity from that circumstance, and in fantastic effect.

Among the dancers was one who danced with peculiar spirit and brilliancy, and her little cry had a ring and a wildness that never failed to set the others going with new inspiration.

She was a slight, dark-haired girl, with a pale, rather mysterious face, and large eyes. Not a word was spoken, and the reel went on for nearly ten minutes. At length the girl with the dark hair gave a final shout, and broke away from the circle.

With her desertion the dance flagged, and presently came to an end. The first breaking of the silence gave a slight shock, in spite of the subdued tones of the speaker.

" It is no use trying to dance a reel without Hadria," said a tall youth, evidently her brother, if one might judge from his almost southern colouring and melancholy eyes. In build and feature he resembled the elder sister, Algitha, who had all the characteristics of a fine northern race.

"Old Maggie said the other day, that Hadria's dancing of the reel was no 'right canny,'" Algitha observed, in the same low tone that all the occupants of the garret instinctively adopted.

"Ah !" cried Fred, "old Maggie has always looked upon Hadria as half bewitched since that night when she found her here 'a wee bit bairn,' as she says, at this very window, in her nightshirt, standing on tiptoe to see the moonlight."

" It frightened the poor old thing out of her wits, of course," said Algitha, who was leaning with crossed arms, in a corner of the deep-set window. The fine outlines of face and form were shewn in the strange light, as in a boldly-executed sketch, without detail. Pride and determination were the dominant qualities so indicated. Her sister stood opposite, the moonshine making the smooth pallor of her face more striking, and emphasizing its mysterious quality.

The whole group of young faces, crowded together by the

window, and lit up by the unsympathetic light, had something characteristic and unusual in its aspect, that might have excited curiosity.

"Tell us the story of the garret, Hadria," said Austin, the youngest brother, a handsome boy of twelve, with curling brown hair and blue eyes.

"Hadria has told it hundreds of times, and you know it as well as she does."

"But I want to hear it again—about the attack upon the keep, and the shouting of the men, while the lady was up here starving to death."

But Algitha shook her head.

"We don't come up here to tell stories, we must get to business."

"Will you have the candle, or can you see?" asked Fred, the second brother, a couple of years younger than Hadria, whom he addressed. His features were irregular; his short nose and twinkling grey eyes suggesting a joyous and whimsical temperament.

"I think I had better have the candle; my notes are very illegible."

Fred drew forth a candle-end from his pocket, stuck it into a quaint-looking stand of antique steel, much eaten with rust, and set the candle-end alight.

Algitha went into the next room and brought in a couple of chairs. Fred followed her example till there were enough for the party. They all took their places, and Hadria, who had been provided with a seat facing them, and with a rickety wooden table that trembled responsively to her slightest movement, laid down her notes and surveyed her audience. The faces stood out strangely, in the lights and shadows of the garret.

"Ladies and gentlemen," she began; "on the last occasion on which the Preposterous Society held its meeting, we had the pleasure of listening to an able lecture on 'Character' by our respected member Demogorgon" (the speaker bowed to

Ernest, and the audience applauded). "My address to-night on 'Fate' is designed to contribute further ideas to this fascinating subject, and to pursue the enquiry more curiously."

The audience murmured approval.

"We were left at loggerheads, at the end of the last debate. I doubted Demogorgon's conclusion, while admiring his eloquence. To-night, I will put before you the view exactly contrary to his. I do not assert that I hold this contrary view, but I state it as well as I am able, because I think that it has not been given due consideration."

"This will be warm," Fred was heard to murmur with a chuckle, to an adjacent sister. The speaker looked at her notes.

"I will read," she said, "a passage from Emerson, which states very strikingly the doctrine that I am going to oppose."

Hadria held her paper aslant towards the candle-end, which threw a murky yellow light upon the background of the garret, contrasting oddly with the thin, clear moonbeams.

"'But the soul contains the event that shall befall it, for the event is only the actualization of its thoughts; and what we pray to ourselves for is always granted. The event is the print of your form. It fits you like your skin. What each does is proper to him. Events are the children of his mind and body.'"

Algitha leant forward. The members of the Preposterous Society settled into attitudes of attention.

Hadria said that this was a question that could not fail to be of peculiar interest to them all, who had their lives before thèm, to make or mar. It was an extremely difficult question, for it admitted of no experiment. One could never go back in life and try another plan. One could never make sure, by such a test, how much circumstance and how much innate ideas had to do with one's disposition. Emerson insisted that man makes his circumstance, and history seemed to support that theory. How untoward had been, in appearance, the surroundings of those who had made all the great movements and done all the great deeds of the world. Let one consider the poverty, persecution, the incessant discouragement, and often the tragic end of our greatest benefactors. Christ was but one of the host of the crucified. In spite of the theory which the lecturer had undertaken to champion, she believed that it was generally those people who had difficult lives who did the beneficent deeds, and generally those people who were encouraged and comfortable who went to sleep, or actively dragged down what the thinkers and actors had piled up. In great things and in small, such was the order of life.

"Hear, hear," cried Ernest, "my particular thunder!"

"Wait a minute," said the lecturer. "I am going to annihilate you with your particular thunder." She paused for a moment, and her eyes rested on the strange white landscape beyond the little group of faces upturned towards her.

"Roughly, we may say that people are divided into two orders : first, the organizers, the able, those who build, who create cohesion, symmetry, reason, economy; and, secondly, the destroyers, those who come wandering idly by, and unfasten, undo, relax, disintegrate all that has been effected by the force and vigilance of their betters. This distinction is carried into even the most trivial things of life. Yet without that organization and coherence, the existence of the destroyers themselves would become a chaos and a misery."

The oak table over which Hadria bent forward towards her audience, appeared to be applauding this sentiment vigorously. It rocked to and fro on the uneven floor with great clamour.

"Thus," the speaker went on, "these relaxed and derivative people are living on the strength of the strong. He who is strong must carry with him, as a perpetual burden, a mass of such pensioners, who are scared and shocked at his rude individuality; and if he should trip or stumble, if he should lose his way in the untrodden paths, in seeking new truth and a broader foundation for the lives of men, then a chorus of censure goes up from millions of little throats."

"Hear, hear!" cried Algitha and Fred, and the table rocked enthusiastically.

"But when the good things are gained for which the upholders have striven and perhaps given their lives, then there are no more greedy absorbers of the bounty than these same innumerable little throats."

The table led the chorus of assent.

"And now," said the lecturer slowly, "consider this in relation to the point at issue. Emerson asserts that circumstance can always be conquered. But is not circumstance, to a large extent, created by these destroyers, as I have called them? Has not the strongest soul to count with these, who weave the web of adverse conditions, whose dead weight has to be carried, whose work of destruction has to be incessantly repaired? Who can dare to say 'I am master of my fate,' when he does not know how large may be the share of the general burden that will fall to him to drag through life, how great may be the number of these parasites who are living on the moral capital of their generation? Surely circumstance consists largely in the inertia, the impenetrability of the destroyers."

Ernest shewed signs of restiveness. He shuffled on his chair, made muttered exclamations.

"Presently," said the lecturer reassuringly.

"Or put it in another way," she went on. "A man may make a thing—circumstance included—but he is not a sort of moral spider; he can't spin it out of his own inside. *He wants something to make it of.* The formative force comes from within, but he must have material, just as much as a sculptor must have his marble before he can shape his statue. There is a subtle relation between character and conditions, and it is this *relation* that determines Fate. Fate is as the statue of the sculptor."

"That's where Hadria mainly differs from you," said Fred, "you make the thing absolute; Hadria makes it a matter of relation."

"Exactly," assented the lecturer, catching the remark.

"Difficulties need not be really obstructive to the best development of a character or a power, nor a smooth path always favourable. Obstacles may be of a kind to stimulate one person and to annihilate another. It is *not* a question of relative strength between character and circumstance, as people are so fond of asserting. That is mere gibberish. It means nothing. The two things cannot be compared, for they are not of the same nature. They can't be reduced to a common denominator."

Austin appreciated this illustration, being head of his class for arithmetic.

"We shall never be able to take a reasonable view of this question till we get rid of that ridiculous phrase, '*If the soul is strong enough, it can overcome circumstance.*' In a room filled with carbonic acid instead of ordinary air, a giant would succumb as quickly as a dwarf, and his strength would avail him nothing. Indeed, if there is a difference, it is in favour of the dwarf."

Ernest frowned. This was all high treason against his favourite author. He had given his sister a copy of Emerson's works last Christmas, in the hope that her views might be enlightened, and *this* was the disgraceful use she made of it!

"Finally," said Hadria, smiling defiantly at her brother, "let us put the question shortly thus: Given (say) great artistic power, given also a conscience and a strong will, is there any combination of circumstances which might prevent the artistic power (assuming it to be of the highest order and strength) from developing and displaying itself, so as to meet with general recognition?"

"No," asserted Ernest, and there was a hesitating chorus on his side.

"There seem to me to be a thousand chances against it," Hadria continued. "Artistic power, to begin with, is a sort of weakness in relation to the everyday world, and so, in some respects, is a nice conscience. I think Emerson is shockingly unjust. His beaming optimism is a worship of success disguised under lofty terms. There is nothing to prove that thousands have not been swamped by maladjustment of character to circumstance, and I would even go so far as to suggest that perhaps the very greatest of all are those whom the world has never known, because the present conditions are inharmonious with the very noblest and the very highest qualities."

No sooner was the last word uttered than the garret became the scene of the stormiest debate that had ever been recorded in the annals of the Preposterous Society, an institution that had lately celebrated its fifth anniversary. Hadria, fired by opposition, declared that the success of great people was due not simply to their greatness, but to some smaller and commoner quality which brought them in touch with the majority, and so gave their greatness a chance.

At this, there was such a howl of indignation that Algitha remonstrated.

" We shall be heard, if you don't take care," she warned.

" My dear Algitha, there are a dozen empty rooms between us and the inhabited part of the house, not to mention the fact that we are a storey above everyone except the ghosts, so I think you may compose yourself."

However, the excited voices were hushed a little as the discussion continued. One of the chief charms of the institution, in the eyes of the members of the Society, was its secrecy. The family, though united by ties of warm affection to their parents, did not look for encouragement from them in this direction. Mr. Fullerton was too exclusively scientific in his bent of thought, to sympathize with the kind of speculation in which his children delighted, while their mother looked with mingled pride and alarm at these outbreaks of individuality on the part of her daughters, for whom she craved the honours of the social world. In this out-of-the-way district, society smiled upon conformity, and glared vindictively at the faintest sign of spontaneous thinking. Cleverness of execution, as in music, tennis, drawing, was forgiven, even commended;

but originality, though of the mildest sort, created the same agonizing disturbance in the select circle, as the sight of a crucifix is wont to produce upon the father of Evil. Yet by some freak of fortune, the whole family at Dunaghee had shewn obstinate symptoms of individuality from their childhood, and, what was more distressing, the worst cases occurred in the girls.

In the debate just recorded, that took place on Algitha's twenty-second birthday, Ernest had been Hadria's principal opponent, but the others had also taken the field against her.

"You have the easier cause to champion," she said, when there was a momentary lull, "for all your evidences can be pointed to and counted; whereas mine, poor things—pale hypotheses, nameless peradventures—lie in forgotten churchyards—unthought of, unthanked, untrumpeted, and all their tragedy is lost in the everlasting silence."

"You will never make people believe in what *might* have been," said Algitha.

"I don't expect to." Hadria was standing by the window looking out over the glimmering fields and the shrouded white hills. "Life is as white and as unsympathetic as this," she said dreamily. "We just dance our reel in our garret, and then it is all over; and whether we do the steps as our fancy would have them, or a little otherwise, because of the uneven floor, or tired feet, or for lack of chance to learn the steps— heavens and earth, what does it matter?"

"Hadria!" exclaimed an astonished chorus.

The sentiment was so entirely unlike any that the ardent President of the Society had ever been known to express before, that brothers and sisters crowded up to enquire into the cause of the unusual mood.

"Oh, it is only the moonlight that has got into my head," she said, flinging back the cloudy black hair from her brow.

Algitha's firm, clear voice vibrated through the room.

"But I think it matters very much whether one's task is done well or ill," she said, "and nobody has taught me to wish to make solid use of my life so much as you have, Hadria.   What possesses you to-night ? "

" I tell you, the moonlight."

" And something else."

" Well, it struck me, as I stood there with my head full of what we have been discussing, that the conditions of a girl's life of our own class are pleasant enough, but they are stifling, absolutely *stifling;* and not all the Emersons in the world will convince me to the contrary.   Emerson never was a girl ! "

There was a laugh.

" No ; but he was a great man," said Ernest.

" Then he must have had something of the girl in him ! " cried Hadria.

" I didn't mean that, but perhaps it is true."

" If he had been a girl, he would have known that conditions *do* count hideously in one's life.   I think that there are more ' destroyers ' to be carried about and pampered in this department of existence than in any other (material conditions being equal)."

" Do you mean that a girl would have more difficulty in bringing her power to maturity and getting it recognized than a man would have ? " asked Fred.

" Yes ; the odds are too heavy."

" A second-rate talent perhaps," Ernest admitted, " but not a really big one."

" I should exactly reverse that statement," said Hadria. " The greater the power and the finer its quality, the greater the inharmony between the nature and the conditions ; therefore the more powerful the leverage against it.   A small comfortable talent might hold its own, where a larger one would succumb.   That is where I think you make your big mistake, in forgetting that the greatness of the power may serve to make the greatness of the obstacles."

" So much the better for me then," said Algitha, with a touch of satire ; " for I have no idea of being beaten."   She folded her arms in a serene attitude of determination.

"Surely it only wants a little force of will to enable you to occupy your life in the manner you think best," said Ernest.

"That is often impossible for a girl, because prejudice and custom are against her."

"But she ought to despise prejudice and custom," cried the brother, nobly.

"So she often would; but then she has to tear through so many living ties that restrain her freedom."

Algitha drew herself up. "If one is unjustly restrained," she said, "it is perfectly right to brave the infliction of the sort of pain that people feel only because they unfairly object to one's liberty of action."

"But what a frightful piece of circumstance *that* is to encounter," cried Hadria, "to have to buy the mere right to one's liberty by cutting through prejudices that are twined in with the very heart-strings of those one loves! Ah! *that* particular obstacle has held many a woman helpless and suffering, like some wretched insect pinned alive to a board throughout a miserable lifetime! What would Emerson say to these cases? That 'Nature magically suits the man to his fortunes by making these the fruit of his character'? Pooh! I think Nature more often makes a man's fortunes a veritable shirt of Nessus which burns and clings, and finally kills him with anguish!"

CHAPTER II.

ONCE more the old stronghold of Dunaghee, inured for centuries to the changes of the elements, received the day's greeting. The hues of dawn tinged the broad hill pastures, or "airds," as they were called, round about the Tower of the Winds. No one was abroad yet in the silent lands, except perhaps a shepherd, tending his flock. The little farmstead of Craw Gill, that lay at a distance of about a couple of miles down the valley, on the side of a ravine, was apparently dead asleep. Cruachmore, the nearest upland farm, could scarcely be seen from the stronghold. The old tower had been added to, perhaps two hundred years ago; a rectangular block projecting from the corner of the original building, and then a second erection at right angles to the first, so as to form three sides of an irregular courtyard. This arrangement afforded some shelter from the winds which seldom ceased to blow in these high regions. The spot had borne the same reputation for centuries, as the name of the old tower implied.

The Tower of the Winds stood desolately, in the midst of a wide-eyed agricultural country, and was approached only by a sort of farm track that ran up hill and down dale, in a most erratic course, to the distant main road.

The country was not mountainous, though it lay in a northern district of Scotland; it was bleak and solitary, with vast bare fields of grass or corn; and below in the valley, a river that rushed sweeping over its rough bed, silent where it ran deep, but chattering busily in the shallows. Here was verdure to one's heart's content; the whole country being a

singular mixture of bleakness on the heights, and woodland
richness in the valleys; bitterly cold in the winter months,
when the light deserted the uplands ridiculously early in the
afternoon, leaving long mysterious hours that held the great
silent stretches of field and hillside in shadow; a circumstance,
which had, perhaps, not been without its influence in the
forming of Hadria's character. She, more than the others,
seemed to have absorbed the spirit of the northern twilights.
It was her custom to wander alone over the broad spaces of
the hills, watching the sun set behind them, the homeward
flight of the birds, the approach of darkness and the rising of
the stars. Every instinct that was born in her with her Celtic
blood—which lurked still in the family to the confounding of
its fortunes—was fostered by the mystery and wildness of her
surroundings.

Dawn and sunset had peculiar attractions for her.

Although the Preposterous Society had not separated until
unusually late on the previous night, the President was up
and abroad on this exquisite morning, summoned by some
" message of range and of sweep——" to the flushing stretches
of pasture and the windy hillside.

In spite of the view that Hadria had expounded in her
capacity of lecturer, she had an inner sense that somehow,
after all, the will *can* perform astonishing feats in Fate's
despite. Her intellect, rather than her heart, had opposed the
philosophy of Emerson. Her sentiment recoiled from admitting the possibility of such tragedy as her expressed belief
implied. This morning, the wonder and the grandeur of the
dawn supplied arguments to faith. If the best in human
nature were always to be hunted down and extinguished, if the
efforts to rise in the scale of being, to bring gifts instead of
merely absorbing benefits, were only by a rare combination of
chances to escape the doom of annihilation, where was one to
turn to for hope, or for a motive for effort? How could one
reconcile the marvellous beauty of the universe, the miracles
of colour, form, and, above all, of music, with such a chaotic

moral condition, and such unlovely laws in favour of dulness, cowardice, callousness, cruelty? One aspired to be an upholder and not a destroyer, but if it were a useless pain and a bootless venture——?

Hadria tried to find some proof of the happier philosophy that would satisfy her intellect, but it refused to be comforted. Yet as she wandered in the rosy light over the awakening fields, her heart sang within her. The world was exquisite, life was a rapture!

She could take existence in her hands and form and fashion it at her will, obviously, easily; her strength yearned for the task.

Yet all the time, the importunate intellect kept insisting that feeling was deceptive, that health and youth and the freshness of the morning spoke in her, and not reason or experience. Feeling was left untouched nevertheless. It was impossible to stifle the voices that prophesied golden things. Life was all before her; she was full of vigour and longing and good will; the world stretched forth as a fair territory, with magical pathways leading up to dizzy mountain tops. With visions such as these, the members of the Preposterous Society had fired their imaginations, and gained impetus for their various efforts and their various ambitions.

Hadria had been among the most hopeful of the party, and had pointed to the loftier visions, and the more impersonal aims. Circumstance must give way, compromise was wrong; we had but a short time in this world, and mere details and prejudices must not be allowed to interfere with one's right to live to the utmost of one's scope. But it was easier to state a law than to obey it; easier to inspire others with faith than to hold fast to it oneself.

The time for taking matters in one's own hands had scarcely come. A girl was so helpless, so tied by custom. One could engage, so far, only in guerilla warfare with the enemy, who lurked everywhere in ambush, ready to harass the wayfarers with incessant petty attack. But life *must* have something more to offer than this—life with its myriad interests, dramas, mysteries, arts, poetries, delights!

By the river, where it had worn for itself a narrow ravine, with steep rocky sides or "clints," as they were called, several short tunnels or passages had been cut in places where the rock projected as far as the bank of the river, which was followed in its windings by a narrow footway, leading to the farmstead of Craw Gill.

In one part, a series of such tunnels, with intervals of open pathway, occurred in picturesque fashion, causing a singular effect of light and shade.

As Hadria stood admiring the glow of the now fully-risen sun, upon the wall of rock that rose beyond the opening of the tunnel which she had just passed through, she heard footsteps advancing along the riverside path, and guessed that Algitha and Ernest had come to fetch her, or to join in any absurd project that she might have in view. Although Algitha was two-and-twenty, and Hadria only a year younger, they were still guilty at times of wild escapades, with the connivance of their brothers. Walks or rides at sunrise were ordinary occurrences in the family, and in summer, bathing in the river was a favourite amusement.

"I thought I recognised your footsteps," said Hadria, as the two figures appeared at the mouth of the tunnel, the low rays of the sun lighting them up, for a moment, as they turned the sharp bend of the narrow path, before entering the shadow.

A quantity of brown dead leaves were strewn upon the floor of the rock-passage, blown in by the wind from the pathway at each end, or perhaps through the opening in the middle of the tunnel that looked out upon the rushing river.

A willow-tree had found footing in the crevice of the rock just outside, and its branches, thinly decked with pale yellow leaves, dipped into the water just in front of the opening. When the wind blew off the river it would sweep the leaves of the willow into the tunnel.

"Let's make a bonfire," suggested Ernest.

They collected the withered harvest of the winds upon the cavern floor, in a big brown heap, and then Ernest struck a match and set light to it. Algitha, in a large black cloak, stood over it with a hazel stick—like a wand—stirring and heaping on the fuel, as the mass began to smoulder and to send forth a thick white smoke that gradually filled the cavern, curling up into the rocky roof and swirling round and out by the square-cut mouth, to be caught there by the slight wind and illumined by the sun, which poured down upon the soft coils of the smoke, in so strange a fashion, as to call forth a cry of wonder from the onlookers. Standing in the interval of open pathway between the two rock-passages, and looking back at the fire-lit cavern, with its black shadows and flickering flame-colours, Hadria was bewildered by what appeared to her a veritable magic vision, beautiful beyond anything that she had ever met in dream. She stood still to watch, with a real momentary doubt as to whether she were awake.

The figures, stooping over the burning heap, moved occasionally across the darkness, looking like a witch and her familiar spirit, who were conjuring, by uncanny arts, a vision of life, on the strange, white, clean-cut patch of smoke that was defined by the sunlit entrance to the tunnel. The witch stirred, and her familiar added fuel, while behind them the smoke, rising and curdling, formed the mysterious background of light: opaque, and yet in a state of incessant movement, as of some white raging fire, thinner and more deadly than any ordinary earthly element, that seemed to sicken and flicker in the blast of a furnace, and then rushed upwards, and coiled and rolled across the tunnel's mouth. Presently, as a puff of wind swept away part of the smoke, a miraculous tinge of rosy colour appeared, changing, as one caught it, into gold, and presently to a milky blue, then liquid green, and a thousand intermediate tints corresponding to the altering density of the smoke—and then! Hadria caught her breath — the blue and the red and the gold melted and moved and formed, under the incantation, into a marvellous vision of distant lands, purple mountains, fair white cities, and wide kingdoms, so many, so great, that the imagination staggered at the vastness revealed, and offered, as it seemed, to him who could grasp and perceive it. Among those blue deeps and faint innumerable mountain-tops, caught through a soft mist that continually moved and lifted, thinned and thickened, with changing tints, all the secrets, all the hopes, all the powers and splendours, of life lay hidden; and the beauty of the vision was as the essence of poetry and of music—of all that is lovely in the world of art, and in the world of the emotions. The question that had been debated so hotly and so often, as to the relation of the good and the beautiful, art and ethics, seemed to be answered by this bewildering revelation of sunlit smoke, playing across the face of a purple-tinted rock, and a few feet of grass-edged pathway.

"Come and see what visions you have conjured up, O witch!" cried Hadria.

Algitha gave a startled exclamation, as the smoke thinned and revealed that bewildering glimpse of distant lands, half seen, as through the atmosphere of a dream. An exquisite city, with slender towers and temples, flashed, for a moment, through the mist curtain.

"If life is like that," she said at length, drawing a long breath, "nothing on this earth ought to persuade us to forego it; no one has the right to hold one back from its possession."

"No one," said Hadria; "but everyone will try!"

"Let them try," returned Algitha defiantly.

CHAPTER III.

ERNEST and his two sisters walked homeward along the banks of the river, and thence up by a winding path to the top of the cliffs. It was mild weather, and they decided to pause in the little temple of classic design, which some ancient owner of the Drumgarran estate, touched with a desire for the exquisiteness of Greek outline, had built on a promontory of the rocks, among rounded masses of wild foliage ; a spot that commanded one of the most beautiful reaches of the river. The scene had something of classic perfection and serenity.

"I admit," said Ernest in response to some remark of one of his sisters, "I admit that I should not like to stay here during all the best years of my life, without prospect of widening my experience; only as a matter of fact, the world is somewhat different from anything that you imagine, and by no means would you find it all beer and skittles. Your smoke and sun-vision is not to be trusted."

"But think of the pride and joy of being able to speak in that tone of experience !" exclaimed Hadria mockingly.

"One has to pay for experience," said Ernest, shaking his head and ignoring her taunt.

"I think one has to pay more heavily for *in*experience," she said.

"Not if one never comes in contact with the world. Girls are protected from the realities of life so long as they remain at home, and that is worth something after all."

Algitha snorted. "I don't know what you are pleased to call realities, my dear Ernest, but I can assure you there are plenty of unpleasant facts, in this protected life of ours."

"Nobody can expect to escape unpleasant facts," said Ernest.

"Then for heaven's sake, let us purchase with them something worth having!" Hadria cried.

"Hear, hear!" assented Algitha.

"Unpleasant facts being a foregone conclusion," Hadria added, "the point to aim at obviously is *interesting* facts—and plenty of them."

Ernest flicked a pebble off the parapet of the balustrade of the little temple, and watched it fall, with a silent splash, into the river.

"I never met girls before, who wanted to come out of their cotton-wool," he observed. "I thought girls loved cotton-wool. They always seem to."

"Girls *seem* an astonishing number of things that they are not," said Hadria, "especially to men. A poor benighted man might as well try to get on to confidential terms with the Sphinx, as to learn the real thoughts and wishes of a girl."

"You two are exceptional, you see," said Ernest.

"Oh, *everybody's* exceptional, if you only knew it!" exclaimed his sister. "Girls," she went on to assert, "are stuffed with certain stereotyped sentiments from their infancy, and when that painful process is completed, intelligent philosophers come and smile upon the victims, and point to them as proofs of the intentions of Nature regarding our sex, admirable examples of the unvarying instincts of the feminine creature. In fact," Hadria added with a laugh, "it's as if the trainer of that troop of performing poodles that we saw, the other day, at Ballochcoil, were to assure the spectators that the amiable animals were inspired, from birth, by a heaven-implanted yearning to jump through hoops, and walk about on their hind legs——"

"But there *are* such things as natural instincts," said Ernest.

"There *are* such things as acquired tricks," returned Hadria.

A loud shout, accompanied by the barking of several dogs, announced the approach of the two younger boys. Boys and dogs had been taking their morning bath in the river.

"You have broken in upon a most interesting discourse," said Ernest. "Hadria was really coming out."

This led to a general uproar.

When peace was restored, the conversation went on in desultory fashion. Ernest and Hadria fell apart into a more serious talk. These two had always been "chums," from the time when they used to play at building houses of bricks on the nursery floor. There was deep and true affection between them.

The day broke into splendour, and the warm rays, rounding the edge of the eastward rock, poured straight into the little temple. Below and around on the cliff-sides, the rich foliage of holly and dwarf oak, ivy, and rowan with its burning berries, was transformed into a mass of warm colour and shining surfaces.

"What always bewilders me," Hadria said, bending over the balustrade among the ivy, "is the enormous gulf between what *might be* and what *is* in human life. Look at the world —life's most sumptuous stage—and look at life! The one, splendid, exquisite, varied, generous, rich beyond description; the other, poor, thin, dull, monotonous, niggard, distressful —is that necessary?"

"But all lives are not like that," objected Fred.

"I speak only from my own narrow experience," said Hadria.

"Oh, she is thinking, as usual, of that unfortunate Mrs. Gordon!" cried Earnest.

"Of her, and the rest of the average, typical sort of people that I know," Hadria admitted. "I wish to heaven I had a wider knowledge to speak from."

"If one is to believe what one hears and reads," said Algitha, "life must be full of sorrow indeed."

"But putting aside the big sorrows," said her sister, "the

ordinary every day existence that would be called prosperous, seems to me to be dull and stupid to a tragic extent."

"The Gordons of Drumgarran once more! I confess I can't see anything particularly tragic there," observed Fred, whose memory recalled troops of stalwart young persons in flannels, engaged for hours, in sending a ball from one side of a net to the other.

"It is more than tragic ; it is disgusting!" cried Hadria with a shiver. Algitha drew herself together. She turned to her eldest brother.

"Look here, Ernest ; you said just now that girls were shielded from the realities of life. Yet Mrs. Gordon was handed over by her protectors, when she was little more than a school-girl, without knowledge, without any sort of resource or power of facing destiny, to—well, to the hateful realities of the life that she has led now for over twenty years. There is nothing to win general sympathy in this case, for Mr. Gordon is good and kind ; but oh, think of the existence that a 'protected,' carefully brought-up girl may be launched into, before she knows what she is pledged to, or what her ideas of life may be ! If *that* is what you call protection, for heaven's sake let us remain defenceless."

Fred and Ernest accused their elder sister of having been converted by Hadria. Algitha, honest and courageous in big things and in small, at once acknowledged the source of her ideas. Not so long ago, Algitha had differed from the daughters of the neighbouring houses, rather in force of character than in sentiment.

She had followed the usual aims with unusual success, giving unalloyed satisfaction to her proud mother. Algitha had taken it as a matter of course that she would some day marry, and have a house of her own to reign in. A home, not a husband, was the important matter, and Algitha had trusted to her attractions to make a good marriage ; that is, to obtain extensive regions for her activities. She craved a roomy stage for her drama, and obviously there was only one method of

obtaining it, and even that method was but dubious. But
Hadria had undermined this matter of fact, take-things-as-you-
find-them view, and set her sister's pride on the track. That
master-passion once aroused in the new direction, Algitha was
ready to defend her dignity as a woman, and as a human being,
to the death. Hadria felt as a magician might feel, who has
conjured up spirits henceforth beyond his control; for obviously, her sister's whole life would be altered by this change
of sentiment, and, alas, her mother's hopes must be disappointed. The laird of Clarenoc—a fine property, of which
Algitha might have been mistress—had received polite
discouragement, much to his surprise and that of the neighbourhood. Even Ernest, who was by no means worldly,
questioned the wisdom of his sister's decision; for the laird
of Clarenoc was a good fellow, and after all, let them talk as
they liked, what was to become of a girl unless she married?
This morning's conversation therefore touched closely on
burning topics.

"Mrs. Gordon's people meant it for the best, I suppose,"
Ernest observed, "when they married her to a good man with
a fine property."

"That is just the ghastly part of it!" cried Hadria; "from
ferocious enemies a girl might defend herself, but what is she
to do against the united efforts of devoted friends?"

"I don't suppose Mrs. Gordon is aware that she is so
ill-used!"

"Another gruesome circumstance!" cried Hadria, with a
half laugh; "for that only proves that her life has dulled her
self-respect, and destroyed her pride."

"But, my dear, every woman is in the same predicament,
if predicament it be!"

"What a consolation!" Hadria exclaimed, "*all* the foxes
have lost their tails!"

"It may be illogical, but people generally are immensely
comforted by that circumstance."

The conversation waxed warmer and more personal. Fred

took a conservative view of the question. He thought that there were instincts implanted by Nature, which inspired Mrs. Gordon with a yearning for exactly the sort of existence that fate had assigned to her. Algitha, who had been the recipient of that lady's tragic confidences, broke into a shout of laughter.

"Well, Harold Wilkins says ——"

This name was also greeted with a yell of derision.

"I don't see why you girls always scoff so at Harold Wilkins," said Fred, slightly aggrieved, "he is generally thought a lot of by girls. All Mrs. Gordon's sisters adore him."

"He needs no further worshippers," said Hadria.

Fred was asked to repeat the words of Harold Wilkins, but to soften them down if too severe.

"He laughs at your pet ideas," said Fred ruthlessly.

"Break it gently, Fred, gently."

"He thinks that a true woman esteems it her highest privilege to—well, to be like Mrs. Gordon."

"Wise and learned youth!" cried Hadria, resting her chin on her hand, and peering up into the blue sky, above the temple.

"*Fool!*" exclaimed Algitha.

"He says," continued Fred, determined not to spare those who were so overbearing in their scorn, "he says that girls who have ideas like yours will never get any fellow to marry them."

Laughter loud and long greeted this announcement.

"Laughter," observed Fred, when he could make himself heard, "is among the simplest forms of argument. Does this merry outburst imply that you don't care a button whether you are able to get some one to marry you or not?"

"It does," said Algitha.

"Well, so I said to Wilkins, as a matter of fact, with my nose in the air, on your behalf, and Wilkins replied, 'Oh, it's all very well while girls are young and good-looking to be so

high and mighty, but some day, when they are left out in the
cold, and all their friends married, they may sing a different
tune.' Feeling there was something in this remark," Fred
continued, "I raised my nose two inches higher, and adopted
the argument that *I* also resort to *in extremis.* I laughed.
'Well, my dear fellow,' Wilkins observed calmly, 'I mean no
offence, but what on earth is a girl to do with herself if she
doesn't marry?'"

"What did you reply?" asked Ernest with curiosity.

"Oh, I said that was an unimportant detail, and changed
the subject."

Algitha was still scornful, but Hadria looked meditative.

"Harold Wilkins has a practical mind," she observed.
"After all, he is right, when you come to consider it."

"*Hadria!*" remonstrated her sister, in dismay.

"We may as well be candid," said Hadria. "There *is*
uncommonly little that a girl can do (or rather that people
will let her do) unless she marries, and that is why she so often
does marry as a mere matter of business. But I wish Harold
Wilkins would remember that fact, instead of insisting that
it is our inherent and particular nature that urges us, one and
all, to the career of Mrs. Gordon."

Algitha was obviously growing more and more ruffled.
Fred tried in vain to soothe her feelings. He joked, but she
refused to see the point. She would not admit that Harold
Wilkins had facts on his side.

"If one simply made up one's mind to walk through all
the hampering circumstances, who or what could stop one?"
she asked.

"Algitha has evidently got some desperate plan in her head
for making mincemeat of circumstances," cried Fred, little
guessing that he had stated the exact truth.

"Do you remember that Mrs. Gordon herself waged a
losing battle in early days, incredible as it may appear?"
asked Hadria.

Algitha nodded slowly, her eyes fixed on the ground.

"She did not originally set out with the idea of being a sort of amiable cow. She once aspired to be quite human ; she really did, poor thing ! "

"Then why didn't she do it?" asked Algitha contemptuously.

"Instead of *doing* a thing, she had to be perpetually struggling for the chance to do it, which she never achieved, and so she was submerged. That seems to be the fatality in a woman's life."

"Well, there is one thing I am very sure of," announced Algitha, leaning majestically against a column of the temple, and looking like a beautiful Greek maiden, in her simple gown, "I do not intend to be a cow. I do not mean to fight a losing battle. I will not wait at home meekly, till some fool holds out his sceptre to me."

All eyes turned to her, in astonishment.

"But what are you going to do?" asked a chorus of voices. Hadria's was not among them, for she knew what was coming. The debate of last night, and this morning's discussion, had evidently brought to a climax a project that Algitha had long had in her mind, but had hesitated to carry out, on account of the distress that it would cause to her mother. Algitha's eyes glittered, and her colour rose.

"I am not going to be hawked about the county till I am disposed of. It does not console me in the least, that *all* the foxes are without tails," she went on, taking short cuts to her meaning, in her excitement. "I am going to London with Mrs. Trevelyan, to help her in her work."

"By *Jove!*" exclaimed Fred. Ernest whistled. Austin stared, with open mouth.

Having recovered from the first shock of surprise, the family plied their sister with questions. She said that she had long been thinking of accepting the post offered her by Mrs. Trevelyan last year, and now she was resolved. The work was really wise, useful work among the poor, which Algitha felt she could do well. At home, there was nothing that she did that the housekeeper could not do better. She felt herself fretting and growing irritable, for mere want of some active employment. This was utterly absurd, in an overworked world. Hadria had her music and her study, at any rate, but Algitha had nothing that seemed worth doing; she did not. care to paint indifferently on china; she was a mere encumbrance—a destroyer, as Hadria put it—while there was so much, so very much, that waited to be done. The younger sister made no comment.

"Next time I meet Harold Wilkins," said Fred, drawing a long breath, "I will tell him that if a girl does not marry, she can devote herself to the poor."

"Or that she can remain to be the family consolation, eh, Hadria? By Jove, what a row there will be!"

The notion of Hadria in the capacity of the family consolation, created a shout of laughter. It had always been her function to upset foregone conclusions, overturn orthodox views, and generally disturb the conformity of the family attitude. Now the sedate and established qualities would be expected of her. Hadria must be the stay and hope of the house!

Fred continued to chuckle, at intervals, over the idea.

"It *does* seem to indicate rather a broken-down family!" said Ernest.

"I wish one of you boys would undertake the position instead of laughing at *me*," exclaimed Hadria in mock resentment. "I wish *you* would go to eternal tennis-parties, and pay calls, and bills, and write notes, and do little useless necessary things, more or less all day. I wish *you* had before you the choice between that existence and the career of Mrs. Gordon, with the sole chance of escape from either fate, in ruthlessly trampling upon the bleeding hearts of two beloved parents!"

"Thank you kindly," said Fred, "but we infinitely prefer to laugh at you."

"Man's eternal reply to woman, admirably paraphrased!" commented Hadria.

Everyone was anxious to know when Algitha intended to go to London. Nobody doubted for a moment that she would hold to her purpose; as Fred said, she was so "beastly obstinate."

Algitha had not fixed any time. It would depend on her mother. She wished to make things as little painful as possible. That it was her duty to spare her pain altogether by remaining at home, Algitha refused to admit. She and Hadria had thought out the question from all sides. The work she was going to do was useful, but she did not justify herself on that ground. She claimed the right to her life and her liberty, apart from what she intended to do with either. She owed it to her own conscience alone to make good use of her liberty. "I don't want to pose as a philanthropist," she added, "though I honestly do desire to be of service. I want to spread my wings. And why should I not? Nobody turns pale when Ernest wants to spread *his*. How do I know what life is like, or how best to use it, if I remain satisfied with my present ignorance? How can I even appreciate what I possess, if I have nothing to compare it with? Of course, the truly nice and womanly thing to do, is to remain at home, waiting to be married. I have elected to be *un*womanly."

"I wonder how all this will turn out," said Ernest, "whether you won't regret it some day when it is too late."

"Don't people *always* regret what they do—some day?" asked Hadria.

"Perhaps so, especially if they do it sooner than other people."

"When are you going to make the announcement at head quarters?" asked Fred.

There was a pause. The colour had left Algitha's cheeks. She answered at length with an effort—

"I shall speak to mother to-day."

CHAPTER IV.

M RS. FULLERTON had gone to the study, to consult
with her husband on some matter of domestic importance. It was a long, low-pitched room, situated in the
part of the house that stood at right angles to the central
block, with long, narrow windows looking on to a rough
orchard. A few old portraits, very yellow and somewhat
grotesque, hung on the walls; a wood fire burnt on the hob-
grate, and beside it stood a vast arm chair, considerably worn,
with depressions shewing where its owner had been leaning
his head, day after day, when he smoked his pipe, or took
his after-dinner nap. The bookshelves were stocked with
scientific works, and some volumes on philosophy of a
materialistic character. With the exception of Robert Burns,
not one poet was represented.

The owner of the house sat before a big writing-table, which
was covered with papers. His face was that of a hard thinker;
the head was fine in form, the forehead broad and high; the
features regular, almost severe. The severity was softened by
a genial expression. Mrs. Fullerton, though also obviously
above the average of humanity, shewed signs of incomplete
development. The shape of the head and brow promised
many faculties that the expression of the face did not encourage one to expect. She was finely built; and carried
herself with dignity. When her daughters accompanied her
on a round of calls in the neighbourhood, they expressed a
certain quality in her appearance, in rough and ready terms:
"Other married women always look such fools beside mother!"

And they did.

Mrs. Fullerton wore her fine black hair brushed neatly over her forehead; her eyes were large, and keen in expression. The mouth shewed determination. It was easy to see that this lady had unbounded belief in her husband's wisdom, except in social matters, for which he cared nothing. On that point she had to keep her ambitions to herself. In questions of philosophy, she had imbibed his tenets unmodified, and though she went regularly every Sunday to the close little Scottish church at Ballochcoil, she had no more respect than her husband had, for the doctrines that were preached there.

"No doubt it is all superstition and nonsense," she used to say, "but in this country, one can't afford to fly in the face of prejudice. It would seriously tell against the girls."

"Well, have your own way," Mr. Fullerton would reply, "but I can't see the use of always bothering about what people will think. What more do the girls want than a good home and plenty of lawn-tennis? They'll get husbands fast enough, without your asphyxiating yourself every Sunday in their interests."

In her youth, Mrs. Fullerton had shewn signs of qualities which had since been submerged. Her husband had influenced her development profoundly, to the apparent stifling of every native tendency. A few volumes of poetry, and other works of imagination, bore testimony to the lost sides of her nature.

Mr. Fullerton thought imagination "all nonsense," and his wife had no doubt he was right, though there was something to be said for one or two of the poets. The buried impulses had broken out, like a half-smothered flame, in her children, especially in her younger daughter. Singularly enough, the mother regarded these qualities, partly inherited from herself, as erratic and annoying. The memory of her own youth taught her no sympathy.

It was a benumbed sort of life that she led, in her picturesque old home, whose charm she perceived but dimly with the remnants of her lost aptitudes.

"Picturesque!" Mr. Fullerton used to cry with a snort;
"why not say 'unhealthy' and be done with it?"

From these native elements of character, modified in so
singular a fashion in the mother's life, the children of this
pair had drawn certain of their peculiarities. The inborn
strength and authenticity of the parents had transmuted itself,
in the younger generation, to a spirit of free enquiry, and an
audacity of thought which boded ill for Mrs. Fullerton's
ambitions. The talent in her daughters, from which she had
hoped so much, seemed likely to prove a most dangerous
obstacle to their success. Why was it that clever people were
never sensible?

The gong sounded for luncheon. Austin put his head in at
the door of the study, to ask if his father would shew him a
drop of ditch-water through the microscope, in the afternoon.

"If you will provide the ditch-water, I will provide the
microscope," promised Mr. Fullerton genially.

Luncheon, usually a merry meal at Dunaghee, passed off
silently. There was a sense of oppression in the air. Algitha
and her sister made spasmodic remarks, and there were long
pauses. The conversation was chiefly sustained by the parents
and the ever-talkative Fred.

The latter had some anecdotes to tell of the ravages made
by wasps.

"If Buchanan would only adopt my plan of destroying
them," said Mr. Fullerton, "we should soon get rid of the pest."

"It's some chemical, isn't it?" asked Mrs. Fullerton.

"Oh, no; that's no use at all! Wasps positively enjoy
chemicals. What you do is this——." And then followed a
long and minute explanation of his plan, which had the merit
of extreme originality.

Mr. Fullerton had his own particular way of doing everything, a piece of presumption which was naturally resented,
with proper spirit, by his neighbours. He found it an expensive luxury. In the management of the estate, he had
outraged the feelings of every landlord and land-agent within

a radius of many miles, but he gained the affection of his tenants, and this he seemed to value more than the approval of his fellow-proprietors. In theory, he stuck out for his privileges; in practice, he was the friend and brother of the poorest on the estate. In his mode of farming he was as eccentric as in his method of management. He had taken Croachmore into his own hands, and this devoted farm had become the subject of a series of drastic scientific experiments, to the great grief and indignation of his bailiff.

Mrs. Fullerton believed implicitly in the value of these experiments, and so long as her husband tried science only on the farm she had no misgivings; but, alas, he had lately taken shares in some company, that was to revolutionize agriculture through an ingenious contrivance for collecting nitrogen from the atmosphere. Mr. Fullerton was confident that the new method was to be a gigantic success. But on this point, his wife uneasily shook her head. She had even tried to persuade Mr. Fullerton to rid himself of his liability. It was so great, she argued, and why should one be made anxious? But her husband assured her that she didn't understand anything about it; women ought not to meddle in business matters; it was a stupendous discovery, sure to make the fortunes of the original shareholders.

"When once the prejudice against a new thing has been got over," said the man of science, "you will see —— the thing will go like wild-fire."

Many years afterwards, these words were remembered by Mrs. Fullerton, and she bitterly regretted that she had not urged the matter more strenuously.

"Well, Algitha," said her father, wondering at her silence, "how are the roses getting on? And I hope you have not forgotten the sweet-brier that you promised to grow for me."

"Oh, no, father, the sweet-brier has been ordered," returned Algitha, without her usual brightness of manner.

"Have you a headache?" enquired Mrs. Fullerton. "I hope you have not all been sitting up talking in Hadria's room, as you are too fond of doing. You have the whole day in which to express your ideas, and I think you might let the remainder wait over till morning."

"We *were* rather late last night," Algitha confessed.

"Pressure of ideas overpowering," added Fred.

"When *I* was young, ideas would never have been tolerated in young people for a moment," said Mrs. Fullerton, "it would have been considered a mark of ill-breeding. You may think yourselves lucky to be born at this end of the century, instead of the other."

"Indeed we do!" exclaimed Ernest. "It's getting jolly interesting!"

"In some respects, no doubt we have advanced," observed his mother, "but I confess I don't understand all your modern notions. Everybody seems to be getting discontented. The poor want to be rich, and the rich want to be millionaires; men want to do their master's work, and women want to do men's; everything is topsy-turvy!"

"The question is: What constitutes being right side up?" said Ernest. "One can't exactly say what is topsy-turvy till one knows *that.*"

"When I was young we thought we *did* know," said Mrs. Fullerton, "but no doubt we are old-fashioned."

When luncheon was over, Mr. Fullerton went to the garden with his family, according to a time-honoured custom. His love of flowers sometimes made Hadria wonder whether her father also had been born with certain instincts, which the accidents of life had stifled or failed to develop. Terrible was the tyranny of circumstance! What had Emerson been dreaming of?

Mr. Fullerton, with a rose-bud in his button-hole, went off with the boys for a farming walk. Mrs. Fullerton returned to the house, and the sisters were left pacing together in the sheltered old garden, between two rows of gorgeous autumn flowers.

Hadria felt sick with dread of the coming interview.

Algitha was buoyed up, for the moment, by a strong conviction that she was in the right.

"It can't be fair even for parents to order one's whole life
according to their pleasure," she said. "Other girls submit,
I know ——"

"And so the world is full of abortive, ambiguous beings,
fit for nothing. The average woman always seem to me to be
muffled——or morbid."

"That's what *I* should become if I pottered about here
much longer," said Algitha—"morbid; and if there is one
thing on the face of the earth that I loathe, it is morbidness."

Both sisters were instinctively trying to buttress up Algitha's
courage, by strengthening her position with additional
arguments.

"Is it fair," Hadria asked, "to summon children into
the world, and then run up bills against them for future
payment? Why should one not see the bearings of the
matter?"

"In theory one can see them clearly enough; but it is poor
comfort when it comes to practice."

"Oh, seeing the bearings of things is *always* poor comfort!"
exclaimed the younger sister, with sudden vehemence.
"Upon my word, I think it is better, after all, to absorb
indiscriminately whatever idiotcy may happen to be around
one, and go with the crowd."

"Nonsense!" cried Algitha, who had no sympathy with
these passionate discouragements that alternated, in Hadria,
with equally passionate exaltations.

"When you have gone, I will ask Mrs. Gordon to teach me
the spirit of acquiescence, and one of those distracting games
—bésique or halma, or some of the other infernal pastimes
that heaven decrees for recalcitrant spirits in need of crushing
discipline."

"I think I see you!" Algitha exclaimed with a dispirited
laugh.

"It will be a trial," Hadria admitted; "but it is said that

suffering strengthens the character. You may look forward
before long, to claiming as sister a creature of iron purpose."

"I wonder, I wonder," cried Algitha, bending her fine
head; "we owe everything to her."

"I know we do. It's of no use disguising the unpleasant
side of the matter. A mother disappointed in her children
must be a desperately unhappy woman. She has nothing
left; for has she not resigned everything for them? But is
sacrifice for ever to follow on sacrifice? Is life to go rolling
after life, like the cheeses that the idiot in the fable sent
running downhill, the one to fetch the other back?"

"Yes, for ever," said Algitha, "until a few dare to break
through the tradition, and then everyone will wonder at its
folly. If only I could talk the matter over, in a friendly spirit,
with mother, but she won't let me. Ah! if it were not that
one is born with feelings and energies and ambitions of one's
own, parents might treat one as a showman treats his marion-
ettes, and we should all be charmed to lie prone on our
backs, or to dance as may be convenient to our creators. But,
as it is, the life of a marionette—however affectionate the
wire-pullers—does become monotonous after a time."

"As to that," said the younger sister, with a little raising of
the brows, as if half shrinking from what she meant to say,
"I think most parents regard their children with such
favourable eyes, not so much because they are *they* as
because they are *theirs*."

The sisters paced the length of the garden without speaking.
Then Hadria came to a standstill at the sun-dial, at the
crossing of the paths, and began absently to trace the figures
of the hours, with the stalk of a rose.

"After all," she said, "parents are presumably not actuated
by humanitarian motives in bringing one into this wild world.
They don't even profess to have felt an unselfish desire to see
one enjoying oneself at their expense (though, as a matter of
fact, what enjoyment one has generally *is* at their expense).
People are always enthusiastically congratulated on the arrival

of a new child, though it be the fourteenth, and the income two hundred a year! This seems to point to a pronounced taste for new children, regardless of the consequences!"

"Oh, of course," said Algitha, "it's one of the canons! Women, above all, are expected to jubilate at all costs. And I think most of them do, more or less sincerely."

"Very well then," cried Hadria, "it is universally admitted that children are summoned into the world to gratify parental instincts. Yet the parents throw all the onus of existence, after all, upon the children, and make *them* pay for it, and apologise for it, and justify it by a thousand sacrifices and an ever-flowing gratitude."

"I am quite ready to give gratitude and sacrifice too," said Algitha, "but I don't feel that I ought to sacrifice *everything* to an idea that seems to me wrong. Surely a human being has a right to his own life. If he has not that, what, in heaven's name, *has* he?"

"Anything but that!" cried Hadria.

*   *   *   *   *   *

While the momentous interview was going on, Hadria walked restlessly up and down the garden, feverishly waiting. The borders were brilliant with vast sunflowers, white lilies, and blazing "red-hot pokers" tangled together in splendid profusion, a very type of richness and glory of life. Such was the sort of existence that Hadria claimed from Fate. Her eyes turned to the bare, forlorn hills that even the August sunshine could not conjure into sumptuousness, and there she saw the threatened reality.

When at last Algitha's fine figure appeared at the further end of the path, Hadria hastened forward and took her sister's arm.

"It was worse than I had feared," Algitha said, with a quiver in her voice. "I *know* I am right, and yet it seems almost more than I am equal for. When I told mother, she turned deadly white, and I thought, for a moment, that she was going to faint. Let's sit down on this seat."

"Oh, it was horrible, Hadria! Mother must have been cherishing hopes about us, in a way that I don't think she quite knew herself. After that first moment of wretchedness, she flew into a passion of rage—that dreadful, tearing anger that people only feel when something of themselves is being wrenched away from them. She said that her children were all bad and unnatural; that she had spent her whole life in their interests; that if it had not been for her, we should all of us have grown up without education or accomplishments, or looks, or anything else; that she watched over us incessantly when we were little children, denying herself, spending her youth in devotion to us, when she might have gone into the world, and had some brightness and pleasure. If we imagined that she had never felt the dulness of her life, and never longed to go about and see people and things, we were much mistaken. But she had renounced everything she cared for, from her girlhood—she was scarcely older than I when her sacrifices began—and now her children gave no consideration to her; they were ready to scatter themselves hither and thither without a thought of her, or her wishes. They even talked scoffingly of the kind of life that she had led for *them* —for *them*, she repeated bitterly."

Hadria's face had clouded.

"Truly parents must have a bad time of it!" she exclaimed, "but does it really console them that their children should have a bad time of it too?"

Algitha was trembling and very pale.

"Mother says I shall ruin my life by this fad. What real good am I going to do? She says it is absurd the way we talk of things we know nothing about."

"But she won't let us know about things; one must talk about *some*thing!" cried Hadria with a dispirited laugh.

"She says she has experience of life, and we are ignorant of it. I reminded her that our ignorance was not exactly our fault."

"Ah! precisely. Parents throw their children's ignorance

in their teeth, having taken precious good care to prevent their knowing anything. I can't understand parents; they must have been young themselves once. Yet they seem to have forgotten all about it. They keep us hoodwinked and infantile, and then launch us headlong into life, with all its problems to meet, and all momentous decisions made for us, past hope of undoing." Hadria rose restlessly in her excitement. "Surely no creature was ever dealt with so insanely as the well-brought-up girl! Surely no well-wisher so sincere as the average parent ever ill-treated his charge so preposterously."

Again there was a long silence, filled with painful thought. "One begins to understand a little, why women do things that one despises, and why the proudest of them so often submit to absolute indignity. You remember when Mrs. Arbuthnot and—"

"Ah, don't!" cried Algitha, flushing. "*Nothing* ought to induce a woman to endure that."

"H'm —— I suspect the world that we know nothing about, Algitha, has ways and means of applying the pressure such as you and I scarcely dream of." Hadria spoke with half-closed eyes that seemed to see deep and far. "I have read and heard things that have almost taken my breath away! I feel as if I could *kill* every man who acquiesces in the present order of things. It is an insult to every woman alive!"

In Hadria's room that night, Algitha finally decided to delay her going for another six months, hoping by that time that her mother would have grown used to the idea, and less opposed to it. Mr. Fullerton dismissed it, as obviously absurd. But this high-handed treatment roused all the determination that Algitha had inherited from her father. The six months had to be extended, in order to procure funds. Algitha had a small income of her own, left her by her godmother, Miss Fortescue. She put aside this, for her purpose. Further delay, through Mrs. Trevelyan, brought the season round again to autumn, before Algitha was able to make her final preparations for departure.

"Do try and reconcile them to the idea," she said to her sister, as they stood on the platform of Ballochcoil station, very white and wretched-looking.

"It breaks my heart to see father look so fixed and angry, and mother so miserable. I am not going away for ever. Dear me, a day's journey will bring me back, at any time.

"I'll do my best," said Hadria, "here's your train; what a clumsy instrument of fate it does look!"

There was not much time for farewells. In a few minutes the train was steaming out of the station. A solitary figure stood on the platform, watching the monster curving and diminishing along the line, with its white smoke soaring merrily into the air, in great rolling masses, that melted, as if by some incantation, from thick, snow-like whiteness to rapid annihilation.

CHAPTER V.

AS Hadria drove over the winding upland road back to her home, her thoughts followed her sister into her new existence, and then turned wistfully backwards to the days that had been marked off into the past by Algitha's departure. How bright and eager and hopeful they had all been, how full of enthusiasm and generous ambitions! Even as they talked of battle, they stretched forth their hands for the crown of victory.

At the last meeting of the Preposterous Society, Ernest had repeated a poem of his favourite Emerson, called *Days*, and the poem, which was familiar to Hadria, sounded in her memory, as the pony trotted merrily along the well-known homeward way.

"Daughters of Time, the hypocritic Days,
Muffled and dumb, like barefoot Dervishes,
And marching single in an endless file,
Bring diadems and faggots in their hands.
To each they offer gifts after his will,
Bread, kingdoms, stars, and sky that holds them all.
I, in my pleached garden, watched the pomp,
Forgot my morning wishes, hastily
Took a few herbs and apples, and the Day
Turned and departed silent. I, too late,
Under her solemn fillet saw the scorn."

In spite of Hadria's memorable lecture of a year ago, it was still the orthodox creed of the Society, that Circumstance is the handmaid of the Will; that one can demand of one's days "bread, kingdoms, stars, or sky," and that the Days will obediently produce the objects desired. If one has but the spirit that can soar high enough to really be resolved upon stars, or the ambition sufficiently vaulting to be determined on

43

kingdoms, then—so ran the dogma—stars and kingdoms would be forthcoming, though obstacles were never so deter- mined. No member except Hadria had ever dreamt of insinuating that one might have a very pronounced taste for stars and kingdoms—nay, a taste so dominant that life would be worthless unless they were achieved—yet might be forced, by the might of events, to forego them. Hadria's own heresy had been of the head rather than of the heart. But to-day, feeling began to share the scepticism of the intellect.

What if one's stars and kingdoms lay on the further side of a crime or a cruelty?

What then was left but to gather up one's herbs and apples, and bear, as best one might, the scorn of the unjust Days?

Hadria cast about in her mind for a method of utilizing to the best advantage possible, the means at her disposal : to force circumstance to yield a harvest to her will. To be the family consolation meant no light task, for Mrs. Fullerton was exacting by nature : she had given much, and she expected much in return. Her logic was somewhat faulty, but that could not be gracefully pointed out to her by her daughter. Having allowed her own abilities to decay, Mrs. Fullerton had developed an extraordinary power of interfering with the employment of the abilities of others. Hadria had rather underrated than exaggerated this difficulty. Her mother would keep her for hours, discussing a trivial point of domestic busi- ness, giving elaborate directions about it, only to do it herself in the end. She spent her whole life in trifles of this kind, or over social matters. Everything was done cumbrously, with an incredible amount of toil and consideration, and without any noticeable results. Hadria, fighting against a multitude of harassing little difficulties, struggled to turn the long winter months to some use. But Mrs. Fullerton broke the good serviceable time into jagged fragments.

"I really can't see," said the mother, when the daughter proposed to set apart certain hours for household duties, and to have other portions of the day to herself, "I really

can't see why a girl's little occupations should be treated
with so much consideration. However, I have no wish for
grudging assistance."

Hadria's temper was far indeed from perfect, and painful
scenes often occurred. But as a rule, she would afterwards
be seized with a fit of remorse, knowing that her mother was
suffering bitterly from her keen disappointment about Algitha.
The failure of a life-long hope must try the endurance of
the bravest. Mrs. Fullerton, seeing that Hadria was more
patient, quickly took advantage of the favourable moment,
with a rapid instinct that had often done her good service in
the management of a niggard destiny. The valuable mood
must not be allowed to die fruitless. The elder girl's defection
thus became, to the mother, a sort of investment, bearing
interest of docility in the younger. Because the heartless
Algitha had left home, it seemed to Mrs. Fullerton that the
very least that Hadria could do, was to carry out her mother's
lightest wish.

And so the weeks went by, in dreary, troublous fashion, cut
into a hundred little barren segments. The mind had no space,
or stretch, or solitude. It was incessantly harassed, and its
impetus was perpetually checked. But Hadria hoped on.
This could not last for ever. Some day, doubtless, if she
sank not in spirit, the stars and the kingdoms would come.

Meanwhile, the position of affairs was decidedly ridiculous.
She was here as the family consolation, and nobody seemed
to be consoled! Her efforts had been sincere and even
enthusiastic, but the boys only laughed at her, in this rôle,
and nobody was apparently in the least gratified (except those
imps of boys!).

For a long time, Mrs. Fullerton seemed to be oblivious of
her daughter's efforts, but one day, when they had been
talking about Algitha, the mother said: "Your father and I
now look to you, Hadria. I do think that you are beginning
to feel a little what your duty is. If *you* also were to turn
deserter in our old age, I think it would kill us."

Hadria felt a thrill of horror. The network of Fate seemed to be fast closing round her. The temporary was to become fixed. She must act all her days according to the conviction of others, or her parents would die of grief!

When she went to the hills that afternoon, she felt as if she must walk on and on into the dreamy distance, away from all these toils and claims, away into the unknown world and never return. But, alas! the night descended and return she must. These wild impulses could never be followed.

The day had been peculiarly harassing and cut up; some neighbours had been to afternoon tea and tennis, and the sight of their faces and the sound of their talk had caused, in Hadria, an unutterable depression. The light, conventional phrases rang in her ears still, the expression of the faces haunted her, and into her heart crept a chill that benumbed every wish and hope and faith that she had ever cherished.

She sat up late into the night. Since freedom and solitude could not be had by day, the nights were often her sole opportunity. At such times she would work out her musical ideas, which in the dead silence of the house were brought forth plentifully. These, from her point of view, were the fruitful hours of the twenty-four. Thoughts would throng the darkness like swarms of living things.

Hadria's mood found expression to-night in a singular and most melancholy composition. She called it *Futility.*

It was unlike anything that she had ever done before, and she felt that it shewed an access of musical power.

She dreamt an absurd dream: That she was herself one of those girls with the high pattering accents, playing tennis without ceasing and with apparent cheerfulness; talking just as they had talked, and about just the same things; and all the time, a vast circle of shadowy forms stood watching, beckoning, and exhorting and warning, and turning away, at last, in sorrowful contempt, because she preferred to spend her youth eternally in futilities. And then they all slowly drifted by with sad eyes fixed on her, and she was still left playing,

playing. And it seemed as if whole weeks passed in that way, and she grew mortally tired, but some power prevented her from resting. The evil spell held her enthralled. Always cheerful, always polite and agreeable, she continued her task, finding herself growing accustomed to it at last, and duly resigned to the necessity, wearisome though it was. Then all hope that the game would ever cease went away, and she played on, mechanically, but always with that same polite cheerfulness, as of afternoon calls. She would not for the world admit that she was tired. But she was so tired that existence became a torture to her, and her heart seemed about to break with the intolerable strain—when she woke up with a start, and found herself lying in a constrained attitude, half-choked by the bed-clothes.

She did not see the comic side of the dream till next morning, when she told it at breakfast for the benefit of the family.

As Hadria was an ardent tennis-player, it struck her brethren as a particularly inappropriate form of nightmare.

Hadria, at this time, went frequently with her father on his farming walks, as he liked to have one or more of the family with him. She enjoyed these walks, for Mr. Fullerton would talk about philosophy and science, often of the most abstruse and entrancing kind. His children were devoted to him. During these expeditions, they always vied with one another to ferret out the most absurd story to tell him, he being held as conqueror who made their father laugh most heartily. Sometimes they all went in a body, armed with wild stories; and occasionally, across the open fields, a row of eccentric-looking figures might be seen, struggling in the grip of hilarious paroxysms; Mr. Fullerton doubled up in the middle of a turnip-field, perhaps, with his family in contortions round him. The air of the hills seemed to run to their heads, like wine. Roulades of laughter, hearty guffaws, might have been heard for surprising distances, much to the astonishment of the sober labourers bending over their toil.

Ernest had to go back to college; Fred and Austin to school.
The house seemed very quiet and sad after the boys left, and
Hadria missed her sister more and more, as time went on.

Algitha wrote most happily.

"With all its drawbacks, this existence of hard work (yet
not too hard) suits me exactly. It uses up my energies; yet,
in spite of the really busy life I lead, I literally have more
leisure than I used to have at home, where all through the
day, there was some little detail to be attended to, some call to
make, some convention to offer incense to, some prejudice to
respect. Here, once my day's work is over, it *is* over, and I
have good solid hours of leisure. I feel that I have earned
those hours when they come; also that I have earned a right
to my keep, as Wilfred Burton, the socialist, puts it somewhat
crudely. When I go to bed at night, I can say: 'Because of
me, this day, heavy hearts have been made a little lighter.'
I hear all sorts of opinions, and see all sorts of people. I
never was so happy in my life."

It was Hadria's habit still to take solitary rambles over the
country. A passionate lover of Nature, she found endless
pleasure in its ever-changing aspects. Yet of late, a new
feeling had begun to mutter angrily within her: a resentment
against these familiar sights and sounds, because they were
the boundaries of her horizon. She hated the line of the
round breezy hills where the row of fir-trees stood against the
sky, because that was the edge of her world, and she wanted
to see what was beyond. She must and would see what was
beyond, some day. Her hope was always vague; for if she
dared to wonder how the curtain of life was to be lifted, she
had to face the fact that there was no reasonable prospect of
such a lifting. Still, the utter horror of living on always, in
this fashion, seemed to prove it impossible.

On one dim afternoon, when the sun was descending,
Hadria's solitary figure was noticed by a white-haired lady,
presumably a tourist, who had stopped to ask a question
of some farm labourers, working in a field. She ceased

to listen to the information, on the subject of Dunaghee, that was given to her in a broad Scottish dialect. The whole scene, which an instant before had impressed her as one of beauty and peace, suddenly focussed itself round the dark figure, and grew sinister in its aspect. At that moment, nothing would have persuaded the onlooker that the hastening figure was not hastening towards misfortune.

A woman of impulse, she set off in purposeless pursuit. Hadria's pace was very rapid ; she was trying to outrun thought. It was impossible to live without hope, yet hope, in this forlorn land, was growing faint and tired.

Her pursuer was a remarkable-looking woman, no longer young, with her prematurely white hair drawn up from her brow with a proud sweep that suited well her sharply defined features and her air of defiance. She was carelessly dressed after the prevailing fashion, and gave the impression of not having her life successfully in hand, but rather of being driven by it, as by a blustering wind, against her inclination.

The impression which had seized her, a moment ago, deepened as she went. Something in the scene and the hastening figure roused a sense of dread. With her, an impression was like a spark to gunpowder. Her imagination blazed up. Life, in its most tragic aspect, seemed before her in the lonely scene, with the lonely figure, moving, as if in pursuit of a lost hope, towards the setting sun.

If Hadria had not paused on the brow of the hill, it is unlikely that she would have been overtaken, but that pause decided the matter. The stranger seemed suddenly to hesitate, wondering, apparently, what she had done this eccentric thing for.

Hadria, feeling a presence behind her, turned nervously round and gave a slight start.

It was so rare to meet anybody on these lonely hills, that the apparition of a striking-looking woman with white hair, dark eyes, and a strange exalted sort of expression, gave a shock of surprise.

As the lady had stopped short, Hadria supposed that she had lost her way, and wished to make some enquiries.

"Can I direct you, or give you any assistance?" she asked, after a second's pause.

"Oh, thank you, you are very kind. I have come over from Ballochcoil to explore the country. I have been trying to find out the history of the old houses of the district. Could you tell me, by the way, anything about that house with the square tower at the end; I have been loitering round it half the afternoon. And I would have given anything to know its history, and what it is like inside."

"Well, I can help you there, for that old house is my home. If you have time to come with me now, I will show you all over it," said Hadria, impulsively.

"That is too tempting an offer. And yet I really don't like to intrude in this way. I am a perfect stranger to you and—your parents I suppose?"

"They will be delighted," Hadria assured her new acquaintance, somewhat imprudently.

"Well, I can't resist the temptation," said the latter, and they walked on together.

Hadria related what she knew about the history of the house. Very scanty records had survived. It had obviously been one of the old Scottish strongholds, built in the lawless days when the country was plunged in feuds and chieftains lived on plunder. A few traditions lingered about it: among them that of a chief who had carried off, by force, the daughter of his bitterest enemy, in revenge for some deed of treachery. He had tortured her with insolent courtship, and then starved her to death in a garret in the tower, while her father and his followers assaulted its thick walls in vain.

"The tradition is, that on stormy nights one can still hear the sound of the attack, the shouts of the men and the father's imprecations."

"A horrible story!"

"When people say the world has not progressed, I always think of that story, and remember that such crimes were common in those days," Hadria remarked.

"I doubt if we are really less ferocious to-day," the other said; "our ferocity is directed against the weakest, now as then, but there are happily not so many weak, so we get the credit of being juster, without expense. As a matter of fact, our opportunities are less, and so we make a virtue of necessity—with a vengeance!"

Hadria looked at her companion with startled interest. "Will you tell me to whom I have the pleasure of speaking?" the lady asked.

"My name is Fullerton—Hadria Fullerton."

"Thank you. And here is my card, at least I think it is. Oh, no, that is a friend's card! How very tiresome! I am reduced to pronouncing my own name—Miss Du Prel, Valeria Du Prel; you may know it."

Hadria came to a sudden standstill. She might know it! she might indeed. Valeria Du Prel had long been to her a name to swear by.

"Miss Du Prel! Is that—are you—may I ask, are you the writer of those wonderful books?"

Miss Du Prel gave a gratified smile. "I am glad they please you."

"Ah! if you could guess how I have longed to know you. I simply can't believe it."

"And so my work has really given you pleasure?"

"Pleasure! It has given me hope, it has given me courage, it has given me faith in all that is worth living for. It was an epoch in my life when I first read your *Parthenia.*"

Miss Du Prel seemed so genuinely pleased by this enthusiasm that Hadria was surprised.

"I have plenty of compliments, but very seldom a word that makes me feel that I have spoken to the heart. I feel as if I had called in the darkness and had no response, or like one who has cried from the house-tops to a city of the dead."

"And I so often thought of writing to you, but did not like to intrude," cried Hadria.

"Ah! if you only *had* written to me!" Miss Du Prel exclaimed.

Hadria gazed incredulously at the familiar scene, as they approached the back of the house, with its round tower and its confusion of picturesque, lichen-covered roofs. An irregular circle of stately trees stood as sentinels round the stronghold.

After all, something did happen, once in a while, in this remote corner of the universe, whose name, Hadria used to think, had been erased from the book of Destiny. She was perhaps vaguely disappointed to find that the author of *Parthenia* wore ordinary human serge, and a cape cut after the fashion of any other person's cape. Still, she had no idea what supersensuous material she could reasonably have demanded of her heroine (unless it were the mythic "bombazine" that Ernest used to talk about, in his ignorant efforts to describe female apparel), or what transcendental form of cape would have satisfied her imagination.

"You have a lovely home," said Valeria Du Prel, "you must be very happy here."

"Would you be happy here?"

"Well, of course that would depend. I am, I fear, too roving by nature to care to stay long in one place. Still I envy girls their home-life in the country; it is so healthy and free."

Hadria, without answering, led her companion round the flank of the tower, and up to the front door. It was situated in the angle of the wings, a sheltered nook, hospitably careful of the guest, whom the winds of the uplands were disposed to treat but roughly.

Hadria and her companion entered a little panelled hall, whence a flight of broad stairs with stout wooden balusters, of quaint design, led to the first floor.

The visitor was charmed with the quiet old rooms, especially with Hadria's bedroom in the tower, whose windows were so deep-set that they had to be approached through a little tunnel cut out of the thickness of the wall. The windows looked on to the orchard at the back, and in front over the hills. Miss Du Prel was taken to see the scene of the tragedy, and the meeting-room of the Preposterous Society.

"You must see the drawing-room," said Hadria.

She opened a door as she spoke, and ushered her visitor into a large, finely-proportioned room with three tall windows of stately form, divided into oblong panes, against which vagrant sprays of ivy were gently tapping.

This room was also panelled with painted wood; its character was quiet and stately and reposeful. Yet one felt that many human lives had been lived in it. It was full of the sentiment of the past, from the old prints and portraits on the walls, to the delicate outlines of the wooden mantel-piece, with its finely wrought urns and garlands.

Before this mantel-piece, with the firelight flickering in her face, sat Mrs. Fullerton, working at a large piece of embroidery.

For the first time, Hadria hesitated. "Mother," she said, "this is Miss Du Prel. We met out on the hills this after-noon, and I have brought her home to see the house, which she admires very much."

Mrs. Fullerton had looked up in astonishment, at this in-cursion into her very sanctuary, of a stranger met at hap-hazard on the hills. Hadria wheeled up an easy-chair for the visitor.

"I fear Miss Du Prel will not find much to see in the old house," said Mrs. Fullerton, whose manner had grown rigid, partly because she was shy, partly because she was annoyed with Hadria for her impulsive conduct, and largely because she disliked the idea of a literary acquaintance for her daughter, who was quite extraordinary enough as it was.

"We have been all over the house," said Hadria hastily, with an anxious glance at Miss Du Prel, whom she half expected to rise and walk out of the room. It must surely be the first time in her life that her presence had not been received as an honour!

"It is all very old and shabby," said Mrs. Fullerton. "I

hope you will take some tea; if you have walked far to-day, you must be cold and in need of something to eat."

"Oh no, no, thank you," returned the visitor; "I ought to be getting back to Ballochcoil to-night."

"To Ballochcoil!" exclaimed mother and daughter in simultaneous dismay. "But it is nearly seven miles off, and the sun is down. You can't get back to-night on foot."

"Dear me, can I not? I suppose I forgot all about getting back, in the interest of the scenery."

"What an extraordinary person!" thought Mrs. Fullerton.

Miss Du Prel glanced helplessly at Hadria; rising then and looking out of the window at the dusk, which had come on so rapidly. "Dear me, how dark it has grown! Still I think I can walk it, or perhaps I can get a fly at some inn on the way."

"Can we offer you a carriage?" asked Mrs. Fullerton.

"Oh no, thank you; that is quite unnecessary. I have already intruded far too long; I shall wend my way back, or what might perhaps be better, I could get a lodging at the farmhouse down the road. I am told that they put travellers up sometimes."

Miss Du Prel hurried off, evidently chilled by Mrs. Fullerton's freezing courtesy. Hadria, disregarding her mother's glance of admonition, accompanied the visitor to the farm of Craw Gill, having first given directions to old Maggie to put together a few things that Miss Du Prel would require for the night. Hadria's popularity at the farm, secured her new friend a welcome. Mrs. McEwen was a fine example of the best type of Scottish character; warm of heart, honest of purpose, and full of a certain unconscious poetry, and a dignity that lingers still in districts where the railway whistle is not too often heard. Miss Du Prel seemed to nestle up to the good woman, as a child to its mother after some scaring adventure. Mrs. McEwen was recommending a hot water-bottle and gruel in case of a chill, when Hadria wended her way homeward to brave her mother's wrath.

CHAPTER VI.

" I CANNOT make you realize that you are an ignorant
girl who knows nothing of the world, and that it is
necessary you should accept my experience, and condescend to
be guided by my wishes. You put me in a most unpleasant
position this afternoon, forcing me to receive a person whom
I have never been introduced to, or heard of——"

"Valeria Du Prel has been heard of throughout the
English-speaking world," said Hadria rhetorically.

"So much the worse," retorted Mrs. Fullerton. "No nicely
brought up woman is ever heard of outside her own circle."

Hadria recalled a similar sentiment among the ancient
Greeks, and thought how hard an old idea dies.

"She might have been some awful person, some unprincipled
adventuress, and that I believe is what she is. What was she
prowling about the back of our house for, I should like to
know?"

"I suspect she wanted to steal chickens or something," Hadria
was goaded into suggesting, and the interview ended painfully.

When Hadria went to Craw Gill, next morning, to enquire
for Miss Du Prel, Mrs. McEwen said that the visitor had break-
fasted in bed. The farmer's wife also informed Miss Fullerton
that the lady had decided to stay on at Craw Gill, for some
time. She had been looking out for a retreat of the kind.

"She seems a nice-like body," said Mrs. McEwen, "and I
see no objection to the arrangement."

Hadria's heart beat faster. Could it be possible that
Valeria du Prel was to be a near neighbour? It seemed too
good to be true!

When Miss Du Prel came down in her walking garments,

55

she greeted Hadria with a certain absence of mind, which smote chill upon the girl's eagerness.

"I wanted to know if you were comfortable, if I could do anything for you." Miss Du Prel woke up.

"Oh no, thank you; you are very kind. I am most comfortable—at least—it is very strange, but I have lost my keys and my umbrella and my hand-bag—I can't think what I can have done with them. Oh, and my purse is gone too!"

Whereupon Mrs. McEwen in dismay, Mr. McEwen (who then appeared), the maid, and Hadria, hunted high and low for the missing properties, which were brought to light, one by one, in places where their owner had already "thoroughly searched," and about which she had long since abandoned hope.

She received them with mingled joy and amazement, and having responded to Mrs. McEwen's questions as to what she would like for dinner, she proposed to Hadria that they should take a walk together.

Hadria beamed. Miss Du Prel seemed both amused and gratified by her companion's worship, and the talk ran on, in a light and pleasant vein, differing from the talk of the ordinary mortal, Hadria considered, as champagne differs from ditch-water.

In recording it for Algitha's benefit that evening, Hadria found that she could not reproduce the exhilarating quality, or describe the influence of Miss Du Prel's personality. It was as if, literally, a private and particular atmosphere had encompassed her. She was "alive all round," as her disciple asserted.

Her love of Nature was intense. Hadria had never before realized that she had been without full sympathy in this direction. She awoke to a strange retrospective sense of solitude, feeling a new pity for the eager little child of years ago, who had wandered up to the garret, late at night, to watch the moonlight spread its white shroud over the hills.

With every moment spent in the society of Valeria Du Prel, new and clearer light seemed to Hadria, to be thrown upon all the problems of existence; not by any means only through what Miss Du Prel directly said, but by what she implied, by what she took for granted, by what she omitted to say.

"It seems like a home-coming from long exile," Hadria wrote to her sister. "I have been looking through a sort of mist, or as one looks at one's surroundings before quite waking. Now everything stands out sharp and cut, as objects do in the clear air of the South. Ah me, the South! Miss Du Prel has spent much of her life there, and my inborn smouldering passion for it, is set flaming by her descriptions! You remember that brief little fortnight that we spent with mother and father in Italy? I seem now to be again under the spell of the languorous airs, the cloudless blue, the white palaces, the grey olive groves, and the art, the art! Oh, Algitha, I must go to the South soon, soon, or I shall die of home sickness! Miss Du Prel says that this is only one side of me breaking out : that I am northern at heart. I think it is true, but meanwhile the thought of the South possesses me. I confess I think mother had some cause to be alarmed when she saw Miss Du Prel, if she wants to keep us in a chastened mood, at home. It seems as if all of me were in high carnival. Life is raised to a higher power. I feel nearly omnipotent. Epics and operas are child's play to me! It is true I have produced comparatively few ; but, oh, those that are to come! I feel fit for anything, from pitch-and-toss to manslaughter. I think of the two, I rather lean to the manslaughter. Oh, I don't mean it in the facetious sense! that would be a terrible downfall from my present altitudes. To such devices the usual wretched girl, who has never drawn rebellious breath, or listened to the discourses of Valeria Du Prel, has to turn for a living, or to keep *ennui* at bay. But *I*, no, the inimical sex may possess their souls in peace, as far as I am concerned. They might retort that they never *had* felt nervous, but a letter has the same advantage as the pulpit : the adversary can never get up and contradict.

"That ridiculous adversary, Harold Wilkins, is staying again at Drumgarren, and I hear from Mrs. Gordon that he thinks it very strange that I should see so much of so extraordinary a person as Miss Du Prel! Opinions differ of course; *I* think it very strange that the Gordons should see so much of so ordinary a person as Mr. Wilkins. Everybody makes much of him here, and, alas! all the girls run after him, and even fall in love with him; why, I can't conceive. For if driven by dire compulsion of fate, to bend one's thoughts upon *some* prosaic example of that prosaic sex, why not choose one of the many far more attractive candidates available—the Gordons, the McKenzies, and so forth? When I go to tennis parties with mother—they are still playing upon the asphalte courts—and see the little dramas that go on, the jealousies and excitements, and general much-ado-about-nothing, I can scarcely believe that Miss Du Prel really belongs to the same planet as ours. But I don't feel so contemptuous as I did; it is so pitiful. Out of my great wealth I can afford to be more generous.

"And when I see those wretched girls fluttering round Mr. Wilkins, I no longer turn up my 'aughty nose' (as old Mrs. Brooks used to say). I only think to myself, 'Heavens and earth! what an aching, empty life those young women must lead, if they are actually reduced for interest and amusement to the utterances of Mr. Wilkins!' They would have the pull of one though, if the utterances of Mr. Wilkins were the only utterances to be heard! Perish the thought of such beggary!"

The talks with Valeria Du Prel grew more intimate, and more deeply interesting to Hadria, every day.

Miss Du Prel used often to look at her companion in amazement. "Where *did* you come from?" she exclaimed on one occasion. "One would suppose you had lived several lives; you seem to *know* things in such a subtle, intimate fashion!"

She used to ponder over the problem, wondering what Professor Fortescue would say to it. There appeared to be more here than mere heredity could account for. But science had never solved this problem; originality seemed always to enter upon its career, uncaused and unaccountable. It was ever a miraculous phenomenon. The Professor had always said so. Still the heritage was rich enough, in this case. Heredity might have some discoverable part in the apparent marvel. Each member of the Fullerton family had unusual ability of some kind. Their knowledge of science, and their familiarity with the problems of philosophy, had often astonished Miss Du Prel. Hadria's accounts of the Preposterous Society made her laugh and exclaim at the same moment. She gave an envious sigh at the picture of the eager little group, with their warmth of affection for one another, and their vivid interests. Miss Du Prel, with all her sadness, was youthful in spirit. Hadria found her far younger than many girls of her own age. This set her thinking. She observed how rigid most people become in a few years, and how the personality grows wooden, in the daily repetition of the same actions and the same ideas. This stiffening process had been attributed to the malice of Time; but now Hadria began to believe that narrow and ungenerous thought lay at the root of the calamity. The entire life of the little world in which she had grown up, on all its sides, in all its ideals and sentiments, stood before her, as if some great painter had made a picture of it. She had never before been able to stand so completely apart from the surroundings of her childhood. And she was able to do so now, not because Miss Du Prel discoursed about it, but because Hadria's point of view had shifted sympathetically to the point of view of her companion, through the instinctive desire to see how these familiar things would look to alien eyes. That which had seemed merely prosaic and dreary, became characteristic; the very things which she had taken most for granted were exactly those which turned out to be the significant and idiomatic facts.

These had made permanent inroads into the mind and character. It was with these that Hadria would have to reckon all her days, under whatever conditions she might hereafter be placed. Daily surroundings were not merely pleasant or unpleasant facts, otherwise of no importance; they were the very material and substance of character; the push and impetus, or the let and hindrance; the guardians or the assassins of the soul.

CHAPTER VII.

MISS DU PREL had promised to allow Hadria to drive her to Darachanarvan, a little town on the banks of the river, about seven miles across country.

Hadria was in high spirits, as they trundled along the white roads with the wind in their faces, the hills and the blue sky spread out before them, the pleasant sound of the wheels and the trotting of the pony setting their thoughts to rhythm.

The trees were all shedding their last yellow leaves, and the air was full of those faded memories of better days, whirling in wild companies across the road, rushing upward on the breast of some vagabond gust, drifting, spinning, shuddering along the roadside, to lie there at last, quiet, among a host of brothers, with little passing tremors, as if (said Valeria) they were silently sobbing because of their banishment from their kingdom of the air.

Miss Du Prel, though she enjoyed the beauty of the day and the scenery, seemed sad of mood. "This weather recalls so many autumns," she said. "It reminds me too vividly of wonderful days, whose like I shall never see again, and friends, many of whom are dead, and many lost sight of in this inexorable coming and going of people and things, this inexorable change that goes on for ever. I feel as if I should go mad at times, because it will not stop, either in myself or others."

"Ah, that is a dreadful thought!"

"It comes to me so insistently, perhaps, because of my roving life," she said.

She paused for a moment, and then she fell into one of her

exalted moods, when she seemed to lose consciousness of the ordinary conditions around her, or rather to pierce deeper into their significance and beauty. Her speech would, at such times, become rhythmic and picturesque; she evidently saw vivid images before her, in which her ideas embodied themselves.

"Most people who live always in one place see the changes creeping on so gradually that they scarcely feel them, but with me this universal flux displays itself pitilessly, I cannot escape. Go where I will, there is something to measure the changes by. A shoal of yellow leaves whispers to me of seasons long ago, and the old past days, with their own intimate character that nothing ever repeats, flash before me again with the vividness of yesterday; and a flight of birds—ah! if I could express what they recall! The dead years pass again in a great procession, a motley company—some like emperors, crowned and richly dowered, with the sound of trumpets and the tramping of many obsequious feet; and others like beggars, despoiled and hungry, trudging along a dusty high road, or like grey pilgrims bound, with bleeding feet, for a far-off shrine."

They entered a little beech-wood, whose leaves made a light of their own, strange and mystical.

"Yours must have been a wonderful life!" said Hadria.

"Yes, I have seen and felt many things," answered Miss Du Prel, stirred by the intoxication of the motion and the wind and the sunlight, "life has been to me a series of intense emotions, as it will be to you, I fear —— "

"You fear?" said Hadria.

"Yes; for that means suffering. If you feel, you are at the mercy of all things. Every wind that blows uses you as an Æolian harp."

"That must be charming, at least for those who live in your neighbourhood," said Hadria.

"No; for often the harp rings false. Its strings get loosened; one hangs slack and jars, and where then is your harmony?"

"One would run the risk of many things rather than let one's strings lie dumb," said Hadria.

"What a dangerous temperament you have!" cried Valeria, looking round at the glowing face beside her.

"I must take my risks," said Hadria.

"I doubt if you know what risks there are."

"Then I must find out," she answered.

"One plays with fire so recklessly before one has been burnt."

Hadria was silent. The words sounded ominous.

"Will can do so much," she said at length. "Do you believe in the power of the human will to break the back of circumstance?"

"Oh, yes; but the effort expended in breaking its back sometimes leaves one prone, with a victory that arrives ironically too late. However I don't wish to discourage you. There is no doubt that human will has triumphed over everything—but death."

Again the sound of the pony's hoofs sounded through the silence, in a cheerful trot upon the white roads. They were traversing an open, breezy country, chequered with wooded hollows, where generally a village sought shelter from the winds. And these patches of foliage were golden and red in the meditative autumn sunshine, which seemed as if it were a little sad at the thought of parting with the old earth for the coming winter.

"I think the impossible lesson to learn would be renouncement," said Hadria. "I cannot conceive how anyone could say to himself, while he had longings and life still in him, 'I will give up this that I might have learnt; I will stop short here where I might press forward; I will allow this or that to curtail me and rob me of my possible experience.'"

"Well, I confess that has been my feeling too, though I admire the spirit that can renounce."

"Admire? Oh, yes, perhaps; though I am not so sure

that the submissive nature has not been too much glorified—
in theory. Nobody pays much attention to it in practice, by
the way."

Miss Du Prel laughed. "What an observant young woman
you are."

"Renunciation is always preached to girls, you know," said
Hadria—"preached to them when as yet they have nothing
more than a rattle and a rag-doll to renounce. And later,
when they set about the business of their life, and resign their
liberty, their talents, their health, their opportunity, their
beauty (if they have it), then people gradually fall away from
the despoiled and obedient being, and flock round the still
unchastened creature who retains what the gods have given
her, and asks for more."

"I fear you are indeed a still unchastened creature!"

"Certainly; there is no encouragement to chasten oneself.
People don't stand by the docile members of Society. They
commend their saints, but they drink to their sinners."

Miss Du Prel smiled.

"It is true," she admitted. "A woman must not renounce
too much if she desires to retain her influence."

"*Pas trop de zèle,*" Hadria quoted.

"There is something truly unmanageable about you, my
dear!" cried Valeria, much amused. "Well, I too have had
just that sort of instinct, just that imperious demand, just
that impatience of restraint. I too regarded myself and my
powers as mine to use as I would, responsible only to my own
conscience. I decided to have freedom though the heavens
should fall. I was unfitted by temperament to face the world,
but I was equally unfitted to pay the price for protection—the
blackmail that society levies on a woman : surrender of body
and of soul. What could one expect, in such a case, but
disaster? I often envy now the simple-minded woman who
pays her price and has her reward—such as it is."

"Ah! such as it is!" echoed Hadria.

"Who was it said, the other day, that she thought a wise

woman always took things as they were, and made the best of them?"

"Some dull spirit."

"And yet a practical spirit."

"I am quite sure," said Hadria, "that the stokers of hell are practical spirits."

"Your mother must have had her work cut out for her when she undertook to bring you up," exclaimed Miss Du Prel.

"So she always insinuates," replied Hadria demurely.

They were spinning down hill now, into a warm bit of country watered by the river, and Hadria drew rein. The spot was so pleasant that they alighted, tied the pony to a tree, and wandered over the grass to the river's edge. Hadria picked her way from stone to slippery stone, into the middle of the river, where there was comparatively safe standing room. Here she was suddenly inspired to execute the steps of a reel, while Valeria stood dismayed on the bank, expecting every moment, to see the dance end in the realms of the trout.

But Hadria kept her footing, and continued to step it with much solemnity. Meanwhile, two young men on horseback were coming down the road; but as a group of trees hid it from the river at this point, they were not noticed. The horsemen stopped suddenly when they cleared the group of trees. The figure of a young woman in mid-stream, dancing a reel with extreme energy and correctness, and without a smile, was sufficiently surprising to arrest them.

"As I thought," exclaimed Hadria, "it is Harold Wilkins!"

"I shall be glad to see this conquering hero," said Valeria.

Hadria, who had known the young man since her child-hood, waited calmly as he turned his horse's head towards the river, and advanced across the grass, raising his hat. "Good morning, Miss Fullerton."

"Good morning," Hadria returned, from her rock.

"You seem to be having rather an agreeable time of it."

"Very. Are you fond of dancing?"

Mr. Wilkins was noted, far and wide, for his dancing, and the question was wounding.

He was tall and loosely built, with brown expressionless eyes, dark hair, a pink complexion, shelving forehead, and a weak yet obstinate mouth. His companion also was tall and dark, but his face was pale, his forehead broad and high, and a black moustache covered his upper lip. He had raised his hat gracefully on finding that the dancer in mid-stream was an acquaintance of his companion, and he shewed great self-possession in appearing to regard the dancing of reels in these circumstances, as an incident that might naturally be expected. Not a sign of surprise betrayed itself in the face, not even a glimmer of curiosity. Hadria was so tickled by this finished behaviour under difficulties, that she took her cue from it, and decided to treat the matter in the same polished spirit. She too would take it all decorously for granted.

Mr. Wilkins introduced his friend : Mr. Hubert Temperley. Hadria bowed gracefully in reply to Mr. Temperley's salute.

"Don't you feel a little cramped out there?" asked Mr. Wilkins.

"Dear me, no," cried Hadria in mock surprise. "What could induce you to suppose I would come out here if I felt cramped?"

"Are you—are you thinking of coming on shore? Can I help you?"

"Thank you," replied Hadria. "This is a merely temporary resting-place. We ought to be getting on ; we have some miles yet to drive," and she hurried her friend away. They were conducted to the pony-cart by the cavaliers, who raised their hats, as the ladies drove off at a merry pace, bowing their farewells.

"The eternal riddle!" Temperley exclaimed, as they turned the corner of the road.

"What is the eternal riddle?" Harold Wilkins enquired.

"Woman, woman!" Temperley replied, a little impatiently. He had not found young Wilkins quick to catch his meaning

during the two hours' ride, and it occurred to him that Miss
Fullerton would have been a more interesting companion.

He made a good many enquiries about her and her family,
on the way back to Drumgarren.

"We are invited to tennis at their house, for next Tuesday,"
said Harold, "so you will have a chance of pursuing the
acquaintance.   For my part, I don't admire that sort of
girl."

"Don't you?   I am attracted by originality.   I like a
woman to have something in her."

"Depends on what it is.   I hate a girl to have a lot of silly
ideas."

"Perhaps you prefer her to have but one," said Temperley,
"that one being that Mr. Harold Wilkins is a charming
fellow."

"Nothing of the kind," cried Harold.   "I can't help it if
girls run after me ; it 's a great bore."

Temperley laughed.   "You, like Achilles, are pursued by
ten thousand girls.   I deeply sympathize, though it is not an
inconvenience that has troubled me, even in my palmiest
days."

"Why, how old are you?   Surely you are not going to talk
as if those days were over?"

"Oh, I am moderately palmy still!" Temperley admitted.
"Still, the hour approaches when the assaults of time will
become more disastrous."

"You and Hadria Fullerton ought to get on well together,
for she is very musical," said Harold Wilkins.

"Ah!" cried Temperley with new interest.   "I could have
almost told that from her face.   Does she play well?"

"Well, I suppose so.   She plays things without any tune
that bore one to death, but I daresay you would admire it.
She composes too, I am told."

"Really?   Dear me, I must make a point of having a talk
with her, on the earliest opportunity."

Meanwhile, the occupants of the pony-cart had arrived at

Darachanarvan, where they were to put up the pony and have luncheon. It was a prosaic little Scottish town, with only a beautiful survival, here and there, from the past.

After luncheon, they wandered down to the banks of the river, and watched the trout and the running water. Hadria had long been wishing to find out what her oracle thought about certain burning questions on which the sisters held such strong, and such unpopular sentiments, but just because the feeling was so keen, it was difficult to broach the subject.

An opportunity came when Miss Du Prel spoke of her past. Hadria was able to read between the lines. When a mere girl, Miss Du Prel had been thrown on the world—brilliant, handsome, impulsive, generous—to pass through a fiery ordeal, and to emerge with aspirations as high as ever, but with her radiant hopes burnt out. But she did not dwell on this side of the picture; she emphasized rather, the possibility of holding on through storm and stress to the truth that is born in one; to belief in "the noblest and wildest hopes (if you like to call them so) that ever thrilled generous hearts."

But she gave no encouragement to certain of her companion's most vehement sentiments. She seemed to yearn for exactly that side of life from which the younger shrank with so much horror. She saw it under an entirely different aspect. Hadria felt thrown back on herself, lonely once more.

"You have seen Mrs. Gordon," she said at length, "what do you think of her?"

"Nothing; she does not inspire thought."

"Yet once she was a person, not a thing."

"If a woman can't keep her head above water in Mrs. Gordon's position, she must be a feeble sort of person."

"I should not dare to say that, until I had been put through the mill myself, and come out unpulverised."

Miss Du Prel failed to see what there was so very dreadful in Mrs. Gordon's lot. She had, perhaps, rather more children than was necessary, but otherwise——

"Oh, Miss Du Prel," cried Hadria, "you might be a mere man! That is just what my brothers say."

"I don't understand what you mean," said Miss Du Prel. " Do explain."

"Do you actually—*you* of all people—not recognize and hate the idea that lies so obviously at the root of all the life that is swarming round us——? "

Valeria studied her companion's excited face.

"Are you in revolt against the very basis of existence? " she asked curiously.

"No : at least . . . but this is not what I am driving at exactly," replied Hadria, turning uneasily away from the close scrutiny. "Don't you know—oh, don't you see—how many women secretly hate, and shrink from this brutal domestic idea that fashions their fate for them? "

Miss Du Prel's interest quickened.

"Nothing strikes me so much as the tamely acquiescent spirit of the average woman, and I doubt if you would find another woman in England to describe the domestic existence as you do."

"Perhaps not; tradition prevents them from using bad language, but they *feel*, they *feel*."

"Young girls perhaps, brought up very ignorantly, find life a little scaring at first, but they soon settle down into happy wives and mothers."

"As the fibre grows coarser," assented Hadria.

"No ; as the affections awaken, and the instincts that hold society together, come into play. I have revolted myself from the conditions of life, but it is a hopeless business—beating one's wings against the bars."

"The bars are, half of them, of human construction," said Hadria, "and against *those* one may surely be allowed to beat."

"Of human construction? "

"I mean that prejudice, rather than instinct, has built up the system that Mrs. Gordon so amiably represents."

"Prejudice has perhaps taken advantage of instinct to

establish a somewhat tyrannical tradition," Miss Du Prel admitted, "but instinct is at the bottom of it. There is, of course, in our society, no latitude for variety of type; that is the fault of so many institutions."

"The ordinary domestic idea may have been suitable when women were emerging from the condition of simple animals," said Hadria, "but now it seems to me to be out of date."

"It can never be entirely out of date, dear Hadria. Nature has asked of women a great and hard service, but she has given them the maternal instinct and its joys, in compensation for the burden of this task, which would otherwise be intolerable and impossible. It can only be undertaken at the instigation of some stupendous impetus, that blinds the victim to the nature of her mission. It must be a sort of obsession; an intense personal instinct, amounting to madness. Nature, being determined to be well served in this direction, has supplied the necessary monomania, and the domestic idea, as you call it, grows up round this central fact."

Hadria moved restlessly to and fro by the river bank. "One presumes to look upon oneself, at first—in one's earliest youth," she said, "as undoubtedly human, with human needs and rights and dignities. But this turns out to be an illusion. It is as an *animal* that one has to play the really important part in life; it is by submitting to the demands of society, in this respect, that one wins rewards and commendation. Of course, if one likes to throw in a few ornamental extras, so much the better; it keeps up appearances and the aspect of refined sentiment—but the main point ——"

"You *are* extravagant!" cried Miss Du Prel. "That is not the right way to look at it."

"It is certainly not the convenient way to look at it. It is doubtless wise to weave as many garlands as you can, to deck yourself for the sacrifice. By that means, you don't quite see which way you are going, because of the masses of elegant vegetation."

"Ah! Hadria, you exaggerate, you distort; you forget so

many things—the sentiments, the affections, the thousand details that hallow that crude foundation which you see only bare and unsoftened."

"A repulsive object tastefully decorated, is to me only the more repulsive," returned Hadria, with suppressed passion.

"There will come a day when you will feel very differently," prophesied Miss Du Prel.

"Perhaps. Why should I, more than the others, remain uninfluenced by the usual processes of blunting, and grinding down, and stupefying, till one grows accustomed to one's function, one's *intolerable* function?"

"My dear, my dear!"

"I am sorry if I shock you, but that is how I feel. I have seen this sort of traditional existence and nothing else, all my life, and I have been brought up to it, with the rest—prepared and decked out like some animal for market—all in the most refined and graceful manner possible; but how can one help seeing through the disguise; how can one be blind to the real nature of the transaction, and to the fate that awaits one—awaits one as inexorably as death, unless by some force of one's own, with all the world—friends and enemies—in opposition, one can avert it?"

Miss Du Prel remained silent.

"You *can* avert it," she said at last; "but at what cost?"

"Miss Du Prel, I would rather sweep a crossing, I would rather beg in the streets, than submit to the indignity of such a life!"

"Then what do you intend to do instead?"

"Ah! there's the difficulty. What *can* one do instead, without breaking somebody's heart? Nothing, except breaking one's own. And even putting that difficulty aside, it seems as if everyone's hand were against a woman who refuses the path that has been marked out for her."

"No, no, it is not so bad as that. There are many openings now for women."

"But," said Hadria, "as far as I can gather, ordinary

ability is not sufficient to enable them to make a scanty living. The talent that would take a man to the top of the tree is required to keep a woman in a meagre supply of bread and butter."

"Allowing for exaggeration, that is more or less the case," Miss Du Prel admitted.

"I have revolted against the common lot," she went on after a pause, "and you see what comes of it; I am alone in the world. One does not think of that when one is quite young."

"Would you rather be in Mrs. Gordon's position than in your own?"

"I doubt not that she is happier."

"But would you change with her, surrendering all that she has surrendered?"

"Yes, if I were of her temperament."

"Ah! you always evade the question. Remaining yourself, would you change with her?"

"I would never have allowed my life to grow like hers."

"No," said Hadria, laughing, "you would probably have run away or killed yourself or somebody, long before this."

Miss Du Prel could not honestly deny this possibility. After a pause she said:

"A woman cannot afford to despise the dictates of Nature. She may escape certain troubles in that way; but Nature is not to be cheated, she makes her victim pay her debt in another fashion. There is no escape. The centuries are behind one, with all their weight of heredity and habit; the order of society adds its pressure — one's own emotional needs. Ah, no! it does not answer to pit oneself against one's race, to bid defiance to the fundamental laws of life."

"Such then are the alternatives," said Hadria, moving close to the river's brink, and casting two big stones into the current. "There stand the devil and the deep sea."

"You are too young to have come to that sad conclusion," said Miss Du Prel.

"But I haven't," cried Hadria. "I still believe in revolt."

The other shook her head.

"And what about love? Are you going through life without the one thing that makes it bearable?"

"I would not purchase it at such a cost. If I can't have it without despoiling myself of everything that is worth possessing, I prefer to go without."

"You don't know what you say!" exclaimed Miss Du Prel.

"But why? Love would be ruined and desecrated. I understand by it a sympathy so perfect, and a reverence so complete, that the conditions of ordinary domestic existence would be impossible, unthinkable, in connection with it."

"So do I understand love. But it comes, perhaps, once in a century, and if one is too fastidious, it passes by and leaves one forlorn; at best, it comes only to open the gates of Paradise, for a moment, and to close them again, and leave one in outer darkness."

"Always?"

"I believe always," answered Miss Du Prel.

The running of the river sounded peacefully in the pause that followed.

"Well," cried Hadria at length, raising her head with a long sigh, "one cannot do better than follow one's own instinct and thought of the moment. Regret may come, do what one may. One cannot escape from one's own temperament."

"One can modify it."

"I cannot even wish to modify mine, so that I should become amenable to these social demands. I stand in hopeless opposition to the scheme of life that I have grown up amongst, to the universal scheme of life indeed, as understood by the world up to this day. Audacious, is it not?"

"I like audacity," returned Miss Du Prel. "As I understand you, you require an altogether new dispensation!"

Hadria gave a half smile, conscious of her stupendous demand. Then she said, with a peculiar movement of the head, as if throwing off a heavy weight, and looking before her steadily: "Yes, I require a new dispensation."

CHAPTER VIII.

HUBERT TEMPERLEY made a point of going to the tennis-party, on Tuesday, at Dunaghee, in order to talk to Miss Fullerton. He had not expected to find original musical talent in this out-of-the-way place.

Hadria was in a happy mood, for her mother had so far overcome her prejudice against Miss Du Prel, as to ask her to join the party.

The festivity had, therefore, lost its usual quality of melancholy.

It was a warm afternoon, and every one seemed cheerful "and almost intelligent," Hadria commented. The first words that Mr. Temperley uttered, made her turn to him, in surprise. She was so unaccustomed to be interested in what the people about here had to say. Even intelligent visitors usually adopted the tone of the inhabitants. Hubert Temperley's manner was very polished. His accent denoted mental cultivation. He spoke with eloquence of literature, and praised enthusiastically most great names dating securely from the hallowed past. Of modern literature he was a stern critic ; of music he spoke with ardour.

"I hear that you not only perform but compose, Miss Fullerton," he said. "As soon as I heard that, I felt that I must make your acquaintance. My friends, the Gordons, are very charming, but they don't understand a note of music, and I am badly off for a kindred spirit."

"My composing is a very mild affair," Hadria answered. "I suppose you are more fortunate."

"Not much. I am pretty busy you see. I have my pro

73

fession. I play a good deal—the piano and the *'cello* are my instruments. But my difficulty is to find someone to accompany me. My sister does when she can, but of course with a house and family to look after——I am sometimes selfish enough to wish she had not married. We used to be such good friends."

"Is that all over?"

"It is different. She always manages to be busy now," said Temperley in a slightly ironical tone.

He plunged once more, into a musical discussion.

Hadria had reluctantly to cut it short, in order to arrange tennis-matches. This task was performed as usual, somewhat recklessly. Polite and amiable in indiscriminate fashion, Hadria ignored the secret jealousies and heart-burnings of the neighbourhood, only to recognise and repent her mistakes when too late. To-day she was even more unchastened than usual in her dealings with inflammable social material.

"Hadria!" cried Mrs. Fullerton, taking her aside, "How *could* you ask Cecilia Gordon to play with young McKenzie? You *know* their families are not on speaking terms!"

Everyone, except the culprit, had remarked the haughty manner in which Cecilia wielded her racket, and the gloomy silence in which the set was played.

Hadria, though not impenitent, laughed. "How does Miss Gordon manage to be energetic and chilling at the same time!" she exclaimed.

The Gordons and the McKenzies, like hostile armies, looked on grimly. Everyone felt awkward, and to feel awkward was nothing less than tragic, in the eyes of the assembly.

"Oh, Hadria, how *could* you?" cried Mrs. Gordon, coming up in her elaborate toilette, which expressed almost as much of the character of its wearer as was indicated by her thin, chattering tones, and unreposeful manner. Her mode of dress was rich and florid—very obvious in its effects, very *naïf*. She was built on a large scale, and might have been graceful, had not her mental constitution refused to permit, or to inspire, that which physical construction seemed to intend. She distributed smiles on all hands, of no particular meaning. Though still a young woman, she looked worn and wearied. However, her *rôle* was cheerfulness, and she smiled on industriously.

"I am so sorry," said Hadria, "the quarrel went clean out of my head. They are so well matched. But your sister-in-law will never forgive me."

"Oh, well, never mind, my dear; it is your way, I know. Only of course it is awkward."

"What can be done? Shall I run in and separate them?"

"Oh, Hadria, you *are* ridiculous!"

"I was not meant for society," she said, in a depressed tone.

"Oh, you will soon get into the way of it," cried Mrs. Gordon encouragingly.

"I am afraid I shall."

Mrs. Gordon stared. "Mr. Temperley, I can never make out what Miss Fullerton really means. Do see if you can."

"How could I expect to succeed where you have failed?"

"Oh, you men are so much cleverer than we poor women," cried the lady archly. Temperley was obviously of the same opinion. But he found some appropriate Chesterfieldian reply, while Hadria, to his annoyance, hurried off to her duties, full of good resolutions.

Having introduced a couple of sisters to their brother, she grew desperate. A set had just ended, and the sisters were asked to play. This time, no mistake had been made in the selection of partners, so far as the question of sentiment was concerned, but they were fatally ill-assorted as to strength. However, Hadria said with a sigh, if their emotions were satisfied, it was really all they could expect. Considering the number of family feuds, she did not see her way to arranging both points, to everyone's satisfaction.

Hadria was surrounded by a small group, among whom

were Temperley, Harold Wilkins, and Mr. Hawkesley, the brother who had been introduced to his sisters.

"How very handsome Hadria is looking this afternoon," said Mrs. Gordon, "and how becoming that dark green gown is."

Mrs. Fullerton smiled. "Yes, she does look her best to-day. I think she has been improving, of late, in her looks."

"That's just what we have all noticed. There is so much animation in her face; she is such a sweet girl."

Miss Du Prel, who was not of the stuff that martyrs are made of, muttered something incoherent and deserted her neighbour. She came up to the group that had gathered round Hadria.

"Ah, Miss Du Prel," cried the latter, "I am so glad to see you at large again. I was afraid you were getting bored."

"I was," said Miss Du Prel frankly, "so I came away."

The young men laughed. "If only everybody could go away when he was bored," cried Hadria, "how peaceful it would be, and what small tennis-parties one would have!"

"Always excepting tennis-parties at *this* house," said Hubert Temperley.

"I don't think any house would survive," said Miss Du Prel. "If people do not meet to exchange ideas, I can't see the object of their meeting at all."

"What a revolutionary sentiment!" cried Temperley, laughing. "Where would society be, on that principle?"

Hadria was called away, at that moment, and the group politely wavered between duty and inclination. Temperley and Miss Du Prel strolled off together, his vast height bent deferentially towards her. This air of deference proved somewhat superficial. Miss Du Prel found that his opinions were of an immovable order, with very defined edges. In some indescribable fashion, those opinions partook of the general elegance of his being. Not for worlds would he have harboured an exaggerated or immoderate idea. In politics he was conservative, but he did not abuse his opponents. He smiled at them; he saw no reason for supposing that they did not mean quite as well as he did, possibly better. What he *did* see reason to doubt, was their judgment. His tolerance was urbane and superior. On all questions, however, whether he knew much about them or little, his judgment was final and absolute., He swept away whole systems of thought that had shaken the world, with a confident phrase. Miss Du Prel looked at him with increasing amazement. He seemed unaccustomed to opposition.

"A vast deal of nonsense is talked in the name of philosophy," he observed, in a tone of gay self-confidence peculiar to him, and more indicative of character than even what he said. "People seem to think that they have only to quote Spencer or Huxley, or take an interest in heredity, to justify themselves in throwing off all the trammels, as they would regard them, of duty and common sense."

"I have not observed that tendency," said Miss Du Prel.

"Really. I regret to say that I notice everywhere a disposition to evade responsibilities which, in former days, would have been honestly and contentedly accepted."

"Our standards are all changing," said Miss Du Prel. "It does not follow that they are changing for the worse."

"It seems to me that they are not so much changing, as disappearing altogether," said Temperley cheerfully, "especially among women. We hear a great deal about rights, but we hear nothing about duties."

"We are perhaps, a little tired of hearing about duties," said Miss Du Prel.

"You admit then what I say," he returned placidly. "Every woman wants to be Mary, and no one will be Martha."

"I make just the opposite complaint," cried Miss Du Prel.

"Dear me, quite a different way of looking at it. I confess I have scant patience with these interfering women, who want to turn everything upside down, instead of quietly minding their duties at home."

"I know it is difficult to make people understand," said Miss Du Prel, with malice.

"I should esteem it a favour to be enlightened," returned Temperley.

"You were just now condemning socialism, Mr. Temperley, because you say that it attempts to ignore the principle of the division of labour. Now, when you lose patience with the few women who are refusing to be Marthas, you ignore that principle yourself. You want all women to do exactly the same sort of work, irrespective of their ability or their bent of· mind. May I ask why?"

"Because I consider that is the kind of work for which they are best fitted," replied Temperley serenely.

"Then *you* are to be judge and jury in the case ; *your* opinion, not theirs, is to decide the matter. Supposing *I* were to take upon myself to judge what *you* were best fitted for, and were to claim, therefore, to decide for you what sort of life you should live, and what sort of work you should undertake——?"

"I should feel every confidence in resigning myself to your able judgment," said Temperley, with a low bow. Miss Du Prel laughed.

"Ah," she said, "you are at present, on the conquering side, and can afford to jest on the subject."

"It is no joke to jest with an able woman," he returned "Seriously, I have considerable sympathy with your view, and no wish to treat it flippantly. But if I am to treat it seriously, I must admit frankly that I think you forget that, after all, *Nature* has something to say in this matter."

Engrossed in their conversation, they had, without thinking what they were doing, passed through the open gate at the end of the avenue, and walked on along the high road.

Swarms of small birds flew out of the hedges, with a whirring sound, to settle further on, while an incessant chatter was kept up on each side.

"I often think that modern women might take example from these little creatures," said Temperley, who, in common with many self-sufficient persons, was fond of recommending humility to others. "*They* never attempt to shirk their lowly tasks on the plea of higher vocations. Not one turns from the path marked out by our great Mother, who also teaches her human children the same lesson of patient duty; but, alas! by them is less faithfully obeyed."

" If our great Mother wanted instinct she should not have bestowed reason," said Miss Du Prel impatiently.

Temperley had fallen into the dulcet strains of one who feels, not only that he stands as the champion of true wisdom and virtue, but that he is sure of support from the vast majority of his fellows. Miss Du Prel's brusqueness seemed to suit her less admirable *rôle*.

Temperley was tolerant and regretful. If Miss Du Prel would think for a moment, she could not fail to see that Nature . . . and so forth, in the same strain of "pious devotion to other people's duties" as his companion afterwards described it. She chafed at the exhortation to "think for a moment."

At that instant, the solitude was broken by the apparition of a dusty wayfarer in knickerbockers and soft felt hat, coming towards them up the road. He was a man of middle height and rather slim. He appeared about five-and-thirty years of age. He had fair hair, and a strange, whimsical face, irregular of feature, with a small moustache covering the upper lip.

Miss Du Prel looked startled, as she caught sight of the travel-stained figure. She flushed deeply, and her expression changed to one of bewilderment and uncertainty, then to one of incredulous joy. She hastened forward, at length, and arrested the wayfarer.

" Professor Fortescue, don't you remember me?" she cried excitedly.

He gazed at her for a second, and then a look of amazement came into his kind eyes, as he held out his hand.

" Miss Du Prel! This is incredible!"

They stood, with hand locked in hand, staring at one another. " By what happy misunderstanding am I thus favoured by the gods?" exclaimed the Professor.

Miss Du Prel explained her presence.

"Prodigious!" cried Professor Fortescue. "Fate must have some strange plots in the making, unless indeed we fall to the discouraging supposition that she deigns to jest."

He said that he was on a walking tour, studying the geology of the district, and that he had written to announce his coming to his old friends, Mr. and Mrs. Fullerton, and to ask them to put him up. He supposed that they were expecting him.

Miss Du Prel was greatly excited. It was so long since they had met, and it was so delightful to meet again. She had a hundred enquiries to make about common friends, and about the Professor's own doings.

She forgot Temperley's name, and 'ler introduction was vague. The Professor held out his hand cordially. Temperley was not allowed to feel an intrusive third. This was in consequence of the new-comer's kindliness of manner, and not at all because of Miss Du Prel, who had forgotten Temperley's elegant existence. She had a look of surprise when he joined in the conversation.

"I can scarcely believe that it is ten years since I was here," cried the Professor, pausing to look over a gate at the stretch of country.

"I used to visit my friends at Dunaghee every autumn, and now if some one were to assure me that I had been to sleep and dreamt a ten years' dream, I should be disposed to credit it. Every detail the same; the very cattle, the very birds— surely just those identical sparrows used to fly before me along the hedgerows, in the good old times, ten years ago! Ah! yes, it is only the human element that changes."

"One is often so thankful for a change in that," Temperley remarked, with an urbane sort of cynicism.

"True," said Miss Du Prel; "but what is so discouraging is that so often the charm goes, like the bloom of a peach, and only the qualities that one regrets remain and prosper."

"I think people improve with time, as often as they fall off," said the Professor.

The others shook their heads.

"To him that hath shall be given, but to him that hath not——" The Professor smiled a little sadly, in quoting the significant words. "Well, well," he said, turning to Miss Du Prel, "I can't say how happy I am to see you again. I have not yet got over my surprise. And so you have made the acquaintance of the family at Dunaghee. I have the warmest respect and affection for those dear folks. Mrs. Fullerton has the qualities of a heroine, kind hostess as she is! And of what fine Scottish stuff the old man is made— and a mind like crystal! What arguments we used to have in that old study of his! I can see him now. And how genial! A man could never forget it, who had once received his welcome."

Such was Miss Du Prel's impression, when ten minutes later the meeting took place between the Professor and his old friend.

It would indeed have been hard to be anything but genial to the Professor. Hadria remembered him and his kindness to her and the rest of the children, in the old days; the stories he used to tell when he took them for walks, stories full of natural lore more marvellous than any fairy tale, though he could tell fairy tales too, by the dozen. He had seemed to them like some wonderful and benevolent magician, and they adored him, one and all. And what friends he used to be with Ruffian, the brown retriever, and with every living creature on the place!

The tennis-party began to break up, shortly after the Professor's arrival. Temperley lingered to the last.

"Is that a son of the celebrated Judge Temperley?" asked one of the bystanders.

"His eldest son," answered Mr. Gordon; "a man who ought to make his mark, for he has splendid chances and good ability."

"I have scarcely had a word with you, the whole afternoon," Temperley said to Hadria, who had sunk upon a seat, tired with making herself agreeable, as she observed.

"That is very sad; but when one has social gatherings, one never does have a word with anybody. I think that must be the object of them—to accustom people to do without human sympathy."

Temperley tried to start a conversation, taking a place beside her, on the seat, and setting himself to draw her out. It was obvious that he found her interesting, either as a study or in a less impersonal sense. Hadria, feeling that her character was being analysed, did what many people do without realizing it: she instinctively arranged its lights and shades with a view to artistic effect. It was not till late that night, when the events of the day passed before her in procession, that she recognized what she had done, and laughed at herself. She had not attempted to appear in a better light than she deserved; quite as often as not, she submitted to appear in a worse light; her effort had been to satisfy some innate sense of proportion or form. The instinct puzzled her.

Also she became aware that she was interested in Hubert Temperley. Or was it that she was interested in his interest in her? She could not be certain. She thought it was direct interest. She felt eager to know more of him; above all, to hear him play.

On returning to the house, after Temperley had, at last, felt compelled to depart, Hadria found her father and mother and their guest, gathered together before the cheery fire in the study. Hearing his daughter's step, her father opened the door and called her in. Till now, the Professor had not seen her, having been hurried into the house, to change his clothes and have something to eat.

As she entered, rather shyly, he rose and gave a gasp of astonishment.

"You mean to tell me that this is the little girl who used to take me for walks, and who had such an inordinate appetite for stories! Good heavens, it is incredible!"

He held out a thin, finely-formed hand, with a kind smile.

"They change so much at that age, in a short time," said Mrs. Fullerton, with a glance of pride; for her daughter was looking brilliantly handsome, as she stood before them, with flushed cheeks and a soft expression, which the mere tones of the Professor's voice had power to summon in most human faces. He looked at her thoughtfully, and then rousing himself, he brought up a chair for her, and the group settled again before the fire.

"Do you know," said the Professor, "I was turning into a French sweet-shop the other day, to buy my usual tribute for the children, when I suddenly remembered that they would no longer be children, and had to march out again, crestfallen, musing on the march of time and the mutability of things human—especially children."

"It's ridiculous," cried Mr. Fullerton. "I am always lecturing them about it, but they go on growing just the same."

"And how they make you feel an old fogey before you know where you are! And I thought I was quite a gay young fellow, upon my word!"

"You, my dear Chantrey! why you'd be a gay young fellow at ninety!" said Mr. Fullerton.

The Professor laughed and shook his head.

"And so this is really my little playfellow!" he exclaimed, nodding meditatively. "I remember her so well; a queer, fantastic little being in those days, with hair like a black cloud, and eyes that seemed to peer out of the cloud, with a perfect passion of enquiry. She used to bewilder me, I remember, with her strange, wise little sayings! I always prophesied great things from her! Ernest, too, I remember: a fine little chap with curly, dark hair—rather like a young Italian, but with features less broadly cast; drawn together and calmed by his northern blood. Yes, yes; it seems but

yesterday," he said, with a smile and a sigh; "and now my
little Italian is at college, with a bored manner and a high
collar."

"Oh, no; Ernest's a dear boy still," cried Hadria.
"Oxford hasn't spoilt him a bit. I do wish he was at home
for you to see him."

"Ah! you mustn't hint at anything against Ernest in
Hadria's presence!" cried Mr. Fullerton, with an approving
laugh.

"Not for the world!" rejoined the Professor. "I was only
recalling one or two of my young Oxford acquaintances. I
might have known that a Fullerton had too much stuff in him
to make an idiot of himself in that way."

"The boy has distinguished himself too," said Mr. Fullerton.

"Everyone says he will do splendidly," added the mother;
"and you can't think how modest he is about himself, and
how anxious to do well, and to please us by his success."

"Ah! that's good."

The Professor was full of sympathy. Hadria was astonished
to see how animated her mother had become under his
influence.

They fell again to recalling old times; little trivial incidents
which had seemed so unimportant at the moment, but now
carried a whole epoch with them, bringing back, with a rush,
the genial memories. Hadria remembered that soon after his
last visit, the Professor had married a beautiful wife, and that
about a year or so later, the wife had died. It was said that
she had killed herself. This set Hadria speculating.

The visitor reminded his companions of various absurd
incidents of the past, sending Mr. Fullerton into paroxysms
of laughter that made the whole party laugh in sympathy.
Mrs. Fullerton too was already wiping her streaming eyes as
the Professor talked on in his old vein, with just that particular
little humorous manner of his that won its way so surely to
the hearts of his listeners. For a moment, in the midst of the
bright talk and the mirth that he had created, the Professor

lost the thread, and his face, as he stared into the glowing centre of the fire, had a desolate look ; but it was so quick to pass away that one might have thought oneself the victim of a fancy. His was the next chuckle, and " Do you remember that day when——? " and so forth, Mr. Fullerton's healthy roar following, avalanche-like, upon the reminiscence.

" We thought him a good and kind magician when we were children," was Hadria's thought, " and now one is grown up, there is no disillusion. He is a good and kind magician still."

He seemed indeed to have the power to conjure forth from their hiding-places, the finer qualities of mind and temperament, which had lain dormant, perhaps for years, buried beneath daily accumulations of little cares and little habits. The creature that had once looked forth on the world, fresh and vital, was summoned again, to his own surprise, with all his ancient laughter and his tears.

"This man," Hadria said to herself, drawing a long, relieved breath, " is the best and the most generous human being I have ever met."

She went to sleep, that night, with a sweet sense of rest and security, and an undefined new hope. If such natures were in existence, then there must be a great source of goodness and tenderness somewhere in heaven or earth, and the battle of life must be worth the fighting.

CHAPTER IX.

THE Professor's presence in the house had a profound influence on the inmates, one and all. The effect upon his hostess was startling. He drew forth her intellect, her sense of humour, her starved poetic sense; he probed down among the dust and rust of years, and rescued triumphantly the real woman, who was being stifled to death, with her own connivance.

Hadria was amazed to see how the new-comer might express any idea he pleased, however heterodox, and her mother only applauded.

His manner to her was exquisitely courteous. He seemed to understand all that she had lost in her life, all its disappointments and sacrifices.

On hearing that Miss Du Prel was among the Professor's oldest friends, Mrs. Fullerton became suddenly cordial to that lady, and could not show her enough attention. The evenings were often spent in music, Temperley being sometimes of the party. He was the only person not obviously among the Professor's admirers.

"However cultivated or charming a person may be," Temperley said to Hadria, "I never feel that I have found a kindred spirit, unless the musical instinct is strong."

"Nor I."

"Professor Fortescue has just that one weak point."

"Oh, but he is musical, though his technical knowledge is small."

But Temperley smiled dubiously.

The Professor, freed from his customary hard work, was like a schoolboy. His delight in the open air, in the freshness of

86

the hills, in the peace of the mellow autumn, was never-ending.

He loved to take a walk before breakfast, so as to enjoy the first sweetness of the morning; to bathe in some clear pool of the river; to come into healthy contact with Nature. Never was there a brighter or a wholesomer spirit. Yet the more Hadria studied this clear, and vigorous, and tender nature, the more she felt, in him, the absence of that particular personal hold on life which so few human beings are without, a grip usually so hard to loosen, that only the severest experience, and the deepest sorrow have power to destroy it.

Hadria's letters to her sister, at this time, were full of enthusiasm. "You cannot imagine what it is, or perhaps you *can* imagine what it is to have the society of three such people as I now see almost every day.

"You say I represent them as impossible angels, such as earth never beheld, but you are wrong. I represent them as they are. I suppose the Professor has faults—though he does not show them to us—they must be of the generous kind, at any rate. Father says that he never could keep a farthing; he would always give it away to undeserving people. Miss Du Prel, I find on closer acqaintance, is not without certain jealousies and weaknesses, but these things just seem to float about as gossamer on a mountain-side, and one counts them in relation to herself, in about the same proportion. Mr. Temperley—I don't know quite what to say about him. He is a tiny bit too precise and finished perhaps—a little wanting in *élan*—but he seems very enlightened and full of polite information; and ah, his music! When he is playing I am completely carried away. If he said then, 'Miss Fullerton, may I have the pleasure of your society in the infernal regions?' I should arise and take his arm and reply, 'Delighted,' and off we would march. But what am I saying? Mr. Temperley would never ask anything so absurd.

"You would have thought that when Miss Du Prel and

Professor Fortescue arrived on the scene, I had about enough privileges; but no, Destiny, waking up at last to her duties, remembers that I have a maniacal passion for music, and that this has been starved. So she hastens to provide for me a fellow maniac, a brother in Beethoven, who comes and fills my world with music and my soul with—— But I must not rave. The music is still in my veins; I am not in a fit state to write reasonable letters. Here comes Mr. Temperley for our practice. No more for the present."

Temperley would often talk to Hadria of his early life, and about his mother and sister. Of his mother he spoke with great respect and affection, the respect perhaps somewhat conventional, and allowing one to see, through its meshes, the simple fact that she was looked up to as a good and dutiful parent, who had worshipped her son from his birth, and perfectly fulfilled his ideas of feminine excellency. From her he had learnt the lesser Catechism and the Lord's Prayer, since discarded, but useful in their proper season. Although he had ceased to be an orthodox Christian, he felt that he was the better for having been trained in that creed. He had a perfect faith in the system which had produced himself.

"I think you would like my mother," said Temperley.

Hadria could scarcely dispute this.

"And I am sure she would like you."

"On that point I cannot offer an opinion."

"Don't you ever come to town?" he asked.

"We go to Edinburgh occasionally," she replied with malice, knowing that he meant London.

He set her right.

"No; my father hates London, and mother never goes away without him."

"What a pity! But do you never visit friends in town?"

"Yes; my sister and I have spent one or two seasons in Park Lane, with some cousins."

"Why don't you come this next season? You ought to hear some good music."

The *tête-a-tête* was interrupted by the Professor. Temperley looked annoyed. It struck Hadria that Professor Fortescue had a very sad expression when he was not speaking. He seemed to her lonely, and in need of the sort of comfort that he brought so liberally to others.

Although he had talked to Hadria about a thousand topics in which they were both interested, there had been nothing personal in their conversation. He was disposed, at times, to treat her in a spirit of affectionate banter.

"To think that I should ever have dared to offer this young lady acidulated drops!" he exclaimed on one occasion, when Hadria was looking flushed and perturbed.

"Ah! shall I ever forget those acidulated drops!" she cried, brightening.

"You don't mean to say that you would stoop to them now?"

"It is not one's oldest friends who always know one best," she replied demurely.

"I shall test you," he said.

And on that same day, he walked into Ballochcoil, and when he returned, he offered her, with a solemn twinkle in his eye, a good-sized paper bag of the seductive sweetmeat; taking up his position on the top of a low dyke, and watching her, while she proceeded to make of that plump white bag, a lank and emaciated bag, surprising to behold. He sat and looked on, enjoying his idleness with the zest of a hard worker. The twinkle of amusement faded gradually from his face, and the sadness that Hadria had noticed the day before, returned to his eyes. She was leaning against the dyke, pensively enjoying her festive meal. The dark fresh blue of her gown, and the unwonted tinge of colour in her cheeks, gave a vigorous and healthful impression, in harmony with the weather-beaten stones and the windy breadth of the northern landscape.

The Professor studied the face with a puzzled frown. He flattered himself that he was a subtle physiognomist, but in this case, he would not have dared to pronounce judgment. Danger and difficulty might have been predicted, for it was a moving face, one that could not be looked upon quite coldly. And the Professor had come to the conclusion, from his experience of life, that the instinct of the average human being whom another has stirred to strong emotion, is to fasten upon and overwhelm that luckless person, to burden him with responsibilities, to claim as much of time, and energy, and existence, as can in any way be wrung from him, careless of the cost to the giver.

Professor Fortescue noticed, as Hadria looked down, a peculiar dreaminess of expression, and something indefinable, which suggested a profoundly emotional nature. At present, the expression was softened. That this softness was not altogether trustworthy, however, the Professor felt sure, for he had seen, at moments, when something had deeply stirred her, expressions anything but soft come into her face. He thought her capable of many things of which the well-brought-up young Englishwoman is not supposed to dream. It seemed to him, that she had at least two distinct natures that were at war with one another: the one greedy and pleasure-loving, careless and even reckless; the other deep-seeing and aspiring. But which of these two tendencies would experience probably foster?

" I wonder what you like best, next to acidulated drops," he said at length, with one of his half-bantering smiles.

"There are few things in this wide world that can be mentioned in the same breath with them, but toffy also has its potency upon the spirit."

" I like not this mocking tone."

" Then I will not mock," she said.

"Yes, Hadria," he went on meditatively, "you have grown up, if an old friend may make such remarks, very much as I expected, from the promise of your childhood. You used to puzzle me even then."

" Do I puzzle you now? " she asked.

" Inexpressibly ! "

" How amusing ! But how ? "

" One can generally see at a glance, or pretty soon, the general trend of a character. But not with you. Nothing that I might hear of you in the future, would very much surprise me. I should say to myself, ' Yes, the germ was there.' "

Hadria paled a little. " Either good or bad you mean ? "

" Well——"

" Yes, I understand." She drew herself together, crossing her arms, and looking over the hills, with eyes that burned with a sort of fear and defiance mingled. It was a singular expression, which the Professor noted with a sense of discomfort.

Hadria slowly withdrew her eyes from the horizon, and bent them on the ground.

" You must have read some of my thoughts," she said. " I often wonder how it is, that the world can drill women into goodness at all." She raised her head, and went on in a low, bitter tone : " I often wonder why it is, that they don't, one and all, fling up their *rôles* and revenge themselves to the best of their ability — intentionally, I mean — upon the world that makes them live under a permanent insult. I think, at times, that I should thoroughly enjoy spending my life in sheer, unmitigated vengeance, and if I did "—she clenched her hands, and her eyes blazed—"if I did, I would not do my work by halves ! "

" I am sure you would not," said the Professor dryly.

" But I shall not do anything of the kind," she added in a different tone ; "women don't. They always try to be good, always, *always*—the more fools they ! And the more they are good, the worse things get."

" Ah ! I thought there was some heterodox sentiment lurking here at high pressure ! " exclaimed the Professor.

Hadria sighed. " I have just been receiving good advice from Mrs. Gordon," she said, flushing at the remembrance, "and I think if you knew the sort of counsel it was, that you would understand one's feeling a little fierce and bitter. Oh, not with her, poor woman! She meant it in kindness. But the most cutting thing of all is, that what she said is *true!*"

"That *is* exactly the worst thing," said the Professor, who seemed to have divined the nature of Mrs. Gordon's advice.

Hadria coloured. It hurt as well as astonished her, that he should guess what had been said.

"Ah! a woman ought to be born without pride, or not at all! I wish to heaven that our fatal sex could be utterly stamped out!"

The Professor smiled, a little sadly, at her vehemence.

"We are accused of being at the bottom of every evil under heaven," she added, "and I think it is true. *That* is some consolation, at any rate!"

In spite of her immense reverence for the Professor, she seemed to have grown reckless as to his opinion.

The next few days went strangely, and not altogether comprehensibly. There was a silent warfare between Professor Fortescue and Hubert Temperley.

"I have never in my life before ventured to interfere in such matters," the Professor said to Miss Du Prel; "but if that fellow marries Hadria, one or both will live to rue it."

"I think it 's the best thing that could happen to her," Miss Du Prel declared.

"But they are not suited to one another," said the Professor.

"Men and women seldom are!"

"Then why ——?" the Professor began.

"He is about as near as she will get," Valeria interrupted. "I will never stand in the way of a girl's marrying a good, honest man. There is not one chance in ten thousand that Hadria will happen to meet exactly the right person. I have made a mistake in my life. I shall do all in my power to urge her to avoid following in my footsteps."

It was useless for the Professor to remonstrate.

"I pity Mr. Temperley, though I am so fond of Hadria," said Miss Du Prel. "If he shatters *her* illusions, she will certainly shatter *his*."

The event that they had been expecting, took place. During one of the afternoon practices, when, for a few minutes, Mrs. Fullerton had left the room, Temperley startled Hadria by an extremely elegant proposal of marriage. He did not seem surprised at her refusal, though he pleaded his cause with no little eloquence. Hadria found it a painful ordeal. She shrank from the ungracious necessity to disappoint what appeared to be a very ardent hope. Happily, the interview was cut short by the entrance of Mr. Fullerton. The old man was not remarkable for *finesse*. He gave a dismayed "Oh!" He coughed, suppressed a smile, and murmuring some lame enquiry as to the progress of the music, turned and marched out of the room. The sound of laughter was presently heard from the dining-room below.

"Father is really too absurd!" cried Hadria, "there is *no* tragedy that he is incapable of roaring at!"

"I fear his daughter takes after him," said Temperley with a tragi-comic smile.

When Hadria next met her father, he asked, with perfect but suspicious gravity, about the music that they had been practising that afternoon. He could not speak too highly of music as a pastime. He regretted having rushed in as he did—it must have been so disturbing to the music. Why not have a notice put up outside the door on these occasions: "Engaged"? Then the meanest intelligence would understand, and the meanest intelligence was really a thing one had to count with, in this blundering world!

CHAPTER X.

HUBERT TEMPERLEY left Drumgarren suddenly.
He said that he had business to attend to in town.

"That foolish girl has refused him!" exclaimed Valeria,
when she heard of it.

"Thank heaven!" ejaculated Professor Fortescue.

Valeria's brow clouded. "Why are you so anxious about
the matter?"

"Because I know that a marriage between those two would
end in misery."

Valeria spoke very seriously to Hadria on the subject of
marriage, urging the importance of it, and the wretchedness
of growing old in solitude.

"Better even that, than to grow old in uncongenial company," said Hadria.

Valeria shrugged her shoulders. "One could go away when
it became oppressive," she suggested, at which Hadria laughed.

"What an ideal existence!"

"Are you still dreaming of an ideal existence?"

"Why not?"

"Well, dream while you may," said Miss Du Prel. "My
time of dreaming was the happiest of all."

On one occasion, when Hadria and the Professor went to
call at Craw Gill, they found Miss Du Prel in the gloomiest of
moods. Affection, love?—the very blood and bones of
tragedy. Solitude, indifference?—its heart. And if for men
the world was a delusion, for women it was a torture-chamber.
Nature was dead against them.

"Why do you say that?" asked Hadria.

"Because of the blundering, merciless way she has made us; because of the needs that she has put into our hearts, and the preposterous payment that she demands for their fulfilment; because of the equally preposterous payment she exacts, if we elect to do without that which she teaches us to yearn for."

Professor Fortescue, admitting the dilemma, laid the blame on the stupidity of mankind.

The discussion was excited, for Valeria would not allow the guilt to be thus shifted. In vain the Professor urged that Nature offers a large choice to humanity, for the developing, balancing, annulling of its various forces of good and evil, and that it is only when the choice is made that heredity steps in and fixes it. This process simulates Necessity, or what we call Nature. "Heredity may be a powerful friend, or a bitter enemy, according as we treat her," he said.

"Then our sex must have treated her very badly!" cried Miss Du Prel.

"Or *our* sex must have obliged yours to treat her badly, which comes to the same thing," said the Professor.

They had agreed to take a walk by the river, towards Ballochcoil. It was hoped that the fresh air and sunshine would cheer Miss Du Prel. The Professor led the conversation to her favourite topic : ancient Greek literature, but this only inspired her to quote the discouraging opinion of the *Medea* of Euripedes.

The Professor laughed. "I see it is a really bad attack," he said. "I sympathize. I have these inconsolable moods myself, sometimes."

They came upon the Greek temple on the cliff-side, and paused there to rest, for a few minutes. It was too cold to linger long under the slender columns. They walked on, till they came in sight of the bare little church of Ballochcoil.

The Professor instinctively turned to compare the two buildings. "The contrast between them is so extraordinary !" he exclaimed.

Nothing could have been more eloquent of the difference in the modes of thought which they respectively represented.

"If only they had not made such fools of their women, I should like to have lived at Athens in the time of Pericles!" exclaimed Hadria.

"I," said Valeria, "would choose rather the Middle Ages, with their mysticism and their romance."

The discussion on this point continued till the church was reached. A psalm was being sung, in a harsh but devout fashion, by the congregation. The sound managed to find its way to the sweet outer air, though the ugly rectangular windows were all jealously closed against its beneficence.

The sky had become overcast, and a few drops of rain having given warning of a shower, it was thought advisable to take shelter in the porch, till it was over. The psalm was ground out slowly, and with apparent fervour, to the end.

Then the voice of the minister was heard wrestling in prayer.

The Professor looked grave and sad, as he stood listening. It was possible to hear almost all the prayer through the red baize door, and the words, hackneyed though they were, and almost absurd in their pious sing-song, had a naïf impressiveness and, to the listener, an intense pathos.

The minister prayed for help and comfort for his congregation. There had been much sickness in the village during the summer, and many were in trouble. The good man put forth his petition to the merciful and mighty Father, that strength might be given to the sufferers to bear all that was sent in chastisement, for they knew that nothing would be given beyond their ability to endure. He assured the great and mighty Lord that He had power to succour, and that His love was without end; he prayed that as His might and His glory were limitless, so might His mercy be to the miserable sinners who had offended Him.

Age after age, this same prayer, in different forms, had besieged the throne of heaven. Age after age, the spirit of

man had sought for help, and mercy, and inspiration, in the
Power that was felt, or imagined, behind the veil of mystery.

From the village at the foot of the hill, vague sounds floated
up, and presently, among them and above them, could be
heard the yelping and howling of a dog.

The minister, at the moment, was glorifying his Creator and
his race at the same time, by addressing Him as "Thou who
hast given unto us, Thy servants, dominion over the beasts
of the field and over every living thing, that they may serve
us and minister unto us ——"

Again, and more loudly, came the cry of distress.

"I must go and see what is the matter," exclaimed the
Professor. At the moment, the howling suddenly ceased, and
he paused. The minister was still appealing to his God for
mercy. "Out of the deep have I cried unto Thee, O Lord
——," and then there was a general prayer, in which the
voices of the congregation joined. Some more singing and
praying took place, before the sound of a sudden rush and
movement announced the conclusion of the service.

"We had better go," said Miss Du Prel.

They had no more than time to leave the porch, before the
doors burst open, and the people streamed forth. A whiff
of evil-smelling air issued from the building, at the same time.
The dog was howling more piteously than ever. Someone
complained of the disturbance that had been caused by the
creature's cries, during worship. The congregation continued
to pour out, dividing into little groups to discuss the sermon
or something of more mundane interest. An appearance of
superhuman respectability pervaded the whole body. The
important people, some of whom had their carriages waiting
to drive them home, lingered a few moments, to exchange
greetings, and to discuss sporting prospects or achievements.
Meanwhile, one of the creatures over whom God had given
them dominion, was wailing in vain appeal.

"I can't stand this," cried the Professor, and he started off.

"I will come too," Hadria announced. Miss Du Prel said

that she could not endure the sight of suffering, and would await their return.

And then occurred the incident that made this afternoon memorable to Hadria. In her last letter to her sister, she had said that she could not imagine the Professor contemptuous or angry. She had reason now to change her mind. His face was at once scornful and sad. For a moment, Hadria thought that he was displeased with her.

"I sometimes feel," he said, with a scornful bitterness that she had not suspected in him, "I sometimes feel that this precious humanity of ours that we are eternally worshipping and exalting, is but a mean, miserable thing, after all, not worth a moment's care or effort. One's sympathy is wasted. Look at these good people whining to their heavenly Father about their own hurts, craving for a pity of which they have not a spark themselves!—puffed up with their little lordship over the poor beasts that they do not hesitate to tear, and hurt, and torture, for their own pleasure, or their own benefit,—to whom they, in their turn, love to play the God. Cowards! And having used their Godhead for purposes of cruelty, they fling themselves howling on their knees before their Almighty Deity and beg for mercy, which He too knows how to refuse!"

"Thank heaven!" exclaimed Hadria. She drew a deep sigh of relief. Without precisely realizing the fact, she had been gradually sinking into an unformulated conviction that human beings are, at heart, ruthless and hard, as soon as they are brought beyond the range of familiar moral claims, which have to be respected on pain of popular censure. Self-initiated pity was nowhere to be found. The merciless coldness of many excellent people (kind and tender, perhaps, within these accepted limits) had often chilled her to the heart, and prompted a miserable doubt of the eventual victory of good over evil in the world, which her father always insisted was ruled by mere brute force, and would be so ruled to the end of time. She had tried to find a wider, more generous, and less conventional standard in her oracle, Miss Du Prel, but to her bitter disappointment, that lady had shrugged her shoulders a little callously, as soon as she was asked to extend her sympathy outside the circle of chartered candidates for her merciful consideration. Hadria's hero-worship had suffered a severe rebuff. Now, as the Professor spoke, it was as if a voice from heaven had bidden her believe and hope fearlessly in her race, and in its destiny.

"I had almost come to shrink a little from people," she said, "as from something cruel and savage, at heart, without a grain of real, untaught pity."

"There is only just enough to swear by," said the Professor sadly. "We are a lot of half-tamed savages, after all, but we may be thankful that a capacity for almost infinite development is within us."

"I wish to heaven we could get on a little faster," exclaimed Hadria.

The incident proved, in the end, a fortunate one for the homeless, and almost starving terrier, of plebeian lineage, whose wail of distress had summoned two friends to the rescue. The creature had been ill-treated by some boys, who found Sunday afternoon hang heavy on their hands. The Professor carried the injured animal across the fields and through the woods, to Dunaghee.

Here the wounds were dressed, and here the grateful creature found a new and blissful home. His devotion to the Professor was unbounded; he followed him everywhere.

Hadria's reverence and admiration rose to the highest pitch of enthusiasm. Her father laughed at her. "Just as if any decent fellow would not have done as much for a wounded brute!"

"There must have been a strange dearth of decent fellows in church that morning then."

It was not merely the action, but the feeling revealed by the Professor's words on that occasion, that had turned Hadria's sentiment towards him, into one of worship.

Algitha warned her that even the Professor was human.

Hadria said she did not believe it, or rather she believed that he was inordinately, tenderly, superlatively human, and that he had gone many steps farther in that direction than the rest of his generation. He was dowered with instincts and perceptions belonging to some kinder, nobler race than ours.

Miss Du Prel looked grave. She took occasion to mention that the Professor had never ceased to grieve for his wife, to whom he had been passionately attached, and that he, almost alone among men, would never love any other woman.

" I admire him only the more for that," said Hadria.

" Don't let yourself care too much for him."

" Too much ! "

" Don't fall in love with him, if I must be frank."

Hadria was silent. "If one *were* to fall in love at all, I don't see how it would be possible to avoid his being the man," she pronounced at last. " I defy any creature with the least vestige of a heart to remain indifferent to him." (Valeria coloured.) " Why there isn't a man, woman, child, or animal about the place who doesn't adore him ; and what can *I* do ? "

CHAPTER XI.

THE autumn was now on the wane; the robins sang clear, wild little songs in the shrubberies, the sunshine fell slanting across the grass. And at night, the stars twinkled with a frosty brilliancy, and the flowers were cut down by cruel invisible hands. The long dark evenings and the shrieking winds of winter were before them.

With the shortening of the days, and the sweeping away of great shoals of leaves, in the frequent gales, Miss Du Prel's mood grew more and more sombre. At last she announced that she could stand the gloom of this wild North no longer. She had made arrangements to return to London, on the morrow. As suddenly as she had appeared on the scene, she vanished, leaving but one day to grieve at the prospect of parting.

It was through an accidental turn in the conversation, on this last day, that the difference between her creed and the Professor's was brought to light, accounting to Hadria for many things, and increasing, if possible, her admiration for the unconscious Professor.

As for her own private and personal justification for hope, Valeria asserted that she had none. Not even the thought of her work—usually a talisman against depression- had any power to comfort. Who cared for her work, unless she perjured herself, and told the lies that the public loved to hear?

"What should we all do," asked Hadria, "if there were not a few people like you and Professor Fortescue, in the world, to keep us true to our best selves, and to point to something infinitely better than that best?"

Miss Du Prel brightened for a moment.

"What does it matter if you do not provide mental food for

the crowd, seeking nourishment for their vulgarity? Let them
go starve."

"But they don't ; they go and gorge elsewhere. Besides,
the question of starvation faces *me* rather than them."

Miss Du Prel was still disposed to find fault with the
general scheme of things, which she regarded as responsible
for her own woes, great and little.   Survival of the fittest!
What was that but another name for the torture and massacre
of the unfit? Nature's favourite instruments were war, slaughter,
famine, misery (mental and physical), sacrifice and brutality
in every form, with a special malignity in her treatment of the
most highly developed and the noblest of the race.

The Professor in vain pointed out that Valeria's own revolt
against the brutality of Nature, was proof of some higher law
in Nature, now in course of development.

"The horror that is inspired in human beings by that
brutality is just as much a part of Nature as the brutality
itself," he said, and he insisted that the supreme business of
man, was to evolve a scheme of life on a higher plane, wherein
the weak shall not be forced to agonize for the strong, so far
as mankind can intervene to prevent it.   Let man follow the
dictates of pity and generosity in his own soul.   They would
never lead him astray.   While Miss Du Prel laid the whole
blame upon natural law, the Professor impeached humanity.
Men, he declared, cry out against the order of things, which
they, in a large measure, have themselves created.

"But, good heavens ! the whole plan of life is one of
rapine.   *We* did not fashion the spider to prey upon the fly,
or the cat to play with the wounded mouse.   *We* did not
ordain that the strong should fall upon the weak, and tear and
torture them for their own benefit.   Surely we are not responsible for the brutalities of the animal creation."

"No, but we are responsible when we *imitate them*," said
the Professor.

Miss Du Prel somewhat inconsequently attempted to defend
such imitation, on the ground that sacrifice is a law of life, a

law of which she had just been bitterly complaining. But at
this, the Professor would only laugh. His opponent indignantly cited scientific authority of the most solemn and
weighty kind; the Professor shook his head. Familiarity with
weighty scientific authorities had bred contempt.

"Vicarious sacrifice!" he exclaimed, with a sudden outbreak
of the scorn and impatience that Hadria had seen in him
on one other occasion, "I never heard a doctrine more
insane, more immoral, or more suicidal!"

Miss Du Prel hugged herself in the thought of her long
list of scouted authorities. They had assured her that our
care of the weak, by interfering with the survival of the fittest,
is injuring the race.

"Go down into the slums of our great cities, or to the
pestilential East, and there observe the survival of the fittest,
undisturbed by human knowledge or human pity," recommended the Professor.

Miss Du Prel failed to see how this proved anything more
than bad general conditions.

"It proves that however bad general conditions may be,
some wretches will always survive; the 'fittest,' of course, to
endure filth and misery. Selection goes on without ceasing;
but if the conditions are bad, the surviving type will be
miserable. Mere unaided natural selection obviously cannot
be trusted to produce a fine race."

Nothing would convince Miss Du Prel that the preservation
of weakly persons was not injurious to the community. To this
the Professor replied, that what is lost by their salvation is more
than paid back by the better conditions that secured it. The
strong, he said, were strengthened and enabled to retain their
strength by that which saves the lives of the weak.

"Besides, do you suppose a race could gain, in the long run, by
defiance of its best instincts? Never! If the laws of health in
body and in mind were at variance, leaving us a hard choice between physical and moral disease, then indeed no despair could
be too black. But all experience and all insight testify to the

exact opposite. Heavens, how short-sighted people are! It is not the protection of the weak, but the evil and stupid deeds that have made them so, that we have to thank for the miseries of disease. And for our redemption—powers of the universe! it is not to the cowardly sacrifice of the unfortunate that we must trust, but to a more brotherly spirit of loyalty, a more generous treatment of all who are defenceless, a more faithful holding together among ourselves—weak and strong, favoured and luckless."

Miss Du Prel was silent for a moment. Her sympathy but not her hope had been roused.

"I wish I could believe in your scheme of redemption," she said; "but, alas! sacrifice has been the means of progress from the beginning of all things, and so I fear it will be to the end."

"I don't know what it will be at the end," said the Professor, dryly; "for the present, I oppose with the whole strength of my belief and my conscience, the cowardly idea of surrendering individuals to the ferocity of a jealous and angry power, in the hope of currying favour for the rest. We might just as well set up national altars and sacrifice victims, after the franker fashion of the ancients. Morally, the principles are precisely the same."

"Scarcely; for *our* object is to benefit humanity."

"And theirs. Poor humanity!" cried the Professor. "What crimes are we not ready to commit in thy name!"

"That cannot be a crime which benefits mankind," argued Miss Du Prel.

"It is very certain that it cannot eventually benefit mankind, if it *be* a crime," he retorted.

"This sequence of ideas makes one dizzy!" exclaimed Hadria.

The Professor smiled. "Moreover," he added, "we know that society has formed the conditions of existence for each of her members; the whole material of his misfortune, if he be ill-born and ill-conditioned. Is society then to turn and rend her unlucky child whose misery was her own birthday gift? Shall we, who are only too ready, as it is, to trample upon others, in our haste and greed—shall we be encouraged in this savage selfishness by what dares to call itself science, to play one another false, instead of standing, with united front, to the powers of darkness, and scorning to betray our fellows, human or animal, in the contemptible hope of gaining by the treachery? Ah! you may quote authorities, wise and good, till you are hoarse!" cried the Professor, with a burst of energy; "but they will not convince me that black is white. I care not who may uphold the doctrine of vicarious sacrifice; it is monstrous, it is dastardly, it is *damnable!*"

There are some sentences and some incidents that fix themselves, once for all, in the memory, often without apparent reason, to remain as an influence throughout life. In this fashion, the afternoon's discussion registered itself in the memory of the silent member of the trio.

In her dreams that night, those three concluding and energetic adjectives played strange pranks, as, in dreams, words and phrases often will. Her deep regret at Miss Du Prel's departure, her dread of her own future, her growing sense of the torment, and horror, and sacrifice that form so large a part of the order of the world, all appeared to be united fantastically in malignant and threatening form, in the final words of the Professor: "It is monstrous, it is dastardly, it is damnable!" The agony of the whole earth seemed to hang over the sleeper, hovering and black and intolerable, crushing her with a sense of hopeless pity and fatigue.

And on waking, though the absurd masquerading of words and thoughts had ceased, she was still weighed down with the horror of the dream, which she knew had a corresponding reality still more awful. And there was no adversary to all this anguish; everybody acquiesced, nay, everybody threw on yet another log to the martyr's pile, and coolly watched the hungry flames at their work, for "Nature," they all agreed, demanded sacrifice.

It was in vain to turn for relief to the wise and good; the "wise" insisted on keeping up the altar fires that they might appease the blood-thirsty goddess by a continuous supply of victims (for the noble purpose of saving the others); the "good" trusted to the decision of the wise; they were humbly content to allow others to judge for them; for by this means would they not secure some of the spoils?

No, no; there was no help anywhere on earth, no help, no help. So ran Hadria's thoughts, in the moments of vivid sensation, between sleeping and waking. "Suffering, sacrifice, oppression: there is nothing else under the sun, under the sun."

Perhaps a brilliant beam that had found its way, like a message of mercy, through the blind, and shone straight on to the pillow, had suggested the form of the last thought.

Hadria moved her hand into the ray, that she might feel the warmth and "the illusion of kindness."

There was one person, and at the moment, only one, whose existence was comforting to remember. The hundreds of kind and good people, who were merely kind and good where popular sentiment expected or commended such conduct, gave no re-assurance; on the contrary, they proved the desperation of our plight, since wisdom and goodness themselves were busy at the savage work.

When the party met at breakfast, an hour later, the Professor caused universal consternation, by announcing that he would be obliged to return to London on that very day, having received a letter, by the morning's post, which left him no choice. The very butler paused, for a perceptible period, while handing ham and eggs to the guest. Forks and knives were laid down; letters remained unopened.

"It's no use your attempting to go, my dear Chantrey," said Mr. Fullerton, "we have grown accustomed to the luxury of your society, and we can't get on without it."

But the Professor explained that his departure was inevitable, and that he must go by the morning train.

He and Hadria had time for a short walk to the river, by the pathway of the tunnels.

"What are your plans for the winter?" the Professor asked. "I hope that you will find time to develop your musical gift. It ought to be used and not wasted, or worse than wasted, as all forces are, unless they find their legitimate outlet. Don't be persuaded to do fancy embroidery, as a better mode of employing energy. You have peculiar advantages of a hereditary kind, if only you can get a reasonable chance to use them. I have unbounded faith in the Fullerton stock. It has all the elements that ought to produce powers of the highest order. You know I have always cherished a warm affection for your parents, but ten years more of experience have taught me better how to value that sterling sincerity and honour in your father, united with so much kindliness, not to mention his qualities of brain; and then your mother's strong sense of duty, her ability, her native love of art, and her wonderful devotion. These are qualities that one does not meet with every day, and the children of such parents start in life with splendid material to fashion into character and power."

"Algitha will be worthy of our parents, I think," said Hadria, "though she has commenced her career by disobeying them."

"And you too must turn your power to account."

"You can't conceive how difficult it is."

"I can very easily. I see that the sacrifice of her own development, which your mother has made for your sakes, is taking its inevitable revenge upon her, and upon you all. One can't doom one's best powers to decay, however excellent the motive, without bringing punishment upon oneself and one's children, in some form or other. You will have to fight against that penalty. I know you will not have a smooth time of it; but who has, except cowards and weaklings? Your safeguard will be in your work."

"And my difficulty," said Hadria. "In the world that I

was born into (for my sins), when one tries to do something
that other people don't do, it is like trying to get up early in a
house where the breakfast-hour is late. Nothing fits in with
one's eccentric custom; everything conspires to discourage it."

"I wish I could give you a helping hand," said the Professor
wistfully; "but one is so powerless. Each of us has to fight
the real battle of life alone. Nobody can see with our eyes,
or feel with our nerves. The crux of the difficulty each bears
for himself. But friendship can help us to believe the struggle
worth while; it can sustain our courage and it can offer
sympathy in victory,—but still more faithfully in defeat."

CHAPTER XII.

HADRIA had determined upon making a strong and patient effort to pursue her work during the winter, while doing her best, at the same time, to please her mother, and to make up to her, as well as she could, for Algitha's departure. She would not be dismayed by difficulties: as the Professor said, only cowards and weaklings escaped these. She treated herself austerely, and found her power of concentration increasing, and her hold on herself greater. But, as usual, her greatest effort had to be given, not to the work itself, but to win opportunity to pursue it. Mrs. Fullerton opposed her daughter's endeavours as firmly as ever. It was not good for a girl to be selfishly pre-occupied. She ought to think of others.

If Hadria yielded the point on any particular occasion, her mood and her work were destroyed: if she resisted, they were equally destroyed, through the nervous disturbance and the intense depression which followed the winning of a liberty too dearly bought. The incessant rising and quelling of her impulse and her courage—like the ebb and flow of tides— represented a vast amount of force not merely wasted, but expended in producing a dangerous wear and tear upon the system. The process told upon her health, and was the beginning of the weakening and unbalancing of the splendid constitution which Hadria, in common with every member of the family, enjoyed as a birthright. The injury was insidious but serious. Hadria, unable to command any certain part of the day, began to sit up at night. This led to a direct clash of wills. Mr. Fullerton said that the girl was doing her best to ruin her health for life; Mrs. Fullerton wished to know why Hadria, who had all the day at her disposal, could not spend the night rationally.

"But I haven't all the day, or any part of it, for certain," said Hadria.

"If you grudge the little services you do for me, pray abandon them," said the mother, genuinely hurt.

Hadria entered her room, one evening, tired out and profoundly depressed. A table, covered with books, stood beside the fire. She gave the top-heavy pile an impatient thrust and the mass fell, with a great crash, to the floor. A heap of manuscript—her musical achievement for the past year—was involved in the fall. She contemplated the wreck gravely.

"Yes, it is I who am weak, not circumstance that is strong. If I could keep my mind unmoved by the irritations; if I could quarrel with mother, and displease father, and offend all the world without a qualm, or without losing the delicate balance of thought and mood necessary for composition, then I should, to some extent, triumph over my circumstances; I should not lose so much time in this wretched unstringing. Only were I so immovably constituted, is it probable that I should be able to compose at all?"

She drew the score towards her. "People are surprised that women have never done anything noteworthy in music. People are so intelligent!" She turned over the pages critically. If only this instinct were not so overwhelmingly strong! Hadria wondered how many other women, from the beginning of history, had cursed the impulse to create! Fortunately, it was sometimes extinguished altogether, as to-night, for instance, when every impression, every desire was swept clean out of her, and her mind presented a creditable blank, such as really ought to satisfy the most exacting social mentor. In such a state, a woman might be induced to accept anything!

Hadria brought out two letters from her pocket; one from the Professor, the other from Miss Du Prel. The latter had been writing frequently of late, pointing out the danger of Hadria's exaggerated ideas, and the probability of their ruining her happiness in life. Valeria had suffered herself from "ideas," and knew how fatal they were. Life *could* not be exactly as one would have it, and it was absolutely necessary, in order to avoid misery for oneself and others, to consent to take things more or less as they were; to make up one's mind to bend a little, rather than have to break, in the end. Things were never quite so shocking as they seemed to one's youthful imagination. The world was made up of compromises. Good was mixed with evil everywhere. The domestic idea, as Hadria called it, might be, in its present phase, somewhat offensive, but it could be redeemed in its application, in the details and "extenuating circumstances." Valeria could not warn Hadria too earnestly against falling into the mistake that Valeria herself had made. She had repudiated the notion of anything short of an ideal union; a perfect comradeship, without the shadow of restraint or bondage in the relationship; and not having found it, she had refused the tie altogether. She could not bring herself to accept the lesser thing, having conceived the possibility of the greater. She now saw her error, and repented it. She was reaping the penalty in a lonely and unsatisfied life. For a long time her work had seemed to suffice, but she felt now that she had been trusting to a broken reed. She was terrified at her solitude. She could not face the thought of old age, without a single close tie, without a home, without a hold upon her race.

She ended by entreating Hadria not to refuse marriage merely because she could not find a man to agree with her in everything, or capable of entering into the spirit of the relationship that perhaps would unite the men and women of the future. It was a pity that Hadria had not been born a generation later, but since she had come into the world at this time of transition, she must try to avoid the tragedy that threatens all spirits who are pointing towards the

new order, while the old is still working out its unexhausted
impetus.

This reiterated advice had begun to trouble Hadria. It
did not convince her, but Valeria's words were incessantly
repeating themselves in her mind; working as a ferment
among her thoughts.

The letters from Miss Du Prel and the Professor were to
her, a source of great pleasure and of great pain. In her
depressed moods, they would often rather increase her de-
spondency, because the writers used to take for granted so
many achievements that she had not been able to accomplish.

"They think I am living and progressing as they are; they
do not know that the riot and stir of intellectual life has
ceased. I am like a creature struggling in a quicksand."

On the Professor's letter, the comments were of a different
character.

He had recommended her to read certain books, and
reminded her that no possessor of good books could lack the
privilege of spiritual sanctuary.

"Ah! yes, I know few pleasures so great as that of finding
one's own idea, or hope, or longing, finely expressed, half-born
thoughts alive and of stately stature; and then the exquisite
touches of art upon quick nerves, the enlarging of the realms
of imagination, knowledge, the heightening of perceptions,
intuitions; finally the blessed power of escaping from oneself,
with the paradoxical reward of greater self-realization! But,
ah, Professor, to me there is a 'but' even here. I am
oppressed by a sense of the discrepancy between the world
that books disclose to me, and the world that I myself inhabit.
In books, the *impossibilities* are all left out. They give you no
sense of the sordid Inevitable that looms so large on the grey
horizon. Another more personal quarrel that I have with books
is on account of their attacking all my pet prejudices, and
sneering at the type of woman that I have the misfortune to
belong to. I am always exhorted to cure myself of being myself.
Nothing less would suffice. Now this is wounding. All my

particular feelings, my strongest beliefs, are condemned, directly or by inference. I could almost believe that there is a literary conspiracy to reform me. The "true women" of literature infallibly think and feel precisely as I do *not* think and feel, while the sentiments that I detest—woe is me—are lauded to the skies. Truly, if we women don't know exactly what we ought to think and feel, it is not for want of telling. Yet you say, Professor, in this very letter, that the sense of having a peculiar experience is always an illusion, that every feeling of ours has been felt before, if not in our own day, then in the crowded past, with its throngs of forgotten lives and unrecorded experiences. I wish to heaven I could meet those who have had exactly mine !"

Hadria did not keep up an active correspondence with Miss Du Prel or with the Professor. She had no idea of adding to the burden of their busy lives, by wails for sympathy. It seemed to her feeble, and contemptible, to ask to be dragged up by their strength, instead of exerting her own. If that were insufficient, why then let her go down, as thousands had gone down before her. As a miser telling his gold, she would read and re-read those occasional letters, written amidst the stress of life at high pressure, and bearing evidence of that life of thought and work, in their tense, full-packed phrases. With what a throb of longing and envy Hadria used to feel the vibration through her own nerves ! It was only when completely exhausted and harassed that the response was lacking. To-night everything seemed to be obliterated. Her hope, her interest were, for the moment, tired out. Her friends would be disappointed in her, but there was no help for it.

She picked up the score of her music, and stood, with a handful of the once precious offspring of her brain held out towards the flames. Then she drew it back, and half closed her eyes in self-scrutinizing thought. " Come now," she said to herself, "are you sincere in your intention of giving up? Are you not doing this in a fit of spite against destiny? as if destiny cared two straws. Heavens ! what a poor little piece of melodrama.   And to think that you should have actually taken yourself in it by it.   One acts so badly with only oneself for audience.   You know perfectly well that you are *not* going to give in, you are *not* going to attempt to stifle that which is the centre of your life; you have not courage for such slow suicide.   Don't add insincerity to the other faults that are laid to your account——"   She mused over the little self-administered lecture.   And probing down into her consciousness, she realized that she could not face the thought of surrender.   She meant to fight on.   The notion of giving in had been seized instinctively, for a moment of rest. Nothing should really make her cease the struggle, until the power itself had been destroyed.   She was sure of it, in her heart, in spite of failures and miserably inadequate expressions of it.   Suddenly, as a shaft of light through parting clouds, came bursting forth, radiant, rejoicing, that sense of power, large, resistless, genial as morning sunshine.   Yes, yes, let them say what they might, discourage, smile, or frown as they would, the faculty was given to her, and she would fight for opportunity to use it while she had breath.

CHAPTER XIII.

AS if it had all been ingeniously planned, the minutest incidents and conditions of Hadria's life conspired towards the event that was to decide its drift for ever.

Often, in the dim afternoon, she would sit by the window and watch the rain sweeping across the country, longing then for Temperley's music, which used to make the wild scene so unspeakably beautiful. Now there was no music, no music anywhere, only this fierce and mournful rush of the wind, which seemed as if it were trying to utter some universal grief. At sunset, braving the cold, she would mount the creaking staircase, pass along the silent upper corridors, and on through the empty rooms to the garret in the tower. The solitude was a relief; the strangeness of the scene appealed to some wild instinct, and to the intense melancholy that lurks in the Celtic nature.

Even at night, she did not shrink from braving the glooms and silences of the deserted upper floor, nor the solitude of the garret, which appeared the deeper, from the many memories of happy evenings that it evoked. She wished Ernest would come home. It was so long since she had seen her favourite brother. She could not bear the thought of his drifting away from her. What talks they had had in this old garret!

These nights in the tower, among the winds, soothed the trouble of her spirit as nothing else had power to do. The mystery of life, the thrill of existence, touched her with a strange joy that ran perilously near to pain. What vast dim possibilities lurked out there, in the hollows of the hills! What inspiration thundered in the voice of the prophet wind!

Once, she had gone downstairs and out, alone, in a tearing storm, to wander across the bleak pastures, wrapt round by the wind as by a flame; at one with the desperate elemental thing.

The wanderer felt herself caught into the heart of some vast unknown power, of which the wind was but a thrall, until she became, for a moment, consciously part of that which was universal. Her personality grew dim; she stood, as it seemed, face to face with Nature, divided from the ultimate truth by only a thin veil, to temper the splendour and the terror. Then the tension of personal feeling was loosened. She saw how entirely vain and futile were the things of life that we grieve and struggle over.

It was not a side, an aspect of existence, but the whole of it that seemed to storm round her, in the darkness. No wonder, when the wind was let loose among the mountains, that the old Highland people thought that their dead were about them. All night long, after Hadria returned to her room in the keep, the wind kept up its cannonade against the walls, hooting in the chimneys with derisive voices, and flinging itself, in mad revolt, against the old-established hills and the stable earth, which changed its forms only in slow obedience to the persuadings of the elements, in the passing of centuries. It cared nothing for the passion of a single storm.

And then came reaction, doubt. After all, humanity was a puny production of the Ages. Men and women were like the struggling animalculæ that her father had so often shewn the boys, in a drop of magnified ditch-water; yet not quite like those microscopic insects, for the stupendous processes of life had at last created a widening consciousness, a mind which could perceive the bewildering vastness of Nature and its own smallness, which could, in some measure, get outside its own particular ditch, and the strife and struggle of it, groping upwards for larger realities—

"Over us stars and under us graves."

To go down next morning to breakfast; to meet the usual homely events, was bewildering after such a night.

Which was dream: this or that? So solid and convincing seemed, at times, the interests and objects of every day, that Hadria would veer round to a sudden conviction that these things, or what they symbolized, were indeed the solid facts of human life, and that all other impressions arose from the disorderly working of overcharged brain-cells. It was a little ailment of youth and would pass off. Had it been possible to describe to her father the impressions made upon her by the world and Nature, as they had presented themselves to her imagination from her childhood, he would have prescribed change of air and gymnastics. Perhaps that was the really rational view of the matter. But what if these hygienic measures cured her of the haunting consciousness of mystery and vastness; what if she became convinced of the essential importance of the Gordon pedigree, or of the amount of social consideration due to the family who had taken Clarenoc? Would that alter the bewildering truths of which she would have ceased to think?

No; it would only mean that the animalcule had returned to the occupations of its ditch, while the worlds and the peoples went spinning to their destiny.

"Do the duty that lies nearest thee," counselled everybody : people of all kinds, books of all kinds. "Cheap, well-sounding advice," thought Hadria, "sure of popularity! Continue to wriggle industriously, O animalcule, in that particular ditch wherein it has pleased heaven to place thee; seek not the flowing stream and the salt ocean ; and if, some clear night, a star finds room to mirror itself in thy little stagnant world, shining through the fat weeds and slime that almost shut out the heavens, pray be careful not to pay too much heed to the high-born luminary. Look to your wriggling ; that is your proper business. An animalcule that does not wriggle must be morbid or peculiar. All will tender, in different forms of varying elegance, the safe and simple admonition : 'Wriggle and be damned to you!'"

*   *   *   *   *   *

It was at this somewhat fevered moment, that Hubert Temperley appeared, once more, upon the scene. Hadria was with her mother, taking tea at Drumgarren, when Mrs. Gordon, catching the sounds of carriage wheels, announced that she was expecting Hubert and his sister for a visit. In another second, the travellers were in the drawing-room.

Hubert's self-possession was equal to the occasion. He introduced his sister to Mrs. Fullerton and Hadria. Miss Temperley was his junior by a year; a slight, neatly-built young woman, with a sort of tact that went on brilliantly up to a certain point, and then suddenly collapsed altogether. She had her brother's self-complacency, and an air of encouragement which Mrs. Gordon seemed to find most gratifying.

She dressed perfectly, in quiet Parisian fashion. Hadria saw that her brother had taken her into his confidence, or she concluded so from something in Miss Temperley's manner. The latter treated Hadria with a certain familiarity, as if she had known her for some time, and she had a way of seeming to take her apart, when addressing her, as if there were a sort of understanding between them. It was here that her instinct failed her; for she seemed unaware that this assumption of an intimacy that did not exist was liable to be resented, and that it might be unpleasant to be expected to catch special remarks sent over the heads of the others, although ostensibly for the common weal.

Hadria thought that she had never seen so strange a contrast as this young woman's behaviour, within and without the circle of her perceptions. It was the more remarkable, since her mind was bent upon the details and niceties of conduct, and the *nuances* of existence.

"I shall come and see you as soon as I can," she promised, when Mrs. Fullerton rose to leave.

Miss Temperley kept her word. She was charmed with the old house, praising authoritatively.

"This is an excellent piece of carving; far superior to the one in the dining-room. Ah, yes, that is charming; so well arranged. You ought to have a touch of blue there to make it perfect."

Hubert shewed good taste in keeping away from Dunaghee, except to pay his call on Mr. and Mrs. Fullerton.

"Hadria," said his sister, "I am going to call you by your pretty Christian name, and I want you to call me Henriette. I feel I have known you much longer than ten days, because Hubert has told me so much about you, and your music. You play charmingly. So much native talent. You want good training, of course; but you really might become a brilliant performer. Hubert is quite distressed that you should not enjoy more advantages. I should like so much if you could come and stay with us in town, and have some good lessons. Do think of it."

Hadria flushed. "Oh, thank you, I could not do that— I——"

"I understand you, dear Hadria," said Henriette, drawing her chair closer to the fire. "You know, Hubert can never keep anything of great importance from me." She looked arch.

Hadria muttered something that might have discouraged a less persistent spirit, but Miss Temperley paid no attention.

"Poor Hubert! I have had to be a ministering angel to him during these last months."

"Why do you open up this subject, Miss Temperley?"

"*Henriette*, if you please," cried that young woman, with the air of a playful potentate who has requested a favoured courtier to drop the ceremonious "Your Majesty" in private conversation.

"It was I who made him accept Mrs. Gordon's invitation. He very nearly refused it. He feared that it would be unpleasant for you. But I insisted on his coming. Why should he not? He would like so much to come here more often, but again he fears to displease you. He is not a Temperley for nothing. They are not of the race of fools who rush in where angels fear to tread."

"Are they not?" asked Hadria absently.

"We both see your difficulty," Miss Temperley went on. "Hubert would not so misunderstand you—the dear fellow is full of delicacy—and I should dearly love to hear him play to your accompaniment; he used to enjoy those practices so much. Would you think him intrusive if he brought his *'cello* some afternoon?"

Hadria, not without an uneasy qualm, agreed to the suggestion, though by no means cordially.

Accordingly brother and sister arrived, one afternoon, for the practice. Henriette took the leadership, visibly employed tact and judgment, talked a great deal, and was surprisingly delicate, as beseemed a Temperley. Hadria found the occasion somewhat trying nevertheless, and Hubert stumbled, at first, in his playing. In a few minutes, however, both musicians became possessed by the music, and then all went well. Henriette sat in an easy chair and listened critically. Now and then she would call out "bravo," or "admirable," and when the performance was over, she was warm in her congratulations.

Hadria was flushed with the effort and pleasure of the performance.

"I never heard Hubert's playing to such advantage," said his sister. "I seem to hear it for the first time. You really ought to practise together often." Another afternoon was appointed; Henriette left Hadria almost no choice.

After the next meeting, the constraint had a little worn off, and the temptation to continue the practising was very strong. Henriette's presence was reassuring. And then Hubert seemed so reasonable, and had apparently put the past out of his mind altogether.

After the practice, brother and sister would linger a little in the drawing-room, chatting. Hubert appeared to advantage in his sister's society. She had a way of striking his best vein. Her own talent ran with his, appealed to it, and created the conditions for its display. Her presence and inspiration seemed to produce, on his ability, a sort of cumulative effect. Henriette set all the familiar machinery in motion ; pressed the right button, and her brother became brilliant.

A slight touch of diffidence in his manner softened the effect of his usual complacency. Hadria liked him better than she had liked him on his previous visit. His innate refinement appealed to her powerfully. Moreover, he was cultivated and well-read, and his society was agreeable. Oh, why did this everlasting matrimonial idea come in and spoil everything? Why could not men and women have interests in common, without wishing instantly to plunge into a condition of things which hampered and crippled them so miserably?

Hadria was disposed to under-rate all defects, and to make the most of all virtues in Hubert, at the present moment. He had come at just the right time to make a favourable impression upon her ; for the loneliness of her life had begun to leave its mark, and to render her extremely sensitive to influence.

She was an alien among the people of her circle ; and she felt vaguely guilty in failing to share their ideas and ambitions. Their glances, their silences, conveyed a world of cold surprise and condemnation.

Hubert was tolerance itself compared with the majority of her associates. She felt almost as if he had done her a personal kindness when he omitted to look astonished at her remarks, or to ignore them as "awkward."

Yet she felt uneasy about this renewal of the practices, and tried to avoid them as often as possible, though sorely against her inclination. They were so great a relief and enjoyment. Her inexperience, and her carelessness of conventional standards, put her somewhat off her guard. Hubert showed no signs of even remembering the interview of last year, that had been cut short by her father's entrance. Why should *she* insist on keeping it in mind? It was foolish. Moreover she had been expressly given to understand, in a most pointed manner, that her conduct would not be misinterpreted if she allowed him to come occasionally.

From several remarks that Temperley made, she saw that he too regarded the ordinary domestic existence with distaste. It offended his fastidiousness. He was fastidious to his finger-tips. It amused Hadria to note the contrast between him and Mr. Gordon, who was a typical father of a family; limited in his interests to that circle; an amiable ruler of a tiny, somewhat absurd little world, pompous and important and inconceivably dull.

The *bourgeois* side of this life was evidently displeasing to Hubert. Good taste was his fetish. From his remarks about women, Hadria was led to observe how subtly critical he was with regard to feminine qualities, and wondered if his preference for herself ought to be regarded as a great compliment.

Henriette congratulated her on having been admired by the fastidious Hubert.

"Let us hope it speaks well for me," Hadria replied with a cynical smile, "but I have so often noticed that men who are very difficult to please, choose for the domestic hearth the most dreary and unattractive woman of their acquaintance! I sometimes doubt if men ever do marry the women they most admire."

"They do, when they can win them," said Henriette.

CHAPTER XIV.

DURING Henriette's visit, one of the meetings of the Preposterous Society fell due, and she expressed a strong wish to be present. She also craved the privilege of choosing the subject of discussion. Finally, she received a formal request from the members to give the lecture herself. She was full of enthusiasm about the Society (such an educating influence !), and prepared her paper with great care. There had been a tendency among the circle, to politely disagree with Henriette. Her ideas respecting various burning topics were at variance with the trend of opinion at Dunaghee, and Miss Temperley was expected to take this opportunity of enlightening the family. The family was equally resolved not to be enlightened.

"I have chosen for my subject to-night," said the lecturer, "one that is beginning to occupy public attention very largely : I mean the sphere of woman in society."

The audience, among whom Hubert had been admitted at his sister's earnest request, drew themselves together, and a little murmur of battle ran along the line. Henriette's figure, in her well-fitting Parisian gown, looked singularly out of place in the garret, with the crazy old candle-holder beside her, the yellow flame of the candle flinging fantastic shadows on the vaulted roof, preposterously distorting her neat form, as if in wicked mockery. The moonlight streamed in, as usual on the nights chosen by the Society for their meetings.

Henriette's paper was neatly expressed, and its sentiments were admirable. She maintained a perfect balance between the bigotry of the past and the violence of the present. Her phrases seemed to rock, like a pair of scales, from excess to excess, on either side. She came to rest in the exact middle. This led to the Johnsonian structure, or, as Hadria afterwards said, to the style of a *Times* leading article: "While we remember on the one hand, we must not forget on the other——"

At the end of the lecture, the audience found themselves invited to sympathize cautiously and circumspectly with the advancement of women, but led, at the same time, to conclude that good taste and good feeling forbade any really nice woman from moving a little finger to attain, or to help others to attain, the smallest fraction more of freedom, or an inch more of spiritual territory, than was now enjoyed by her sex. When, at some future time, wider privileges should have been conquered by the exertions of someone else, then the really nice woman could saunter in and enjoy the booty. But till then, let her leave boisterous agitation to others, and endear herself to all around her by her patience and her loving self-sacrifice.

"That pays better for the present," Hadria was heard to mutter to an adjacent member.

The lecturer, in her concluding remarks, gave a smile of ineffable sweetness, sadly marred, however, by the grotesque effect of the flickering shadows that were cast on her face by the candle. After all, *duty* not *right* was the really important matter, and the lecturer thought that it would be better if one heard the former word rather oftener in connection with the woman's question, and the latter word rather more seldom. Then, with new sweetness, and in a tone not to be described, she went on to speak of the natural responsibilities and joys of her sex, drawing a moving, if somewhat familiar picture of those avocations, than which she was sure there could be nothing higher or holier.

For some not easily explained cause, the construction of this sentence gave it a peculiar unctuous force: "than which," as Fred afterwards remarked, "would have bowled over any but the most hardened sinner."

For weeks after this memorable lecture, if any very lofty

altitude had to be ascended in conversational excursions, the aspirant invariably smiled with ineffable tenderness and lightly scaled the height, murmuring "than which" to a vanquished audience.

The lecture was followed by a discussion that ráther took the stiffness out of Miss Temperley's phrases. The whole party was roused. Algitha had to whisper a remonstrance to the boys, for their solemn questions were becoming too preposterous. The lecture was discussed with much warmth. There was a tendency to adopt the form "than which" with some frequency. Bursts of laughter startled a company of rats in the wainscoting, and there was a lively scamper behind the walls. No obvious opposition was offered. Miss Temperley's views were examined with gravity, and indeed in a manner almost pompous. But by the end of that trying process, they had a sadly bedraggled and plucked appearance, much to their parent's bewilderment. She endeavoured to explain further, and was met by guilelessly intelligent questions, which had the effect of depriving the luckless objects of their solitary remaining feather. The members of the society continued to pine for information, and Miss Temperley endeavoured to provide it, till late into the night. The discussion finally drifted on to dangerous ground. Algitha declared that she considered that no man had any just right to ask a woman to pledge herself to love him and live with him for the rest of her life. How *could* she? Hubert suggested that the woman made the same claim on the man.

"Which is equally absurd," said Algitha. "Just as if any two people, when they are beginning to form their characters, could possibly be sure of their sentiments for the rest of their days. They have no business to marry at such an age. They are bound to alter."

"But they must regard it as their duty not to alter with regard to one another," said Henriette.

"Quite so; just as they ought to regard it as their duty among other things, not to grow old," suggested Fred.

"Then, Algitha, do you mean that they may fall in love elsewhere?" Ernest inquired.

"They very likely *will* do so, if they make such an absurd start," Algitha declared.

"And if they do?"

"Then, if the sentiment stands test and trial, and proves genuine, and not a silly freak, the fact ought to be frankly faced. Husband and wife have no business to go on keeping up a bond that has become false and irksome."

Miss Temperley broke into protest. "But surely you don't mean to defend such faithlessness."

Algitha would not admit that it *was* faithlessness. She said it was mere honesty. She could see nothing inherently wrong in falling in love genuinely after one arrived at years of discretion. She thought it inherently idiotic, and worse, to make a choice that ought to be for life, at years of *in*discretion. Still, people *were* idiotic, and that must be considered, as well as all the other facts, such as the difficulty of really knowing each other before marriage, owing to social arrangements, and also owing to the training, which made men and women always pose so ridiculously towards one another, pretending to be something that they were not.

"Well done, Algitha," cried Ernest, laughing; "I like to hear you speak out. Now tell me frankly: supposing you married quite young, before you had had much experience; supposing you afterwards found that you and your husband had both been deceiving yourselves and each other, unconsciously perhaps; and suppose, when more fully awakened and developed, you met another fellow and fell in love with him genuinely, what would you do?"

"Oh, she would just mention it to her husband casually," Fred interposed with a chuckle, "and disappear."

"I should certainly not go through terrific emotions and self-accusations, and think the end of the world had come," said Algitha serenely. "I should calmly face the situation."

"Calmly! She by supposition being madly in love!" ejaculated Fred, with a chuckle.

"Calmly," repeated Algitha. "And I should consider carefully what would be best for all concerned. If I decided, after mature consideration and self-testing, that I ought to leave my husband, I should leave him, as I should hope he would leave me, in similar circumstances. That is my idea of right."

"And is this also your idea of right, Miss Fullerton?" asked Temperley, turning, in some trepidation, to Hadria.

"That seems to me right in the abstract. One can't pronounce for particular cases where circumstances are entangled."

Hubert sank back in his chair, and ran his hand over his brow. He seemed about to speak, but he checked himself.

"Where did you get such extraordinary ideas from?" cried Miss Temperley.

"They were like Topsy; they growed," said Fred.

"We have been in the habit of speculating freely on all subjects," said Ernest, "ever since we could talk. This is the blessed result!"

"I am not quite so sure now, that the Preposterous Society meets with my approval," observed Miss Temperley.

"If you had been brought up in the bosom of this Society, Miss Temperley, you too, perhaps, would have come to this. Think of it!"

"Does your mother know what sort of subjects you discuss?"

There was a shout of laughter. "Mother used often to come into the nursery and surprise us in hot discussion on the origin of evil," said Hadria.

"Don't you believe what she says, Miss Temperley," cried Fred; "mother never could teach Hadria the most rudimentary notions of accuracy."

"Her failure with my brothers, was in the department of manners," Hadria observed.

"Then she does *not* know what you talk about?" persisted Henriette.

"You ask her," prompted Fred, with undisguised glee.

"She never attends our meetings," said Algitha.

"Well, well, I cannot understand it!" cried Miss Temperley. "However, you don't quite know what you are talking about, and one mustn't blame you."

"No, don't," urged Fred; "we are a sensitive family."

"Shut up!" cried Ernest with a warning frown.

"Oh, you are a coarse-grained exception; I speak of the family average," Fred answered with serenity.

Henriette felt that nothing more could be done with this strange audience. Her business was really with the President of the Society. The girl was bent on ruining her life with these wild notions. Miss Temperley decided that it would be better to talk to Hadria quietly in her own room, away from the influence of these eccentric brothers and that extraordinary sister. After all, it was Algitha who had originated the shocking view, not Hadria, who had merely agreed, doubtless out of a desire to support her sister.

"I have not known you for seven years, but I am going to poke your fire," said Henriette, when they were established in Hadria's room.

"I never thought you would wait so long as that," was Hadria's ambiguous reply.

Then Henriette opened her batteries. She talked without interruption, her companion listening, agreeing occasionally with her adversary, in a disconcerting manner; then falling into silence.

"It seems to me that you are making a very terrible mistake in your life, Hadria. You have taken up a fixed idea about domestic duties and all that, and are going to throw away your chances of forming a happy home of your own, out of a mere prejudice. You may not admire Mrs. Gordon's existence; for my part I think she leads a very good, useful life, but there is no reason why all married lives should be like hers."

"Why are they, then?"

"I don't see that they are."

" It is the prevailing type. It shows the way the domestic wind blows. Fancy having to be always resisting such a wind. What an oblique, shorn-looking object one would be after a few years ! "

Henriette grew eloquent. She recalled instances of women who had fulfilled all their home duties, and been successful in other walks as well; she drew pictures in attractive colours of Hadria in a home of her own, with far more liberty than was possible under her parents' roof; and then she drew another picture of Hadria fifteen years hence at Dunaghee.

Hadria covered her face with her hands. "You who uphold all these social arrangements, how do you feel when you find yourself obliged to urge me to marry, not for the sake of the positive joys of domestic existence, but for the merely negative advantage of avoiding a hapless and forlorn state? You propose it as a *pis-aller*. Does *that* argue that all is sound in the state of Denmark ? "

" If you had not this unreasonable objection to what is really a woman's natural destiny, the difficulty would not exist."

" Have women no pride ? "

Henriette did not answer.

" Have they no sense of dignity? If one marries (accepting things on the usual basis, of course) one gives to another person rights and powers over one's life that are practically boundless. To retain one's self-direction in case of dispute would be possible only on pain of social ruin. I have little enough freedom now, heaven knows; but if I married, why my very thoughts would become the property of another. Thought, emotion, love itself, must pass under the yoke ! There would be no nook or corner entirely and indisputably my own."

" I should not regard that as a hardship," said Henriette, "if I loved my husband."

" I should consider it not only a hardship, but beyond endurance."

"But, my dear, you are impracticable."

"That is what I think domestic life is!" Hadria's quiet tone was suddenly changed to one of scorn. "You talk of love; what has love worthy of the name to do with this preposterous interference with the freedom of another person? If *that* is what love means—the craving to possess and restrain and demand and hamper and absorb, and generally make mince-meat of the beloved object, then preserve me from the master-passion."

Henriette was baffled. "I don't know how to make you see this in a truer light," she said. "There is something to my mind so beautiful in the close union of two human beings, who pledge themselves to love and honour one another, to face life hand in hand, to share every thought, every hope, to renounce each his own wishes for the sake of the other."

"That sounds very elevating; in practice it breeds Mr. and Mrs. Gordon."

"Do you mean to tell me you will never marry on this account?"

"I would never marry anyone who would exact the usual submissions and renunciations, or even desire them, which I suppose amounts almost to saying that I shall never marry at all. What man would endure a wife who demanded to retain her absolute freedom, as in the case of a close friendship? The man is not born!"

"You seem to forget, dear Hadria, in objecting to place yourself under the yoke, as you call it, that your husband would also be obliged to resign part of *his* independence to you. The prospect of loss of liberty in marriage often prevents a man from marrying ("Wise man!" ejaculated Hadria), so you see the disadvantage is not all on one side, if so you choose to consider it."

"Good heavens! do you think that the opportunity to interfere with another person would console me for being interfered with myself? I don't want my share of the constraining power. I would as soon accept the lash of a slave-driver. This moral lash is almost more odious than the other, for its thongs are made of the affections and the domestic 'virtues,' than which there can be nothing sneakier or more detestable!"

Henriette heaved a discouraged sigh. "You are wrong, my dear Hadria," she said emphatically; "you are wrong, wrong, wrong."

"How? why?"

"One can't have everything in this life. You must be willing to resign part of your privileges for the sake of the far greater privileges that you acquire."

"I can imagine nothing that would compensate for the loss of freedom, the right to oneself."

"What about love?" murmured Henriette.

"Love!" echoed Hadria scornfully. "Do you suppose I could ever love a man who had the paltry, ungenerous instinct to enchain me?"

"Why use such extreme terms? Love does not enchain."

"Exactly what I contend," interrupted Hadria.

"But naturally husband and wife have claims."

"Naturally. I have just been objecting to them in what you describe as extreme terms."

"But I mean, when people care for one another, it is a joy to them to acknowledge ties and obligations of affection."

"Ah! one knows what *that* euphemism means!"

"Pray what does it mean?"

"That the one serious endeavour in the life of married people is to be able to call each other's souls their own."

Henriette stared.

"My language may not be limpid."

"Oh, I see what you mean. I was only wondering who can have taught you all these strange ideas."

Hadria at length gave way to a laugh that had been threatening for some time.

"My mother," she observed simply.

Henriette gave it up.

CHAPTER XV.

THE family had reassembled for the New Year's festivities. The change in Algitha since her departure from home was striking. She was gentler, more affectionate to her parents, than of yore. The tendency to grow hard and fretful had entirely disappeared. The sense of self was obviously lessened with the need for self-defence. Hadria discovered that an attachment was springing up between her sister and Wilfred Burton, about whom she wrote so frequently, and that this development of her emotional nature, united with her work, had given a glowing centre to her life which showed itself in a thousand little changes of manner and thought. Hadria told her sister that she felt herself unreal and fanciful in her presence. "I go twirling things round and round in my head till I grow dizzy. But you compare ideas with fact; you even turn ideas into fact; while I can get no hold on fact at all. Thoughts rise as mists rise from the river, but nothing happens. I feel them begin to prey upon me, working inwards."

Algitha shook her head. "It is a mad world," she said. "Week after week goes by, and there seems no lifting of the awful darkness in which the lives of these millions are passed. We want workers by the thousand. Yet, as if in mockery, the Devil keeps these well-fed thousands eating their hearts out in idleness or artificial occupations till they become diseased merely for want of something to do. Then," added Algitha, "His Majesty marries them, and sets them to work to create another houseful of idle creatures, who have to be supported by the deathly toil of those who labour too much."

"The devil is full of resources!" said Hadria.

Miss Temperley had been asked to stay at Dunaghee for

132

the New Year. Algitha conceived for her a sentiment almost vindictive. Hadria and the boys enjoyed nothing better than to watch Miss Temperley giving forth her opinions, while Algitha's figure gradually stiffened and her neck drew out, as Fred said, in truly telescopic fashion, like that of Alice in Wonderland. The boys constructed a figure of cushions, stuffed into one of Algitha's old gowns, the neck being a padded broom-handle, made to work up and down at pleasure; and with this counterfeit presentment of their sister, they used to act the scene amidst shouts of applause, Miss Temperley entering, on one occasion, when the improvised cocoa-nut head had reached its culminating point of high disdain, some-where about the level of the curtain-poles.

On New-Year's-eve, Dunaghee was full of guests. There was to be a children's party, to which however most of the grown-up neighbours were also invited.

"What a charming sight!" cried Henriette, standing with her neat foot on the fender in the hall, where the children were playing blind man's buff.

Mrs. Fullerton sat watching them with a dreamy smile. The scene recalled many an old memory. Mr. Fullerton was playing with the children.

Everyone remarked how well the two girls looked in their new evening gowns. They had made them themselves, in consequence of a wager with Fred, who had challenged them to combine pink and green satisfactorily.

"The gowns are perfect!" Temperley ventured to remark. "So much distinction!"

"All my doing," cried Fred. "I chose the colours."

"Distinction comes from within," said Temperley. "I should like to see what sort of gown in pink and green Mrs. ——." He stopped short abruptly.

Fred gave a chuckle. Indiscreet eyes wandered towards Mrs. Gordon's brocade and silver.

Later in the evening, that lady played dance music in a florid manner, resembling her taste in dress. The younger children had gone home, and the hall was filled with spinning couples.

"I hope we are to have some national dances," said Miss Temperley. "My brother and I are both looking forward to seeing a true reél danced by natives of the country."

"Oh, certainly!" said Mr. Fullerton. "My daughters are rather celebrated for their reels, especially Hadria." Mr. Fullerton executed a step or two with great agility.

"The girl gets quite out of herself when she is dancing," said Mrs. Fullerton. "She won't be scolded about it, for she says she takes after her father!"

"That's the time to get round her," observed Fred. "If we want to set her up to some real fun, we always play a reel and wait till she's well into the spirit of the thing, and then, I'll wager, she would stick at nothing."

"It's a fact," added Ernest. "It really seems to half mesmerise her."

"How very curious!" cried Miss Temperley.

She and her brother found themselves watching the dancing a little apart from the others.

"I would try again to-night, Hubert," she said in a low voice.

He was silent for a moment, twirling the tassel of the curtain.

"There is nothing to be really alarmed at in her ideas, regretable as they are. She is young. That sort of thing will soon wear off after she is married."

Temperley flung away the tassel.

"She doesn't know what she is talking about. These high-flown lectures and discussions have filled all their heads with nonsense. It will have to be rooted out when they come to face the world. No use to oppose her now. Nothing but experience will teach her. She must just be humoured for the present They have all run a little wild in their notions. Time will cure that."

"I am sure of it," said Hubert tolerantly. "They don't know the reàl import of what they say." He hugged this sentence with satisfaction.

"They are like the young Russians one reads about in Turgenieff's novels," said Henriette—"all ideas, no common-sense."

" And you really believe —— ? "

Henriette's hand was laid comfortingly on her brother's arm.

" Dear Hubert, I know something of my sex. After a year of married life, a woman has too many cares and responsibilities to trouble about ideas of this kind, or of any other."

" She strikes me as being somewhat persistent by nature," said Hubert, choosing a gentler word than *obstinate* to describe the quality in the lady of his affections.

" Let her be as persistent as she may, it is not possible for any woman to resist the laws and beliefs of Society. What can she do against all the world ? She can't escape from the conditions of her epoch. Oh ! she may talk boldly now, for she does not understand ; she is a mere infant as regards knowledge of the world, but once a wife —— "

Henriette smiled and shook her head, by way of finish to her sentence. Hubert mused silently for some minutes.

" I could not endure that there should be any disturbance —any eccentricity—in our life —— "

" My dear boy, if you don't trust to the teaching of experience to cure Hadria of these fantastic notions, rely upon the resistless persuasions of our social facts and laws. Nothing can stand against them—certainly not the fretful heresies of an inexperienced girl, who, remember, is really good and kind at heart."

" Ah ! yes," cried Hubert ; " a fine nature, full of good instincts, and womanly to her finger-tips."

" Oh ! if she were not that, *I* would never encourage you to think of her," cried Henriette with a shudder. " It is on this essential goodness of heart that I rely. She would never be able, try as she might, to act in a manner that would really distress those who were dear to her. You may count upon that securely."

" Yes ; I am sure of it," said Hubert, " but unluckily " (he shook his head and sighed) " I am not among those who are dear to her."

He rose abruptly, and Henriette followed him.

" Try to win her to-night," she murmured, "and be sure to express no opposition to her ideas, however wild they may be. Ignore them, humour her, plead your cause once more on this auspicious day—the last of the old year. Something tells me that the new year will begin joyously for you. Go now, and good luck to you."

"Ah! here you are," cried Mr. Fullerton, "we were wondering what had become of you. You said you wished to see a reel. Mrs. McPherson is so good as to play for us."

The kindly old Scottish dame had come, with two nieces, from a distance of ten miles.

A thrill ran through the company when the strange old tune began. Everyone rushed for a partner, and two long rows of figures stood facing one another, eager to start. Temperley asked Hadria to dance with him. Algitha had Harold Wilkins for a partner. The two long rows were soon stepping and twirling with zest and agility. A new and wilder spirit began to possess the whole party. The northern blood took fire and transfigured the dancers. The Temperleys seemed to be fashioned of different clay; they were able to keep their heads. Several elderly people had joined in the dance, performing their steps with a conscientious dexterity that put some of their juniors to shame. Mr. Fullerton stood by, looking on and applauding.

"How your father seems to enjoy the sight!" said Temperley, as he met his partner for a moment.

" He likes nothing so well, and his daughters take after him."

Hadria's reels were celebrated, not without reason. Some mad spirit seemed to possess her. It would appear almost as if she had passed into a different phase of character. She lost caution and care and the sense of external events.

When the dance was ended, Hubert led her from the hall. She went as if in a dream. She would not allow herself to be taken beyond the sound of the grotesque old dance music that was still going on, but otherwise she was unresisting.

He sat down beside her in a corner of the dining-room.

Now and then he glanced at his companion, and seemed about to speak. " You seem fond of your national music," he at last remarked.

" It fills me with bewildering memories," she said in a dreamy tone. " It seems to recall—it eludes description— some wild, primitive experiences—mountains, mists—I can't express what northern mysteries. It seems almost as if I had lived before, among some ancient Celtic people, and now, when I hear their music—or sometimes when I hear the sound of wind among the pines—whiffs and gusts of some-thing intensely familiar return to me, and I cannot grasp it. It is very bewildering."

" The only thing that happens to me of the kind is that curious sense of having done a thing before. Strange to say, I feel it now. This moment is not new to me."

Hadria gave a startled glance at her companion, and shuddered.

" I suppose it is all pre-ordained," she said. He was puzzled, but more hopeful than usual. Hadria might almost have accepted him in sheer absence of mind. He put the thought in different terms. He began to speak more boldly. He gave his view of life and happiness, his philosophy and religion. Hadria lazily agreed. She lay under a singular spell. The bizarre old music smote still upon the ear. She felt as if she were in the thrall of some dream whose events followed one another, as the scenes of a moving panorama unfold them-selves before the spectators. Temperley began to plead his cause. Hadria, with a startled look in her eyes, tried to check him. But her will refused to issue a vigorous command. Even had he been hateful to her, which he certainly was not, she felt that she would have been unable to wake out of the nightmare, and resume the conduct of affairs. The sense of the importance of personal events had entirely disappeared. What did it all matter? " Over us stars and under us graves." The graves would put it all right some day. As for attempting to direct one's fate, and struggle out of the highways of the

world—midsummer madness! It was not only the Mrs.
Gordons, but the Valeria Du Prels who told one so. Everybody said (but in discreeter terms), " Disguise from yourself
the solitude by setting up little screens of affections, and little
pompous affairs about which you must go busily, and with all
the solemnity that you can muster."

The savage builds his mud hut to shelter him from the
wind and the rain and the terror of the beyond. Outside is
the wilderness ready to engulf him. Rather than be left
alone at the mercy of elemental things, with no little hut,
warm and dark and stuffy, to shelter one, a woman will
sacrifice everything—liberty, ambition, health, power, her very
dignity. There was a letter in Hadria's pocket at this
moment, eloquently protesting in favour of the mud hut.

Hadria must have been appearing to listen favourably to
Temperley's pleading, for he said eagerly, " Then I have not
spoken this time quite in vain. I may hope that perhaps
some day——"

"Some day," repeated Hadria, passing her hand across her
eyes. " It doesn't really matter. I mean we make too much
fuss about these trifles; don't you think so?" She spoke
dreamily. The music was jigging on with strange merriment.

"To me it matters very much indeed. I don't consider it
a trifle," said Temperley, in some bewilderment.

"Oh, not to ourselves. But of what importance are we?"

"None at all, in a certain sense," Temperley admitted;
" but in another sense we are all important. I cannot help
being intensely personal at this moment. I can't help grasping
at the hope of happiness. Hadria, it lies in your hand.
Won't you be generous?"

She gave a distressed gesture, and seemed to make some
vain effort, as when the victim of a nightmare struggles to
overcome the paralysis that holds him.

"Then I may hope a little, Hadria—I *must* hope."

Still the trance seemed to hold her enthralled. The music
was diabolically merry. She could fancy evil spirits tripping

to it in swarms around her. They seemed to point at her, and wave their arms around her, and from them came an influence, magnetic in its quality, that forbade her to resist. All had been pre-arranged. Nothing could avert it. She seemed to be waiting rather than acting. Against her inner judgment, she had allowed those accursed practices to go on. Against her instinct, she had permitted Henriette to become intimate at Dunaghee; indeed it would have been hard to avoid it, for Miss Temperley was not easy to discourage. Why had she assured Hadria so pointedly that Hubert would not misinterpret her consent to renew the practices? Was it not a sort of treachery? Had not Henriette, with her larger knowledge of the world, been perfectly well aware that whatever might be said, the renewal of the meetings would be regarded as encouragement? Did she not know that Hadria herself would feel implicated by the concession?

Temperley's long silence had been misleading. The danger had crept up insidiously. And had she not been treacherous to herself? She had longed for companionship, for music, for something to break the strain of her wild, lonely life. Knowing, or rather half-divining the risk, she had allowed herself to accept the chance of relief when it came. Lack of experience had played a large part in the making of to-night's dilemma. Hadria's own strange mood was another ally to her lover, and for that, old Mrs. McPherson and her reels were chiefly responsible. Of such flimsy trifles is the human fate often woven.

"Tell me, did you ask your sister to —— ? "

"No, no," Hubert interposed. "My sister knows of my hopes, and is anxious that I should succeed."

"I thought that she was helping you."

"She would take any legitimate means to help me," said Hubert. "You cannot resent that. Ah, Hadria, why will you not listen to me?" He bent forward, covering his face with his hands in deep dejection. His hope had begun to wane.

"You know what I think," said Hadria. "You know how

I should act if I married. Surely that ought to cure you of all ——."

He seized her hand.

"No, no, nothing that you may think could cure me of the hope of making you my wife. I care for what you *are*, not for what you *think*. You know how little I cling to the popular version of the domestic story. I have told you over and over again that it offends me in a thousand ways. I hate the *bourgeois* element in it. What have we really to disagree about?"

He managed to be very convincing. He shewed that for a woman, life in her father's house is far less free than in her own home ; that existence could be moulded to any shape she pleased. If Hadria hesitated only on this account her last reason was gone. It was not fair to him. He had been patient. He had kept silence for many months. But he could endure the suspense no longer. He took her hand. Then suddenly she rose.

"No, no. I can't, I can't," she cried desperately.

"I will not listen to denial," he said following her. "I cannot stand a second disappointment. You have allowed me to hope."

"How? When? Never!" she exclaimed.

"Ah, yes, Hadria. I am older than you and I have more experience. Do you think a man will cease to hope while he continues to see the woman he loves?"

Hadria turned very pale.

"You seemed to have forgotten—your sister assured me— Ah, it was treacherous, it was cruel. She took advantage of my ignorance, my craving for companionship."

"No, it is you who are cruel, Hadria, to make such accusations. I do not claim the slightest consideration because you permitted those practices. But you cannot suppose that my feeling has not been confirmed and strengthened since I have seen you again. Why should you turn from me? Why may I not hope to win you? If you have no repugnance to me, why should not I have a chance? Hadria, Hadria,

answer me, for heaven's sake. Oh, if I could only understand
what is in your mind !"

She would have found it a hard task to enlighten him. He
had succeeded, to some extent, in lulling her fears, not in
banishing them, for a sinister dread still muttered its warning
beneath the surface thoughts.

The strength of Temperley's emotion had stirred her. The
magic of personal influence had begun to tell upon her.
It was so hard not to believe when some one insisted with
such certainty, with such obvious sincerity, that everything
would be right. He seemed so confident that she could
make him happy, strange as it appeared. Perhaps after
all——? And what a release from the present difficulties.
But could one trust? A confused mass of feeling struggled
together. A temptation to give the answer that would cause
pleasure was very strong, and beneath all lurked a trembling
hope that perhaps this was the way of escape. In apparent
contradiction to this, or to any other hope, lay a sense of
fatality, a sad indifference, interrupted at moments by flashes
of very desperate caring, when suddenly the love of life,
the desire for happiness and experience, for the exercise of
her power, for its use in the service of her generation, became
intense, and then faded away again, as obstacles presented
their formidable array before the mind. In the midst of
the confusion the thought of the Professor hovered vaguely,
with a dim distressing sense of something wrong, of something
within her lost and wretched and forlorn.

Mrs. Fullerton passed through the room on the arm of
Mr. Gordon. How delighted her mother would be if she were
to give up this desperate attempt to hold out against her
appointed fate. What if her mother and Mrs. Gordon and all
the world were perfectly right and far-seeing and wise ? Did it
not seem more likely, on the face of it, that they *should* be
right, considering the enormous majority of those who would
agree with them, than that she, Hadria, a solitary girl, un-
supported by knowledge of life or by fellow-believers, should

have chanced upon the truth? Had only Valeria been on her side, she would have felt secure, but Valeria was dead against her.

"We are not really at variance, believe me," Temperley pleaded. "You state things rather more strongly than I do— a man used to knocking about the world—but I don't believe there is any radical difference between us." He worked himself up into the belief that there never were two human beings so essentially at one, on all points, as he and Hadria.

"Do you remember the debate that evening in the garret? Do you remember the sentiments that scared your sister so much?" she asked.

Temperley remembered.

"Well, I don't hold those sentiments merely for amusement and recreation. I mean them. I should not hesitate a moment to act upon them. If things grew intolerable, according to my view of things, I should simply go away, though twenty marriage-services had been read over my head. Neither Algitha nor I have any of the notions that restrain women in these matters. We would brook no such bonds. The usual claims and demands we would neither make nor submit to. You heard Algitha speak very plainly on the matter. So you see, we are entirely unsuitable as wives, except to the impossible men who might share our rebellion. Please let us go back to the hall. They are just beginning to dance another reel."

"I cannot let you go back. Oh, Hadria, you can't be so unjust as to force me to break off in this state of uncertainty. Just give me a word of hope, however slight, and I will be satisfied."

Hadria looked astonished. "Have you really taken in what I have just said?"

"Every word of it.'

"And you realise that I mean it, *mean* it, with every fibre of me."

"I understand; and I repeat that I shall not be happy until

you are my wife. Have what ideas you please, only be my
wife."

She gazed at him in puzzled scrutiny. "You don't think I
am really in earnest. Let us go."

"I know you are in earnest," he cried, eagerly following her,
"and still I ——"

At that moment Harold Wilkins came up to claim Hadria
for a promised dance. Temperley gave a gesture of impatience.
But Harold insisted, and Hadria walked with her partner into
the hall where Mrs. Gordon was now playing a sentimental
waltz, with considerable poetic license as to time. As everyone
said : Mrs. Gordon played with so much expression.

Temperley stood about in corners watching Hadria. She
was flushed and silent, dancing with a still gliding movement
under the skilful guidance of her partner.

Temperley tried to win a glance as she passed round, but
her eyes were resolutely fixed on the floor.

Algitha followed her sister's movements uneasily. She had
noticed her absence during the last reel, and observed that
Temperley also was not to be seen. She felt anxious. She
knew Hadria's emotional susceptibility. She knew Temperley's
convincing faculty, and also Hadria's uneasy [feeling that she
had done wrong in allowing the practices to be resumed.

Henriette had not failed to notice the signs of the times,
and she annoyed Algitha beyond endurance by her obviously
sisterly manner of addressing the family. She had taken to
calling the boys by their first names.

Fred shared his sister's dislike to Henriette. "Tact !" he
cried with a snort, "why a Temperley rushes in where a bull
in a china-shop would fear to tread !"

Algitha saw that Hubert was again by Hadria's side before
the evening was out. The latter looked white, and she
avoided her sister's glance. This last symptom seemed to
Algitha the worst.

"What's the matter with Hadria?" asked Fred, "she will
scarcely speak to me. I was just telling her the best joke
I've heard this year, and, will you believe me, she didn't see

the point! Yes, you may well stare! I tried again and she
gave a nervous giggle; I am relating to you the exact truth.
Do any of the epidemics come on like that?"

"Yes, one of the worst," said Algitha gloomily.   Fred
glared enquiry.

"I am afraid she has been led into accepting Hubert
Temperley."

Fred opened his mouth and breathed deep.   "Stuff!
Hadria would as soon think of selling her soul to the devil."

"Oh, she is quite capable of that too," said Algitha,
shaking her head.

"Well, I'm blowed," cried Fred.

Not long after this, the guests began to disperse.   Mrs.
Gordon and her party were among the last to leave, having
a shorter distance to go.

Hubert Temperley was quiet and self-possessed, but Algitha
felt sure that she detected a look of suppressed exultation in
his demeanour, and something odiously brotherly in his mode
of bidding them all good-night.

When everyone had left, and the family were alone, they
gathered round the hall fire for a final chat, before dispersing
for the night.

"What a delightful evening we have had, Mrs. Fullerton,"
said Miss Temperley.   "It was most picturesque and characteristic.   I shall always remember the charm and kindliness of
Scottish hospitality."

"And I," said Ernest, *sotto voce* to Algitha, "shall always
remember the calm and thoroughness of English cheek!"

"Why, we had almost forgotten that the New Year is just
upon us," exclaimed Mr. Fullerton.   The first stroke of
twelve began to sound almost as he spoke.   He threw up the
window and disclosed a night brilliant with stars.   ("And
under us graves," said Hadria to herself.)

They all crowded up, keeping silence as the slow strokes of
the clock told the hour.

"A Happy New Year to all!" cried Mr. Fullerton heartily.

Part II.

CHAPTER XVI.

" . . . when the steam
Floats up from those dim fields about the homes
Of happy men that have the power to die."
Tithonius, TENNYSON.

A COUNTRYMAN with stooping gait touched his cap and bid good-day to a young woman who walked rapidly along the crisp high road, smiling a response as she passed.

The road led gradually upward through a country blazing with red and orange for rolling miles, till the horizon closed in with the far-off blue of English hills.

The old man slowly turned to watch the wayfarer, whose quick step and the look in her eyes of being fixed on objects beyond their owner's immediate ken, might have suggested to the observant, inward perturbation. The lissom, swiftly moving figure was almost out of sight before the old man slowly wheeled round and continued on his way towards the hamlet of Craddock Dene, that lay in the valley about a mile further on. Meanwhile the young woman was speeding towards the village of Craddock on the summit of the gentle slope before her. A row of broad-tiled cottages came in sight, and on the hill-side the Vicarage among trees, and a grey stone church which had seen many changes since its tower first looked out from the hill-top over the southern counties.

The little village seemed as if it had forgotten to change with the rest of the country, for at least a hundred years. The spirit of the last century lingered in its quiet cottages, in the little ale-house with half-obliterated sign, in its air of absolute repose and leisure. There was no evidence of contest any-where—except perhaps in a few mouldy advertisements of a circus and of a remarkable kind of soap, that were half peeling off a moss-covered wall. There were not even many indications of life in the place. The sunshine seemed to have the village street to itself. A couple of women stood gossiping over the gate of one of the cottages. They paused in their talk as a quick step sounded on the road.

"There be Mrs. Temperley again!" one matron exclaimed. "Why this is the second time this week, as she's come and sat in the churchyard along o' the dead. Don't seem nat'ral to my thinking."

Mrs. Dodge and Mrs. Gullick continued to discuss this gloomy habit with exhaustive minuteness, involving themselves in side issues regarding the general conduct of life on the part of Mrs. Temperley, that promised solid material for conversation for the next week. It appeared from the observations of Mrs. Gullick, whose husband worked on Lord Engleton's model farm, that about five years ago Mr. Temperley had rented the Red House at Craddock Dene, and had brought his new wife to live there. The Red House belonged to Professor Fortescue, who also owned the Priory, which had stood empty, said Mrs. Gullick, since that poor Mrs. Fortescue killed herself in the old drawing-room. Mr. Temperley went every day to town to attend to his legal business, and returned by the evening train to the bosom of his family. That family now consisted in his wife and two small boys; pretty little fellows, added Mrs. Dodge, the pride of their parents' hearts; at least, so she had heard Mr. Joseph Fleming say, and he was intimate at the Red House. Mrs. Gullick did not exactly approve of Mrs. Temperley. The Red House was not, it would seem, an everflowing fount of sustaining port wine and spiritually nourishing literature. The moral evolution of the village had proceeded on those lines. The prevailing feeling was vaguely hostile ; neither Mrs. Gullick nor Mrs. Dodge exactly knew why. Mrs. Dodge said that her husband (who was the sexton and gravedigger) had found Mrs. Temperley always ready for a chat. He spoke well of her. But Dodge was not one of many. Mrs. Temperley was perhaps too sensitively respectful of the feelings of her poorer neighbours to be very popular among them. At any rate, her habits of seclusion did not seem to village philosophy to be justifiable in the eyes of God or man. Her apparent fondness for the society of the dead also caused displeasure. Why she went to the churchyard could not be imagined : one would think she had a family buried there, she who was, "as one might say, a stranger to the place," and could not be supposed to have any interest in the graves, which held for her nor kith nor kin !

Mrs. Temperley, however, appeared to be able to dispense with this element of attraction in the "grassy barrows." She and a company of youthful Cochin-China fowls remained for hours among them, on this cheerful morning, and no observer could have determined whether it was the graves or the fowls that riveted her attention. She had perched herself on the stile that led from the churchyard to the fields : a slender figure in serviceable russet and irresponsible-looking hat, autumn-tinted too, in sympathy with the splendid season. In her ungloved left hand, which was at once sensitive and firm, she carried a book, keeping a forefinger between the pages to mark a passage.

Her face bore signs of suffering, and at this moment, a look of baffled and restless longing, as if life had been for her a festival whose sounds came from a hopeless distance. Yet there was something in the expression of the mouth, that suggested a consistent standing aloof from herself and her desires. The lines of the face could never have been drawn by mere diffusive, emotional habits. Thought had left as many traces as feeling in the firm drawing. The quality of the face was of that indefinable kind that gives to all characteristic things their peculiar power over the imagination.

The more powerful the quality, the less can it be rendered into terms. It is the one marvellous, remaining, musical fact not to be defined that makes the Parthenon, or some other master-piece of art, translate us to a new plane of existence, and inspire, for the time being, the pessimist with hope and the sceptic with religion.

The Cochin-Chinas pecked about with a contented mien among the long grass, finding odds and ends of nourishment, and here and there eking out their livelihood with a dart at a passing fly. Their long, comic, tufted legs, which seemed to form a sort of monumental pedestal whereon the bird itself was elevated, stalked and scratched about with an air of industrious serenity.

There were few mornings in the year which left unstirred the grass which grew long over the graves, but this was one of the few. Each blade stood up still and straight, bearing its string of dewdrops. There were one or two village sounds that came subdued through the sunshine. The winds that usually haunted the high spot had fallen asleep, or were lying somewhere in ambush among the woodlands beyond.

The look of strain had faded from the face of Mrs. Temperley, leaving only an expression of sadness. The removal of all necessity for concealing thought allowed her story to write itself on her face. The speculative would have felt some curiosity as to the cause of a sadness in one seemingly so well treated by destiny. Neither poverty nor the cares of great wealth could have weighed upon her spirit; she had beauty, and a quality more attractive than beauty, which must have placed many things at her command; she had evident talent—her very attitude proclaimed it—and the power over Fortune that talent ought to give. Possibly, the observer might reflect, the gift was of that kind which lays the possessor peculiarly open to her outrageous slings and arrows. Had Mrs. Temperley shown any morbid signs of self-indulgent emotionalism the problem would have been simple enough; but this was not the case.

The solitude was presently broken by the approach of an old man laden with pickaxe and shovel. He remarked upon the fineness of the day, and took up his position at a short distance from the stile, where the turf had been cleared away in a long-shaped patch. Here, with great deliberation he began his task. The sound of his steady strokes fell on the stillness. Presently, the clock from the grey tower gave forth its announcement—eleven. One by one, the slow hammer sent the waves of air rolling away, almost visibly, through the sunshine, their sound alternating with the thud of the pickaxe, so as to produce an effect of intentional rhythm. One might have fancied that clock and pickaxe iterated in turn, "Time, Death! Time, Death! Time, Death!" till the clock had come to the end of its tale, and then the pickaxe went on alone in the stillness—"Death! Death! Death! Death!"

A smile, not easy to be accounted for, flitted across the face of Mrs. Temperley.

The old gravedigger paused at last in his toil, leaning on his pickaxe, and bringing a red cotton handkerchief out of his hat to wipe his brow.

"That seems rather hard work, Dodge," remarked the onlooker, leaning her book upright on her knee and her chin on her hand.

"Ay, that it be, mum; this clay's that stiff! Lord! folks is almost as much trouble to them as buries as to them as bears 'em; it's all trouble together, to my thinkin'."

She assented with a musing nod.

"And when a man's not a troublin' o' some other body, he's a troublin' of hisself," added the philosopher.

"You are cursed with a clear-sightedness that must make life a burden to you," said Mrs. Temperley.

"Well, mum, I do sort o' see the bearin's o' things better nor most," Dodge modestly admitted. The lady knew, and liked to gratify, the gravedigger's love of long-worded discourse.

"Some people," she said, "are born contemplative, while others never reflect at all, whatever the provocation."

"Yes 'm, that's just it; folks goes on as if they was to live for ever, without no thought o' dyin'. As you was a sayin' jus' now, mum, there's them as contemflecs natural like, and there's them as is born without provocation——"

"Everlastingly!" assented Mrs. Temperley with a sudden laugh. "You evidently, Dodge, are one of those who strive to read the riddle of this painful earth. Tell me what you think it is all about."

Gratified by this appeal to his judgment, Dodge scratched his head, and leant both brawny arms upon his pickaxe.

"Well, mum," he said, "I s'pose it's the will o' th' Almighty as we is brought into the world, and I don't say nothin' agin it —'t isn't my place—but it do come over me powerful at times, wen I sees all the vexin' as folks has to go through, as God A'mighty might 'a found somethin' better to do with His time; not as I wants to find no fault with His ways, which is past finding out," added the gravedigger, falling to work again.

A silence of some minutes was broken by Mrs. Temperley's enquiry as to how long Dodge had followed this profession.

"Nigh on twenty year, mum, come Michaelmas," replied Dodge. "I've lain my couple o' hundred under the sod, easy; and a fine lot o' corpses they was too, take 'em one with another." Dodge was evidently prepared to stand up for the average corpse of the Craddock district against all competitors.

"This is a very healthy neighbourhood, I suppose," observed Mrs. Temperley, seemingly by way of supplying an explanation of the proud fact.

"Lord bless you, as healthy as any place in the kingdom. There wasn't one in ten as was ill when he died, as one may say."

"But that scarcely seems an unmixed blessing," commented the lady musingly, "to go off suddenly in the full flush of health and spirits; it would be so discouraging."

"Most was chills, took sudden," Dodge explained; "chills is wot chokes up yer churchyards for yer. If we has another hard winter this year, we shall have a job to find room in here. There's one or two in the village already, as I has my eye on, wot——"

"Was this one a chill?" interrupted Mrs. Temperley, with a nod towards the new grave.

"Wot, this here? Lord bless you, no, mum. This here's our schoolmarm. Didn't you never hear tell about *her?*" This damning proof of his companion's aloofness from village gossip seemed to paralyse the gravedigger.

"Why everybody's been a talkin' about it. Over varty, she war, and ought to 'a knowed better."

"But, with advancing years, it is rare that people *do* get to know better—about dying," Mrs. Temperley suggested, in defence of the deceased schoolmistress.

"I means about her conduc'," Dodge explained; "scand'lous thing. Why, she's been in Craddock school since she war a little chit o' sixteen."

"That seems to me a trifle dull, but scarcely scandalous," Mrs. Temperley murmured.

". . . And as steady and respectable a young woman as you'd wish to see . . . pupil teacher she was, and she rose to be schoolmarm," Dodge went on.

"It strikes me as a most blameless career," said his companion. "Perhaps, as you say, considering her years, she ought to have known better, but ——"

"She sort o' belongs to the place, as one may say," Dodge proceeded, evidently quite unaware that he had omitted to give the clue to the situation. "She's lived here all her life."

"Then much may be forgiven her," muttered Mrs. Temperley.

"And everybody respected of her, and the parson he thought a deal o' her, he did, and used to hold her up as a sample to the other young women, and nobody dreamt as she'd go and bring this here scandal on the place; nobody knows who the man was, but it *is* said as there's someone *not* twenty miles from here as knows more about it nor he didn't ought to,"

Dodge added with sinister meaning. This dark hint conveyed absolutely no enlightenment to the mind of Mrs. Temperley, from sheer lack of familiarity, on her part, with the rumours of the district. Dodge applied himself with a spurt to his work.

"When she had her baby, she was like one out of her mind," he continued; "she couldn't stand the disgrace and the neighbours talkin', and that. Mrs. Walker she went and saw her, and brought her nourishin' things, and kep' on a-telling her how she must try and make up for what she had done, and repent and all that; but she never got up her heart again like, and the poor soul took fever from grievin', the doctor says, and raved on dreadful, accusin' of somebody, and sayin' he'd sent her to hell; and then Wensday morning, ten o'clock, she died. Didn't you hear the passing bell a-tolling, mum?"

"Yes, the wind brought it down the valley; but I did not know whom it was tolling for."

"That's who it was," said Dodge.

"This is an awfully sad story," cried Mrs. Temperley.

Dodge ran his fingers through his hair judicially. "I don't hold with them sort o' goings on for young women," he observed.

"Do you hold with them for young men?"

Dodge puckered. up his face into an odd expression of mingled reflection and worldly wisdom. "You can't prevent young fellers bein' young fellers," he at length observed.

"It seems almost a pity that being young fellows should also mean being blackguards," observed Mrs. Temperley calmly.

"Well, there's somethin' to be said for that way o' lookin' at it," Dodge was startled into agreeing.

"I suppose *she* gets all the blame of the thing," the lady went on, with quiet exasperation. Dodge seemed thrown off his bearings.

"Everybody in Craddock was a-talking about it, as was only to be expected," said the gravedigger. "Well, well, we're all sinners. Don't do to be too hard on folks. 'Pears sad like after keepin' 'spectable for all them years too—sort o' waste."

Mrs. Temperley gave a little laugh, which seemed to Dodge rather eccentric.

"Who is looking after the baby?" she asked.

"One of the neighbours, name o' Gullick, as her husband works for Lord Engleton, which she takes in washing," Dodge comprehensively explained.

"Had its mother no relatives?"

"Well, she had an aunt down at Southampton, I've heard tell, but she didn't take much notice of her, not *she* didn't. Her mother only died last year, took off sudden before her daughter could get to her."

"Your schoolmistress has known trouble," observed Mrs. Temperley. "Had she no one, no sister, no friend, during all this time that she could turn to for help or counsel?"

"Not as I knows of," Dodge replied.

There was a long pause, during which the stillness seemed to weigh upon the air, as if the pressure of Fate were hanging there with ruthless immobility.

"She ain't got no more to suffer now," Dodge remarked, nodding with an aspect of half apology towards the grave. "They sleeps soft as sleeps here."

"Good heavens, I hope so!" Mrs. Temperley exclaimed.

The grave had made considerable progress before she descended from the stile and prepared to take her homeward way. On leaving, she made Dodge come with her to the gate, and point out the red-roofed cottage covered with monthly roses and flaming creeper, where the schoolmistress had passed so many years, and where she now lay with her work and her days all over, in the tiny upper room, at whose latticed window the sun used to wake her on summer mornings, or the winter rain pattered dreary prophecies of the tears that she would one day shed.

CHAPTER XVII.

" I F you please, ma'am, the cook says as the meat hasn't come for lunch, and what is she to do?"

"Without," replied Mrs. Temperley automatically.

The maid waited for more discreet directions. She had given a month's notice that very morning, because she found Craddock Dene too dull.

"Thank goodness, that barbarian is going!" Hubert had exclaimed.

"We shall but exchange a Goth for a Vandal," his wife replied.

Mrs. Temperley gazed intently at her maid, the light of intelligence gradually dawning in her countenance. "Is there anything else in the house, Sapph—Sophia?"

"No, ma'am," replied Sophia.

"Oh, tell the cook to make it into a fricassee, and be sure it is well flavoured." The maid hesitated, but seeing from the wandering expression of her employer's eye that her intellect was again clouded over, she retired to give the message to the cook—with comments.

The library at the Red House was the only room that had been radically altered since the days of the former tenants, whose taste had leant towards the florid rather than the classic. The general effect had been toned down, but it was impossible to disguise the leading motive; or what Mrs. Temperley passionately described as its brutal vulgarity. The library alone had been subjected to *peine forte et dure*. Mrs. Temperley said that it had been purified by suffering. By dint of tearing down and dragging out offending objects ("such a pity!" cried the neighbours) its prosperous and complacent

154

absurdity had been humbled. Mrs. Temperley retired to this refuge after her encounter with Sophia. That perennially aggrieved young person entered almost immediately afterwards and announced a visitor, with an air that implied— "She'll stay to lunch; see if she don't, and what'll you do then? Yah!"

The pronunciation of the visitor's name was such, that, for the moment, Mrs. Temperley did not recognize it as that of Miss Valeria Du Prel.

She jumped up joyfully. "Ah, Valeria, this *is* delightful!"

The visit was explained after a characteristic fashion. Miss Du Prel realized that over two years had passed since she had seen Hadria, and moreover she had been seized with an overwhelming longing for a sight of country fields and a whiff of country air, so she had put a few things together in a handbag, which she had left at Craddock station by accident, and come down. Was there anyone who could go and fetch her handbag? It was such a nuisance; she laid it down for a moment to get at her ticket—she never could find her pocket, dressmakers always hid them in such an absurd way; could Hadria recommend any dressmaker who did not hide pockets? Wasn't it tiresome? She had no time-table, and so she had gone to the station that morning and waited till a Craddock train started, and by this arrangement it had come to pass that she had spent an hour and a half on the platform: she did not think she ever had such an unpleasant time; why didn't they have trains oftener? They did to Putney.

Mrs. Temperley sat down and laughed. Whereupon the other's face lightened and she joined in the laugh at her own expense, settling into the easy chair that her hostess had prepared for her, with a gesture of helplessness and comfort.

"Well, in spite of that time at the station, I'm glad I came. It seems so long since I have seen you, dear Hadria, and the last time you know you were very unhappy, almost mad——"

"Yes, yes; never mind about that," interposed Mrs. Temperley hastily, setting her teeth together.

"You take things too hard, too hard," said Miss Du Prel. "I used to think *I* was bad in that way, but I am phlegmatic compared with you. One would suppose that——"

"Valeria, don't, don't, don't," cried Mrs. Temperley. "I can't stand it." Her teeth were still set tight and hard, her hands were clenched.

"Very well, very well. Tell me what you have been making of this ridiculous old world, where everything goes wrong and everybody is stupid or wicked, or both."

Mrs. Temperley's face relaxed a little, though the signs of some strong emotion were still visible.

"Well, to answer the general by the particular, I have spent the morning, accompanied by a nice young brood of Cochin-China fowls, in Craddock churchyard."

"Oh, I hate a churchyard," exclaimed Miss Du Prel, with a shudder. "It makes one think of the hideous mockery of life, and the more one would like to die, the worse seems the brutality of death and his hideous accompaniments. It is such a savage denial of all human aspirations and affections and hopes. Ah, it is horrible!" The sharply-outlined face grew haggard and white, as its owner crouched over the fire.

"Heaven knows! but it was very serene and very lovely up there this morning."

"Ah!" exclaimed Valeria with a burst of strange enthusiasm and sadness, that revealed all the fire and yearning and power that had raised her above her fellows in the scale of consciousness, with the penalty of a life of solitude and of sorrow.

"Surely it is not without meaning that the places of the dead are the serenest spots on earth," said Mrs. Temperley. "If I could keep myself in the mood that the place induces, I think I should not mind anything very much any more. The sunshine seems to rest more tenderly there than elsewhere, and the winds have a reverence for the graves, as if they felt it time that the dead were left in peace—the 'happier dead,' as poor immortal Tithonius calls them, who has not the gift of death. And the grey old tower and the weather stains on the stones ; there is a conspiracy of beauty in the place, that holds one as one is held by music."

"Ah ! I know the magic of these things ; it tempts one to believe at times that Nature is *not* all blind and unpitying. But that is a delusion : if there were any pity in Nature, the human spirit would not be dowered with such infinite and terrible longings and such capacities and dreams and prayers and then—then insulted with the mockery of death and annihilation."

"If there should be no Beyond," muttered Mrs. Temperley. "That to me is inconceivable. When we die we fall into an eternal sleep. Moreover, I can see no creed that does not add the fear of future torments to the certainties of these."

Mrs. Temperley was seized with a bitter mood. "You should cultivate faith," she said ; "it acts the part of the heading 'Sundries omitted' in one's weekly accounts ; one can put down under it everything that can't be understood— but you don't keep weekly accounts, so it's no use pointing out to you the peace that comes of that device."

The entrance of Sophia with firewood turned the current of conversation. "Good heavens ! I don't think we have anything for lunch !" Mrs. Temperley exclaimed. "Are you very hungry? What is to be done? It was the faithlessness of our butcher that disturbed the serenity of my mood this morning. Perhaps the poor beast whose carcase we were intending to devour will feel serene instead of me : but, alas ! I fear he has been slaughtered *quand même*. That is one of the unsatisfactory things about life : that all its worst miseries bring good to no one. One may deny oneself, but not a living thing is necessarily the better for it—generally many are the worse. The wheels of pain go turning day by day, and the gods stand aloof—they will not help us, nor will they stay the 'wild world' in its course. No, no," added Mrs. Temperley with a laugh, "I am not tired of life, but I am tired *with* it ; it won't give me what I want. That is perhaps because I want so much."

The sound of male footsteps in the hall broke up the colloquy.

"Good heavens ! Hubert has brought home a crowd of people to lunch," exclaimed Hadria, "a thing he scarcely ever does. What fatality can have induced him to choose to-day of all others for this orgy of hospitality?"

"Does the day matter?" enquired Valeria, astonished at so much emotion.

"*Does the day matter!* Oh irresponsible question of the unwedded! When I tell you the butcher has not sent the meat."

"Oh . . . can't one eat fish?" suggested Miss Du Prel.

Hadria laughed and opened the door.

"My dear, I have brought Fleming home to lunch."

"Thank heaven, *only one !*"

Temperley stared.

"I could not conveniently have brought home several," he said.

"I thought you would be at least seven," cried the mistress of the house, "and with all the pertinacity of Wordsworth's little girl."

"What *do* you mean, if one may ask for simple English?"

"Merely that that intolerable Sanders has broken his word —*hinc illæ lacrimæ.*"

Hubert Temperley turned away in annoyance. He used to be amused by his wife's flippancy before her marriage, but he had long since grown to dislike it. He retired to get out some wine, while Hadria went forward to welcome the guest, who now came in from the garden, where he had lingered to talk to the children.

"I am delighted to see you, Mr. Fleming; but I am grieved to say that we have unluckily only a wretched luncheon to give you, and after your long walk over the fields too ! I am *so* sorry. The fact is we are left, this morning, with a gaping larder, at the mercy of a haughty and inconstant butcher, who grinds down his helpless dependents without mercy, overbearing creature that he is! We must ask you to be very tolerant."

"Oh! please don't trouble about that; it doesn't matter in the least," cried Mr. Fleming, pulling at his yellowish whiskers. He was a man of about five-and-thirty, of medium height, dressed in knickerbockers and Norfolk jacket that had seen some service.

"What is the difficulty?" asked Hubert.

"I was explaining to Mr. Fleming how inhospitably we are forced to treat him, on account of that traitor Sanders."

Hubert gave a gesture of annoyance.

"I suppose there is something cold in the house."

"Pudding, perhaps," said his wife hopelessly. "It is most unlucky."

"My dear, surely there must be something cold that isn't pudding."

"I fear, very little; but I will go and see the cook, though, alas! she is not easy to inspire as regards her particular business. She is extremely entertaining as a conversationalist, but I think she was meant for society rather than the kitchen. I am sure society would be more diverting if she were in it."

Hadria was just turning to seek this misplaced genius, when she paused in the doorway.

"By the way, I suppose Sapphira has——"

"Do try and cure yourself of the habit of calling the girl by that absurd name, Hadria."

"Oh, yes; but the name is so descriptive. She has told you of Miss Du Prel's arrival?"

"She has told me nothing of the sort."

Temperley did not look overjoyed. There had never been much cordiality between him and Valeria since the afternoon when they had met at Dunaghee, and found their sentiments in hopeless opposition.

Miss Du Prel took no interest in Hubert, though she admired his character. She had every wish to make herself agreeable to him, but her efforts in that direction were somewhat neutralized by an incurable absence of mind.   If she was not interested, as Hadria said, she was seldom affable.

Possibly Hubert's request to her, years ago at Dunaghee, to "think for a moment" had not been forgiven.

"Where is she?   Oh !——"

The exclamation was in consequence of Miss Du Prel's appearing at the door of the library, whence she surveyed the group with absent-minded intentness.

Valeria woke up with a start, and responded to Hubert's greeting in an erratic fashion, replying tragically, to a casual enquiry as to her health, that she had been *frightfully* ill.

"I thought I was dying.   But one never dies," she added in a disgusted tone, whereat Hadria heartlessly laughed, and hurried the visitor upstairs to help her to unpack.

"Valeria," said Mrs. Temperley, while that lady was confusedly trying to disentangle hat and hair, hat-pin and head, without involving the entire system in a common ruin— "Valeria, we are not a remarkable people at Craddock Dene. We may be worthy, we may have our good points, but we are not brilliant (except the cook).   Should Mr. Fleming fail to impress you as a person of striking personality, I ask you, as a favour, *not* to emblazon that impression on every feature : should he address to you a remark that you do not find interesting, and it is quite conceivable that he may—do not glare at him scornfully for a moment, and——"

Hadria was not allowed to finish the sentence.

"As if I ever did any such thing—and people are so dull," said Miss Du Prel.

A few "curried details," as the hostess dejectedly described the fare, had been supplemented with vegetables, fruit, and impromptu preparations of eggs, and the luncheon was pronounced excellent and ample.

Miss Du Prel said that she hoped the butcher would always forget to send the meat.   She liked these imaginative meals.

Temperley purposely misunderstood her to say "imaginary

meals," and hoped that next time she came, Hadria would not have an oratorio in course of composition. Miss Du Prel expressed a fiery interest in the oratorio.

" I judge the presence of oratorio by the absence of food," Temperley explained suavely.

Hadria watched the encounter with a mingled sense of amusement and discomfort.

Valeria was in no danger. To be morally crushed by an adversary, it is necessary that one should be at least aware that the adversary is engaged in crushing one : a consciousness that was plainly denied to Miss Du Prel. Many a man far less able than Hubert had power to interest her, while he could not even hold her attention. She used to complain to Professor Fortescue that Temperley's ideas never seemed to have originated in his own brain : they had been imported ready-made. Hubert was among the many who shrink and harden into mental furrows as time passes. What he had thought at twenty, at thirty-five had acquired sanctity and certainty, from having been the opinion of Hubert Temperley for all those favoured years. He had no suspicion that the views which he cherished in so dainty and scholarly a fashion were simply an *edition de luxe* of the views of everybody else. But his wife had made that discovery long ago. He smiled at the views of everybody else : his own were put forth as something choice and superior. He had the happy knack of being *bourgeois* with the air of an artist. If one could picture one's grocer weighing out sugar in a Spanish cloak and brigand's hat, it would afford an excellent symbol of his spiritual estate. To be perfectly commonplace in a brilliantly original way, is to be notable after all.

Mr. Fleming seemed puzzled by Miss Du Prel, at whom he glanced uneasily from time to time, wondering what she would say next. At Craddock Dene, ladies usually listened with a more or less breathless deference when Temperley spoke. This new-comer seemed recklessly independent.

Mrs. Temperley endeavoured to lead the conversation in

ways of peace, but Valeria was evidently on the war-path. Temperley was polite and ironical, with undermeanings for Hadria's benefit.

"If one asks impossible things of life, one is apt to be disappointed, I fear," he said serenely. "Ask for the possible and natural harvest of a woman's career, and see if you don't get it."

"Let a canary plead for its cage, in short, and its commendable prayer will be answered!"

"If you like to put it thus ungraciously. I should say that one who makes the most of his opportunities, as they stand, fares better than he who sighs for other worlds to conquer."

"I suppose that is what his relatives said to Columbus," observed Miss Du Prel.

."And how do you know they were not right?" he retorted.

Mrs. Temperley gave the signal to rise. "Let's go for a walk," she suggested, "the afternoon invites us. Look at it."

The brilliant sunshine and the exercise brought about a more genial mood. Only once was there anything approaching friction, and then it was Hadria herself who caused it.

"Yes, we all flatter ourselves that we are observing life, when we are merely noting the occasions when some musty old notion of ours happens, by chance, to get fulfilled."

Hubert Temperley at once roused Miss Du Prel's interest by the large stores of information that he had to pour forth on the history of the district, from its earliest times to the present. He recalled the days when these lands that looked so smooth and tended had been mere wastes of marsh and forest.

How quickly these great changes were accomplished! Valeria stood on the brow of a wide corn-field, looking out over the sleeping country. A century, after all, was not much more than one person's lifetime, yet in scarcely nine of these —nine little troubled lifetimes—what incredible things had occurred in this island of ours! How did it all come about? "Not assuredly," Valeria remarked with sudden malice, "by taking things as they stood, and making the best of them with imbecile impatience. If everyone had done that, what sort of an England should I have had stretching before my eyes at this moment?"

"You would not have been here to see," said Hadria, lazily rolling stones down the hill with her foot. "We should all of us have been dancing round some huge log-fire on the borders of a primeval forest, and instead of browsing on salads, as we did to-day, we should be sustaining ourselves on the unholy nourishment of boiled parent or grilled aunt."

Mr. Temperley's refined appearance and manner seemed to raise an incarnate protest against this revolting picture. For some occult reason, the imagination of all was at work especially and exclusively on the figure of that polished gentleman in war-paint and feathers, sporting round the cauldron that contained the boiled earthly remains of his relations.

Mr. Fleming betrayed the common thought by remarking that it would be very becoming to him.

"Ah! I wish we *were* all savages in feathers and war-paint, dancing on the edge of some wild forest, with nothing but the sea and the sky for limits!"

Miss Du Prel surprised her audience by this earnest aspiration.

"Do you feel inclined to revert?" Hadria enquired. "Because if so, I shall be glad to join you."

"I think there *is* a slight touch of the savage about Mrs. Temperley," observed Fleming pensively. "I mean, don't you know—of course——."

"You are quite right!" cried Valeria. "I have often noticed a sort of wildness that crops up now and then through a very smooth surface. Hadria may sigh for the woodlands, yet——!"

CHAPTER XVIII.

THE first break in the unity of the Fullerton family had occurred on the occasion of Hadria's marriage. The short period that elapsed between that memorable New-Year's-Eve and the wedding had been a painful experience for Dunaghee. Hadria's conduct had shaken her brothers' faith in her and in all womankind. Ernest especially had suffered disillusion. He had supposed her above the ordinary, pettier weaknesses of humanity. Other fellows' sisters had seemed to him miserable travesties of their sex compared with her. (There was one exception only, to this rule.) But now, what was he to think? She had shattered his faith. If she hadn't been "so cocksure of herself," he wouldn't have minded so much; but after all she had professed, to go and marry, and marry a starched specimen like that!

Fred was equally emphatic. For a long time he had regarded it all as a joke. He shook his head knowingly, and said that sort of thing wouldn't go down. When he was at length convinced, he danced with rage. He became cynical. He had no patience with girls. They talked for talking's sake. It meant nothing.

Algitha understood, better than her brothers could understand, how Hadria's emotional nature had been caught in some strange mood, how the eloquent assurances of her lover might have half convinced her. Algitha's own experience of proposals set her on the track of the mystery.

"It is most misleading," she pointed out, to her scoffing brothers. "One would suppose that marrying was the simplest thing in the world—nothing perilous, nothing to object to about it. A man proposes to you as if he were asking you for the sixth waltz, only his manner is perfervid. And my belief is that half the girls who accept don't realize that they are agreeing to anything much more serious."

"The more fools they!"

"True; but it really is most bewildering. Claims, obligations, all the ugly sides of the affair are hidden away; the man is at his best, full of refinement and courtesy and unselfishness. And if he persuades the girl that he really does care for her, how can she suppose that she cannot trust her future to him— if he loves her? And yet she can't!"

"How can a man suppose that one girl is going to be different from every other girl?" asked Fred.

"Different, you mean, from what he *supposes* every other girl to be," Algitha corrected. "It's his own look-out if he's such a fool."

"I believe Hadria married because she was sick of being the family consolation," said Ernest.

"Well, of course, the hope of escape was very tempting. You boys don't know what she went through. We all regret her marriage to Hubert Temperley—though between ourselves, not more than *he* regrets it, if I am not much mistaken—but it is very certain that she could not have gone on living at home much longer, as things were."

Fred said that she ought to have broken out after Algitha's fashion, if it was so bad as all that.

"I think mother would have died if she had," said the sister.

"Hadria *was* awkwardly placed," Fred admitted.

"Do you remember that evening in the garret when we all told her what we thought?" asked Ernest.

Nobody had forgotten that painful occasion.

"She said then that if the worst came to the worst, she would simply run away. What could prevent her?"

"That wretched sister of his!" cried Algitha. "If it hadn't been for her, the marriage would never have taken place. She got the ear of mother after the engagement, and I am certain it was through her influence that mother hurried the wedding on so. If only there had been a little more time, it could have been prevented. And Henriette knew that. She is as *knowing*——!"

"I wish we had strangled her."

"I shall never forget," Algitha went on, "that night when Hadria was taken with a fit of terror—it was nothing less—and wrote to break off the engagement, and that woman undertook to deliver the letter and lost it, *on purpose* I am always convinced, and then the favourable moment was over."

"What made her so anxious for the marriage beats me," cried Ernest. "It was not a particularly good match from a mercenary point of view."

"She thought us an interesting family to marry into," suggested Fred, "which is undeniable."

"Then she must be greatly disappointed at seeing so little of us!" cried Ernest.

In the early days, Miss Temperley had stayed frequently at the Red House, and Hadria had been cut off from her own family, who detested Henriette.

For a year or more, there had been a fair promise of a successful adjustment of the two incongruous natures in the new conditions. They both tried to keep off dangerous ground and to avoid collisions of will. They made the most of their one common interest, although even here they soon found themselves out of sympathy. Hubert's instincts were scholastic and lawful, Hadria was disposed to daring innovation. Her bizarre compositions shocked him painfully. The two jarred on one another, in great things and in small. The halcyon period was short-lived. The dream, such as it was, came to an end. Hubert turned to his sister, in his bewilderment and disappointment. They had both counted so securely on the effect of experience and the pressure of events to teach Hadria the desirable lesson, and they were dismayed to find that, unlike other women, she had failed to learn it. Henriette was in despair. It was she who had brought about the ill-starred union. How could she ever forgive herself? How repair the error she had made? Only by devoting herself to her brother, and trying patiently to bring his wife to a wiser frame of mind.

A considerable time had elapsed, during which Hadria saw her brothers and sister only at long intervals. Ernest had become estranged from her, to her great grief. He was as courteous and tender in his manner to her as of yore, but there was a change, not to be mistaken. She had lost the brother of her girlhood for ever. While it bitterly grieved, it did not surprise her. She acknowledged in dismay the inconsistency of her conduct. She must have been mad! The universal similarity in the behaviour of girls, herself included, alarmed her. Was there some external will that drove them all, in hordes, to their fate? Were all the intricacies of event and circumstance, of their very emotion, merely the workings of that ruthless cosmic will by which the individual was hypnotised and ruled?

As usual at critical moments, Hadria had been solitary in her encounter with the elements of Fate. There were conflicts that even her sister knew nothing about, the bewilderments and temptations of a nature hampered in its action by its own voluminous qualities and its caprice.

Her brothers supposed that in a short time Hadria would be "wearing bonnets and a card-case, and going the rounds with an elegant expression like the rest of them."

How different were the little local facts of life—the little chopped-up life that accumulates in odds and ends from moment to moment—from the sun-and-smoke vision of early irresponsible days!

Mrs. Fullerton was pleased with the marriage, not merely because Hubert's father, Judge Temperley, could secure for his son a prosperous career, but because she was so thankful to see a strange, unaccountable girl like Hadria settling quietly down, with a couple of children to keep her out of mischief.

That was what it had come to! Perhaps they calculated a little too surely. Possibly even two children might not keep her entirely out of mischief. Out of what impulse of malice had Fate pitched upon the most essentially mutinous and erratic of the whole brood, for the sedatest *rôle*? But perhaps Fate, too, had calculated unscientifically. Mischief was always possible, if one gave one's mind to it. Or was she growing too old to have the spirit for thorough-going devilry? Youth seemed rather an affair of mental outlook than of years. She felt twenty years older since her marriage. She wondered why it was that marriage did not make all women wicked,—openly and actively so. If ever there was an arrangement by which every evil instinct and every spark of the devil was likely to be aroused and infuriated, surely the customs and traditions that clustered round this estate constituted that dangerous combination! Hardship, difficulty, tragedy could be faced, but not the humiliating, the degrading, the contemptible. Hadria had her own particular ideas as to what ought to be set down under these headings. Most women, she found, ranked certain elements very differently, with lavish use of halos and gilding in their honour, feeling perhaps, she hinted, the dire need of such external decoration.

Good heavens! Did no other woman realize the insult of it all? Hadria knew so few women intimately; none intimately enough to be convinced that no such revolt lay smouldering beneath their smiles. She had a lonely assurance that she had never met the sister-soul (for such there must be by the score, as silent as she), who shared her rage and her detestations. Valeria, with all her native pride, regarded these as proof of a big flaw in an otherwise sound nature. Yet how deep, how passionately strong, these feelings were, how gigantic the flaw!

What possessed people that they did not see what was so

brutally clear? As young girls led forth unconscious into the battle, with a bandage over their eyes, and cotton-wool in their ears—yes, then it was inevitable that they should see and hear nothing. Had they been newly imported from the moon they could scarcely have less acquaintance with terrestrial conditions; but afterwards, when ruthlessly, with the grinning assistance of the onlookers, the facts of the social scheme were cynically revealed, and the *rôle* imperiously allotted — with much admonition and moving appeals to conscience and religion, and all the other aides-de-camp at command—after all that, how in the name of heaven could they continue to " babble of green fields "? Was it conceivable that among the thousands of women to whom year after year the facts were disclosed, not one understood and not one—*hated?*

A flame sprang up in Hadria's eyes. There *must* be other women somewhere at this very moment, whose whole being was burning up with this bitter, this sickening and futile hatred! But how few, how few! How vast was the meek majority, fattening on indignity, proud of their humiliation! Yet how wise they were after all. It hurt so to hate—to hate like this. Submission was an affair of temperament, a gift of birth. Nature endowed with a serviceable meekness those whom she designed for insult. Yet it might not be meekness so much as mere brutal necessity that held them all in thrall— the inexorable logic of conditions. Fate knew better than to assail the victim point blank, and so put her on her guard. No; she lured her on gently, cunningly, closing behind her, one by one, the doors of escape, persuading her, forcing her to fasten on her own tethers, appealing to a thousand qualities, good and bad ; now to a moment's weakness or pity, now to her eternal fear of grieving others (*that* was a well-worked vein !), now to her instinct of self-sacrifice, now to grim necessity itself, profiting too by the increasing discouragements, the vain efforts, the physical pain and horrible weariness, the crowding of little difficulties, harassments, the troubles of others—ah ! how infinite were these ! so that there was no

interval for breathing, and scarcely time or space to cope with
the legions of the moment; the horizon was black with their
advancing hosts !

And this assuredly was no unique experience. Hadria
remembered how she had once said that if the worst came to
the worst, it would be easy to run away. To her inexperience
desperate remedies had seemed so simple, so feasible—the
factors of life so few and unentwined. She had not understood how prolific are our deeds, how an act brings with it
a large and unexpected progeny, which surround us with new
influences and force upon us unforeseen conditions. Yet
frequent had been the impulse to adopt that girlish solution
of the difficulty. She had no picturesque grievances of the
kind that would excite sympathy. On the contrary, popular
feeling would set dead against her; she would be acting on an
idea that nobody shared, not even her most intimate friend.

Miss Du Prel had arrived at the conclusion that she did not
understand Hadria. She had attributed many of her peculiarities to her unique education and her inexperience.
Hadria had indeed changed greatly since her marriage, but
not in the manner that might have been expected. On the
contrary, a closer intimacy with popular social ideals had
fired her with a more angry spirit of rebellion. Miss Du
Prel had met examples of every kind of eccentricity, but she
had never before come upon so marked an instance of this
particular type. Hadria's attitude towards life had suggested
to Miss Du Prel the idea of her heroine, *Caterina*. She
remonstrated with Hadria, assuring her that no insult towards
women was intended in the general scheme of society, and
that it was a mistake to regard it in so resentful a spirit.

"But that is just the most insulting thing about it," Hadria
exclaimed. "Insult is so much a matter of course that
people are surprised if one takes umbrage at it. Read this
passage from Aristotle that I came upon the other day. He
is perfectly calm and amiable, entirely unconscious of offence,
when he says that 'a wife ought to shew herself even more

oɒedient to the rein than if she entered the house as a pur-
chased slave. For she has been bought at a high price, for
the sake of sharing life and bearing children, than which no
higher or holier tie can possibly exist.' (Henriette to the very
life !) "

Miss Du Prel laughed, and re-read the passage from the
Politics, in some surprise.

" Do you suppose insult is deliberately intended in that
graceful sentiment ? " asked Hadria. " Obviously not. If any
woman of that time had blazed up in anger at the well-meant
speech, she would have astonished and grieved her contemporaries. Aristotle doubtless professed a high respect for women
who followed his precepts—as men do now when we are
obedient."

" Of course, our society in this particular has not wandered
far from the Greek idea," Miss Du Prel observed pensively.

Hadria pronounced the paradox, " The sharpness of the
insult lies in its not being intended."

Miss Du Prel could not prevail upon her to modify the
assertion. Hadria pointed out that the Greeks also meant
no offence in regarding their respectable women as simple
reproductive agents of inferior human quality.

" And though our well-brought-up girls shrink from the
frank speech, they do not appear to shrink from the ideas
of the old Greeks. They don't mind playing the part of
cows so long as one doesn't mention it."

About eighteen months ago, the village had been full of talk
and excitement in consequence of the birth of an heir to
the house of Engleton, Lady Engleton's mission in life being
frankly regarded as unfulfilled during the previous three or
four years, when she had disappointed the hopes of the
family. Hadria listened scornfully. In her eyes, the crowning
indignity of the whole affair was Lady Engleton's own smiling
acceptance of the position, and her complacent eagerness to
produce the tardy inheritor of the property and honours.
This expression of sentiment had, by some means, reached the
Vicarage and created much consternation.

Mrs. Walker asserted that it was right and Christian of the lady to desire that which gave every one so much pleasure. "A climax of feminine abjectness!" Hadria had exclaimed in Henriette's presence.

Miss Temperley, after endeavouring to goad her sister-in-law into the expression of jubilant congratulations, was met by the passionate declaration that she felt more disposed to weep than to rejoice, and more disposed to curse than to weep.

Obviously, Miss Temperley had reason to be uneasy about her part in bringing about her brother's marriage.

These sudden overflows of exasperated feeling had become less frequent as time went on, but the neighbours looked askance at Mrs. Temperley. Though a powder-magazine may not always blow up, one passes it with a grave consciousness of vast stores of inflammable material lying somewhere within, and who knows what spark might set the thing spouting to the skies?

When the occasional visitors had left, life in the village settled down to its normal level, or more accurately, to its normal flatness as regarded general contours, and its petty inequalities in respect to local detail. It reminded Hadria of the landscape which stretched in quiet long lines to the low horizon, while close at hand, the ground fussed and fretted itself into minor ups and downs of no character, but with all the trouble of a mountain district in its complexities of slope and hollow. Hadria suffered from a gnawing home-sickness; a longing for the rougher, bleaker scenery of the North.

The tired spirit translated the homely English country, so deeply reposeful in its spirit, into an image of dull unrest. If only those broken, stupid lines could have been smoothed out into the grandeur of a plain, Hadria thought that it would have comforted her, as if a song had moved across it with the long-stretching winds. As it was, to look from her window only meant to find repeated the trivialities of life, more picturesque indeed, but still trivialities. It was the estimable and domestic qualities of Nature that presented themselves:

Nature in her most maternal and uninspired mood—Mother earth submissive to the dictatorship of man, permitting herself to be torn, and wounded, and furrowed, and harrowed at his pleasure, yielding her substance and her life to sustain the produce of his choosing, her body and her soul abandoned supine to his caprice. The sight had an exasperating effect upon Hadria. Its symbolism haunted her. The calm, sweet English landscape affected her at times with a sort of disgust. It was, perhaps, the same in kind as the far stronger sensation of disgust that she felt when she first saw Lady Engleton with her new-born child, full of pride and exultation. It was as much as she could do to shake hands with the happy mother.

When Valeria expressed dismay at so strange a feeling Hadria had refused to be treated as a solitary sinner. There were plenty of fellow-culprits, she said, only they did not dare to speak out. Let Valeria study girls and judge for herself.

Hadria was challenged to name a girl.

Well, Algitha for one. Hadria also suspected Marion Jordan, well-drilled though she was by her dragoon of a mother.

Valeria would not hear of it. Marion Jordan! the gentlest, timidest, most typical of young English girls! Impossible!

"I am almost sure of it, nevertheless," said Hadria. "Oh, believe me, it is common enough! Few grasp it intellectually perhaps, but thousands feel the insult; of that I am morally certain."

"What leads you to think so in Marion's case?"

"Some look, or tone, or word; something slight, but to my mind conclusive. Fellow-sinners detect one another, you know."

"Well, I don't understand what the world is coming to!" exclaimed Miss Du Prel. "Where are the natural instincts?"

"Sprouting up for the first time perhaps," Hadria suggested.

"They seem to be disappearing, if what you say has the slightest foundation."

"Oh, you are speaking of only *one* kind of instinct. The others have all been suppressed. Perhaps women are not altogether animals after all. The thought is startling, I know. Try to face it."

"I never supposed they were," cried Valeria, a little annoyed.

"But you never made allowance for the suppressed instincts," said Hadria.

"I don't believe they *can* be suppressed."

"I believe they can be not merely suppressed, but killed past hope of recovery. And I also believe that there may be, that there *must* be, ideas and emotions fermenting in people's brains, quite different from those that they are supposed and ordered to cherish, and that these heresies go on working in secret for years before they become even suspected, and then suddenly the population exchange confessions."

"After that the Deluge!" exclaimed Miss Du Prel. "You describe the features of a great revolution."

"So much the better," said Hadria; "and when the waters sink again, a nice fresh clean world!"

CHAPTER XIX.

ON the lawn of the Red House, a little group was collected under the big walnut tree. The sunlight fell through the leaves on the singing tea-kettle and the cups and saucers, and made bright patches on the figures and the faces assembled round the tea-table.

Hubert Temperley had again brought his friend Joseph Fleming, in the forlorn hope, he said, of being able to give him something to eat and drink. Ernest and Algitha and Fred were of the party. They had come down from Saturday till Monday. Ernest was studying for the Bar. Fred had entered a merchant's office in the city, and hated his work cordially. Miss Du Prel was still at the Red House.

Lady Engleton had called by chance this afternoon, and Mrs. Walker, the vicar's wife, with two of her countless daughters, had come by invitation. Mrs. Walker was a middle-aged, careworn, rather prim-looking woman. Lady Engleton was handsome. Bright auburn hair waved back in picturesque fashion from a piquant face, and constituted more than half her claim to beauty. The brown eyes were bright and vivacious. The mouth was seldom quite shut. It scarcely seemed worth while, the loquacious lady had confessed. She showed a delicate taste in dress. Shades of brown and russet made a fine harmony with her auburn hair, and the ivory white and fresh red of her skin.

She and Temperley always enjoyed a sprightly interchange of epigrams. Lady Engleton had the qualities that Hubert had admired in Hadria before their marriage, and she was

175

entirely free from the other characteristics that had exasperated him so desperately since that hideous mistake that he had made. Lady Engleton had originality and brilliancy, but she knew how to combine these qualities with perfect obedience to the necessary conventions of life. She had the sparkle of champagne, without the troublesome tendency of that delicate beverage to break bounds, and brim over in iridescent, swelling, joyous foam, the discreet edges of such goblets as custom might decree for the sunny vintage. Lady Engleton sparkled, glowed, nipped even at times, was of excellent dry quality, but she never frothed over. She always knew where to stop; she had the genius of moderation. She stood to Hadria as a correct rendering of a cherished idea stands to a faulty one. She made Hubert acutely feel his misfortune, and shewed him his lost hope, his shattered ideal.

"Is the picture finished?" he enquired, as he handed Lady Engleton her tea.

"What, the view from your field? Not quite. I was working at it when Claude Moreton and Mrs. Jordan and Marion arrived, and I have been rather interrupted. That's the worst of visitors. One's little immortal works do get put aside, poor things."

Lady Engleton broke into the light laugh that had become almost mechanical with her.

"Your friends grudge the hours you spend in your studio," said Temperley.

"Oh, they don't mind, so long as I give them as much time as they want," she said. "I have to apologise and compromise, don't you know, but, with a little management, one can get on. Of course, society does ask a good deal of attention, doesn't it? and one has to be so careful."

"Just a little tact and thought," said Temperley with a sigh.

Lady Engleton admired Algitha, who was standing with Ernest a little apart from the group.

"She is like your wife, and yet there is a singular difference in the expression."

Lady Engleton was too discreet to say that Mrs. Temperley lacked the look of contentment and serenity that was so marked in her sister's face.

"Algitha is a thoroughly sensible girl," said the brother-in-law.

"I hear you have not long returned from a visit to Mr. Fullerton's place in Scotland, Mr. Temperley," observed the vicar's wife when her host turned to address her.

"Yes," he said, "we have been there half the summer. The boys thoroughly enjoyed the freedom and the novelty. The river, of course, was a source of great joy to them, and of hideous anxiety to the rest of us."

"Of course, of course," assented Mrs. Walker. "Ah, there are the dear little boys. Won't you come and give me a kiss, darling?"

"Darling" did what was required in a business-like manner, and stood by, while the lady discovered in him a speaking likeness to his parents, to his Aunt Algitha and his Uncle Fred, not to mention the portrait of his great-grandfather, the Solicitor-General, that hung in the dining-room. The child seemed thoroughly accustomed to be thought the living image of various relations, and he waited indifferently till the list was ended.

"Do you know, we are half hoping that Professor Fortescue may be able to come to us for a week or ten days?" said Lady Engleton. "We are so looking forward to it."

"Professor Fortescue is always a favourite," remarked Mrs. Walker. "It is such a pity he does not return to the Priory, is it not?—a great house like that standing empty. Of course it is very natural after the dreadful event that happened there"—Mrs. Walker lowered her voice discreetly—"but it seems a sin to leave the place untenanted."

Lady Engleton explained that there was some prospect of the house being let at last to a friend and colleague of the

Professor. Mrs. Walker doubtless would remember Professor Theobald, who used to come and stay at Craddock Place rather frequently some years ago, a big man with beard and moustache, very learned and very amusing.

Mrs. Walker remembered him perfectly. Her husband had been so much interested in his descriptions of a tour in Palestine, all through the scenes of the New Testament. He was a great archæologist. Was he really coming to the Priory? How very delightful. John would be so glad to hear it.

"Oh, it is not settled yet, but the two Professors are coming to us some time soon, I believe, and Professor Theobald will look over the house and see if he thinks it would be too unmanageably big for himself and his old mother and sister. I hope he will take the place. He would bring a new and interesting element into the village. What do you think of it, Mrs. Temperley?"

" Oh, I hope the learned and amusing Professor will come," she said. " The worst of it is, from my point of view, that I shall have to give up my practices there. Professor Fortescue allows me to wake the old piano from its long slumbers in the drawing-room."

" Oh, of course. Marion Jordan was telling me that she was quite startled the other day, in crossing the Priory garden, to hear music stealing out of the apparently deserted house. She had heard the country people say that the ghost of poor Mrs. Fortescue walks along the terrace in the twilight, and Marion looked quite scared when she came in, for the music seemed to come from the drawing-room, where its mistress used to play so much after she was first married. I almost wonder you can sit alone there in the dusk, considering the dreadful associations of the place."

" I am used to it now," Mrs. Temperley replied, "and it is so nice and quiet in the empty house. One knows one can't be interrupted—unless by ghosts."

"Well, that is certainly a blessing," cried Lady Engleton.

" I think I shall ask Professor Fortescue to allow me also to
go to the Priory to pursue my art in peace and quietness ; a
truly hyperborean state, beyond the region of visitors ! "

" There would be plenty of room for a dozen unsociable
monomaniacs like ourselves," said Mrs. Temperley.

" I imagine you are a God-send to poor Mrs. Williams, the
caretaker," said Joseph Fleming. "She is my gamekeeper's
sister, and I hear that she finds the solitude in that vast house
almost more than she can stand."

" Poor woman ! " said Lady Engleton. "Well, Mr. Fleming,
what are the sporting prospects this autumn ? "

He pulled himself together, and his face lighted up. On
that subject he could speak for hours.

Of Joseph Fleming his friends all said : The best fellow in
the world. A kinder heart had no man. He lived on his
little property from year's end to year's end, for the sole and
single end of depriving the pheasants and partridges which he
bred upon the estate, of their existence. He was a confirmed
bachelor, living quietly, and taking the world as he found it
(seeing that there was a sufficiency of partridges in good
seasons) ; trusting that there was a God above who would not
let the supply run short, if one honestly tried to do one's
duty and lived an upright life, harming no man, and women
only so much as was strictly honourable and necessary. He
spoke ill of no one. He was diffident of his own powers,
except about sport, wherein he knew himself princely, and
cherished that sort of respect for woman, thoroughly sincere,
which assigns to her a pedestal in a sheltered niche, and offers
her homage on condition of her staying where she is put, even
though she starve there, solitary and esteemed.

" Do tell me, Mr. Fleming, if you know, who is that very
handsome woman with the white hair ? " said Lady Engleton.
"She is talking to Mrs. Walker. I seem to know the
face."

" Oh, that is Miss Valeria Du Prel, the authoress of those
books that Mrs. Walker is so shocked at."

"Oh, of course; how stupid of me. I should like to have some conversation with her."

"That's easily managed. I don't think she and Mrs. Walker quite appreciate each other."

Lady Engleton laughed.

Mrs. Walker was anxiously watching her daughters, and endeavouring to keep them at a distance from Miss Du Prel, who looked tragically bored.

Joseph Fleming found means to release her, and Lady Engleton's desire was gratified. "I admire your books so much, Miss Du Prel, and I have so often wished to see more of you; but you have been abroad for the last two years, I hear."

Lady Engleton, after asking the authoress to explain exactly what she meant by her last book, enquired if she had the latest news of Professor Fortescue. Lady Engleton had heard, with regret, that he had been greatly worried about that troublesome nephew whom he had educated and sent to Oxford.

"The young fellow had been behaving very badly," Miss Du Prel said.

"Ungrateful creature," cried Lady Engleton. "Running into debt I suppose."

Miss Du Prel feared that the Professor was suffering in health. He had been working very hard.

"Oh, yes; what was that about some method of killing animals instantaneously to avoid the horrors of the slaughter-house? Professor Theobald has been saying what a pity it is that a man so able should waste his time over these fads. It would never bring him fame or profit, only ridicule. Every man had his little weakness, but this idea of saving pain to animals, Professor Theobald said, was becoming a sort of mania with poor Fortescue, and one feared that it might injure his career. He was greatly looked up to in the scientific world, but this sort of thing of course——

"Though it is nice of him in a way," added Lady Engleton.

"His weaknesses are nobler than most people's virtues," said Miss Du Prel.

"Then you number this among his weaknesses?"

Algitha, who had joined the group, put this question.

"I would rather see him working in the cause of humanity," Miss Du Prel answered.

Ernest surprised everyone by suggesting that possibly humanity was well served, in the long run, by reminding it of the responsibility that goes with power, and by giving it an object lesson in the decent treatment of those who can't defend themselves.

"You must have sat at the Professor's feet," cried Miss Du Prel, raising her eyebrows.

"I have," said Ernest, with a little gesture of pride.

Lady Engleton shook her head. "I fear he flies too high for ordinary mortals," she said; "and I doubt if even he can be quite consistent at that altitude."

"Better perhaps fly fairly high, and come down now and again to rest, if one must, than grovel consistently and always," observed Ernest.

Lady Engleton gave a little scream. "Mrs. Temperley, come to the rescue. Your brother is calling us names. He says we grovel consistently and always."

Ernest laughed, and protested. Lady Engleton pretended to be mortally offended. Mrs. Temperley was sorry she could give no redress. She had suffered from Ernest's painful frankness from her youth upwards.

The conversation grew discursive. Lady Engleton enjoyed the pastime of lightly touching the edges of what she called "advanced" thought. She sought the society of people like the two Professors and Miss Du Prel, in order to hear what dreadful and delightful things they really would say. She read all the new books, and went to the courageous plays that Mrs. Walker wouldn't mention.

"Your last book, *Caterina*, is a mine of suggestion, Miss Du Prel," she said. "It raises one most interesting point that

has puzzled me greatly. I don't know if you have all read the
book? The heroine finds herself differing in her view of life
from everyone round her. She is married, but she has made
no secret of her scorn for the old ideals, and has announced
that she has no intention of being bound by them."

Mrs. Temperley glanced uneasily at Miss Du Prel.

"Accordingly she does even as she had said," continued
Lady Engleton. "She will not brook that interference with
her liberty which marriage among us old-fashioned people
generally implies. She refuses to submit to the attempt that
is of course made (in spite of a pre-nuptial understanding)
to bring her under the yoke, and so off she goes and lives
independently, leaving husband and relatives lamenting."

The vicar's wife said she thought she must be going home.
Her husband would be expecting her.

"Oh, won't you wait a little, Mrs. Walker? Your daughters
would perhaps like a game of tennis with my brothers
presently."

Mrs. Walker yielded uneasily.

"But before *Caterina* takes the law into her own hands, in
this way," Lady Engleton continued, "she is troubled with
doubts. She sometimes wonders whether she ought not, after
all, to respect the popular standards (notwithstanding the com-
pact), instead of disturbing everybody by clinging to her own.
Now was it strength of character or obstinate egotism that
induced her to stick to her original colours, come what
might? That is the question which the book has stated but
left unanswered."

Miss Du Prel said that the book showed, if it showed anything, that one must be true to one's own standard, and not
attempt to respect an ideal in practice that one despises in
theory. We are bound, she asserted, to produce that which
is most individual within us ; to be ourselves, and not a poor
imitation of someone else; to dare even apparent wrong-doing,
rather than submit to live a life of devotion to that which we
cannot believe.

Mrs. Walker suggested to her daughters that they might go and have a look at the rose-garden, but the daughters preferred to listen to the conversation.

"In real life," said the practical Algitha, "*Caterina* would not have been able to follow her idea so simply. Supposing she had had children and complicated circumstances, what could she have done?"

Miss Du Prel thought that a compromise might have been made.

"A compromise by which she could act according to two opposite standards?"

Valeria was impatient of difficulties. It was not necessary that a woman should leave her home in order to be true to her conscience. It was the best method in *Caterina's* case, but not in all.

Miss Du Prel did not explain very clearly what she meant. Women made too much of difficulties, she thought. Somehow people *had* managed to overcome obstacles. Look at— and then followed a list of shining examples.

"I believe you would blame a modern woman who imitated them," said Mrs. Temperley. "These women have the inestimable advantage of being dead."

"Ah, yes," Lady Engleton agreed, with a laugh, "we women may be anything we like—in the last century."

"The tides of a hundred years or so sweeping over one's audacious deed, soften the raw edges. Then it is tolerated in the landscape; indeed, it grows mossy and picturesque." Mrs. Temperley made this comparison.

"And then think how useful it becomes to prove that a daring deed *can* be done, given only the necessary stuff in brain and heart."

Mrs. Walker looked at Algitha in dismay.

"One can throw it in the teeth of one's contemporaries," added Algitha, "if they fail to produce a dramatic climax of the same kind."

"Only," said Mrs Temperley, "if they *do* venture upon

their own dreadful deed—the deed demanded by their particular modern predicament—then we all shriek vigorously."

"Oh, we shriek less than we used to," said Lady Engleton. "It is quite a relief to be able to retain one's respectability on easier terms."

"In such a case as Miss Du Prel depicts? I doubt it. *Caterina*, in real life, would have a lively story to tell. How selfish we should think her! How we should point to the festoons of bleeding hearts that she had wounded—a dripping cordon round the deserted home! No; I believe Miss Du Prel herself would be horrified at her own *Caterina* if she came upon her unexpectedly in somebody's drawing-room."

There was a laugh.

"Of course, a great deal is to be said for the popular way of looking at the matter," Lady Engleton observed. "This fascinating heroine must have caused a great deal of real sorrow, or at least she *would* have caused it, were it not that her creator had considerably removed all relatives, except a devoted couple of unorthodox parents, who are charmed at her decision to scandalize society, and wonder why she doesn't do it sooner. Parents like that don't grow on every bush."

Mrs. Walker glanced nervously at her astonished girls.

Lady Engleton pointed out that had *Caterina* been situated in a more ordinary manner, she would have certainly broken her parents' hearts and embittered their last years, to say nothing of the husband and perhaps the children, who would have suffered for want of a mother's care.

"But why should the husband suffer?" asked Algitha. "*Caterina's* husband cordially detested her."

"It is customary to regard the occasion as one proper for suffering," said Mrs. Temperley, "and every well-regulated husband would suffer accordingly."

"Clearly," assented Lady Engleton. "When the world congratulates us we rejoice, when it condoles with us we weep."

"That at least, would not affect the children," said Algitha. "I don't see why of necessity *they* should suffer."

"Their share of the woe would be least of all, I think," Mrs. Temperley observed. "What ogre is going to ill-treat them? And since few of us know how to bring up so much as an earth-worm reasonably, I can't see that it matters so very much which particular woman looks after the children. Any average fool would do."

Mrs. Walker was stiffening in every limb.

"The children would have the usual chances of their class; neither more nor less, as it seems to me, for lack of a maternal burnt-offering."

Mrs. Walker rose, gathered her daughters about her, and came forward to say good-bye. She was sure her husband would be annoyed if she did not return. She retired with nervous precipitation.

"Really you will depopulate this village, Mrs. Temperley," cried Lady Engleton with a laugh; "it is quite dangerous to bring up a family within your reach. There will be a general exodus. I must be going myself, or I shan't have an orthodox sentiment left."

CHAPTER XX.

HENRIETTE had secured Mrs. Fullerton for an ally, from the beginning. When Hadria's parents visited the Red House, Miss Temperley was asked to meet them, by special request. Henriette employed tact on a grand scale, and achieved results in proportion. She was sorry that dear Hadria did not more quickly recover her strength. Her health was not what it ought to be. Mrs. Fullerton sighed. She was ready to play into Miss Temperley's hands on every occasion.

The latter had less success in her dealings with Miss Du Prel. She tried to discover Hadria's more intimate feelings by talking her over with Valeria, ignoring the snubs that were copiously administered by that indignant lady. Valeria spoke with sublime scorn of this attempt.

"To try and pump information out of a friend! Why not listen at the key-hole, and be done with it!"

Henriette's neat hair would have stood on end, had she heard Miss Du Prel fit adjectives to her conduct.

"I have learnt not to expect a nice sense of honour from superior persons with unimpeachable sentiments," said Hadria.

"You are certainly a good hater!" cried Valeria, with a laugh.

"Oh, I don't hate Henriette; I only hate unimpeachable sentiments."

The sentiments that Henriette represented had become, to Hadria, as the walls of a prison from which she could see no means of escape.

She had found that life took no heed either of her ambitions or of her revolts. "And so I growl," she said. She might hate and chafe in secret to her heart's content; external conformity was the one thing needful.

186

"Hadria will be so different when she has children," everyone had said. And so she was; but the difference was alarmingly in the wrong direction. Throughout history, she reflected, children had been the unfailing means of bringing women into line with tradition. Who could stand against them? They had been able to force the most rebellious to their knees. An appeal to the maternal instinct had quenched the hardiest spirit of revolt. No wonder the instinct had been so trumpeted and exalted! Women might harbour dreams and plan insurrections; but their children—little ambassadors of the established and expected—were argument enough to convince the most hardened sceptics. Their help-lessness was more powerful to suppress revolt than regiments of armed soldiers.

Such were the thoughts that wandered through Hadria's mind as she bent her steps towards the cottage near Craddock Church, where, according to the gravedigger's account, the baby of the unhappy schoolmistress was being looked after by Mrs. Gullick.

It would have puzzled the keenest observer to detect the unorthodox nature of Mrs. Temperley's reflections, as she leant over the child, and made enquiries as to its health and temperament.

Mrs. Gullick seemed more disposed to indulge in remarks on its mother's conduct than to give the desired information; but she finally admitted that Ellen Jervis had an aunt at Southampton who was sending a little money for the support of the child. Ellen Jervis had stayed with the aunt during the summer holidays. Mrs. Gullick did not know what was to be done. She had a large family of her own, and the cottage was small.

Mrs. Temperley asked for the address of the aunt.

"I suppose no one knows who the father is? He has not acknowledged the child!"

No; that was a mystery still.

About a week later, Craddock Dene was amazed by the news that Mrs. Temperley had taken the child of Ellen Jervis under her protection. A cottage had been secured on the road to Craddock, a trustworthy nurse engaged, and here the babe was established, with the consent and blessing of the aunt.

"You are the most inconsistent woman I ever met!" exclaimed Miss Du Prel.

"Why inconsistent?"

"You say that children have been the means, from time immemorial, of enslaving women, and here you go and adopt one of your enslavers!"

"But this child is not legitimate."

Valeria stared.

"Whatever the wrongs of Ellen Jervis, at least there were no laws written, and unwritten, which demanded of her as a duty that she should become the mother of this child. In that respect she escapes the ignominy reserved for the married mother who produces children that are not even hers."

"You do manage to ferret out the unpleasant aspects of our position!" Miss Du Prel exclaimed. "But I want to know why you do this, Hadria. It is good of you, but totally unlike you."

"You are very polite!" cried Hadria. "Why should I not lay up store for myself in heaven, as well as Mrs. Walker and the rest?"

"You were not thinking of heaven when you did this deed, Hadria."

"No; I was thinking of the other place."

"And do you hope to get any satisfaction out of your *protégée?*"

Hadria shrugged her shoulders.

"I don't know. The child is the result of great sorrow and suffering; it is the price of a woman's life; a woman who offended the world, having lived for nearly forty weary obedient years, in circumstances dreary enough to have turned twenty saints into as many sinners. No; I am no Lady Bountiful. I feel in defending this child—a sorry defence I know—that I am, in so far, opposing the world and the system of things that I hate——. Ah! *how* I hate it!"

"Is it then hatred that prompts the deed?"

Hadria looked thoughtfully towards the church tower, in whose shadow the mother of the babe lay sleeping.

"Can you ever quite unravel your own motives, Valeria? Hatred? Yes; there is a large ingredient of hatred. Without it, probably this poor infant would have been left to struggle through life alone, with a mill-stone round its neck, and a miserable constitution into the bargain. I hope to rescue its constitution. But that poor woman's story touched me closely. It is so hard, so outrageous! The emptiness of her existence; the lack of outlet for her affections; the endless monotony; and then the sudden new interest and food for the starved emotions; the hero-worship that is latent in us all; and then—good heavens!—for a touch of poetry, of romance in her life, she would have been ready to believe in the professions of the devil himself—and this man was a very good understudy for the devil! Ah! If ever I should meet him!"

"What would you do?" Valeria asked curiously.

"Avenge her," said Hadria with set lips.

"Easier said than done, my dear!"

Gossip asserted that the father of the child was a man of some standing, the bolder spirits even accusing Lord Engleton himself. But this was conjecture run wild, and nobody seriously listened to it.

Mrs. Walker was particularly scandalized with Mrs. Temperley's ill-advised charity. Hadria had the habit of regarding the clergyman's wife as another of society's victims. She placed side by side the schoolmistress in her sorrow and disgrace, and the careworn woman at the Vicarage, with her eleven children, and her shrivelled nature, poor and dead as an autumn leaf that shivers before the wind. They had both suffered—so Mrs. Temperley dared to assert—in the same cause. They were both victims of the same creed. It was a terrible cultus, a savage idol that had devoured them both, as cruel and insatiable as the brazen god of old, with his internal fires, which the faithful fed devoutly, with shrinking girls and screaming children.

"I still fail to understand why you adopt this child," said Valeria. "My *Caterina* would never have done it."

"The little creature interests me," said Hadria. "It is a tiny field for the exercise of the creative forces. Every one has some form of active amusement. Some like golf, others flirtation. I prefer this sort of diversion."

"But you have your own children to interest you, surely far more than this one."

Hadria's face grew set and defiant.

"They represent to me the insult of society—my own private and particular insult, the tribute exacted of my womanhood. It is through them that I am to be subdued and humbled. Just once in a way, however, the thing does not quite 'come off.'"

"What has set you on edge so, I wonder."

"People, traditions, unimpeachable sentiments."

"*Yours* are not unimpeachable at any rate!" Valeria cried laughing. "*Caterina* is an angel compared with you, and yet my publisher has his doubts about her."

"*Caterina* would do as I do, I know," said Hadria. "Those who are looked at askance by the world appeal to my instincts. I shall be able to teach this child, perhaps, to strike a blow at the system which sent her mother to a dishonoured grave, while it leaves the man for whose sake she risked all this, in peace and the odour of sanctity."

Time seemed to be marked, in the sleepy village, by the baby's growth. Valeria, who thought she was fond of babies, used to accompany Hadria on her visits to the cottage, but she treated the infant so much as if it had been a guinea-pig or a rabbit that the nurse was indignant.

The weeks passed in rapid monotony, filled with detail and leaving no mark behind them, no sign of movement or progress. The cares of the house, the children, left only limited time for walking, reading, correspondence, and such music as could be wrung out of a crowded day. An effort on Hadria's part, to make serious use of her musical talent had been frustrated. But a pathetic, unquenchable hope always survived that presently, when this or that corner had been turned, this or that difficulty overcome, conditions would be conquered and opportunity arrive. Not yet had she resigned her belief that the most harassing and wearying and unceasing business that a human being can undertake, is compatible with the stupendous labour and the unbounded claims of an artist's career. The details of practical life and petty duties sprouted up at every step. If they were put aside, even for a moment, the wheels of daily existence became clogged and then all opportunity was over. Hope had begun to alternate with a fear lest that evasive corner should never be turned, that little crop of interruptions never cease to turn up. And yet it was so foolish. Each obstacle in itself was paltry. It was their number that overcame one, as the tiny arrows of the Lilliputs overcame Gulliver.

One of Hadria's best friends in Craddock Dene was Joseph Fleming, who had become very intimate at the Red House during the last year or two. Hadria used to tire of the necessity to be apparently rational (such was her own version), and found it a relief to talk nonsense, just as she pleased, to Joseph Fleming, who never objected or took offence, if he occasionally looked surprised. Other men might have thought she was laughing at them, but Joseph made no such mistake when Mrs. Temperley broke out, as she did now and then, in fantastic fashion.

She was standing, one morning, on the little bridge over the stream that ran at a distance of a few hundred yards from the Red House. The two boys were bespattering themselves in the meadow below, by the water's verge. They called up at intervals to their mother the announcement of some new discovery of flower or insect.

Watching the stream sweeping through the bridge, she seemed the centre of a charming domestic scene to Joseph Fleming, who chanced to pass by with his dogs. He addressed himself to her maternal feelings by remarking what handsome and clever boys they were.

"Handsome and clever?" she repeated. "Is *that* all you can say, Mr. Fleming? When you set about it, I think you might provide a little better food for one's parental sentiment. I suppose you will go and tell Mrs. Walker that *her* dozen and a half are all handsome and clever too!"

"Not so handsome and clever as yours," replied Mr. Fleming, a little aghast at this ravenous maternal vanity.

"What wretched poverty of expression!" Hadria complained. "I ask for bread, and truly you give me a stone."

Joseph Fleming eyed his companion askance. "I—I admire your boys immensely, as you know," he said.

"Not enough, not enough."

"What can I say more?"

"A mother has to find in her children all that she can hope to find in life, and she naturally desires to make the most of them, don't you see?"

"Ah! yes, quite so," said Joseph dubiously.

"Nobody, I suppose, likes to be commonplace all round; one must have some poetry somewhere—so most women idealize their children, and if other people won't help them in the effort, don't you see? it is most discouraging."

"Are you chaffing, or what?" Joseph enquired.

"No, indeed; I am perilously serious."

"I can well understand how a mother must get absorbed in her children," said Joseph. "I suppose it's a sort of natural provision."

"Think of Mrs. Allan with her outrageous eight—all making mud-pies!" cried Hadria; "a magnificent 'natural provision!' A small income, a small house, with those pervasive eight. You know the stampede when one goes to call; the aroma of bread and butter (there are few things more inspiring); the cook always about to leave; Mrs. Allan with a racking headache. It is indeed not difficult to understand how a mother would get absorbed in her children. Why, their pinafores alone would become absorbing."

"Quite so," said Mr. Fleming. Then a little anxious to change the subject: "Oh, by the way, have you heard that

the Priory is really to be inhabited at last? Professor Theobald
has almost decided to take it."

"Really? that will be exciting for Craddock Dene. We
shall have another household to dissect and denounce.
Providence watches over us all, I verily believe."

"I hope so," Joseph replied gravely.

"Truly I hope so too," Hadria said, no less seriously, "for
indeed we need it."

Joseph was too simple to be greatly surprised at anything
that Mrs. Temperley might say. He had decided that she was
a little eccentric, and that explained everything; just as he
explained instances of extraordinary reasoning power in a dog
by calling it "instinct." Whatever Mrs. Temperley might do
was slightly eccentric, and had she suddenly taken it into her
head to dance a fandango on the public road, it would have
merely put a little extra strain on that word.

By dint of not understanding her, Joseph Fleming had
grown to feel towards Mrs. Temperley a genuine liking, conscious, in his vague way, that she was kind at heart, however
bitter or strange she might sometimes be in her speech.
Moreover, she was not always eccentric or unexpected. There
would come periods when she would say and do very much
as her neighbours said and did; looking then pale and lifeless, but absolutely beyond the reach of hostile criticism, as
her champion would suggest to carping neighbours.

Not the most respected of the ladies who turned up
their disapproving noses, was more dull or more depressing
than Hadria could be, on occasion, as she had herself pointed
out; and would not *this* soften stony hearts?

When she discovered that her kindly neighbour had been
fighting her battles for her, she was touched; but she asked
him not to expend his strength on her behalf. She tried in
vain to convince him that she did not care to be invited
too often to submit to the devitalizing processes of social
intercourse, to which the families of the district shrank not
from subjecting themselves. If Joseph Fleming chanced to
call at the Red House after her return from one of these

entertainments, he was sure to find Mrs. Temperley in one of her least comprehensible moods. But whatever she might say, he stood up for her among the neighbours with persistent loyalty. He decked her with virtues that she did not possess, and represented her to the sceptical district, radiant in domestic glory. Hadria thus found herself in an awkwardly uncertain position; either she was looked at askance, as eccentric, or she found herself called upon to make good expectations of saintliness, such as never were on land or sea.

Saintly? Hadria shook her head. She could imagine no one further from such a condition than she was at present, and she felt it in her, to swing down and down to the very opposite pole from that serene altitude. She admitted that, from a utilitarian point of view, she was making a vast mistake. As things were, Mrs. Walker and Mrs. Allan, laboriously spinning their ponderous families on their own axes, in a reverent spirit, had chosen the better part. But Hadria did not care. She would *not* settle down to make the best of things, as even Algitha now recommended, "since there she was, and there was no helping it."

"I will *never* make the best of things," she said. "I know nothing that gives such opportunities to the Devil."

Hadria had characteristically left the paradox unjustified.

"What do you mean?" asked Algitha. "Surely the enemy of good has most hold over the discontented spirit."

Hadria likened the contented to stagnant pools, wherein corruptions grow apace. "It is only the discontented ocean that remains, for all its storms, fresh and sane to the end."

But though she said this, for opposition's sake perhaps, she had her doubts about her own theory. Discontent was certainly the initiator of all movement; but there was a kind of sullen discontent that stagnated and ate inwards, like a disease. Better a cheerful sin or two than allow *that* to take hold!

"But then there is this sickly feminine conscience to deal with!" she exclaimed. "It clings to the worst of us still, and prevents the wholesome big catastrophes that might bring salvation."

CHAPTER XXI.

ANOTHER year had blundered itself away, leaving little trace behind it, in Craddock Dene. The schoolmistress's grave was greener and her child rosier than of yore. Little Martha had now begun to talk, and promised to be pretty and fair-haired like her mother.

The boys and Algitha had come to spend Saturday and Sunday at the Red House. Hadria hunted out a stupendous card-case (a wedding gift from Mrs. Gordon), erected on her head a majestic bonnet, and announced to the company that she was going for a round of visits.

There was a yell of laughter. Hadria advanced across the lawn with quiet dignity, bearing her card-case as one who takes part in a solemn ceremony.

"Where did you fall in with that casket?" enquired Fred.

"And who was the architect of the cathedral?" asked Ernest.

"This casket, as you call it, was presented to me by Mrs. Gordon. The cathedral I designed myself."

They all crowded round to examine the structure. There were many derisive comments.

"Gothic," said Ernest, "pure Gothic."

"I should have described it as 'Early Perpendicular,'" objected Fred.

"Don't display your neglected education; it's beyond all question Gothic. Look at the steeple and the gargoyles and the handsome vegetation. Ruskin would revel in it!"

"Are you really going about in that thing?" asked Algitha.

Hadria wished to know what was the use of designing a Gothic cathedral if one couldn't go about in it.

The bonnet was, in truth, a daring caricature of the prevailing fashion, just sufficiently serious in expression to be wearable.

"Well, I never before met a woman who would deliberately flout her neighbours by wearing preposterous millinery!" Ernest exclaimed.

Hadria went her round of calls, and all eyes fixed themselves on her bonnet. Mrs. Allan, who had small opportunity of seeing the fashions, seemed impressed if slightly puzzled by it. Mrs. Jordan evidently thought it "loud." Mrs. Walker supposed it fashionable, but regretted that this sort of thing was going to be worn this season. She hoped the girls would modify the style in adopting it.

Mrs. Walker had heard that the two Professors had arrived at Craddock Place yesterday afternoon, and the Engletons expected them to make a visit of some weeks. Hadria's face brightened.

"And so at last we may hope that the Priory will be inhabited," said the vicar's wife.

"Of course you know," she added in the pained voice that she always reserved for anecdotes of local ill-doing, "that Mrs. Fortescue committed suicide there."

Madame Bertaux, the English wife of a French official, had chanced to call, and Mrs. Walker gave the details of the story for the benefit of the new-comer.

Madame Bertaux was a brisk, clever, good-looking woman, with a profound knowledge of the world and a corresponding contempt for it.

It appeared that the Professor's wife, whom Madame Bertaux had happened to meet in Paris, was a young, beautiful, and self-willed girl, passionately devoted to her husband. She was piqued at his lack of jealousy, and doubted or pretended to doubt his love for her. In order to put him to the test, she determined to rouse his jealousy by violent and systematic flirtation. This led to an entanglement, and finally, in a fit of reckless anger, to an elopement with a Captain Bolton who was staying at the Priory at the time. Seized with remorse, she had returned home to kill herself. This was the tragedy that had kept the old house for so many years tenantless. Hadria's music was the only sound that had disturbed its silence, since the day when the dead body of its mistress was found in the drawing-room, which she was supposed to have entered unknown to anyone, by the window that gave on to the terrace.

Valeria Du Prel was able to throw more light on the strange story. She had difficulty in speaking without rancour of the woman who had thrown away the love of such a man. She admitted that the girl was extremely fascinating, and had seemed to Valeria to have the faults of an impetuous rather than of a bad nature. She cherished that singular desire of many strong-willed women, to be ruled and mastered by the man she loved, and she had entirely failed to understand her husband's attitude towards her. She resented it as a sign of indifference. She was like the Chinese wives, who complain bitterly of a husband's neglect when he omits to beat them. She taunted the Professor for failing to assert his "rights."

"Morally, I have no rights, except such as you choose to give me of your own free will," he replied. "I am not your gaoler."

"And even that did not penetrate to her better nature till it was too late," Valeria continued. "But after the mischief was done, that phrase seems to have stung her to torment. Her training had blinded her, as one is blinded in coming out of darkness into a bright light. She was used to narrower hearts and smaller brains. Her last letter—a terrible record of the miseries of remorse—shews that she recognized at last what sort of a man he was whose heart she had broken. But even in her repentance, she was unable to conquer her egotism. She could not face the horrors of self-accusation ; she preferred to kill herself."

"What a shocking story!" cried Hadria.

"And all the more so because the Professor clings to her memory so faithfully. He blames himself for everything. He ought, he says, to have realized better the influence of her training; he ought to have made her understand that he could not assert what she called his 'rights' without insulting her and himself."

"Whenever one hears anything new about the Professor, it is always something that makes one admire and love him more than ever!" cried Hadria.

Her first meeting with him was in the old Yew Avenue in the Priory garden. He was on his way to call at the Red House. She stood on a patch of grass by a rustic seat commanding the vista of yews, and above them, a wilderness of lilacs and laburnums, in full flower. It looked to her like a pathway that led to some exquisite fairy palace of one's childhood.

Almost with the first word that the Professor uttered, Hadria felt a sense of relief and hope. The very air seemed to grow lighter, the scent of the swaying flowers sweeter. She always afterwards associated this moment of meeting with the image of that avenue of mourning yews, crowned with the sunlit magnificence of an upper world of blossom.

What had she been thinking of to run so close to despair during these years? A word, a smile, and the dead weight swerved, swung into balance, and life lifted up its head once more. She remembered now, not her limitations, but the good things of her lot; the cruelties that Fate had spared her, the miseries that the ruthless goddess had apportioned to others. But the Professor's presence did not banish, but rather emphasized, the craving to take part in the enriching of that general life which was so poor and sad. He strengthened her disposition to revolt against the further impoverishment of it, through the starving of her own nature. He would not blame her simply on account of difference from others. She felt sure of that. He would not be shocked if she had not answered to the stimulus of surroundings as faithfully as most women seemed to answer to them. Circumstance had done its usual utmost to excite her instinct to beat down the claims of her other self, but for once, circumstance had failed. It was a solitary failure among a creditable multitude of victories. But if instinct had not responded to the imperious summons, the other self had been suffering the terrors of a siege, and the garrison had grown'starved and weakly. What would be the end of it? And the little cynical imp that peeped among her thoughts, as a monkey among forest boughs, gibbered his customary "What matters it? One woman's destiny is but a small affair. If I were you I would make less fuss about it." The Professor would understand that she did not wish to make a fuss. He would not be hard upon any human being. He knew that existence was not such an easy affair to manage. She wished that she could tell him every-thing in her life—its struggle, its desperate longing and ambition, its hatred, its love : only *he* would understand all the contradictions and all the pain. She would not mind his blame, because he would understand, and the blame would be just.

They walked together down the avenue towards the beau-tiful old Tudor house, which stood on the further side of a broad lawn.

The Professor looked worn and thin. He owned to being very tired of the hurry and struggle of town. He was sick of the conflict of jealousies and ambitions. It seemed so little worth while, this din of voices that would so soon be silenced.

"I starve for the sight of a true and simple face, for the grasp of a brotherly hand."

" *You ?* " exclaimed Hadria.

"There are so few, so very few, where the throng is thick and the battle fierce. It saddens me to see good fellows trampling one another down, growing hard and ungenerous. And then the vulgarity, the irreverence : they are almost identical, I think. One grows very sick and sorry at times amidst the cruelty and the baseness that threaten to destroy

one's courage and one's hope. I know that human nature has
in it a germ of nobility that will save it, in the long run, but
meanwhile things seem sadly out of joint."

" Is that the order of the universe ? " asked Hadria.

"No, I think it is rather the disorder of man's nature,"
he replied.

Hadria asked if he would return to tea at the Red House.
The Professor said he would like to call and see Hubert, but
proposed a rest on the terrace, as it was still early in the
afternoon.

" I used to avoid the place," he said, "but I made a
mistake. I have resolved to face the memories : it is better."

It was the first time that he had ever referred, in Hadria's
presence, to the tragedy of the Priory.

" I have often wished to speak to you about my wife," he
said slowly, as they sat down on the old seat, on the terrace.
" I have felt that you would understand the whole sad story,
and I hoped that some day you would know it." He paused
and then added, "It has often been a comfort to me to
remember that you were in the world, for it made me feel less
lonely. I felt in you some new—what can I call it ? instinct,
impulse, inspiration, which ran you straight against all the
hardest stone walls that intersect the pathways of this
ridiculous old world. And, strange to say, it is the very
element in you that sets you at loggerheads with others, that
enabled me to understand you."

Hadria looked bewildered.

" To tell you the truth, I have always wondered why women
have never felt as I am sure you feel towards life. You
remember that day at Dunaghee when you were so annoyed
at my guessing your thoughts. They were unmistakeable to
one who shared them. Your sex has always been a riddle to
me ; there seemed to be something abject in their nature,
even among the noblest of them. But you are no riddle.
While I think you are the least simple woman I ever met, you
are to me the easiest to understand."

"And yet I remember your telling me the exact contrary," said Hadria.

"That was before I had caught the connecting thread. Had I been a woman, I believe that life and my place in it would have affected me exactly as it affects you."

Hadria coloured over cheek and brow. It was so strange, so startling, so delicious to find, for the first time in her life, this intimate sympathy.

"I wish my wife had possessed your friendship," he said. "I believe you would have saved us." He passed his hands over his brow, looking round at the closed windows of the drawing-room. "I almost feel as if she were near us now on this old terrace that she loved so. She planted these roses herself—how they have grown!" They were white cluster roses and yellow banksias, which had strayed far along the balustrade, clambering among the stone pillars.

"You doubtless know the bare facts of her life, but nothing is so misleading as bare fact. My wife was one of the positive natures, capable of great nobility, but liable to glaring error and sin! She held ideas passionately. She had the old barbaric notion that a husband was a sort of master, and must assert his authority and rights. It was the result of her training. I saw that a great development was before her. I pleased myself with the thought of watching and helping it. She was built on a grand scale. To set her free from prejudice, from her injustice to herself, from her dependence on me ; to teach her to breathe deep with those big lungs of hers and think bravely with that capacious brain : that was my dream. I hoped to hear her say to me some day, what I fear no woman has yet been able to say to her husband, 'The day of our marriage was the birthday of my freedom.'"

Hadria drew a long breath. It seemed to overwhelm her that a man, even the Professor, could utter such a sentiment. All the old hereditary instincts of conquest and ownership appeared to be utterly dead in him.

No wonder he had found life a lonely pilgrimage! He lived before his time. His wife had taunted him because he would not treat her as his legal property, or rule her through the claims and opportunities that popular sentiment assigned to him.

When a woman as generous as himself, as just, as gentle-hearted, had appeared on the horizon of the world, the advent of a nobler social order might be hoped for. The two were necessary for the new era.

Then, not only imagination, but cold reason herself grew eloquent with promises.

"It was in there, in the old drawing-room, where we had sat together evening after evening, that they found her dead, the very type of all that is brilliant and exquisite and living. To me she was everything. All my personal happiness was centred in her. I cared for nothing so long as she was in the same world as myself, and I might love her. In the darkness that followed, I was brought face to face with the most terrible problems of human fate. I had troubled myself but little about the question of the survival of the personality after death; I had been pre-occupied with life. Now I realized out of what human longings and what human desperation our religions are built. For one gleam of hope that we should meet again—what would I not have given? But it never came. The trend of my thought made all such hopes impossible. I have grown charier of the word 'impossible' now. We know so infinitesimally little. I had to learn to live on comfortless. All that was strongly personal in me died. All care about myself went out suddenly, as in other cases I think it goes out slowly, beaten down by the continued buffetings of life. I gave myself to my work, and then a curious decentralizing process took place. I ceased to be the point round which the world revolved, in my own consciousness. We all start our career as pivots, if I am not mistaken. The world span, and I, in my capacity of atomic part, span with it. I mean that this was a continuous, not an occasional state of consciousness. After that came an unexpected peace."

" You have travelled a long and hard road to find it !"
cried Hadria.

" Not a unique fate," he said with a smile.

" It must be a terrible process that quite kills the personal
in one, it is so strong. With me the element is clamorous."

" It has its part to play."

" Surely the gods must be jealous of human beings. Why
did they destroy the germ of such happiness as you might
have had?"

" The stern old law holds for ever; wrong and error have
to be expiated."

The Professor traced the history of his wife's family,
shewing the gradual gathering of Fate to its culmination in
the tragedy of her short life. Her father and grandfather had
both been men of violent and tyrannical temper, and tradition
gave the same character to their forefathers. Eleanor's
mother was one of the meek and saintly women who almost
invariably fall to the lot of overbearing men. She had made
a virtue of submitting to tyranny, and even to downright
cruelty, thus almost repeating the story of her equally meek
predecessor, of whose ill-treatment stories were still current
in the district.

" When death put an end to their wretchedness, one would
suppose that the evil of their lives was worked out and over,
but it was not so. The Erinnys were still unsatisfied. My
poor wife became the victim of their fury. And every new
light that science throws upon human life shews that this *must*
be so. The old Greeks saw that unconscious evil-doing is
punished as well as that which is conscious. These poor
unselfish women, piling up their own supposed merit, at the
expense of the character of their tyrants, laid up a store of
misery for their descendant, my unhappy wife. Imagine the
sort of training and tradition that she had to contend with; her
mother ignorant and supine, her father violent, bigoted, almost
brutal. Eleanor's nature was obscured and distorted by it.
Having inherited the finer and stronger qualities of her father's

race, with much of its violence, she was going through a
struggle at the time of our marriage : training, native vigour
and nobility all embroiled in a desperate civil war. It was too
much. There is no doubt as to the ultimate issue, but the
struggle killed her. It is a common story : a character
militant which meets destruction in the struggle for life. The
past evil pursues and throttles the present good."

"This takes away the last consolation from women who
have been forced to submit to evil conditions," said Hadria.

"It is the truth," said the Professor. "The Erinnys are no
mere fancy of the Greek mind. They are symbols of an
awful fact of life that no one can afford to ignore."

"What insensate fools we all are!" Hadria exclaimed.
"I mean women."

The Professor made no polite objection to the statement.

As they were wending their way towards the Red House,
the Professor reminded his companion of the old friendship
that had existed between them, ever since Hadria was a little
girl. He had always cherished towards her that sentiment of
affectionate good-fellowship. She must check him if he
seemed to presume upon it, in seeking sympathy or offering it.
He watched her career with the deepest interest and anxiety.
He always believed that she would give some good gift to the
world. And he still believed it. Like the rest of us, she
needed sympathy at the right moment.

"We need to feel that there is someone who believes in us,
in our good faith, in our good will, one who will not judge
according to outward success or failure. Remember," he
said, "that I have that unbounded faith in you. Nothing can
move it. Whatever happens and wherever you may be led by
the strange chances of life, don't forget the existence of one old
friend, or imagine that anything can shake his friendship or his
desire to be of service."

CHAPTER XXII.

"THE worst thing about the life of you married people," said Valeria, "is its ridiculous rigidity. It takes more energy to get the dinner delayed for a quarter of an hour in most well-regulated houses, or some slight change in routine, than to alter a frontier, or pass an Act of Parliament."

Hadria laughed. "Until you discovered this by personal inconvenience, you always scolded me for my disposition to jeer at the domestic scheme."

"It *is* a little geometrical," Valeria admitted.

"Geometrical! It is like a gigantic ordnance map palmed off on one instead of a real landscape."

"Come now, to be just, say an Italian garden."

"That flatters it, but the simile will do. The eye sees to the end of every path, and knows that it leads to nothing."

"Ah! dear Hadria, but all the pathways of the world have that very same goal."

"At least some of them have the good taste to wind a little, and thus disguise the fact. And think of the wild flowers one may gather by the wayside in some forest track, or among the mountain passes; but in these prim alleys what natural thing can one know? Brain and heart grow tame and clipped to match the hedges, or take on grotesque shapes——"

"That one must guard against."

"Oh, I am sick of guarding against things. To be always warding off evil, is an evil in itself. Better let it come."

Valeria looked at her companion anxiously.

"One knows how twirling round in a circle makes one giddy, or following the same path stupifies. How does the

205

polar bear feel, I wonder, after he has walked up and down in his cage for years and years? "

" Used to it, I imagine," said Valeria.

" But before he gets used to it, that is the bad time. And then it is all so confusing——"

Hadria sat on the low parapet of the terrace at the Priory. Valeria had a place on the topmost step, where the sun had been beating all the morning. Hadria had taken off her hat to enjoy the warmth. The long sprays of the roses were blown across her now and then. Once, a thorn had left a mark of blood upon her hand.

Valeria gathered a spray, and nodded slowly.

" I don't want to allow emotion to get the better of me, Valeria. I don't want to run rank like some overgrown weed, and so I dread the accumulation of emotion—emotion that has never had a good explosive utterance. One has to be so discreet in these Italian gardens; no one shouts or says ' damn.' "

" Ah! you naturally feel out of your element."

Hadria laughed. " It 's all very well to take that superior tone. *You* don't reside on an ordnance map."

There was a pause. Miss Du Prel seemed lost in thought.

" It is this dead silence that oppresses one, this hushed endurance of the travail of life. How do these women stand it? "

Valeria presently woke up, and admitted that to live in an English village would drive her out of her mind in a week.

" And yet, Valeria, you have often professed to envy me, because I had what you called a place in life—as if a place in Craddock Dene were the same thing !"

" It is well that you do not mean all you say."

" Or say all I mean."

Valeria laid her hand on Hadria's with wistful tenderness.

" I don't think anyone will ever quite understand you, Hadria."

" Including perhaps myself. I sometimes fancy that when

it became necessary to provide me with a disposition, the
material had run out, for the moment, nothing being left but
a few remnants of other people's characters; so a living
handful of these was taken up, roughly welded together, and
then the mixture was sent whirling into space, to boil and
sputter itself out as best it might."

Miss Du Prel turned to her companion.

"I see that you are incongruously situated, but don't you
think that you may be wrong yourself? Don't you think you
may be making a mistake?"

Hadria was emphatic in assent.

"Not only do I think I may be wrong, but I don't see how
—unless by pure chance—I can be anything else. For I
can't discover what is right. I see women all round me
actuated by this frenzied sense of duty; I see them toiling
submissively at their eternal treadmill; occupying their best
years in the business of filling their nurseries; losing their
youth, narrowing their intelligence, ruining their husbands,
and clouding their very moral sense at last. Well, I know that
such conduct is supposed to be right and virtuous. But I
can't see it. It impresses me simply as stupid and degrading.
And from my narrow little point of observation, the more I
see of life, the more hopelessly involved become all questions
of right and wrong where our confounded sex is concerned."

"Why? Because the standards are changing," asserted
Miss Du Prel.

"Because—look, Valeria, our present relation to life is *in
itself* an injury, an insult—you have never seriously denied
that—and how can one make for oneself a moral code that
has to lay its foundation-stone in that very injury? And if
one lays one's foundation-stone in open ground beyond, then
one's code is out of touch with present fact, and one's
morality consists in sheer revolt all along the line. The whole
matter is in confusion. You have to accept Mrs. Walker's and
Mrs. Gordon's view of the case, plainly and simply, or you
get off into a sort of morass and blunder into quicksands."

"Then what happens?"

"That's just what I don't know. That's just why I say that I am probably wrong, because, in this transition period, there seems to be no clear right."

"To cease to believe in right and wrong would be to founder morally, altogether," Valeria warned.

"I know, and yet I begin to realize how true it is that there is no such thing as absolute right or wrong. It is related to the case and the moment."

"This leads up to some desperate deed or other, Hadria," cried her friend, "I have feared it, or hoped it, I scarcely know which, for some time. But you alarm me to-day."

"If I believed in the efficacy of a desperate deed, Valeria, I should not chafe as I do, against the conditions of the present scheme of things. If individuals could find a remedy for themselves, with a little courage and will, there would be less occasion to growl."

"But can they not?"

"Can they?" asked Hadria. "A woman without means of livelihood, breaks away from her moorings—well, it is as if a child were to fall into the midst of some gigantic machinery that is going at full speed. Let her try the feat, and the cracking of her bones by the big wheels will attest its hopelessness. And yet I long to try!" Hadria added beneath her breath.

Miss Du Prel admitted that success was rare in the present delirious state of competition. Individuals here and there pulled through.

"I told you years ago that Nature had chosen our sex for ill-usage. Try what we may, defeat and suffering await us, in one form or another. You are dissatisfied with your form of suffering, I with mine. A creature in pain always thinks it would be more bearable if only it were on the other side."

"Ah, I know you won't admit it," said Hadria, "but some day we shall all see that this is the result of human cruelty

and ignorance, and that it is no more 'intended' or inherently necessary than that children should be born with
curvature of the spine, or rickets. Some day it will be as
clear as noon, that heartless 'some day' which can never
help you or me, or any of us who live now. It is we, I
suppose, who are required to help the 'some day.' Only how,
when we are ourselves *in extremis ?* "

"The poor are helpers of the poor," said Valeria.

"But if they grow too poor, to starvation point, then they
can help no more; they can only perish slowly."

"I hoped," said Valeria, "that Professor Fortescue would
have poured oil upon the troubled waters."

"He does in one sense. But in another, he makes me feel
more than ever what I am missing."

Miss Du Prel's impulsive instincts could be kept at bay no
longer.

"There is really nothing for it, but some deed of daring,"
she cried. "I believe, if only your husband could get over
his horror of the scandal and talk, that a separation would
be best for you both. It is not as if he cared for you. One
can see he does not. You are such a strange, inconsequent
being, Hadria, that I believe you would feel the parting far
more than he would (conventions apart)."

"No question of it," said Hadria. "Our disharmony,
radical and hopeless as it is, does not prevent my having
a strong regard for Hubert. I can't help seeing the
admirable sides of his character. He is too irritated and
aggrieved to feel anything but rancour against me. It is
natural. I understand."

"Ah, it will only end in some disaster, if you try to
reconcile the irreconcilable. Of course I think it is a great
pity that you have not more of the instincts on which homes
are founded, but since you have not —— "

Hadria turned sharply round. "Do you really regret that
just for once the old, old game has been played unsuccess-
fully? Therein I can't agree with you, though I am the loser

by it." Hadria grasped a swaying spray that the wind blew towards her, and clasped it hard in her hand, regardless of the thorns. "It gives me a keen, fierce pleasure to know that for all their training and constraining and incitement and starvation, I have *not* developed masses of treacly instinct in which mind and will and every human faculty struggle, in vain, to move leg or wing, like some poor fly doomed to a sweet and sticky death. At least the powers of the world shall not prevail with me by *that* old device. Mind and will and every human faculty may die, but they shall not drown, in the usual applauded fashion, in seas of tepid, bubbling, up-swelling instinct. I will dare anything rather than endure that. They must take the trouble to provide instruments of death from without; they must lay siege and starve me; they must attack in soldierly fashion; I will not save them the exertion by developing the means of destruction from within. There I stand at bay. They shall knock down the citadel of my mind and will, stone by stone."

"That is a terrible challenge!" exclaimed Miss Du Prel.

A light laugh sounded across the lawn.

The afternoon sunshine threw four long shadows over the grass : of a slightly-built woman, of a very tall man, and of two smaller men.

The figures themselves were hidden by a group of shrubs, and only the shadows were visible. They paused, for a moment, as if in consultation; the lady standing, with her weight half leaning on her parasol. The tall man seemed to be talking to her vivaciously. His long, shadow-arms shot across the grass, his head wagged.

"The shadows of Fate!" cried Valeria fantastically.

Then they moved into sight, advancing towards the terrace.

"Who are they I wonder? Oh, Professor Fortescue, for one !"

"Lady Engleton and Joseph Fleming. The other I don't know."

He was very broad and tall, having a slight stoop, and a curious way of carrying his head, craned forward. The attitude suggested a keen observer. He was attired in knickerbockers and rough tweed Norfolk jacket, and he looked robust and powerful, almost to excess. The chin and mouth were concealed by the thick growth of dark hair, but one suspected unpleasant things of the latter. As far as one could judge his age, he seemed a man of about five-and-thirty, with vigour enough to last for another fifty years.

"That," said Valeria, "must be Professor Theobald. He has probably come to see the house."

"I am sure I shall hate that man," exclaimed Hadria. "He is not to be trusted; what nonsense he is talking to Lady Engleton !"

"You can't hear, can you?"

"No; I can see. And she laughs and smiles and bandies words with him. He is amusing certainly; there is that excuse for her; but I wonder how she can do it."

"What an extraordinary creature you are ! To take a prejudice against a man before you have spoken to him."

"He is cruel, he is cruel !" exclaimed Hadria in a low, excited voice. "He is like some cunning wild animal. Look at Professor Fortescue ! his opposite pole — why it is all clearer, at this distance, than if we were under the confusing influence of their speech. See the contrast between that quiet, firm walk, and the insinuating, conceited tread of the other man. Joseph Fleming comes out well too, honest soul !"

"He is carrying a fishing-rod. They have been fishing," said Valeria.

"Not Professor Fortescue, I am certain. *He* does not find his pleasure in causing pain."

"This hero-worship blinds you. Depend upon it, he is not without the primitive instinct to kill."

"There are individual exceptions to all savage instincts, or the world would never move."

"Instinct rules the world," said Miss Du Prel. "At least it is obviously neither reason nor the moral sense that rules it."

"Then why does it produce a Professor Fortescue now and then?"

"Possibly as a corrective."

"Or perhaps for fun," said Hadria.

CHAPTER XXIII.

"PROFESSOR THEOBALD, if you are able to resist the fascinations of this old house you are made of sterner stuff than I thought."

"I can never resist fascinations, Lady Engleton."

"Do you ever try?"

"My life is spent in the endeavour."

"How foolish!" Whether this applied to the endeavour or to the remark, did not quite appear. Lady Engleton's graceful figure leant over the parapet.

"Do you know, Mrs. Temperley," she said in her incessantly vivacious manner, "I have scarcely heard a serious word since our two Professors came to us. Isn't it disgraceful? I naturally expected to be improved and enlightened, but they are both so frivolous, I can't keep them for a moment to any important subject. They refuse to be profound. It is *I* who have to be profound."

"While *we* endeavour to be charming," said Professor Theobald.

"You may think that flattering, but I confess it seems to me a beggarly compliment (as men's to women usually are)."

"You expect too much of finite intelligence, Lady Engleton."

"This is how I am always put off! If it were not that you are both such old friends—you are a sort of cousin I think, Professor Fortescue—I should really feel aggrieved. One has to endure so much more from relations. No, but really; I appeal to Mrs. Temperley. When one is hungering for erudition, to be offered compliments! Not that I can

accuse Professor Fortescue of compliments," she added with a
laugh; "wild horses would not drag one from him. I angle
vainly. But he is so ridiculously young. He enjoys things
as if he were a schoolboy. Does one look for that in one's
Professors? He talks of the country as if it were *Paradise
Regained.*"

"So it is to me," he said with a smile.

"But that is not your *rôle.* You have to think, not to enjoy."

"Then you must not invite us to Craddock Place," Professor
Theobald stipulated.

"As usual, a halting compliment."

"To take you seriously, Lady Engleton," said Professor
Fortescue, "(though I know it is a dangerous practice) one of
the great advantages of an occasional think is to enable one
to relish the joys of mental vacuity, just as the pleasure of
idleness is never fully known till one has worked."

"Ah," sighed Lady Engleton, "I know I don't extract the
full flavour out of *that!*"

"It is a neglected art," said the Professor. "After worrying
himself with the problems of existence, as the human being
is prone to do, as soon as existence is more or less secure and
peaceful, a man can experience few things more enjoyable
than to leave aside all problems and go out into the fields,
into the sun, to feel the life in his veins, the world at the
threshold of his five senses."

"Ah, now you really are profound at last, Professor!"

"I thought it was risky to take you seriously."

"No, no, I am delighted. The world at the threshold of
one's five senses. One has but to look and to listen and the
beauty of things displays itself for our benefit. Yes, but that
is what the artists say, not the Professors."

"Even a Professor is human," pleaded Theobald.

Valeria quoted some lines that she said expressed Professor
Fortescue's idea.

> " Carry me out into the wind and the sunshine,
>   Into the beautiful world!"

Lady Engleton's artistic instinct seemed to occupy itself less with the interpretation of Nature than with the appreciation of the handiwork of man. The lines did not stir her. Professor Theobald shared her indifference for the poetic expression, but not for the reality expressed.

"I quarrel with you about art," said Lady Engleton. "Art is art, and nature is nature, both charming in their way, though I prefer art."

"Our old quarrel!" said the Professor.

"Because a wild glade is beautiful in its quality of wild glade, you can't see the beauty in a trim bit of garden, with its delightful suggestion of human thought and care."

"I object to stiffness," said Professor Theobald.

His proposals to improve the stately old gardens at the Priory by adding what Lady Engleton called "fatuous wriggles to all the walks, for mere wrigglings' sake," had led to hot discussions on the principles of art and the relation of symmetry to the sensibilities of mankind. Lady Engleton thought the Professor crude in taste, and shallow in knowledge, on this point.

"And yet you appreciate so keenly my old enamels, and your eye seeks out, in a minute, a picturesque roof or gable."

"Perhaps Theobald leans to the picturesque and does not care for the classic," suggested his colleague; "a fundamental distinction in mental bias."

"Then why does he enjoy so much of the *Renaissance* work on caskets and goblets? He was raving about them last night in the choicest English."

Lady Engleton crossed over to speak to Miss Du Prel. Professor Theobald approached Mrs. Temperley and Joseph Fleming. Hadria knew by some instinct that the Professor had been waiting for an opportunity to speak to her. As he drew near, a feeling of intense enmity arose within her, which reached its highest pitch when he addressed her in a fine, low-toned voice of peculiarly fascinating quality. Every instinct rose up as if in warning. He sat down beside her, and began to talk about the Priory and its history. His ability was obvious, even in his choice of words and his selection of incidents. He had the power of making dry archæological facts almost dramatic. His speech differed from that of most men, in the indefinable manner wherein excellence differs from mediocrity. Yet Hadria was glad to notice some equally indefinable lack, corresponding perhaps to the gap in his consciousness that Lady Engleton had come upon in their discussions on the general principles of art. What was it? A certain stilted, unreal quality? Scarcely. Words refused to fit themselves to the evasive form. Something that suggested the term "second class," though whether it were the manner or the substance that was responsible for the impression, was difficult to say.

Sometimes his words allowed two possible interpretations to be put upon a sentence. He was a master of the ambiguous. Obviously it was not lack of skill that produced the double-faced phrases.

He did not leave his listeners long in doubt as to his personal history. He enjoyed talking about himself. He was a Professor of archæology, and had written various learned books on the subject. But his studies had by no means been confined to the one theme. History had also interested him profoundly. He had published a work on the old houses of England. The Priory figured among them. It was not difficult to discover from the conversation of this singular man, whose subtle and secretive instincts were contradicted, at times, by a strange inconsequent frankness, that his genuine feeling for the picturesque was accompanied by an equally strong pre-dilection for the appurtenances of wealth and splendour; his love of great names and estates being almost of the calibre of the housemaid's passion for lofty personages in her penny periodical. He seemed to be a man of keen and cunning ability, who studied and played upon the passions and weak-nesses of his fellows, possibly for their good, but always as a magician might deal with the beings subject to his power.

By what strange lapse did he thus naïvely lay himself open to their smiles?

Hadria was amused at his occasional impulse of egotistic frankness (or what appeared to be such), when he would solemnly analyse his own character, admitting his instinct to deceive with an engaging and scholarly candour.

His penetrating eyes kept a watch upon his audience. His very simplicity seemed to be guarded by his keenness.

Hadria chafed under his persistent effort to attract and interest her. She gave a little inward shiver on finding that there was a vague, unaccountable, and unpleasant fascination in the personality of the man.

It was not charm, it was nothing that inspired admiration; it rather inspired curiosity and stirred the spirit of research, a spirit which evidently animated himself. She felt that, in order to investigate the workings of her mind and her heart, the Professor would have coolly pursued the most ruthless psychical experiments, no matter at what cost of anguish to herself. In the interests of science and humanity, the learned Professor would certainly not hesitate to make one wretched individual agonize.

His appeal to the intellect was stimulatingly strong; it was like a stinging wind, that made one walk at a reckless pace, and brought the blood tingling through every vein. That intellectual force could alone explain the fact of his being counted by Professor Fortescue as a friend. Even then it was a puzzling friendship. Could it be that to Professor Fortescue, he shewed only his best side? His manner was more respectful towards his colleague than towards other men, but even with him he was irreverent in his heart, as towards mankind in general.

To Hadria he spoke of Professor Fortescue with enthusiasm—praising his great power, his generosity, his genial qualities, and his uprightness; then he laughed at him as a modern Don Quixote, and sneered at his efforts to save animal suffering when he might have made a name that would

never be forgotten, if he pursued a more fruitful branch of
research.

Hadria remarked that Professor Theobald's last sentence
had added the crowning dignity to his eulogium.

He glanced at her, as if taking her measure.

"Fortescue," he called out, "I envy you your champion.
You point, Mrs. Temperley, to lofty altitudes. I, as a mere
man, cannot pretend to scale them."

Then he proceeded to bring down feminine loftiness with
virile reason.

"In this world, where there are so many other evils to
combat, one feels that it is more rational to attack the more
important first."

"Ah! there is nothing like an evil to bolster up an evil,"
cried Professor Fortescue; "the argument never fails. Every
abuse may find shelter behind it. The slave trade, for instance;
have we not white slavery in our midst? How inconsistent to
trouble about negroes till our own people are truly free!
Wife-beating? Sad; but then children are often shamefully
ill-used. Wait till *they* are fully protected before fussing about
wives. Protect children? Foolish knight-errant, when you
ought to know that drunkenness is at the root of these crimes!
Sweep away *this* curse, before thinking of the children. As for
animals, how can any rational person consider *their* sufferings,
when there are men, women, and children with wrongs to be
redressed?"

Professor Theobald laughed.

"My dear Fortescue, I knew you would have some
ingenious excuse for your amiable weaknesses."

"It is easier to find epithets than answers, Theobald," said
the Professor with a smile. "I confess I wonder at a man of
your logical power being taken in with this cheap argument, if
argument it can be called."

"It is my attachment to logic that makes me crave for con-
sistency," said Theobald, not over pleased at his friend's attack.

Professor Fortescue stared in surprise.

" But do you really mean to tell me that you think it logical to excuse one abuse by pointing to another ? "

" I think that while there are ill - used women and children, it is certainly inconsistent to consider animals," said Theobald.

" It does not occur to you that the spirit in man that permits abuse of power over animals is precisely the same devil inspired spirit that expresses itself in cruelty towards children. Ah," continued Professor Fortescue, shaking his head, " then you really are one of the many who help wrong to breed wrong, and suffering to foster suffering, all the world over. It is you and those who reason as you reason, who give to our miseries their terrible vitality. What arguments has evil ever given to evil ! What shelter and succour cruelty offers eternally to cruelty ! "

" I can't attempt to combat this hobby of yours, Fortescue."

" Again a be-littling epithet in place of an argument ! But I know of old that on this subject your intellectual acumen deserts you, as it deserts nearly all men. You sink suddenly to lower spiritual rank, and employ reasoning that you would laugh to scorn in connection with every other topic."

" You seem bent on crushing me," exclaimed Theobald. " And Mrs. Temperley enjoys seeing me mangled. Talk about cruelty to animals ! I call this cold-blooded devilry ! Mrs. Temperley, come to my rescue ! "

" So long as other forms of cruelty can be instanced, Professor Theobald, I don't see how, on your own shewing, you can expect any consistent person to raise a finger to help you," Hadria returned. Theobald laughed.

" But I consider myself too important and valuable to be made the subject of this harsh treatment."

" That is for others to decide. If it affords us amusement to torment you, and amusement benefits our nerves and digestion, how can you justly object ? We must consider the greatest good of the greatest number; and we are twice as numerous as you."

"You are delicious!" he exclaimed. Mrs. Temperley's manner stiffened.

Acute as the Professor was in many directions, he did not appear to notice the change.

His own manner was not above criticism.

"It is strange," said Lady Engleton, in speaking of him afterwards to Hadria, "it is strange that his cleverness does not come to the rescue; but so far from that, I think it leads him a wild dance over boggy ground, like some will-o'-the-wisp, but for whose freakish allurements the good man might have trodden a quiet and inoffensive way."

The only means of procuring the indispensable afternoon tea was to go on to the Red House, which Mrs. Temperley proposed that they should all do.

"And is there no shaking your decision about the Priory, Professor Theobald?" Lady Engleton asked as they descended the steps.

The Professor's quick glance sought Mrs. Temperley's before he answered. "I confess to feeling less heroic this afternoon."

"Oh, good! We may perhaps have you for a neighbour after all."

CHAPTER XXIV.

HADRIA tried to avoid Professor Theobald, but he was not easily avoided. She frequently met him in her walks. The return of spring had tempted her to resume her old habit of rising with the sun. But she found, what she had feared, that her strength had departed, and she was fatigued instead of invigorated, as of yore. She did not. regard this loss in a resigned spirit. Resignation was certainly not her strong point. The vicar's wife and the doctor's wife and the rest of the neighbours compared their woes and weariness over five o'clock tea, and these appeared so many and so severe that Hadria felt half ashamed to count hers at all. Yet why lower the altars of the sane goddess because her shrine was deserted? Health was health, though all the women of England were confirmed invalids. And with nothing less ought reasonable creatures to be satisfied. As for taking enfeeblement as a natural dispensation, she would as soon regard delirium tremens in that light.

She chafed fiercely against the loss of that blessed sense of well-being and overflowing health, that she used to have, in the old days. She resented the nerve-weariness, the fatigue that she was now more conscious of than ever, with the coming of the spring. The impulse of creative energy broke forth in her. The pearly mornings and the birds' songs stirred every instinct of expression. The outburst did not receive its usual check. The influences of disenchantment were counteracted by Professor Fortescue's presence. His sympathy was marvellous in its penetration, brimming the cold

hollows of her spirit, as a flooded river fills the tiniest chinks
and corners about its arid banks. He called forth all her
natural buoyancy and her exulting sense of life, which was
precisely the element which charged her sadness with such
a fierce electric quality, when she became possessed by it, as a
cloud by storm.

Valeria too was roused by the season.

"What a parable it all is, as old as the earth, and as fresh,
each new year, as if a messenger-angel had come straight
from heaven, in his home-spun of young green, to tell us that
all is well."

If Hadria met Professor Theobald in her rambles, she
always cut short her intended walk. She and Valeria with
Professor Fortescue wandered together, far and wide. They
watched the daily budding greenery, the gleams of daffodils
among their sword-blades of leaves, the pushing of sheaths
and heads through the teeming soil, the bursts of sunshine
and the absurd childish little gushes of rain, skimming the
green country like a frown.

"Truly a time for joy and idleness."

"If only," said Hadria, when Professor Theobald thus grew
enthusiastic on the subject, "if only my cook had not given
a month's notice."

She would not second his mood, be it what it might.
Each day, as they passed along the lanes, the pale green
had spread, like fire, on the hedges, caught the chestnuts, with
their fat buds shining in the sun, which already was releasing
the close-packed leaflets.

Hadria (apparently out of sheer devilry, said Professor
Theobald) kept up a running commentary on the season, and
on her hapless position, bound to be off on the chase for a
cook at this moment of festival. Nor was this all. Crockery,
pots and pans, clothes for the children, clothes for herself,
were urgently needed, and no experienced person, she declared,
could afford to regard the matter as simple because it was
trivial.

"One of the ghastliest mistakes in this trivial and laborious world."

Valeria thought that cooks had simply to be advertised for, and they came.

"What *naïveté !*" exclaimed Hadria. "Helen was persuaded to cross the seas from her Spartan home to set Troy ablaze, and tarnish her fair fame, but it would take twenty sons of Priam to induce a damsel to come over dry land to Craddock Dene, to cook our dinners and retain her character."

"You would almost imply that women don't so very much care about their characters," said Valeria.

"Oh, they do! but sometimes the dulness that an intelligent society has ordained as the classic accompaniment to social smiles, gets the better of a select few—Helen *par exemple.*"

It frequently happened that Hadria and Miss Du Prel came across Lady Engleton and her guests, in the Priory garden. From being accidental, the meetings had become intentional.

"I like to fancy we are fugitives—like Boccaccio's merry company—from the plague of our daily prose, to this garden of sweet poetry !" cried Miss Du Prel.

They all kindled at the idea. Valeria made some fanciful laws that she said were to govern the little realm. Everyone might express himself freely, and all that he said would be held as sacred, as if it were in confidence. To speak ill or slightingly of anyone, was forbidden. All local and practical topics were to be dropped, as soon as the moss-grown griffins who guarded the Garden of Forgetfulness were passed.

Hadria was incorrigibly flippant about the banishment of important local subjects. She said that the kitchen-boiler was out of order, and yet she had to take part in these highly-cultivated conversations and smile, as she complained, with that kitchen-boiler gnawing at her vitals. She claimed to be set on a level with the Spartan boy, if not above him.

Valeria might scoff, as those proverbially did who never felt a wound. Hadria found a certain lack of tender feeling among the happy few who had no such tragic burdens to sustain.

Not only were these prosaic subjects banished from within the cincture of the gentle griffins, but also the suspicions, spites, petty jealousies, vulgar curiosities, and all the indefinable little darts and daggers that fly in the social air, destroying human sympathy and good-will. Each mind could expand freely, no longer on the defensive against the rain of small stabs. There grew up a delicate, and chivalrous code among the little group who met within the griffins' territory.

"It is not for us to say that, individually, we transcend the average of educated mortals," said Professor Theobald, "but I do assert that collectively we soar high above that depressing standard."

Professor Fortescue observed that whatever might be said about their own little band, it was a strange fact that bodies of human beings were able to produce, by union, a condition far above or far below the average of their separate values. "There is something chemical and explosive in human relationships," he said.

These meetings stood out as a unique experience in the memory of all who took part in them. Chance had brought them to pass, and they refused to answer to the call of a less learned magician.

Lady Engleton and Mrs. Temperley alternately sent tea and fruit to the terrace, on the days of meeting, and there the little company would spend the afternoon serenely, surrounded by the beauties of the garden with its enticing avenues, its chaunting birds, its flushes of bloom, and its rich delicious scents.

"Why do we, in the nineteenth century, starve ourselves of these delicate joys?" cried Valeria. "Why do we so seldom leave our stupid pre-occupations and open our souls to the sun, to the spring, to the gentle invitations of gardens, to the charm of conversation? We seem to know nothing of the serenities, the urbanities of life."

" We live too fast; we are too much troubled about outward things — cooks and dressmakers, Mrs. Temperley," said Professor Theobald.

" Poor cooks and dressmakers ! " murmured Professor Fortescue, "where are *their* serenities and urbanities?"

" I would not deprive any person of the good things of life," cried Valeria; " but at present, it is only a few who can appreciate and contribute to the delicate essence that I speak of. I don't think one could expect it of one's cook, after all."

" One is mad to expect anything of those who have had no chance," said Professor Fortescue. " That nevertheless we consistently do,—or what amounts to the same thing : we plume ourselves on what chance has enabled us to be and to achieve, as if between us and the less fortunate there were some great difference of calibre and merit. Nine times in ten, there is nothing between us but luck."

" Oh, dear, you *are* democratic, Professor ! " cried Lady Engleton.

" No ; I am merely trying to be just."

"To be just you must apply your theory to men and women, as well as to class and class," Valeria suggested.

" *Mon Dieu !* but so I do ; so I always have done, as soon as I was intellectually short-coated."

" And would you excuse all our weaknesses on that ground?" asked Lady Engleton, with a somewhat ingratiating upward gaze of her blue eyes.

" I would account for them as I would account for the weaknesses of my own sex. As for excusing, the question of moral responsibility is too involved to be decided off-hand."

The atmosphere of Griffin-land, as Professor Theobald called it, while becoming to his character, made him a little recklessly frank at times.

He admitted that throughout his varied experience of life, he had found flattery the most powerful weapon in a skilled hand, and that he had never known it fail. He related instances of the signal success which had followed its application with the trowel. He reminded his listeners of Lord Beaconsfield's famous saying, and chuckled over the unfortunate woman, "plain as a pike-staff," who had become his benefactress, in consequence of a discreet allusion to the "power of beauty" and a well-placed sigh.

"The woman must have been a fool!" said Joseph Fleming.

"By no means; she was of brilliant intellect. But praises of that were tame to her; she knew her force, and was perhaps tired of the solitude it induced." Professor Theobald laughed mightily at his own sarcasm. "But when the whisper of 'beauty' came stealing to her ear (which was by no means like a shell) it was surpassing sweet to her. I think there is no yearning more intense than that of a clever woman for the triumphs of mere beauty. She would give all her powers of intellect for the smallest tribute to personal and feminine charm. What is your verdict, Mrs. Temperley?"

Mrs. Temperley supposed that clever women had something of human nature in them, and valued overmuch what they did not possess.

Professor Theobald had perhaps looked for an answer that would have betrayed more of the speaker's secret feelings.

"It is the fashion, I know," he said, "to regard woman as an enigma. Now, without professing any unusual acuteness, I believe that this is a mistake. Woman is an enigma certainly, because she is human, but that ends it. Her conditions have tended to cultivate in her the power of dissimulation, and the histrionic quality, just as the peaceful ilex learns to put forth thorns if you expose it to the attacks of devouring cattle. It is this instinct to develop thorns in self-defence, and yet to live a little behind the prickly outposts, that leads to our notion of mystery in woman's nature. Let a man's subsistence and career be subject to the same powers and chances as the success of a woman's life now hangs on, and see whether he too does not become a histrionic enigma."

Professor Fortescue observed that the clergy, at times, developed qualities called feminine, because in some respects their conditions resembled those of women.

Theobald assented enthusiastically to this view. He had himself entered the church as a young fellow (let not Mrs. Temperley look so inconsiderately astonished), and had left it on account of being unable to conscientiously subscribe to its tenets.

" But not before I had acquired some severe training in that sort of strategy which is incumbent upon women, in the conduct of their lives. Whatever I might privately think or feel, my office required that I should only express that which would be more or less grateful to my hearers. (Is not this the woman's case, in almost every position in life?) Even orthodoxy must trip it on tiptoe; there was always some prejudice, some susceptibility to consider. What was frankness in others was imprudence in me; other men's minds might roam at large; mine was tethered, if not in its secret movements, at least in its utterance; and it is a curious and somewhat sinister law of Nature, that perpetual denial of utterance ends by killing the power or the feeling so held in durance."

Hadria coloured.

" That experience and its effect upon my own nature, which has lasted to this day," added Theobald, " served to increase my interest in the fascinating study of character in its relation to environment."

" Ah !" exclaimed Hadria, " then *you* don't believe in the independent power of the human will? "

" Certainly not. To talk of character overcoming circumstance is to talk of an effect without a cause. Yet this phrase is a mere commonplace in our speech. A man no more overcomes his circumstance than oxygen overcomes nitrogen when it combines with it to form the air we breathe. If the nitrogen is present, the combination takes place; but if there is no nitrogen to be had, all the oxygen in the world will not produce our blessed atmosphere ! "

Joseph Fleming caused a sort of anti-climax by mentioning simply that he didn't know that any nitrogen was required in the atmosphere.   One always heard about the oxygen.

Professor Theobald remarked, with a chuckle, that this was one of the uses of polite conversation ; one picked up information by the way-side.   Joseph agreed that it was wonderfully instructive, if the speakers were intelligent.

"That helps," said the Professor, tapping Joseph familiarly on the shoulder.

"When shall we have our next meeting?" enquired Lady Engleton, when the moment came for parting.

"The sooner the better," said Valeria.   "English skies have Puritan moods, and we may as well profit by their present jocund temper.   I never saw a bluer sky in all Italy."

"I certainly shall not be absent from the next meeting," announced Theobald, with a glance at Hadria.

"Nor I," said Lady Engleton.   "Such opportunities come none too often."

"I," Hadria observed, "shall be cook-hunting."

Professor Theobald's jaw shut with a snap, and he turned and left the group almost rudely.

CHAPTER XXV.

HADRIA thought that Professor Theobald had not spoken at random, when he said that the sweetest tribute a woman can receive is that paid to her personal charm. This unwilling admission was dragged out of her by the sight of Valeria Du Prel, as the central figure of an admiring group, in the large drawing-room at Craddock Place.

She was looking handsome and animated, her white hair drawn proudly off her brow, and placed as if with intention beside the silken curtains, whose tint of misty pale green was so becoming to her beauty.

Valeria was holding her little court, and thoroughly enjoying the admiration.

"If we have had to live by our looks for all these centuries, surely the instinct that Professor Theobald thinks himself so penetrating to have discovered in clever women, is accounted for simply enough by heredity," Hadria said to herself, resentfully.

Professor Theobald was bending over Miss Du Prel with an air of devotion. Hadria wished that she would not take his compliments so smilingly. Valeria would not be proof against his flattery. She kindled with a child's frankness at praise. It stung Hadria to think of her friend being carelessly classed by the Professor among women whose weakness he understood and could play upon. He would imagine that he had discovered the mystery of the sun, because he had observed a spot upon it, not understanding the nature of the very spot. Granted that a little salve to one's battered and scarified self-love was soft and grateful, what did that prove of the woman

who welcomed it, beyond a human craving to keep the inner
picture of herself as bright and fine as might be? The man
who, out of contempt or irreverence, set a bait for the universal
appetite proved himself, rather than his intended victim, of
meagre quality. Valeria complimented him generously by
supposing him sincere.

Occasional bursts of laughter came from her court.
Professor Theobald looked furtively round, as if seeking some
one, or watching the effect of his conduct on Mrs. Temperley.

Could he be trying to make her jealous of Valeria?

Hadria gave a sudden little laugh while Lord Engleton—
a shy, rather taciturn man—was shewing her his wife's last
picture. Hadria had to explain the apparent discourtesy as
best she could.

The picture was of English meadows at sunset.

"They are the meadows you see from your windows," said
Lord Engleton. "That village is Masham, with the spire
shewing through the trees. I daresay you know the view
pretty well."

"I doubt," she answered, with the instinct of extravagance
that annoyed Hubert, "I doubt if I know anything else."

Lord Engleton brought a portfolio full of sketches for her
to see.

"Lady Engleton has been busy."

As Hadria laid down the last sketch, her eyes wandered
round the softly-lighted, dimly beautiful room, and suddenly
she was seized with a swift, reasonless, overpowering sense
of happiness that she felt to be atmospheric and parenthetical
in character, but all the more keen for that reason, while it
lasted. The second black inexorable semicircle was ready to
enclose the little moment, but its contents had the condensed
character of that which stands within limits, and reminded her,
with a little sting, as of spur to horse, of her sharp, terrible
aptitude for delight and her hunger for it. Why not, why
not? What pinched, ungenerous philosophy was it that
insisted on voluntary starvation? One saw its offspring in the

troops of thin white souls that hurry, like ghosts, down the avenues of Life.

Again Professor Theobald's stealthy glance was directed towards Mrs. Temperley.

"He is as determined to analyse me as if I were a chemical compound," she said to herself.

"Perhaps we may as well join the group," suggested Lord Engleton.

It opened to admit the new comers, disclosing Miss Du Prel, in a gown of pale amber brocade, enthroned upon a straight-backed antique sofa. The exquisiteness of the surroundings which Lady Engleton had a peculiar gift in arranging, the mellow candlelight, the flowers and colours, seem to have satisfied in Valeria an inborn love of splendour that often opened hungry and unsatisfied jaws.

She had never looked so brilliant or so handsome.

Professor Theobald's face cleared. He explained to Mrs. Temperley that they had been discussing the complexity of human character, and had come to the conclusion that it was impossible to really understand even the simplest man or woman alive. Professor Theobald said that it was a dispensation of Providence which intended the human race for social life. Lady Engleton upbraided the author of the cynical utterance.

"Which of us can dare to face his own basest self?" the culprit demanded. "If any one is so bold, I fear I must accuse him (or even her) of lack of self-knowledge rather than give praise for spotlessness."

"Oh, I don't believe all these dreadful things about my fellows!" cried Miss Du Prel, flinging up her fine head defiantly; "one is likely to find in them more or less what one expects. It's the same everywhere. If you go seeking mole-hills and worms, and put nose to ground on the scent for carrion, you will find them all, with the range of snow-capped Alps in full view, and the infinite of blue above your blind head!"

Hadria, in justice, could not refuse to acknowledge that Professor Theobald was open-minded.

"True," he said, "it is dangerous to seek for evil, unless you naturally love it, and then——"

"You are past praying for," said Professor Fortescue.

"Or at least you never pray," added Hadria.

Both Professors looked at her, each with an expression of enquiry. It was difficult to understand from exactly what sources of experience or intuition the singular remark could have sprung.

The conversation took a slight swerve.

Professor Theobald contended that all our fond distinctions of vice and virtue, right and wrong, were mere praise and blame of conditions and events.

"We like to fancy the qualities of character inherent, while really they are laid on by slow degrees, like paint, and we name our acquaintance by the colour of his last coat."

This view offended Miss Du Prel. Joseph Fleming and Lord Engleton rallied round her. Hubert Temperley joined them. Man, the sublime, the summit of the creation, the end and object of the long and painful processes of nature; sin-spotted perhaps, weak and stumbling, but still the masterpiece of the centuries—was this great and mysterious creature to be thought of irreverently as a mere plain surface for *paint?* Only consider it! Professor Theobald's head went down between his shoulders as he laughed.

"The sublime creature would not look well *un*painted, believe me."

"He dare not appear in that plight even to himself, if Theobald be right in what he stated just now," said Professor Fortescue.

"Life to a character is like varnish to wood," asserted Miss Du Prel; "it brings out the grain."

"Ah!" cried Professor Theobald. "Then *you* insist on varnish, I on paint."

"There is a difference."

"And it affects your respective views throughout," added Professor Fortescue, "for if the paint theory be correct, then it is true that to know one's fellows is impossible, you can only know the upper coat; whereas if the truth lies in varnish, the substance of the nature is revealed to you frankly, if you have eyes to trace the delicacies of the markings, which tell the secrets of sap and fibre, of impetus and check : all the inner marvels of life and growth that go forward in that most botanic thing, the human soul."

"Professor Fortescue is eloquent, but he makes one feel distressingly vegetable," said Temperley.

"Oh! not unless one has a human soul," Lady Engleton reassured him.

"Am I to understand that you would deprive me of mine?" he asked, with a courtly bow.

"Not at all; souls are private property, or ought to be."

"I wish one could persuade the majority of that!" cried Professor Fortescue.

"Impossible," said Theobald. "The chief interest of man is the condition of his neighbour's soul."

"Could he not be induced to look after his own?" Hadria demanded.

"All fun would be over," said Professor Fortescue.

"I wish one could have an Act of Parliament, obliging every man to leave his neighbour's soul in peace."

"You would sap the very source of human happiness and enterprise," Professor Fortescue asserted, fantastically.

"I should be glad if I could think the average human being had the energy to look after *any* business; even other people's!" cried Lady Engleton.

"I believe that, as a matter of fact, the soul is a hibernating creature," said Theobald, with a chuckle.

"It certainly has its drowsy winters," observed Hadria.

"Ah! but its spring awakenings!" cried Miss Du Prel.

The chime of a clock startled them with its accusation of

lingering too long. The hostess remonstrated at the breaking
up the party. Why should they hurry away?

"The time when we could lay claim to have 'hurried' has
long since passed, Lady Engleton," said Hubert, "we can only
plead forgiveness by blaming you for making us too happy."

Professor Theobald went to the window. "What splendid
moonlight! Lady Engleton, don't you feel tempted to walk
with your guests to the end of the avenue?"

The idea was eagerly adopted, and the whole party sallied
forth together into the brilliant night. Long black shadows
of their forms stalked on before them, as if, said Valeria, they
were messengers from Hades come to conduct each his victim
to the abode of the shades.

Professor Theobald shuddered.

"I hate that dreadful chill idea of the Greeks. I have
much too strong a hold on this pleasant earth to relish the
notion of that gloomy under-world yet a while. What do you
say, Mrs. Temperley?"

She made some intentionally trite answer.

Professor Theobald's quick eyes discovered a glow-worm,
and he shouted to the ladies to come and see the little green
lantern of the spring. The mysterious light was bright
enough to irradiate the blades of grass around it, and even to
cast a wizard-like gleam on the strange face of the Professor
as he bent down close to the ground.

"Fancy being a lamp to oneself!" cried Lady Engleton.

"It's as much as most of us can do to be a lamp to
others," commented Hadria.

"Some one has compared the glow-worm's light to Hero's,
when she waited, with trimmed lamp, for her Leander," said
Professor Theobald. "Look here, Mr. Fleming, if you stoop
down just here, you will be able to see the little animal."
The Professor resigned his place to him. When Joseph rose
from his somewhat indifferent survey of the insect, Professor
Theobald had established himself at Mrs. Temperley's right
hand, and the rest of the party were left behind.

"Talking of Greek ideas," said the Professor, "that wonderful people perceived more clearly thàn we Christians have ever done, with all our science, the natural forces of Nature. What we call superstitions were really great scientific intuitions or prophecies. Of course I should not dare to speak in this frank fashion to the good people of Craddock Dene, but to *you* I need not be on my guard."

"I appreciate your confidence."

"Ah, now, Mrs. Temperley, you are unkind. It is of no use for you to try to persuade me that you are *of* as well as in the village of Craddock Dene."

"I have never set out upon that task."

"Again I offend!"

Hadria, dropping the subject, enquired whether the Professor was well acquainted with this part of the country.

He knew it by heart. A charming country; warm, luxuriant, picturesque, the pick of England to his mind. What could beat its woodlands, its hills, its relics of the old world, its barns and churches and smiling villages?

"Then it is not only Tudor mansions that attract you?" Hadria could not resist asking.

Tudor mansions? There was no cottage so humble, provided it were picturesque, that did not charm him.

"Really!" exclaimed Hadria, with a faintly emphasized surprise.

"Have I put my luckless foot into it again?"

"May I not be impressed by magnanimity?"

The Professor's mouth shut sharply.

"Mrs. Temperley is pleased to deride me. Craddock Dene must shrivel under destroying blasts like these."

"Not so much as one might think."

The sound of their steps on the broad avenue smote sharply on their ears. Their absurd-looking shadows stretched always in front of them. "A splendid night," Hadria observed, to break the silence.

"Glorious !" returned her companion, as if waking from thought.

"Spring is our best season here, the time of blossoming."

"I am horribly tempted to take root in the lovely district, in the hope of also blossoming. Can you imagine me a sort of patriarchal apple-tree laden with snowy blooms ? "

"You somewhat burden my imagination."

"I have had to work hard all my life, until an unexpected legacy from an admirable distant relation put me at the end of a longer tether. I still have to work, but less hard. I have always tried not to ossify, keeping in view a possible serene time to come, when I might put forth blossoms in this vernal fashion that tempts my middle-aged fancy. And where could I choose a sweeter spot for these late efforts to be young and green, than here in this perfect south of England home?"

"It seems large," said Hadria.

Professor Theobald grinned. "You don't appear to take a keen interest in my blossoming."

Why in heaven's name *should* she?

"I cannot naturally expect it," Professor Theobald continued, reading her silence aright, "but I should be really obliged by your counsel on this matter. You know the village; you know from your own experience whether it is a place to live in always. Advise me, I beg."

"Really, Professor Theobald, it is impossible for me to advise you in a matter so entirely depending on your own taste and your own affairs."

"You can at least tell me how you like the district yourself; whether it satisfies you as to society, easy access of town, influence on the mind and the spirits, and so forth."

"We are considered well off as to society. There are a good many neighbours within a radius of five miles; the trains to town are not all that could be wished. There are only two in the day worth calling such."

"And as to its effect upon the general aspect of life; is it rousing, cheering, inspiring, invigorating?"

Hadria gave a little laugh. "I must refer you to other inhabitants on this point. I think Lady Engleton finds it fairly inspiring."

"Lady Engleton is not Mrs. Temperley."

"I doubt not that same speech has already done duty as a compliment to Lady Engleton."

"You are incorrigible!"

"I wish you would make it when she is present," said Hadria, "and see us both bow!" The Professor laughed delightedly.

"I don't know what social treasures may be buried within your radius of five miles, but the mines need not be worked. An inhabitant of the Priory would not need them. Mrs. Temperley is a society in herself."

"An inhabitant of the Priory might risk disappointment, in supposing that Mrs. Temperley had nothing else to do than to supply her neighbours with society."

· The big jaw closed, with a snap.

"I don't think, on the whole, that I will take the Priory," he said, after a considerable pause; "it is, as you say, large."

Mrs. Temperley made no comment.

"I suppose I should be an unwelcome neighbour," he said, with a sigh.

"I fear any polite assurance, after such a challenge, would be a poor compliment. As for entreating you to take the Priory, I really do not feel equal to the responsibility."

"I accept in all humility," said the Professor, as he opened the gate of the Red House, "a deserved reproof."

CHAPTER XXVI.

" A SINGULAR character !" said Professor Theobald.
"There is a lot of good in her," Lady Engleton
asserted.

Lord Engleton observed that people were always speaking
ill of Mrs. Temperley, but he never could see that she was
worse than her neighbours. She was cleverer ; that might be
her offence.

Madame Bertaux observed in her short, decisive way that
Craddock Dene might have settled down with Mrs. Temperley
peaceably enough, if it hadn't been for her action about the
schoolmistress's child.

"Yes ; that has offended everybody," said Lady Engleton.

"What action was that?" asked Theobald, turning slowly
towards his hostess.

"Oh, haven't you heard? That really speaks well for this
house. You can't accuse us of gossip."

Lady Engleton related the incident. "By the way, you
must remember that poor woman, Professor. Don't you
know you were here at the school-feast that we gave one
summer in the park, when all the children came and had
tea and games, and you helped us so amiably to look after
them?"

The Professor remembered the occasion perfectly.

"And don't you recollect a very pretty, rather timid, fair-
haired woman who brought the children? We all used to
admire her. She was a particularly graceful, refined-looking
creature. She had read a great deal and was quite cultivated.
I often used to think she must feel very solitary at Craddock,

238

with not a soul to sympathize with her tastes. Mr. and
Mrs. Walker used to preach to her, poor soul, reproving
her love of reading, which took her thoughts away from her
duties and her sphere."

Madame Bertaux snorted significantly. Lady Engleton
had remarked a strange, sad look in Ellen Jervis's eyes, and
owned to having done her best to circumvent the respected
pastor and his wife, by lending her books occasionally, and
encouraging her to think her own thoughts, and get what
happiness she could out of her communings with larger
spirits than she was likely to find in Craddock. Of course
Mrs. Walker now gave Lady Engleton to understand that she
was partly responsible for the poor woman's misfortune. She
attributed it to Ellen's having had "all sorts of ideas in her
head!"

"I admit that if *not* having all sorts of ideas in one's head
is a safeguard, the unimpeachable virtue of a district is amply
accounted for."

Professor Theobald chuckled. He enquired if Lady
Engleton knew Mrs. Temperley's motive in adopting the
child.

"Oh, partly real kindness; but I think, between ourselves,
that Mrs. Temperley likes to be a little eccentric. Most
people have the instinct to go with the crowd. Hadria
Temperley has the opposite fault. She loves to run counter
to it, even when it is pursuing a harmless course."

Some weeks had now passed since the arrival of the two
Professors. The meetings in the Priory garden had been
frequent. They had affected for the better Professor Theobald's manner. Valeria's laws had curbed the worst side
of him, or prevented it from shewing itself so freely. He
felt the atmosphere of the little society, and acknowledged
that it was "taming the savage beast." As for his intellect
it took to blazing, as if, he said, without false modesty, a
torch had been placed in pure oxygen.

"My brain takes fire here and flames. I should make a

very creditable beacon if the burning of brains and the
burning of faggots were only of equal value."

The little feud between him and Mrs. Temperley had been
patched up. She felt that she had been rude to him, on one
occasion at any rate, and desired to make amends. He had
become more cautious in his conduct towards her.

During this period of the Renaissance, as Hadria afterwards
called the short-lived epoch, little Martha was visited frequently. Her protectress had expected to have to do battle
with hereditary weakness on account of her mother's sufferings,
but the child shewed no signs of this. Either the common
belief that mental trouble in the mother is reflected in the
child, was unfounded, or the evil could be overcome by the
simple beneficence of pure air, good food, and warm clothing.

Hadria had begun to feel a more personal interest in her
charge. She had taken it under her care of her own choice,
without the pressure of any social law or sentiment, and in
these circumstances of freedom, its helplessness appealed to
her protective instincts. She felt the relationship to be a true
one, in contradistinction to the more usual form of protectorate
of woman to child.

"There is nothing in it that gives offence to one's dignity
as a human being," she asserted, "which is more than can
be said of the ordinary relation, especially if it be legal."

She was issuing from little Martha's cottage on one splendid
morning, when she saw Professor Theobald coming up the
road from Craddock Dene. He caught sight of Hadria,
hesitated, coloured, glanced furtively up the road, and then,
seeing he was observed, came forward, raising his cap.

"You can't imagine what a charming picture you make;
the English cottage creeper-covered and smiling; the nurse
and child at the threshold equally smiling, yourself a very
emblem of spring in your fresh gown, and a domestic tabby
to complete the scene."

"I wish I could come and see it," said Hadria. She was
waving a twig of lavender, and little Martha was making grabs

at it, and laughing her gurgling laugh of babyish glee. Professor Theobald stood in the road facing up hill towards Craddock, whose church tower was visible from here, just peeping through the spring foliage of the vicarage garden. He only now and again looked round at the picture that he professed to admire.

"Do you want to see a really pretty child, Professor Theobald? Because if so, come here."

He hesitated, and a wave of dark colour flooded his face up to the roots of his close-clipped hair.

He paused a moment, and then bent down to open the little gate. His stalwart figure, in the diminutive enclosure, reduced it to the appearance of a doll's garden.

"Step carefully or you will crush the young *ménage*," Hadria advised. The rosy-cheeked nurse looked with proud expectancy at the face of the strange gentleman, to note the admiration that he could not but feel.

His lips were set.

The Professor evidently knew his duty and proceeded to admire with due energy. Little Martha shrank away a little from the bearded face, and her lower lip worked threateningly, but the perilous moment was staved over by means of the Professor's watch, hastily claimed by Hannah, who dispensed with ceremony in the emergency.

Martha's eyes opened wide, and the little hands came out to grasp the treasure. Hadria stood and laughed at the sight of the gigantic Professor, helplessly tethered by his own chain to the imperious baby, in whose fingers the watch was tightly clasped. The child was in high delight at the loquacious new toy—so superior to foolish fluffy rabbits that could not tick to save their skins. Martha had no notion of relinquishing her hold, so they need not tug in that feeble way; if they pulled too hard, she would yell!

She evidently meant business, said her captive. So long as they left her the watch, they might do as they pleased; she was perfectly indifferent to the accidental human accompaniments

of the new treasure, but on that one point she was firm. She
proceeded to stuff the watch into her mouth as far as it would
go. The Professor was dismayed.

"It's all right," Hadria reassured him. "You have hold of
the chain."

"Did you entice me into this truly ridiculous position in
order to laugh at me?" enquired the prisoner.

"I would not laugh at you for the world."

"Really this young person has the most astonishing grip!
How long does her fancy generally remain faithful to a new
toy?"

"Well—I hope you are not pressed for time," said Hadria
maliciously.

The Professor groaned, and struggled in the toils.

"Come, little one, open the fingers. Oh no, no, we mustn't
cry." Martha kept her features ready for that purpose at
a moment's notice, should any nonsense be attempted.

The victim looked round miserably.

"Is there nothing that will set me free from these tender
moorings?"

Hadria shook her head and laughed. "You are chained by
the most inflexible of all chains," she said: "your own compunction."

"Oh, you little tyrant!" exclaimed the Professor, shaking
his fist in the baby's face, at which she laughed a taunting and
triumphant laugh. Then, once more, the object of dispute
went into her mouth. Martha gurgled with joy.

"What *am* I to do?" cried her victim helplessly.

"Nothing. She has you securely because you fear to hurt
her."

"Little imp! Come now, let me go please. Oh, *please*,
Miss Baby—your Majesty: will nothing soften you? She is
beginning early to take advantage of the chivalry of the
stronger sex, and I doubt not she will know how to pursue
her opportunity later on."

"Oh! is *that* your parable? Into my head came quite a

different one—*à propos* of what we were talking of yesterday in
Griffin-land."

"Ah, the eternal feminine!" cried the Professor. "Yes,
you were very brilliant, Mrs. Temperley."

"You now stand for an excellent type of woman, Professor:
strong, but chained."

"Oh, thank you! (Infant, I implore!)"

"The baby ably impersonates Society with all its sentiments
and laws, written and unwritten."

"Ah!—and my impounded property?"

"Woman's life and freedom."

"Ingenious! And the chain? (Oh, inexorable babe, have
mercy on the sufferings of imprisoned vigour!)"

"Her affections, her pity, her compunction, which forbid her
to wrench away her rightful property, because ignorant and
tender hands are grasping it. The analogy is a little mixed,
but no matter."

"I should enjoy the intellectual treat that is spread before
me better, in happier circumstances, Mrs. Temperley."

"Apply your remark to your prototype—intelligently," she
added.

"My intelligence is rapidly waning; I am benumbed. I
fail to follow the intricacies of analogy, in this constrained
position."

"Ah, so does she!"

"Oh, pitiless cherub, my muscles ache with this monotony."

"And hers," said Hadria.

"Come, come, life is passing; I have but one; relax these
fetters, or I die."

Martha frowned and fretted. She even looked shocked,
according to Hadria, who stood by laughing. The baby, she
pointed out, failed to understand how her captive could so far
forget himself as to desire to regain his liberty.

"She reminds you, sternly, that this is your proper sphere."

"Perdition!" he exclaimed.

"As a general rule," she assented.

The Professor laughed, and said he was tired of being a Type.

At length a little gentle force had to be used, in spite of furious resentment on the part of the baby. A more injured and ill-treated mortal could not have been imagined. She set up a heaven-piercing wail, evidently overcome with indignation and surprise at the cruel treatment that she had received. What horrid selfishness to take oneself and one's property away, when an engaging innocent enjoys grasping it and stuffing it into its mouth!

"Don't you feel a guilty monster?" Hadria enquired, as the lament of the offended infant followed them up the road.

"I feel as if I were slinking off after a murder!" he exclaimed ruefully. "I wonder if we oughtn't to go back and try again to soothe the child." He paused irresolutely.

Hadria laughed. "You *do* make a lovely allegory!" she exclaimed. "This sense of guilt, this disposition to go back—this attitude of apology—it is speaking, inimitable!"

"But meanwhile that wretched child is shrieking itself into a fit!" cried the allegory, with the air of a repentant criminal.

"Whenever you open your mouth, out falls a symbol," exclaimed Hadria. "Be calm; Hannah will soon comfort her, and it is truer kindness not to remind her again of her grievance, poor little soul. But we will go back if you like (you are indeed a true woman!), and you can say you are sorry you made so free with your own possessions, and you wish you had done your duty better, and are eager to return and let Her Majesty hold you captive. Your prototype always does, you know, and she is nearly always pardoned, on condition that she never does anything of that kind again."

Professor Theobald seemed too much concerned about the child, who was still wailing, to pay much attention to any other topic. He turned to retrace his steps.

"I think you make a mistake," said Hadria. "As soon as she sees you she will want the watch, and then you will be placed between the awful alternatives of voluntarily surrender

ing your freedom, and heartlessly refusing to present yourself
to her as a big plaything. In one respect you have not yet
achieved a thorough fidelity to your model; you don't seem
to enjoy sacrifice for its own sake. That will come with
practice."

"I wish that child would leave off crying."

Hadria stopped in the road to laugh at the perturbed
Professor.

"She will presently. That is only a cry of anger, not of
distress. I would not leave her, if it were. Yes; your
vocation is clearly allegorical. Feminine to your finger-tips,
in this truly feminine predicament. We are all—*nous autres
femmes*—like the hero of the *White Ship*, who is described by
some delightful boy in an examination paper as being 'melted
by the shrieks of a near relation.'"

The Professor stumbled over a stone in the road, and
looked back at it vindictively.

"The near relation does so want to hold one's watch and
to stuff it into his mouth, and he shrieks so movingly if one
brutally removes one's property and person!"

"Alas! I am still a little bewildered by my late captivity.
I can't see the bearings of things."

"As allegory, you are as perfect as ever."

"I seem to be a sort of involuntary *Pilgrim's Progress!*"
he exclaimed.

"Ah, indeed!" cried Hadria, "and how the symbolism of
that old allegory would fit this subject!"

"With me for wretched hero, I suppose!"

"Your archetype;—with a little adaptation—yes, and
wonderfully little—the Slough of Despond, Doubting Castle,
the Valley of the Shadow of Death—they all fall into place.
Ah! the modern *Pilgrim's Progress* would read strangely and
significantly with woman as the pilgrim! But the end—that
would be a difficulty."

"One for your sex to solve," said the Professor.

When they arrived at the cottage the wails were dying

away, and Hadria advised that they should leave well alone.
So the baby's victim somewhat reluctantly retired.

"After all, you see, if one has strength of purpose, one *can*
achieve freedom," he observed.

"At the expense of the affections, it would seem," said
Hadria.

The walk was pursued towards Craddock.   Hadria said
she had to ask Dodge, the old gravedigger, if he could give
a few days' work in the garden at the Red House.

The Professor was walking for walking's sake.

"She is a pretty child, isn't she?" said Hadria.

"Very; an attractive mite; but she has a will of her own."

"Yes; I confess I have a moment of exultation when that
child sets up one of her passionate screams—the thrilling
shriek of a near relation!"

"Really, why?"

"She has to make her way in the world.   She must not be
too meek.   Her mother was a victim to the general selfishness and stupidity.   She was too gentle and obedient; too
apt to defer to others, to be able to protect herself.   I want
her child to be strengthened for the battle by a good long
draught of happiness, and to be armed with that stoutest of
all weapons—perfect health."

"You are very wise, Mrs. Temperley," murmured the
Professor.

"*Mon Dieu!* if one had always to judge for others and
never for oneself, what Solons we should all be!"

"I hear that you have taken the child under your protection.   She may think herself fortunate.   It is an act of real
charity."

Hadria winced.   "I fear not.   I have grown very much
attached to Martha now, poor little soul; but when I decided
to adopt her, I was in a state of red-hot fury."

"Against whom, may I ask?"

"Against the child's father," Hadria replied shortly.

CHAPTER XXVII.

"YES, mum, I see un go up to the churchyard. He's tidyin' up the place a bit for the weddin'."

"The wedding?" repeated Hadria vaguely. Mrs. Gullick looked at her as at one whose claims to complete possession of the faculties there seems sad reason to doubt.

"Oh, Miss Jordan's, yes. When is it?"

"Why, it's this mornin', ma'am!" cried Mrs. Gullick.

"Dear me, of course. I *thought* the village looked rather excited."

People were all standing at their doors, and the children had gathered at the gate of the church, with hands full of flowers. The wedding party was, it appeared, to arrive almost immediately. The children set up a shout as the first carriage was heard coming up the hill.

The bride appeared to be a popular character in Craddock. "Dear, dear, she will be missed, she will, she was a real lady, she was; did her duty too to rich *and* poor."

The Professor asked his companion if she remarked that the amiable lady was spoken of universally in the past tense, as some one who had passed from the light of day.

Hadria laughed. "Whenever I am in a cynical mood I come to Craddock and talk to the villagers."

Dodge was found resting on a broom-handle, with a flower in his button-hole. Marion Jordan had supplied him with port wine when he was "took bad" in the winter. Dodge found it of excellent quality. He approved of the institution of landed property, and had a genuine regard for the fair-haired, sweet-voiced girl who used to come in her pony-cart to

247

distribute her bounty to the villagers. Her class in the Sunday-school, as he remarked, was always the best behaved.

The new schoolmistress, a sour and uncompromising looking person, had issued from her cottage in her Sunday best to see the ceremony.

"That's where little Martha's mother used to live," said Hadria, "and that is where she died."

"Indeed, yes. I think Mr. Walker pointed it out to me."

"Ah! of course, and then you know the village of old."

"'Ere they comes!" announced a chorus of children's voices, as the first carriage drove up. The excitement was breathless. The occupants alighted and made their way to the church. After that, the carriages came in fairly quick succession. The bridegroom was criticised freely by the crowd. They did not think him worthy of his bride. "They du say as it was a made up thing," Dodge observed, "and that it wasn't '*im* as she'd like to go up to the altar with."

"Well, *I* don't sort o' take to 'im neither," Mrs. Gullick observed, sympathizing with the bride's feeling. "I do hope he'll be kind to the pore young thing; that I do."

"She wouldn't never give it 'im back; she's that good," another woman remarked.

"Who's the gentleman as she had set her heart on?" a romantic young woman enquired.

"Oh, it's only wot they say," said Dodge judicially; "it's no use a listening to all one hears—not by a long way."

"You 'ad it from Lord Engleton's coachman, didn't you?" prompted Mrs. Gullick.

"Which he heard it said by the gardener at Mr. Jordan's, as Miss Marion was always about with Mr. Fleming."

The murmur of interest at this announcement was drowned by the sound of carriage wheels. The bride had come.

"See the ideal and ethereal being whom you have been so faithfully impersonating all the afternoon!" exclaimed Hadria.

A fair, faint, admirably gentle creature, floating in a mist of tulle, was wafted out of the brougham, the spring sunshine burnishing the pale hair, and flashing a dazzling sword-like glance on the string of diamonds at her throat.

It seemed too emphatic, too keen a greeting for the faint ambiguous being, about to put the teaching of her girlhood, and her pretty hopes and faiths, to the test.

She gave a start and shiver as she stepped out into the brilliant day, turning with a half-scared look to the crowd of faces. It seemed almost as if she were seeking help in a blind, bewildered fashion.

Hadria had an impulse. "What would she think if I were to run down those steps and drag her away?" Professor Theobald shook his head.

Within the church, the procession moved up the aisle, to the sound of the organ. Hadria compared the whole ceremony to some savage rite of sacrifice: priest and people with the victim, chosen for her fairness, decked as is meet for victims.

"But she may be happy," Lady Engleton suggested when the ceremony was over, and the organ was pealing out the wedding march.

"That does not prevent the analogy. What a magnificent hideous thing the marriage-service is! and how exactly it expresses the extraordinary mixture of the noble and the brutal that is characteristic of our notions about these things!"

"The bride is certainly allowed to remain under no misapprehension as to her function," Lady Engleton admitted, with a laugh that grated on Hadria. Professor Theobald had fallen behind with Joseph Fleming, who had turned up among the crowd.

"But, after all, why mince matters?"

"Why indeed?" said Hadria. Lady Engleton seemed to have expected dissent.

"I think," she said, "that we are getting too squeamish nowadays as to speech. Women are so frightened to call a spade a spade."

"It is the *spade* that is ugly, not the name."

" But, my dear ? "

" Oh, it is not a question of squeamishness, it is the insult of the thing. One insult after another, and everyone stands round, looking respectable."

Lady Engleton laughed and said something to lead her companion on.

She liked to listen to Mrs. Temperley when she was thoroughly roused.

" It is the hideous mixture of the delicately civilised with the brutally savage that makes one sick. A frankly barbarous ceremony, where there was no pretence of refinement and propriety and so forth, would be infinitely less revolting."

" Which your language is plain," observed Lady Engleton, much amused.

" I hope so. Didn't you see how it all hurt that poor girl ? One of her training too—suspended in mid air—not an earthward glance. You know Mrs. Jordan's views on the education of girls. Poor girls. They are morally skinned, in such a way as to make contact with Fact a veritable torture, and then suddenly they are sent forth defenceless into Life to be literally curry-combed."

" They adjust themselves," said Lady Engleton.

" Adjust themselves ! " Hadria vindictively flicked off the head of a dandelion with her parasol. " They awake to find they have been living in a Fool's Paradise—a little upholstered corner with stained glass windows and rose-coloured light. They find that suddenly they are expected to place in the centre of their life everything that up to that moment they have scarcely been allowed even to know about ; they find that they must obediently veer round, with the amiable adaptability of a well-oiled weather-cock. Every instinct, every prejudice must be thrown over. All the effects of their training must be instantly overcome. And all this with perfect subjection and cheerfulness, on pain of moral avalanches and deluges, and heaven knows what convulsions of conventional nature ! "

"There certainly is some curious incongruity in our training," Lady Engleton admitted.

"Incongruity! Think what it means for a girl to have been taught to connect the idea of something low and evil with that which nevertheless is to lie at the foundation of all her after life. That is what it amounts to, and people complain that women are not logical."

Lady Engleton laughed. "Fortunately things work better in practice than might be expected, judging them in the abstract. How bashful Professor Theobald seems suddenly to have become! Why doesn't he join us, I wonder? However, so much the better; I do like to hear you talk heresy."

"I do more than talk it, I *mean* it," said Hadria. "I fail utterly to get at the popular point of view."

"But you misrepresent it—there *are* modifying facts in the case"

"I don't see them. Girls are told: 'So and so is not a nice thing for you to talk about. Wait, however, until the proper signal is given, and then woe betide you if you don't cheerfully accept it as your bounden duty.' If *that* does not enjoin abject slavishness and deliberate immorality of the most cold-blooded kind, I simply don't know what does."

Lady Engleton seemed to ponder somewhat seriously, as she stood looking down at the grave beside her.

"How we ever came to have tied ourselves into such an extraordinary mental knot is what bewilders me," Hadria continued, "and still more, why it is that we all, by common consent, go on acting and talking as if the tangled skein ran smooth and straight through one's fingers."

"Chiefly, perhaps, because women won't speak out," suggested Lady Engleton.

"They have been so drilled," cried Hadria, "so gagged, so deafened, by 'the shrieks of near relations.'"

Lady Engleton was asking for an explanation, when the

wedding-bells began to clang out from the belfry, merry and roughly rejoicing. "Tom-boy bells," Hadria called them. They seemed to tumble over one another and pick themselves up again, and give chase, and roll over in a heap, and then peal firmly out once more, laughing at their romping digression, joyous and thoughtless and simple-hearted. ."Evidently without the least notion what they are celebrating," said Hadria.

The bride came out of church on her husband's arm. The children set up a shout. Hadria and Lady Engleton, and, farther back, Professor Theobald and Joseph Fleming, could see the two figures pass down to the carriage and hear the carriage drive away. Hadria drew a long breath.

"I am afraid she was in love with Joseph Fleming," remarked Lady Engleton. "I hoped at one time that he cared for her, but that Irish friend of Marion's, Katie O'Halloran, came on the scene and spoilt my little romance."

"I wonder why she married this man? I wonder why the wind blows?" was added in self-derision at the question.

The rest of the party were now departing. "O sleek wedding guests," Hadria apostrophized them, "how solemnly they sat there, like all-knowing sphinxes, watching, watching, and that child so helpless—handcuffed, manacled! How many prayers will be offered at the shrine of the goddess of Duty within the next twelve months!"

Mrs. Jordan, a British matron of solid proportions, passed down the path on the arm of a comparatively puny cavalier. The sight seemed to stir up some demon in Hadria's bosom. Fantastic, derisive were her comments on that excellent lady's most cherished principles, and on her well-known and much-vaunted mode of training her large family of daughters.

"Only the traditional ideas carried out by a woman of narrow mind and strong will," said Lady Engleton.

"Oh those traditional ideas! They might have issued fresh and hot from an asylum for criminal lunatics."

"You are deliciously absurd, Hadria."

"It is the criminal lunatics who are absurd," she retorted. "Do you remember how those poor girls used to bewail the restrictions to their reading?"

"Yes, it was really a *reductio ad absurdum* of our system. The girls seemed afraid to face anything. They would rather die than think. (I wonder why Professor. Theobald lingers so up there by the chancel? The time must be getting on.)"

Hadria glanced towards him and made no comment. She was thinking of Mrs. Jordan's daughters.

"What became of their personality all that time I cannot imagine : their woman's nature that one hears so much about, and from which such prodigious feats were to be looked for, in the future."

"Yes, *that* is where the inconsistency of a girl's education strikes me most," said Lady Engleton. "If she were intended for the cloister one could understand it. But since she is brought up for the express purpose of being married, it does seem a little absurd not to prepare her a little more for her future life."

"Exactly," cried Hadria, "if the orthodox are really sincere in declaring that life to be so sacred and desirable, why on earth don't they treat it frankly and reverently and teach their girls to understand and respect it, instead of allowing a furtive, sneaky, detestable spirit to hover over it?"

"Yes, I agree with you there," said Lady Engleton.

"And if they *don't* really in their hearts think it sacred and so on (and how they *can*, under our present conditions, I fail to see), why do they deliberately bring up their girls to be married, as they bring up their sons to a profession? It is inconceivable, and yet good people do it, without a suspicion of the real nature of their conduct, which it wouldn't be polite to describe."

Mrs. Jordan—her face irradiated with satisfaction—was acknowledging the plaudits of the villagers, who shouted more or less in proportion to the eye-filling properties of the departing guests.

Hadria was seized with a fit of laughter. It was an awkward fact, that she never could see Mrs. Jordan's majestic form and noble bonnet without feeling the same overwhelming impulse to laugh.

"This is disgraceful conduct !" cried Lady Engleton.

Hadria was clearly in one of her most reckless moods to-day.

"You have led me on, and must take the consequences !" she cried. "Imagine," she continued with diabolical delibera- tion, "if Marion, on any day *previous* to this, had gone to her mother and expressed an overpowering maternal instinct—a deep desire to have a child !"

"Good heavens !" exclaimed Lady Engleton.

"Why so shocked, since it is so holy?"

"But that is different."

"Ah ! then it is holy only when the social edict goes forth, and proclaims the previous evil good and the previous good evil."

"Come, come; the inconsistency is not quite so bad as that. (How that man does dawdle !) "

Hadria shrugged her shoulders. "It seems to me so ; for now suppose, on the other hand, that this same Marion, on any day *subsequent* to this, should go to that same mother, and announce an exactly opposite feeling—a profound objection to the maternal function—how would she be received? Heavens, with what pained looks, with what platitudes and proverbs, with what reproofs and axioms and sentiments ! She would issue forth from that interview like another St. Sebastian, stuck all over with wounds and arrows. 'Sacred mission,' 'tenderest joy,' 'holiest mission,' 'highest vocation'—one knows the mellifluous phrases."

"But after all she would be wrong in her objection. The instinct is a true one," said Lady Engleton.

"Oh, then why should she be pelted for expressing it previously, if the question is not indiscreet?"

"Well, it would seem rather gruesome, if girls were to be overpowered with that passion."

"So we are all to be horribly shocked at the presence of an instinct to-day, and then equally shocked and indignant at its absence to-morrow; our sentiment being determined by the performance or otherwise of the ceremony we have just witnessed. It really shows a touching confidence in the swift adaptability of the woman's sentimental organization !"

Lady Engleton gave an uneasy laugh, and seemed lost in uncomfortable thought. She enjoyed playing with unorthodox speculations, but she objected to have her customary feelings interfered with, by a reasoning which she did not see her way to reduce to a condition of uncertainty. She liked to leave a question delicately balanced, enjoying all the fun of "advanced" thought without endangering her favourite sentiments. Like many women of talent, she was intensely maternal, in the instinctive sense ; and for that reason had a vague desire to insist on all other women being equally so ; but the notion of the instinct becoming importunate in a girl revolted her ; a state of mind that struggled to justify itself without conscious entrenchment behind mere tradition. Lady Engleton sincerely tried to shake off prejudice.

"You are in a mixed condition of feeling, I see," Hadria said. "I am not surprised. Our whole scheme of things indeed is so mixed, that the wonder only is we are not all in a state of chronic lunacy. I believe, as a matter of fact, that we *are;* but as we are all lunatics together, there is no one left to put us into asylums."

Lady Engleton laughed.

" The present age is truly a strange one," she exclaimed.

" Do you think so ? It always seems to me that the present age is finding out for the first time how very strange all the *other* ages have been."

" However that may be, it seems to me, that a sort of shiver is going through all Society, as if it had suddenly become very much aware of things and couldn't make them out—nor itself."

" Like a creature beginning to struggle through a bad illness. I do think it is all extremely remarkable, especially the bad illness."

" You are as strange as your epoch," cried Lady Engleton.

" It is a sorry sign when one remarks health instead of disease."

" Upon my word, you have a wholesome confidence in yourself ! "

" I do not, in that respect, differ from my kind," Hadria returned calmly.

" It is that which *was* that seems to you astonishing, not that which is to be," Lady Engleton commented, pensively.   " For my part I confess I am frightened, almost terrified at times, at that which is to be."

" I am frightened, terrified, so that the thought becomes unbearable, at that which *is*," said Hadria.

There was a long silence.   Lady Engleton appeared to be again plunged in thought.

" The maternal instinct—yes ; it seems to be round that unacknowledged centre that the whole storm is raging."

" A desperate question that Society shrinks from in terror : whether women shall be expected to conduct themselves as if the instinct had been weighed out accurately, like weekly stores, and given to all alike, or whether choice and individual feeling is to be held lawful in this matter—*there* is the red-hot heart of the battle."

" Remember men of science are against freedom in this respect.   (I do wish *our* man of science would make haste.)"

" They rush to the rescue when they see the sentimental defences giving way," said Hadria.   " If the 'sacred privilege' and 'noblest vocation' safeguards won't hold, science must throw up entrenchments."

" I prefer the more romantic and sentimental presentment of the matter," said Lady Engleton.

"Naturally. Ah! it is pathetic, the way we have tried to make things decorative; but it won't hold out much longer. Women are driving their masters to plain speaking—the ornaments are being dragged down. And what do we find? Bare and very ugly fact. And if we venture to hint that this unsatisfactory skeleton may be modified in form, science becomes stern. She wishes things, in this department, left as they are. Women are made for purposes of reproduction; let them clearly understand that. No picking and choosing."

"Men pick and choose, it is true," observed Lady Engleton in a musing tone, as if thinking aloud.

"Ah, but that's different—a real scientific argument, though a superficial observer might not credit it. At any rate, it is quite sufficiently scientific for this particular subject. Our leaders of thought don't bring out their Sunday-best logic on this question. They lounge in dressing-gown and slippers. One gets to know the oriental pattern of that dressing-gown and the worn-down heels of those old slippers."

"They may be right though, notwithstanding their logic," said Lady Engleton.

"By good luck, not good guidance. I wonder what her Serene Highness Science would say if she heard us?"

"That we two ignorant creatures are very presumptuous."

"Yes, people always fall back on that, when they can't refute you."

Lady Engleton smiled.

"I should like to hear the question discussed by really competent persons. (Well, if luncheon is dead cold it will be his own fault.)"

"Oh, really competent persons will tell us all about the possibilities of woman: her feelings, desires, capabilities, and limitations, now and for all time to come. And the wildly funny thing is that women are ready, with open mouths, to reverently swallow this male verdict on their inherent nature, as if it were gospel divinely inspired. I may appear a little

inconsistent," Hadria added with a laugh, "but I do think
women are fools!"

They had strolled on along the path till they came to the
schoolmistress's grave, which was green and daisy-covered, as
if many years had passed since her burial. Hadria stood, for
a moment, looking down at it.

"Fools, fools, unutterable, irredeemable fools!" she burst
out.

"My dear, my dear, we are in a churchyard," remonstrated
Lady Engleton, half laughing.

"We are at this grave," said Hadria.

"The poor woman would have been among the first to
approve of the whole scheme, though it places her here
beneath the daisies."

"Exactly. Am I not justified then in crying 'fool'?
Don't imagine that I exclude myself," she added.

"I think you might be less liable to error if you *were*
rather more of a fool, if I may say so," observed Lady
Engleton.

"Oh error! I daresay. One can guard against that, after
a fashion, by never making a stretch after truth. And the
reward comes, of its kind. How green the grave is. The
grass grows so fast on graves."

Lady Engleton could not bear a churchyard. It made one
think too seriously.

"Oh, you needn't unless you like!" said Hadria with a
laugh. "Indeed a churchyard might rather teach us what
nonsense it is to take things seriously—our little affairs.
This poor woman, a short while ago, was dying of grief and
shame and agony, and the village was stirred with excitement,
as if the solar system had come to grief. It all seemed so
stupendous and important, yet now—look at that tall grass
waving in the wind!"

CHAPTER XXVIII.

PROFESSOR THEOBALD had been engaged, for the last ten minutes, in instructing Joseph Fleming and a few stragglers, among whom was Dodge, in the characteristics of ancient architecture. He was pointing out the fine Norman window of the south transept, Joseph nodding wearily, Dodge leaning judicially on his broom and listening with attention. Joseph, as Lady Engleton remarked, was evidently bearing the Normans a bitter grudge for making interesting arches. The Professor seemed to have no notion of tempering the wind of his instruction to the shorn lambs of his audience.

"I *can't* understand why he does not join us," said Lady Engleton. "It must be nearly luncheon time. However, it doesn't much matter, as everyone seems to be up here. I wonder," she went on after a pause, "what the bride would think if she had heard our conversation this morning ! "

"Probably she would recognize many a half-thought of her own," said Hadria.

Lady Engleton shook her head.

"They alarm me, all these ideas. For myself, I feel bound to accept the decision of wise and good men, who have studied social questions deeply."

Personal feeling had finally overcome her desire to fight off the influence of tradition.

"I do not feel competent to judge in a matter so complex, and must be content to abide by the opinions of those who have knowledge and experience."

Lady Engleton thus retreated hastily behind cover. That was a strategic movement always available in difficulties, and it left one's companion in speculation alone in the open, arrogantly sustaining an eagle-gaze in the sun's face. The

259

advantages of feminine humility were obvious. One could come out for a skirmish and then run for shelter, in awkward moments. No woman ought to venture out on the bare plain without a provision of the kind.

Hadria had a curious sensation of being so exposed, when Lady Engleton retreated behind her "good and wise men," and she had the usual feminine sense of discomfort in the feeling of presumption that it produced. Heredity asserted itself, as it will do, in the midst of the fray, just when its victim seems to have shaken himself free from the mysterious obsession. But Hadria did not visibly flinch. Lady Engleton received the impression that Mrs. Temperley was too sure of her own judgment to defer even to the wisest.

She experienced a pleasant little glow of humility, wrapping herself in it, as in a protecting garment, and unconsciously comparing her more moderate and modest attitude favourably with her companion's self-confidence. Just at that moment, Hadria's self-confidence was gasping for breath. But her sense of the comic in her companion's tactics survived, and set her off in an apparently inconsequent laugh, which goaded Lady Engleton into retreating further, to an encampment of pure orthodoxy.

" I fear there is an element of the morbid, in all this fretful revolt against the old-established destiny of our sex," she said.

The advance-guard of Professor Theobald's party was coming up. The Professor himself still hung back, playing the Ancient Mariner to Joseph Fleming's Wedding Guest. Most unwilling was that guest, most pertinacious that mariner.

Hadria had turned to speak to Dodge, who had approached, broom in hand. "Seems only yesterday as we was a diggin' o' that there grave, don't it, mum?" he remarked pleasantly, including Hadria in the credit of the affair, with native generosity.

" It does indeed, Dodge. I see you have been tidying it up and clearing away the moss from the name. I can read it now. *Ellen Jervis.—Requiescat in pace.*"

" We was a wonderin' wot that meant, me and my missus."

Hadria explained.

"Oh indeed, mum. She didn't die in peace, whatever she be a doin' now, not *she* didn't, pore thing. I was jest a tellin' the gentleman" (Dodge indicated Professor Theobald with a backward movement of the thumb), "about the schoolmarm. He was talkin' like a sermon—beautiful—about the times wen the church was built; and about them as come over from France and beat the English—shameful thing for our soldiers, 'pears to me, not as I believes all them tales. Mr. Walker says as learnin' is a pitfall, wich I don't swaller everything as Mr. Walker says neither. Seems to me as it don't do to be always believin' wot's told yer, or there's no sayin' wot sort o' things you wouldn't come to find inside o' yer, before you'd done."

Hadria admitted the danger of indiscriminate absorption, but pointed out that if caution were carried too far, one might end by finding nothing inside of one at all, which also threatened to be attended with inconvenience.

Dodge seemed to feel that the *désagréments* in this last case were trivial as compared with those of the former.

"Dodge is a born sceptic," said Lady Engleton. "What would you say, Dodge, if some tiresome, reasonable person were to come and point out something to you that you couldn't honestly deny, and yet that seemed to upset all the ideas that you had felt were truest and best?"

Dodge scratched his head. "I should say as what he said wasn't true," replied Dodge.

"But if you couldn't help seeing that it was true?"

"That ud be arkard," Dodge admitted.

"Then what would you do?"

Dodge leant upon the broom-handle, apparently in profound thought. His words were waited for.

"I think," he announced at last, "as I shouldn't do nothin' partic'lar."

"Dodge, you really are an oracle!" Hadria exclaimed. "What could more simply describe the action of our Great Majority?"

"You are positively impish in your mood to-day!" exclaimed Lady Engleton. "What should we do without our Great

Majority, as you call it? It is absolutely necessary to put some curb on the wild impulses of pure reason "—a sentiment that Hadria greeted with chuckles of derision.

Joseph Fleming was looking longingly towards the grave, but his face was resigned, for the Ancient Mariner had him button-holed securely.

"What *are* they lingering for so long, I wonder?" cried Lady Engleton impatiently. "Professor Theobald is really too instructive to-day. I will go and hurry him."

Joseph welcomed her as his deliverer.

"I was merely waiting for you two ladies to move; I would have come on with Mr. Fleming. I am extremely sorry," said the Professor.

He followed Lady Engleton down the path between the graves, with something of the same set expression that had been on his face when he came up the path of the cottage garden to admire the baby.

"It appears that we were all waiting for each other," said Lady Engleton.

"This 'ere's the young woman's grave, sir—Ellen Jervis— 'er as I was a tellin' you of," said Dodge, pointing an earth-stained finger at the mound.

"Oh, yes; very nice," said the Professor vaguely. Hadria's laugh disconcerted him. "I mean—pretty spot—well chosen —well made."

Hadria continued to laugh. "I never heard less skilled comment on a grave!" she exclaimed. "It might be a pagoda!"

"It's not so easy as you seem to imagine to find distinctive epithets. I challenge you. Begin with the pagoda."

"One of the first canons of criticism is never to attempt the feat yourself; jeer rather at others."

"The children don't like the new schoolmarm near so well as this 'un," observed Dodge, touching the grave with his broom. "Lord, it was an unfort'nate thing, for there wasn't a better girl nor she were in all Craddock (as I was a tellin' of you, sir), not when she fust come as pupil teacher. It was all along of her havin' no friends, and her mother far away.

She used to say to me at times of an afternoon wen she was a passin' through the churchyard —'Dodge,' says she, 'do you know I have no one to care for, or to care for me, in all the world?' I used to comfort her like, and say as there was plenty in Craddock as cared for her, but she always shook her head, sort o' sad."

"Poor thing !" Lady Engleton exclaimed.

"And one mornin' a good time after, I found her a cryin' bitter, just there by her own grave, much about where the gentleman 'as his foot at this moment" (the Professor quickly withdrew it). "It was in the dusk o' the evenin', and she was a settin' on the rail of old Squire Jordan's grave, jes' where you are now, sir. We were sort o' friendly, and wen I heard 'er a taking on so bad, I jes' went and stood alongside, and I sez, 'Wy Ellen Jervis,' I sez, 'wot be you a cryin' for?' But she kep' on sobbin' and wouldn't answer nothin'. So I waited, and jes' went on with my work a bit, and then I sez again, 'Ellen Jervis, wot be you a cryin' for?' And then she took her hands from her face and she sez, 'Because I am that miserable,' sez she, and she broke out cryin' wuss than ever. 'Dear, dear,' I sez, 'wot is it? Can't somebody do nothin' for you?'

"'No; nobody in the world can help me, and nobody wants to; it would be better if I was under there.' And she points to the ground just where she lies now—I give you my word she did—and sure enough, before another six months had gone by, there she lay under the sod, 'xacly on the spot as she had pointed to. She was a sinner, there's no denyin', but she 'ad to suffer for it more nor most."

"Very sad," observed Professor Theobald nervously, with a glance at Hadria, as if expecting derision.

"It is a hard case," said Lady Engleton, "but I suppose error *has* to be paid for."

"Well, I don't know 'xacly," said Dodge, "it depends."

"On the sex," said Hadria.

"I have known them as spent all their lives a' injurin' of others, and no harm seemed to come to 'em. And I've seed them as wouldn't touch a fly and always doin' their neighbours a kind turn, wot never 'ad a day's luck."

"Let us hope it will be made up in the next world," said Lady Engleton. Dodge hoped it would, but there was something in the turn of his head that seemed to denote a disposition to base his calculations on this, rather than on the other world. He was expected home by his wife, at this hour, so wishing the company good day, and pocketing the Professor's gratuity with a gleam of satisfaction in his shrewd and honest face, he trudged off with his broom down the path, and out by the wicket-gate into the village street.

"I never heard that part of the story before," said Lady Engleton, when the gravedigger had left.

It was new to everybody. "It brings her nearer, makes one realize her suffering more painfully."

Hadria was silent.

Professor Theobald cast a quick, scrutinizing glance at her.

"I can understand better now how you were induced to take the poor child, Mrs. Temperley," Lady Engleton remarked.

They were strolling down the path, and Professor Theobald was holding open the gate for his companions to pass through. His hand seemed to shake slightly.

"I don't enjoy probing my motives on that subject," said Hadria.

"Why? I am sure they were good."

"I can't help hoping that that child may live to avenge her mother; to make some man know what it is to be horribly miserable—but, oh, I suppose it's like trying to reach the feelings of a rhinoceros!"

"There you are much mistaken, Mrs. Temperley," said the Professor. "Men are as sensitive, in some respects, as women."

"So much the better."

"Then do you think it quite just to punish one man for the sin of another?"

"No; but there is a deadly feud between the sexes: it is

a hereditary vendetta : the duty of vengeance is passed on from generation to generation."

"Oh, Mrs. Temperley!" Lady Engleton's tone was one of reproach.

"Yes, it is vindictive, I know ; one does not grow tender towards the enemy at the grave of Ellen Jervis."

"At least, there were *two* sinners, not only one."

"Only one dies of a broken heart."

"But why attempt revenge ? "

"Oh, a primitive instinct. And anything is better than this meek endurance, this persistent heaping of penalties on the scapegoat."

"No good ever came of mere revenge, however," said Professor Theobald.

"Sometimes that is the only form of remonstrance that is listened to," said Hadria. "When people have the law in their own hands and Society at their back, they can afford to be deaf to mere verbal protest."

"As for the child," said Lady Engleton, "she will be in no little danger of a fate like her mother's."

Hadria's face darkened.

"At least then, she shall have some free and happy hours first ; at least she shall not be driven to it by the misery of moral starvation, starvation of the affections. She shall be protected from the solemn fools—with sawdust for brains and a mechanical squeaker for heart—who, on principle, cut off from her mother all joy and all savour in life, and then punished her for falling a victim to the starved emotional condition to which they had reduced her."

"The matter seems complex," said Lady Engleton, "and I don't see how revenge comes in."

"It is a passion that has never been eradicated. Oh, if I could but find that man ! "

"A man is a hard thing to punish,—unless he is in love with one."

"Well, let him be in love ! " cried Hadria fiercely.

CHAPTER XXIX.

THE sound of music stole over the gardens of the Priory, at sunset. It was the close of one of the most exquisite days of Spring. A calm had settled over the country with the passing away of the sun-god. His attendant winds and voices had been sacrificed on his funeral pyre.

Two figures sat on the terrace by the open window of the drawing-room, listening to the utterance, in music, of a tumultuous, insurgent spirit. In Professor Fortescue, the musical passion was deeply rooted, as it is in most profoundly sympathetic and tender natures. Algitha anxiously watched the effect of her sister's playing on her companion.

The wild power of the composer was not merely obvious, it was overwhelming. It was like "a sudden storm among mountains," "the wind-swept heavens at midnight," "the lonely sea": he struggled for the exactly-fitting simile. There was none, because of its many-sidedness. Loneliness remained as an ever-abiding quality. There were moon-glimpses and sun-bursts over the scenery of the music; there was sweetness, and a vernal touch that thrilled the listeners as with the breath of flowers and the fragrance of earth after rain, but always, behind all fancy and grace and tenderness, and even passion, lurked that spectral loneliness. The performer would cease for some minutes, and presently begin again in a new mood. The music was always characteristic, often wild and strange, yet essentially sane.

"There is a strong Celtic element in it," said the Professor. "This is a very wonderful gift. I suppose one never does really know one's fellows: her music to-night reveals to me new sides of Hadria's character."

"I confess they alarm me," said Algitha.

"Truly, this is not the sort of power that can be safely shut up and stifled. It is the sort of power for which everything ought to be set aside. That is my impression of it."

"I am worried about Hadria," Algitha said. "I know her better than most people, and I know how hard she takes things and what explosive force that musical instinct of hers has. Yet, it is impossible, as things are, for her to give it real utterance. She can only open the furnace door now and then."

The Professor shook his head gravely. "It won't do : it isn't safe. And why should such a gift be lost?"

"That's what I say! Yet what is to be done? There is no one really to blame. As for Hubert, I am sorry for him. He had not the faintest idea of Hadria's character, though she did her best to enlighten him. It is hard for him (since he feels it so) and it is desperate for her. You are such an old friend, that I feel I may speak to you about it. You see what is going on, and I know it is troubling you as it does me."

"It is indeed. If I am not very greatly mistaken, here is real musical genius of the first order, going to waste : strong forces being turned in upon the nature, to its own destruction ; and, as you say, it seems as if nothing could be done. It is the more ironically cruel, since Hubert is himself musical."

"Oh, yes, but in quite a different way. His fetish is good taste, or what he thinks such. Hadria's compositions set his teeth on edge. His nature is conventional through and through. He fears adverse comment more than any earthly thing. And yet the individual opinions that compose the general 'talk' that he so dreads, are nothing to him. He despises them heartily. But he would give his soul (and particularly Hadria's) rather than incur a whisper from people collectively."

"That is a very common trait. If we feared only the opinions that we respect, our fear would cover but a small area."

The music stole out again through the window. The thoughts of the listeners were busy. It was not until quite lately that Professor Fortescue had fully realised the nature of Hadria's present surroundings. It had taken all his acuteness and his sympathy to enable him to perceive the number and strength of the little threads that hampered her spontaneity. As she said, they were made of heart-strings. A vast spider's web seemed to spread its tender cordage round each household, for the crippling of every winged creature within its radius. Fragments of torn wings attested the struggles that had taken place among the treacherous gossamer.

"And the maddening thing is," cried Algitha, "that there is nobody to swear at. Swearing at systems and ideas, as Hadria says, is a Barmecide feast to one's vindictiveness."

"It is the tyranny of affection that has done so much to ruin the lives of women," the Professor observed, in a musing tone.

Then after a pause : "I fear your poor mother has never got over *your* little revolt, Algitha."

"Never, I am sorry to say. If I had married and settled in Hongkong, she would scarcely have minded, but as it is, she feels deserted. Of course the boys are away from home more than I am, yet she is not grieved at that. You see how vast these claims are. Nothing less than one's entire life and personality will suffice."

"Your mother feels that you are throwing your life away, remember. But truly it seems, sometimes, as if people were determined to turn affection into a curse instead of a blessing!"

"I never think of it in any other light," Algitha announced serenely.

The Professor laughed. "Oh, there are exceptions, I hope," he said. "Love, like everything else that is great, is very, very rare. We call the disposition to usurp and absorb another person by that name, but woe betide him or her who is the object of such a sentiment. Yet happily, the real thing *is* to be found now and again. And from that arises freedom."

Hadria was playing some joyous impromptu, which seemed to express the very spirit of Freedom herself.

"I think Hadria has something of the gipsy in her," said

Algitha. "She is so utterly and hopelessly unfitted to be the wife of a prim, measured, elegant creature like Hubert—good fellow though he is—and to settle down for life at Craddock Dene."

"Yes," returned the Professor, "it has occurred to me, more than once, that there must be a drop of nomad blood some-where among the ancestry."

"Hadria always says herself, that she is a vagabond in disguise."

He laughed. Then, as he drew out a tobacco-pouch from his pocket and proceeded to light his pipe, he went on, in quiet meditative fashion, as if thinking aloud: "The fact of the matter is, that in this world, the dead weight of the mass bears heavily upon the exceptional natures. It comes home to one vividly, in cases like this. The stupidity and blindness of each individual goes to build up the dead wall, the impassable obstacle, for some other spirit. The burden that we have cast upon the world has to be borne by our fellow man or woman, and perhaps is doomed to crush a human soul."

"It seems to me that most people are engaged in that crushing industry," said Algitha with a shrug. "Don't I know their bonnets, and their frock-coats and their sneers!"

The Professor smiled. He thought that most of us were apt to take that attitude at times. The same spirit assumed different forms. "While we are sneering at our fellow mortal, and assuring him loftily that he can certainly prevail, if only he is strong enough, it may be *our* particular dulness or *our* hardness that is dragging him down to a tragic failure, before our eyes."

The sun was low when the player came out to the terrace and took her favourite seat on the parapet. The gardens were steeped in profound peace. One could hear no sound for miles round. The broad country made itself closely felt by its stirring silence. The stretches of fields beyond fields, the woodlands in their tender green, the long, long sweep of the quiet land, formed a benign circle round the garden, and led the sense of peace out and out to the horizon, where the liquid light of the sky touched the hills.

The face of the Professor had a transparent look and a

singular beauty of expression, such as is seen on the faces of
the dead, or on the faces of those who are carried beyond
themselves by some generous enthusiasm.

They watched, in silence, the changes creeping over the
heavens, the subtle transmutations of tint; the fairylands of
cloud, growing like dreams, and melting in golden annihilation; the more delicate and exquisite, the sooner the end.

The first pale hints of splendour had spread, till the whole
West was throbbing with the radiance. But it was short-
lived. The soul of the light, with its vital vibrating quality,
seemed to die, and then slowly the glow faded, till every
sparkle was gone, and the amphitheatre of the sky lay cold,
and dusk, and empty. It was not till the last gleam had
melted away that a word was spoken.

"It is like a prophecy," said Hadria.

"To-morrow the dawn, remember."

Hadria's thoughts ran on in the silence.

The dawn? Yes; but all that lost splendour, those winged
islands, those wild ranges of mountain where the dreams
dwell; to-morrow's dawn brings no resurrection for them.
Other pageants there will be, other cloud-castles, but never
again just those.

Had the Professor been following her thoughts?

"Life," he said, "offers her gifts as the Sibyl her books;
they grow fewer as we refuse them."

"Ah! that is the truth that clamours in my brain, warning
and pointing to an empty temple, like the deserted sky, a
little while ahead."

"Be warned then."

"Ah! but what to do? I am out of myself now with the
spring; there are so many benign influences. I too have
winged islands, and wild ranges where the dreams dwell; life
is a fairy-tale; but there is always that terror of the departure
of the sun."

"*Carpe diem.*"

Hadria turned a startled and eager face towards the Professor, who was leaning back in his chair, thoughtfully smoking. The smoke curled away serenely through the calm air of the evening.

"You have a great gift," he said.

"One is afraid of taking a thing too seriously because it is one's own."

The Professor turned almost angrily.

"Good heavens, what does it matter whose it is? There may be a sort of inverted vanity in refusing fair play to a power, on that ground. Alas! here is one of the first morbid signs of the evil at work upon you. If you had been wholesomely moving and striving in the right direction, do you think you would have been guilty of that piece of egotism?"

"Vanity pursues one into hidden corners of the mind. I am so used to that sort of spirit among women. Apparently I have caught the infection."

"I would not let it go farther," advised the Professor.

"To do myself justice, I think it is superficial," said Hadria with a laugh. "I would dare anything, *any*thing for a chance of freedom, for ——," she broke off, hesitating. "I remember once—years ago, when I was quite a girl—seeing a young ash-tree that had got jammed into a chink so that it couldn't grow straight, or spread, as its inner soul, poor stripling, evidently inspired it to grow. Outside, there were hundreds of upright, vigorous, healthful young trees, fulfilling that innate idea in apparent gladness, and with obvious general advantage, since they were growing into sound, valuable trees, straight of trunk, nobly developed. I felt like the poor sapling in the cranny, that had just the same natural impetus of healthy growth as all the others, but was forced to become twisted, and crooked, and stunted and wretched. I think most women have to grow in a cranny. It is generally known as their Sphere." Algitha gave an approving chuckle. "I noticed," Hadria added, "that the desperate struggle to grow of that young tree had begun to loosen the masonry of the edifice that cramped it. There was a great dangerous-looking crack right across the building.

The tree was not saved from deformity, *but* it had its revenge! Some day that noble institution would come down by the run."

"Yes. Well, the thing to do is to get out of it," said the Professor.

"You really advise that?"

"Advise? One dare not advise. It is too perilous. No general theories will hold in all instances."

"Tell me," said Hadria, "what are the qualities in a human being that make him most serviceable, or least harmful?"

"What qualities?" Professor Fortescue watched the smoke of his pipe curling away, as if he expected to find the answer in its coils. He answered slowly, and with an air of reflection.

"Mental integrity, and mercy. A resolute following of reason (in which I should include insight) to its conclusion, though the heavens fall, and an unfailing fellow-feeling for the pain and struggle and heartache and sin that life is so full of. But one must add the quality of imagination. Without imagination and its fruits, the world would be a howling wilderness."

"I wish you would come down with me, some day, to the East End and hold out the hand of fellowship to some of the sufferers there," cried Algitha. "I am, at times, almost in despair at the mass of evil to be fought against, but somehow you always make me feel, Professor, that the race has all the qualities necessary for redemption enfolded within itself."

"But assuredly it has!" cried the Professor. "And assuredly those redeeming qualities will germinate. Otherwise the race would extinguish itself in cruelty and corruption. Let people talk as they please about the struggle for existence, it is through the development of the human mind and the widening of human mercy that better things will come."

"One sees, now and then, in a flash, what the world may some day be," said Hadria. "The vision comes, perhaps, with the splendour of a spring morning, or opens, scroll-like, in a flood of noble music. It sounds unreal, yet it brings a sense of conviction that is irresistible."

"I think it was Pythagoras who declared that the woes of men are the work of their own hands," said the Professor. "So are their joys. Nothing ever shakes my belief that what the mind of man can imagine, that it can achieve."

"But there are so many pulling the wrong way," said Algitha sadly.

"Ah, one man may be miserable through the deeds of others; the race can only be miserable through its own."

After a pause, Algitha put a question : How far was it justifiable to give pain to others in following one's own idea of right and reasonable ? How far might one attempt to live a life of intellectual integrity and of the widest mercy that one's nature would stretch to ?

Professor Fortescue saw no limits but those of one's own courage and ability. Algitha pointed out that in most lives the limit occurred much sooner. If " others "—those tyrannical and absorbent " others "—had intricately bound up their notions of happiness with the prevention of any such endeavour, and if those notions were of the usual negative, home-comfort-and-affection order, narrowly personal, fruitful in nothing except a sort of sentimental egotism that spread over a whole family—what Hadria called an *egotism à douze*—how far ought these ideas to be respected, and at what cost ?

Professor Fortescue was unqualified in his condemnation of the sentiment which erected sacrificial altars in the family circle. He spoke scornfully of the doctrine of renunciation, so applied, and held the victims who brought their gifts of power and liberty more culpable than those who demanded them, since the duty of resistance to recognised wrong was obvious, while great enlightenment was needed to teach one to forego an unfair privilege or power that all the world concurred in pressing upon one.

"Then you think a person—even a feminine person— justified in giving pain by resisting unjust demands ? "

"I certainly think that all attempts to usurp another person's life on the plea of affection should be stoutly resisted. But I recognise that cases must often occur when resistance is practically impossible."

" One ought not to be too easily melted by the ' shrieks of a near relation,' " said Hadria. "Ah, I have a good mind to try. I don't fear any risk for myself, nor any work; the stake is worth it. I don't want to grow cramped and crooked, like my poor ash-tree. Perhaps this may be a form of vanity too ; I don't know, I was going to say I don't care."

The scent of young leaves and of flowers came up, soft and rich from the garden, and as Hadria leant over the parapet, a gust of passionate conviction of power swept over her ; not merely of her own personal power, but of some vast, flooding, beneficent well-spring from which her own was fed. And with the inrush, came a glimpse as of heaven itself.

"I wonder," she said after a long silence, "why it is that when we *know* for dead certain, we call it faith."

"Because, I suppose, our certainty is certainty only for ourselves. If you have found some such conviction to guide you in this wild world, you are very fortunate. We need all our courage and our strength—— "

"And just a little more," Hadria added.

"Yes ; sometimes just a little more, to save us from its worst pitfalls."

It struck both Hadria and her sister that the Professor was looking very ill and worn this evening.

"You are always giving help and sympathy to others, and you never get any yourself!" Hadria exclaimed.

But the Professor laughed, and asserted that he was being spoilt at Craddock Dene. They had risen, and were strolling down the yew avenue. A little star had twinkled out.

"I am very glad to have Professor Fortescue's opinion of your composition, Hadria. I was talking to him about you, and he quite agrees with me."

"What? that I ought to—— ?"

"That you ought not to go on as you are going on at present."

"But that is so vague."

"I suppose you have long ago tried all the devices of self-discipline?" said the Professor. "There are ways, of course, of arming oneself against minor difficulties, of living within a sort of citadel. Naturally much force has to go in keeping up the defences, but it is better than having none to keep up."

Hadria gave a quiet smile. "There is not a method, mental or other, that I have not tried, and tried hard. If it had not been for the sternest self-discipline, my mind at this moment, would be so honeycombed with small pre-occupations (pleasant and otherwise), that it would be incapable of consecutive ideas of any kind. As it is, I feel a miserable number of holes here"—she touched her brow—"a loss of absorbing power, at times, and a mental slackness that is really alarming. What remains of me has been dragged ashore as from a wreck, amidst a rush of wind and wave. But just now, thanks greatly to your sympathy and Algitha's, I seem restored to myself. I can never describe the rapture of that sensation to one who has never felt himself sinking down and down into darkness, to a dim hell, where the doom is a slow decay instead of the fiery pains of burning."

"This is all wrong, wrong!" cried the Professor anxiously.

"Ah! but I feel now, such certainty, such courage. It seems as if Fate were giving me one more chance. I have often run very close to making a definite decision—to dare everything rather than await this fool's disaster. But then comes that everlasting feminine humility, sneaking up with its simper: 'Is not this presumptuous, selfish, mistaken, wrong? What business have *you*, one out of so many, to break roughly through the delicate web that has been spun for your kindly detention?' Of course my retort is: 'What business have they to spin the web?' But one can never get up a real sense of injured innocence. It is always the spiders who seem injured and innocent. However, this time I am going to try, though the heavens fall!"

A figure appeared, in the dusk, at the further end of the avenue. It proved to be Miss Du Prel, who had come to find Hadria. Henriette had arrived unexpectedly by the late afternoon train, and Valeria had volunteered to announce her arrival to her sister-in-law.

"Ah!" exclaimed Hadria, "heaven helps him who helps himself! This will fit in neatly with my plans."

CHAPTER XXX.

VALERIA DU PREL, finding that. Miss Temperley proposed a visit of some length, returned to town by the early morning train.

"Valeria, do you know anyone in Paris to whom you could give me a letter of introduction?" Hadria asked, at the last moment, when there was just time to write the letter, and no more.

"Are you going to Paris?" Valeria asked, startled.

"Please write the letter and I will tell you some day what I want it for."

"Nothing very mad, I hope?"

"No, only a little—judiciously mad."

"Well, there is Madame Bertaux, in the Avenue Kleber, but her you know already. Let me see. Oh yes, Madame Vauchelet, a charming woman; very kind and very fond of young people. She is about sixty; a widow; her husband was in the diplomatic service."

Valeria made these hurried comments while writing the letter.

"She is musical too, and will introduce you, perhaps, to the great Joubert, and others of that set. You will like her, I am sure. She is one of the truly good people of this world. If you really are going to Paris, I shall feel happier if I know that Madame Vauchelet is your friend."

Sophia's successor announced that the pony-cart was at the door.

Miss Du Prel looked rather anxiously at Hadria and her sister-in-law, as they stood on the steps to bid her good-bye. There was a look of elation mixed with devilry, in Hadria's

276

face. The two figures turned and entered the house together, as the pony-cart passed through the gate.

Hadria always gave Miss Temperley much opportunity for the employment of tact, finding this tact more elucidating than otherwise to the designs that it was intended to conceal; it affected them in the manner of a magnifying-glass. About a couple of years ago, the death of her mother had thrown Henriette on her own resources, and set free a large amount of energy that cravèd a legitimate outlet. The family with whom she was now living in London, not being related to her, offered but limited opportunities.

Henriette's eye was fixed, with increasing fondness, upon the Red House. *There* lay the callow brood marked out by Nature and man, for her ministrations. With infinite adroitness, Miss Temperley questioned her sister-in-law, by inference and suggestion, about the affairs of the household. Hadria evaded the attempt, but rejoiced, for reasons of her own, that it was made. She began to find the occupation diverting, and characteristically did not hesitate to allow her critic to form most alarming conclusions as to the state of matters at the Red House. She was pensive, and mild, and a little surprised when Miss Temperley, with a suppressed gasp, urged that the question was deeply serious. It amused Hadria to reproduce, for Henriette's benefit, the theories regarding the treatment and training of children that she had found current among the mothers of the district.

Madame Bertaux happened to call during the afternoon, and that outspoken lady scoffed openly at these theories, declaring that women made idiots of themselves on behalf of their children, whom they preposterously ill-used with unflagging devotion.

"The moral training of young minds is such a problem," said Henriette, after the visitor had left, "it must cause you many an anxious thought."

Hadria arranged herself comfortably among cushions, and let every muscle relax.

"The boys are so young yet," she said drowsily. "I have no doubt that will all come, later on."

"But, my dear Hadria, unless they are trained now——"

"Oh, there is plenty of time!"

"Do you mean to say——?"

"Only what other people say. Nothing in the least original, I assure you. I see the folly and the inconvenience of that now. I have consulted hoary experience. I have sat reverently at the feet of old nurses. I have talked with mothers in the spirit of a disciple, and I have learnt, oh, so much!"

"Mothers are most anxious about the moral training of their little ones," said Henriette, in some bewilderment.

"Of course, but they don't worry about it so early. One can't expect accomplished morality from poor little dots of five and six. The charm of infancy would be gone."

Miss Temperley explained, remonstrated. Hadria was limp, docile, unemphatic. Perhaps Henriette was right, she didn't know. A sense of honour? (Hadria suppressed a smile.) Could one, after all, expect of six what one did not always get at six and twenty? Morals altogether seemed a good deal to ask of irresponsible youth. Henriette could not overrate the importance of early familiarity with the difference between right and wrong. Certainly it was important, but Hadria shrank from an extreme view. One must not rush into it without careful thought.

"But meanwhile the children are growing up!" cried Henriette, in despair.

Hadria had not found that experienced mothers laid much stress on that fact. Besides, there was considerable difficulty in the matter. Henriette did not see it. The difference between right and wrong could easily be taught to a child.

Perhaps so, but it seemed to be thought expedient to defer the lesson till the distant future; at least, if one might judge from the literature especially designed for growing minds, wherein clever villainy was exalted, and deeds of ferocious cruelty and revenge occurred as a daily commonplace among heroes. The same policy was indicated by the practice of allowing children to become familiar with the sight of slaughter, and of violence of every kind towards animals, from earliest infancy. Hadria concluded from all this, that it was thought wise to postpone the moral training of the young till a more convenient season.

Henriette looked at her sister-in-law, with a sad and baffled mien. Hadria's expression was solemn, and as much like that of Mrs. Walker as she could make it, without descending to obvious caricature.

"Do you think it quite wise, Henriette, to run dead against the customs of ages? Do you think it safe to ignore the opinion of countless generations of those who were older and wiser than ourselves?"

"Dear me, how you *have* changed!" cried Miss Temperley.

"Advancing years; the sobering effects of experience," Hadria explained. She was grieved to find Henriette at variance with those who had practical knowledge of education. As the child grew up, one could easily explain to him that the ideas and impressions that he might have acquired, in early years, were mostly wrong, and had to be reversed. That was quite simple. Besides, unless he were a born idiot of criminal tendencies, he was bound to find it out for himself.

"But, my dear Hadria, it is just the early years that are the impressionable years. Nothing can quite erase those first impressions."

"Oh, do you think so?" said Hadria mildly.

"Yes, indeed, I think so," cried Henriette, losing her temper.

"Oh, well of course you may be right."

Hadria had brought out a piece of embroidery (about ten years old), and was working peacefully.

On questions of hygiene, she was equally troublesome. She had taken hints, she said, from mothers of large families. Henriette laid stress upon fresh air, even in the house.

Hadria believed in fresh air; but was it not going a little far to have it in the house?

Henriette shook her head.

Fresh air was *always* necessary. In moderation, perhaps, Hadria admitted. But the utmost care was called for, to avoid taking cold. She laid great stress upon that. Children were naturally so susceptible. In all the nurseries that she had visited, where every possible precaution was taken against draughts, the children were incessantly taking cold.

"Perhaps the precautions made them delicate," Henriette suggested. But this paradox Hadria could not entertain. "Take care of the colds, and the fresh air will take care of itself," was her general maxim.

"But, my dear Hadria, do you mean to tell me that the people about here are so benighted as really not to understand the importance to the system of a constant supply of pure air?"

Hadria puckered up her brow, as if in thought. "Well," she said, "several mothers *have* mentioned it, but they take more interest in fluid magnesia and tonics."

Henriette looked dispirited.

At any rate, there was no reason why Hadria should not be more enlightened than her neighbours, on these points. Hadria shook her head deprecatingly. She hoped Henriette would not mind if she quoted the opinion of old Mr. Jordan, whose language was sometimes a little strong. He said that he didn't believe all that "damned nonsense about fresh air and drains!" Henriette coughed.

"It is certainly not safe to trust entirely to nurses, however devoted and experienced," she insisted. Hadria shrugged her shoulders. If the nurse *did* constitutionally enjoy a certain stuffiness in her nurseries—well the children were out half the day, and it couldn't do them much harm. (Hadria bent low over her embroidery.)

The night?

"Oh! then one must, of course, expect to be a little stuffy."

" But," cried Miss Temperley, almost hopeless, " impure air breathed, night after night, is an incessant drain on the strength, even if each time it only does a little harm."

Hadria smiled over her silken arabesques. "Oh, nobody ever objects to things that only do a little harm." There was a moment of silence.

Henriette thought that Hadria must indeed have changed very much during the last years. Well, of course, when very young, Hadria said, one had extravagant notions: one imagined all sorts of wild things about the purposes of the human brain: not till later did one realize that the average brain was merely an instrument of adjustment, a sort of spirit-level which enabled its owner to keep accurately in line with other people. Henriette ought to rejoice that Hadria had thus come to bow to the superiority of the collective wisdom.

But Henriette had her doubts.

Hadria carefully selected a shade of silk, went to the light to reassure herself of its correctness, and returned to her easy chair by the fire. Henriette resumed her knitting. She was making stockings for her nephews.

" Henriette, don't you think it would be rather a good plan if you were to come and live here and manage affairs—morals, manners, hygiene, and everything ? "

Henriette's needles stopped abruptly, and a wave of colour came into her face, and a gleam of sudden joy to her eyes.

" My dear, what do you mean ? "

" Hubert, of course, would be only too delighted to have you here, and I want to go away."

" For heaven's sake——"

" Not exactly for heaven's sake. For my own sake, I suppose : frankly selfish. It is, perhaps, the particular form that my selfishness takes—an unfortunately conspicuous form. So many of us can have a nice cosy pocket edition that doesn't show. However, that's not the point. I know you would be happier doing this than anything else, and that you would do it perfectly. You have the kind of talent, if I may say so, that

makes an admirable ruler. When it has a large political field
we call it 'administrative ability'; when it has a small
domestic one, we speak of it as 'good housekeeping.' It is a
precious quality, wherever it appears. You have no scope
for it at present."

Henriette was bewildered, horrified, yet secretly thrilled
with joy on her own account. Was there a quarrel? Had
any cloud come over the happiness of the home? Hadria
laughed and assured her to the contrary. But where was
she going, and for how long? What did she intend to do?
Did Hubert approve? And could she bear to be away
from her children? Hadria thought this was all beside the
point, especially as the boys were shortly going to school.
The question was, whether Henriette would take the charge.

Certainly, if Hadria came to any such mad decision, but
that, Henriette hoped, might be averted. What *would* people
say? Further discussion was checked by a call from Mrs.
Walker, whom Hadria had the audacity to consult on
questions of education and hygiene, leading her, by dexterous
generalship, almost over the same ground that she had
traversed herself, inducing the unconscious lady to repeat, with
amazing accuracy, Hadria's own reproduction of local views.

"Now *am* I without authority in my ideas?" she asked,
after Mrs. Walker had departed. Henriette had to admit that
she had at least one supporter.

"But I believe," she added, "that your practice is better
than your preaching."

"It seems to be an ordinance of Nature," said Hadria,
"that these things shall never correspond."

CHAPTER XXXI.

HADRIA said nothing more about her project, and when Henriette alluded to it, answered that it was still unfurnished with detail. She merely wished to know, for certain, Henriette's views. She admitted that there had been some conversation on the subject between Hubert and herself, but would give no particulars. Henriette had to draw her own conclusions from Hadria's haggard looks, and the suppressed excitement of her manner.

Henriette always made a point of being present when Professor Fortescue called, as she did not approve of his frequent visits. She noticed that he gave a slight start when Hadria entered. In a few days, she had grown perceptibly thinner. Her manner was restless. A day or two of rain had prevented the usual walks. When it cleared up again, the season had taken a stride. Still more glorious was the array of tree and flower, and their indescribable freshness suggested the idea that they were bathed in the mysterious elixir of life, and that if one touched them, eternal youth would be the reward. Professor Theobald gazed at Hadria with startled and enquiring eyes, when they met again.

" You look tired," he said.

" I am, rather. The spring is always a little trying."

" Especially *this* spring, I find."

The gardens of the Priory were now at the very perfection of their beauty. The supreme moment had come of flowing wealth of foliage and delicate splendour of blossom, yet the paleness of green and tenderness of texture were still there.

Professor Theobald said suddenly, that Hadria looked as if

283

she were turning over some project very anxiously in her mind—a project on which much depended.

"You are very penetrating," she replied, after a moment's hesitation, "that is exactly what I *am* doing. When I was a girl, my brothers and sisters and I used to discuss the question of the sovereignty of the will. Most of us believed in it devoutly. We regarded circumstance as an annoying trifle, that no person who respected himself would allow to stand in his way. I want to try that theory and see what comes of it."

"You alarm me, Mrs. Temperley."

"Yes, people always do seem to get alarmed when one attempts to put their favourite theories in practice."

"But really—for a woman——"

"The sovereignty of the will is a dangerous doctrine?"

"Well, as things are ; a young woman, a beautiful woman."

"You recall an interesting memory," she said.

"Ah, that is unkind."

Her smile checked him.

"When you fall into a mocking humour, you are quite impracticable."

"I merely smiled," she said, "sweetly, as I thought."

"It is really cruel ; I have not had a word with you for days, and the universe has become a wilderness."

"A pleasant wilderness," she observed, looking round.

"Nature is a delightful background, but a poor subject."

"Do you think so? I often fancy one's general outlook would be nicer, if one had an indistinct human background and a clear foreground of unspoiled Nature. But that may be a jaundiced view."

Hadria went off to meet Lady Engleton, who was coming down the avenue with Madame Bertaux. Professor Theobald instinctively began to follow and then stopped, reddening, as he met the glance of Miss Temperley. He flung himself into conversation with her, and became especially animated when he was passing Hadria, who did not appear to notice him. As both Professors were to leave Craddock Dene at the end of the week, this was the last meeting in the Priory gardens.

Miss Temperley found Professor Theobald entertaining, but at times a little incoherent.

"Why, there is Miss Du Prel!" exclaimed Henriette. "What an erratic person she is. She went to London the day before yesterday, and now she turns up suddenly without a word of warning."

This confirmed Professor Theobald's suspicions that something serious was going on at the Red House.

Valeria explained her return to Hadria, by saying that she had felt so nervous about what the latter might be going to attempt, that she had come back to see if she could be of help, or able to ward off any rash adventure.

There was a pleasant open space among the shrubberies, where several seats had been placed to command a dainty view of the garden and lawns, with the house in the distance, and here the party gradually converged, in desultory fashion, coming up and strolling off again, as the fancy inspired them.

Cigars were lighted, and a sense of sociability and enjoyment suffused itself, like a perfume, among the group.

Lady Engleton was delighted to see Miss Du Prel again. She did so want to continue the hot discussion they were having at the Red House that afternoon, when Mr. Temperley *would* be so horridly logical. He smiled and twisted his moustache.

"We were interrupted by some caller, and had to leave the argument at a most exciting moment."

"An eternally interesting subject!" said Temperley; "what woman is, what she is not."

"My dread is that presently, the need for dissimulation being over, all the delightful mystery will have vanished," said Professor Theobald. "I should tire, in a day, of a woman I could understand."

"You tempt one to enquire the length of the reign of a satisfactory enigma," cried Lady Engleton.

"Precisely the length of her ability to mystify me," he replied.

"Your future wife ought to be given a hint."

"Oh! a wife, in no case, could hold me: the mere fact that it was my duty to adore her, would be chilling. And when added to that, I knew that she had placed it among the list of her obligations to adore *me*—well, that would be the climax of disenchantment."

Hubert commended his wisdom in not marrying.

"The only person I could conceivably marry would be my cook; in that case there would be no romance to spoil, no vision to destroy."

"I fear this is a cloak for a poor opinion of our sex, Professor."

"On the contrary. I admire your sex too much to think of subjecting them to such an ordeal. I could not endure to regard a woman I had once admired, as a matter of course, a commonplace in my existence."

Henriette plunged headlong into the fray, in opposition to the Professor's heresy. The conversation became general.

Professor Theobald fell out of it. He was furtively watching Hadria, whose eyes were strangely bright. She was sitting on the arm of a seat, listening to the talk, with a little smile on her lips. Her hand clasped the back of the seat rigidly, as if she were holding something down.

The qualities and defects of the female character were frankly canvassed, each view being held with fervour, but expressed with urbanity. Women were *always* so and so; women were absolutely *never* so and so: women felt, without exception, thus and thus; on the contrary, they were entirely devoid of such sentiments. A large experience and wide observation always supported each opinion, and eminent authorities swarmed to the standard.

"I do think that women want breadth of view," said Lady Engleton.

"They sometimes want accuracy of statement," observed

Professor Theobald, with a possible second meaning in his words.

"It seems to me they lack concentration. They are too versatile," was Hubert's comment.

"They want a sense of honour," was asserted.

"And a sense of humour," some one added.

"They want a feeling of public duty."

"They want a spice of the Devil!" exclaimed Hadria.

There was a laugh.

Hubert thought this was a lack not likely to be felt for very long. It was under rapid process of cultivation.

"Why, it is a commonplace; that if a woman *is* bad, she is always *very* bad," cried Lady Engleton.

"A new and intoxicating experience," said Professor Fortescue. "I sympathize."

"New?" his colleague murmured, with a faint chuckle.

"You distress me," said Henriette.

Professor Fortescue held that woman's "goodness" had done as much harm in the world as men's badness. The one was merely the obverse of the other.

"This is strange teaching!" cried Lady Engleton.

The Professor reminded her that truth was always stranger than fiction.

"To the best men," observed Valeria, "women show all their meanest qualities. It is the fatality of their training."

Professor Theobald had noted the same trait in other subject races.

"Pray, don't call us a subject race!" remonstrated Lady Engleton.

"Ah, yes, the truth," cried Hadria, "we starve for the truth."

"You are courageous, Mrs. Temperley."

"Like the Lady of Shallott, I am sick of shadows."

"The bare truth, on this subject, is hard for a woman to face."

"It is harder, in the long run, to waltz eternally round it with averted eyes."

"But, dear me, why is the truth about ourselves hard to face?" demanded Valeria.

"I am placed between the horns of a dilemma: one lady clamours for the bare truth: another forbids me to say anything unpleasing."

"I withdraw my objection," Valeria offered.

"The ungracious task shall not be forced upon unwilling chivalry," said Hadria. "If our conditions have been evil, some scars must be left and may as well be confessed. Among the faults of women, I should place a tendency to trade upon and abuse real chivalry and generosity when they meet them: a survival perhaps from the Stone Age, when the fittest to bully were the surviving elect of society."

Hadria's eyes sparkled with suppressed excitement.

"Freedom alone teaches us to meet generosity, generously," said Professor Fortescue; "you can't get the perpendicular virtues out of any but the really free-born."

"Then do you describe women's virtues as horizontal?" enquired Miss Du Prel, half resentfully.

"In so far as they follow the prevailing models. Women's love, friendship, duty, the conduct of life as a whole, speaking very roughly, has been lacking in the quality that I call perpendicular; a quality implying something more than *upright.*"

"You seem to value but lightly the woman's acknowledged readiness for self-sacrifice," said Lady Engleton. "That, I suppose, is only a despised horizontal virtue."

"Very frequently."

"Because it is generally more or less abject," Hadria put in. "The sacrifice is made because the woman is a woman. It is the obeisance of sex; the acknowledgment of servility; not a simple desire of service."

"The adorable creature is not always precisely obeisant," observed Theobald.

"No; as I say, she may be capricious and cruel enough to those who treat her justly and generously" (Hadria's eyes

instinctively turned towards the distant Priory, and Valeria's
followed them); "but ask her to sacrifice herself for nothing;
ask her to cherish the selfishness of some bully or fool; assure
her that it is her duty to waste her youth, lose her health, and
stultify her mind, for the sake of somebody's whim, or somebody's fears, or somebody's absurdity, *then* she needs no persuasion. She goes to the stake smiling. She swears the flames
are comfortably warm, no more. Are they diminishing her in
size? Oh no—not at all—besides she *was* rather large, for a
woman. She smiles encouragement to the other chained figures,
at the other stakes. Her reward? The sense of exalted
worth, of humility; the belief that she has been sublimely
virtuous, while the others whom she serves have been—well
the less said about them the better. She has done her duty,
and sent half a dozen souls to hell!"

Henriette uttered a little cry.

"Where one expects to meet her!" Hadria added.

Professor Theobald was chuckling gleefully.

Lady Engleton laughed. "Then, Mrs. Temperley, you *do*
feel rather wicked yourself, although you don't admire our nice,
well-behaved, average woman."

"Oh, the mere opposite of an error isn't always truth," said
Hadria.

"The weather has run to your head!" cried Henriette.

Hadria's eyes kindled. "Yes, it is like wine; clear, intoxicating sparkling wine, and its fumes are mounting! Why does
civilisation never provide for these moments?"

"What would you have? A modified feast of Dionysius?"

"Why not? The whole earth joins in the festival and sings,
except mankind. Some frolic of music and a stirring dance!—
But ah! I suppose, in this tamed England of ours, we should
feel it artificial; we should fear to let ourselves go. But in
Greece—if we could fancy ourselves there, shorn of our little
local personalities—in some classic grove, on sunlit slopes, all
bubbling with the re-birth of flowers and alive with the light,
the broad all-flooding light of Greece that her children dreaded

to leave more than any other earthly thing, when death threatened—could one not imagine the loveliness of some garlanded dance, and fancy the naïads, and the dryads, and all the hosts of Pan gambolling at one's heels?"

"Really, Mrs. Temperley, you were not born for an English village. I should like Mrs. Walker to hear you!"

"Mrs. Walker knows better than to listen to me. She too hides somewhere, deep down, a poor fettered thing that would gladly join the revel, if it dared. We all do."

Lady Engleton dwelt joyously on the image of Mrs. Walker, cavorting, garlanded, on a Greek slope, with the nymphs and water-sprites for familiar company.

Lady Engleton had risen laughing, and proposed a stroll to Hadria.

Henriette, who did not like the tone the conversation was taking, desired to join them.

"I never quite know how far you are serious, and how far you are just amusing yourself, Hadria," said Lady Engleton. "Our talking of Greece reminds me of some remark you made the other day, about Helen. You seemed to me almost to sympathize with her."

Hadria's eyes seemed to be looking across miles of sea to the sunny Grecian land.

"If a slave breaks his chains and runs, I am always glad," she said.

"I was talking about Helen."

"So was I. If a Spartan wife throws off her bondage and defies the laws that insult her, I am still more glad."

"But not if she sins?" Henriette coughed, warningly.

"Yes; if she sins."

"Oh, Hadria," remonstrated Henriette, in despair.

"I don't see that it follows that Helen *did* sin, however; one does not know much about her sentiments. She revolted against the tyranny that held her shut in, enslaved, body and soul, in that wonderful Greek world of hers. I am charmed to think that she gave her countrymen so much trouble to

assert her husband's right of ownership. It was at *his* door
that the siege of Troy ought to be laid. I only wish elope-
ments always caused as much commotion !" Lady Engleton
laughed, and Miss Temperley tried to catch Hadria's eye.

"Well, that *is* a strange idea ! And do you really think
Helen did not sin ? Seriously now."

"I don't know. There is no evidence on that point."
Lady Engleton laughed again.

"You do amuse me. Assuming that Helen did not sin, I
suppose you would (if only for the sake of paradox) accuse
the virtuous Greek matrons—who sat at home, and wove, and
span, and bore children—of sinning against the State !"

"Certainly," said Hadria, undismayed. "It was they who
insidiously prepared the doom for their country, as they wove
and span and bore children, with stupid docility. As surely
as an enemy might undermine the foundations of a city till
it fell in with a crash, so surely they brought ruin upon
Greece."

"Oh, Hadria, you are quite beside yourself to-day !" cried
Henriette.

"A love of paradox will lead you far !" said Lady Engleton.
"We have always been taught to think a nation sound and
safe whose women were docile and domestic."

"What nation, under those conditions, has ever failed to
fall in with a mighty crash, like my undermined city? Greece
herself could not hold out. Ah, yes ; we have our revenge !
a sweet, sweet revenge !"

Lady Engleton was looking much amused and a little
dismayed, when she and her companions rejoined the party.

"I never heard anyone say so many dreadful things in so
short a space of time," she cried. "You are distinctly
shocking."

"I am frank," said Hadria. "I fancy we should all go
about with our hair permanently on end, if we spoke out in
chorus."

"I don't quite like to hear you say that, Hadria.'

"I mean no harm—merely that every one thinks thoughts and feels impulses that would be startling if expressed in speech. Don't we all know how terrifying a thing speech is, and thought? a chartered libertine."

"Why, you are saying almost exactly what Professor Theobald said the other day, and we were so shocked."

"And yet my meaning has scarcely any relation to his," Hadria hastened to say. "He meant to drag down all belief in goodness by reminding us of dark moments and hours; by placarding the whole soul with the name of some shadow that moves across it, I sometimes think from another world, some deep under-world that yawns beneath us and sends up blackness and fumes and strange cries." Hadria's eyes had wandered far away. "Are you never tormented by an idea, an impression that you know does not belong to you?"

Lady Engleton gave a startled negative. "Professor Fortescue, come and tell me what you think of this strange doctrine?"

"If we had to be judged by our freedom from rushes of evil impulse, rather than by our general balance of good and evil wishing, I think those would come out best, who had fewest thoughts and feelings of any kind to record." The subject attracted a small group.

"Unless goodness is only a negative quality," Valeria pointed out, "a mere *absence*, it must imply a soul that lives and struggles, and if it lives and struggles, it is open to the assaults of the devil."

"Yes, and it is liable to go under too sometimes, one must not forget," said Hadria, "although most people profess to believe so firmly in the triumph of the best—how I can't conceive, since the common life of every day is an incessant harping on the moral: the smallest, meanest, poorest, thinnest, vulgarest qualities in man and woman are those selected for survival, in the struggle for existence."

There was a cry of remonstrance from idealists.

"But what else do we mean when we talk by common

consent of the world's baseness, harshness, vulgarity, injustice?
It means surely—and think of it!—that it is composed of men
and women with the best of them killed out, as a nerve burnt
away by acid ; a heart won over to meaner things than it set
out beating for; a mind persuaded to nibble at edges of dry
crust that might have grown stout and serviceable on generous
diet, and mellow and inspired with noble vintage."

"You really are shockingly Bacchanalian to-day," cried
Lady Engleton.

Hadria laughed. "Metaphorically, I am a toper. The
wonderful clear sparkle, the subtle flavour, the brilliancy of
wine, has for me a strange fascination ; it seems to signify so
much in life that women lose."

"True. What beverage should one take as a type of what
they gain by the surrender?" asked Lady Engleton, who was
disposed to hang back towards orthodoxy, in the presence of
her uncompromising neighbour.

"Oh, toast and water!" replied Hadria.

Part III.

CHAPTER XXXII.

THE speed was glorious. Back flashed field and hill and copse, and the dear "companionable hedgeways." Back flew iterative telegraph posts with Herculean swing, into the Past, looped together in rhythmic movement, marking the pulses of old Time. On, with rack and roar, into the mysterious Future. One could sit at the window and watch the machinery of Time's foundry at work; the hammers of his forge beating, beating, the wild sparks flying, the din and chaos whirling round one's bewildered brain;—Past becoming Present, Present melting into Future, before one's eyes. To sit and watch the whirring wheels; to think " Now it is thus and thus; presently, another slice of earth and sky awaits me"—ye Gods, it is not to be realized !

The wonder of the flying land—England, England with her gentle homesteads, her people of the gentle voices; and the unknown wonder of that other land, soon to change its exquisite dream-features for the still more thrilling, appealing marvel of reality—could it all be true? Was this the response of the genius of the ring, the magic ring that we call *will?* And would the complaisant genius always appear and obey one's behests, in this strange fashion?

Thoughts ran on rhythmically, in the steady, flashing movement through verdant England. The Real! *that* was the truly exquisite, the truly great, the true realm of the imagination ! What imagination was ever born to conceive or compass it ?

A rattle under a bridge, a roar through a tunnel, and on again, through Kentish orchards. A time of blossoming. Disjointed, delicious impressions followed one another in swift succession, often superficially incoherent, but threaded deep, in the stirred consciousness, on a silver cord :—the unity of the creation was as obvious as its multiplicity.

Images of the Past joined hands with visions of the Future. In these sweet green meadows, men had toiled, as thralls, but a few lifetimes ago, and they had gathered together, as Englishmen do, first to protest and reasonably demand, and then to buy their freedom with their lives. Their country-woman sent a message of thanksgiving, backward through the centuries, to these stout champions of the land's best heritage, and breathed an aspiration to be worthy of the kinship that she claimed.

The rattle and roar grew into a symphony—full, rich, magnificent, and then, with a rush, came a stirring musical conception : it seized the imagination.

Oh, why were they stopping? It was a little country station, but many passengers were on the platform. A careworn looking woman and a little girl entered the carriage, and the little girl fixed her eyes on her fellow-traveller with singular per-sistence. Then the more practical features of the occasion came into view, and all had an enthralling quality of reality—poetry. The sound of the waiting engine breathing out its white smoke into the brilliant air, the powerful creature quiescent but ready, with the turn of a handle, to put forth its slumbering might; the crunching of footsteps on the gravel, the wallflowers and lilacs in the little station garden, the blue of the sky, and ah! the sweetness of the air when one leant out to look along the interminable straight line of rails, leading—whither? Even the very details of one's travelling gear : the tweed gown meet for service, the rug and friendly umbrella, added to the feeling of overflowing satisfaction. The little girl stared more fixedly than ever. A smile and the offer of a flower made her look down, for a minute, but the gaze was resumed. Wherefore?

Was the inward tumult too evident in the face? Well, no matter. The world was beautiful and wide!

The patient monster began to move again, with a gay whistle, as if he enjoyed this chase across country, on the track of Time. He was soon at full speed again, on his futile race : a hapless idealist in pursuit of lost dreams. The little girl watched the dawn of a smile on the face of the kind, pretty lady who had given her the flower. A locomotive figuring as an idealist! Where would one's fancy lead one to next?

Ah the sea! heaving busily, and flashing under the morning radiance. Would they have a good crossing? The wind was fresh. How dreamy and bright and windy the country looked, and how salt was the sea-breeze! Very soon they would arrive at Folkestone. Rugs and umbrellas and hand-bags must be collected. The simple, solid commonplace of it all, touched some wholesome spring of delight. What a speed the train was going at! One could scarcely stand in the jolting carriage. Old Time must not make too sure of his victory. One felt a wistful partisanship for his snorting rival, striving for ever to accomplish the impossible. The labouring visionary was not without significance to aspiring mortals.

The outskirts of the town were coming in sight; grey houses bleakly climbing chalky heights. It would be well to put on a thick overcoat at once. It was certain to be cold in the Channel.

Luckily Hannah had a head on her shoulders, and could be trusted to follow the directions that had been given her.

The last five minutes seemed interminable, but they did come to an end. There was an impression of sweet salt air, of wind and voices, of a hurrying crowd; occasionally a French sentence pronounced by one of the officials, reminis-cent of a thousand dreams and sights of foreign lands ; and then the breezy quay and waiting steamboat.

The sound of that quiet, purposeful hiss of the steam sent

a thrill along the nerves. Hannah and her charge were safely on board; the small luggage followed, and lastly Hadria traversed the narrow bridge, wondering when the moment would arrive for waking up and finding herself in her little bedroom at Craddock Dene? What was she thinking of? Dream? *This* was no dream, this bold, blue, dancing water, this living sunshine, this salt and savour and movement and brilliancy!

The *other* was the dream; it seemed to be drifting away already. The picture of the village and the house and the meadows, and the low line of the hills was recalled as through a veil; it would not stand up and face the emphatic present. At the end of a few months, would there be anything left of her connexion with the place where she had passed six— seven years of her life? and such years! They had put scars on her soul, as deep and ghastly as ever red-hot irons had marked on tortured flesh. Perhaps it was because of this rabid agony undergone, that now she seemed to have scarcely any clinging to her home,—for the present at any rate. And she knew that she left only sorrow for conventional disasters behind her. The joy of freedom and its intoxication drowned every other feeling. It was sheer relief to be away, to stretch oneself in mental liberty and leisure, to look round at earth and sky and the hurrying crowds, in quiet enjoyment; to possess one's days, one's existence for the first time, in all these long years! It was as the home-coming of a dis-possessed heir. This freedom did not strike her as strange, but as obvious, as familiar. It was the first condition of a life that was worth living. And yet never before had she known it. Ernest and Fred and even Austin had enjoyed it from boyhood, and in far greater completeness than she could ever hope to possess it, even now.

Yet even this limited, this comparative freedom, which a man could afford to smile at, was intoxicating. Heavens! under what a leaden cloud of little obligations and restraints, and loneliness and pain, she had been living! And for what purpose? To make obeisance to a phantom public, not because she cared one iota for the phantom or its opinions, but because husband and parents and relations were terrified at the prospect of a few critical and disapproving remarks, that they would not even hear! How mad it all was! It was not true feeling, not affection, that prompted Hubert's opposition; it was not care for his real happiness that inspired Henriette with such ardour in this cause; they would both be infinitely happier and more harmonious in Hadria's absence. The whole source of their distress was the fear of what people would say when the separation became known to the world. That was the beginning and the end of the matter. Why could not the stupid old world mind its own business, in heaven's name? Good people, especially good women of the old type, would all counsel the imbecile sacrifice. They would all condemn this step. Indeed, the sacrifice that Hadria had refused to make, was so common, so much a matter of course, that her refusal appeared startling and preposterous : scarcely less astonishing than if a neighbour at dinner, requesting one to pass the salt, had been met with a rude " I shan't."

" A useful phrase at times, of the nature of a tonic, amidst our enervating civilisation," she reflected.

There was a tramping of passengers up and down the deck. People walked obliquely, with head to windward. Draperies fluttered; complexions verged towards blue. Only two ladies who had abandoned hope from the beginning, suffered from the crossing. The kindly sailors occupied their leisure in bringing tarpaulins to the distressed.

" Well, Hannah, how are you getting on? "

Hannah looked forward ardently to the end of the journey, but her charge seemed delighted with the new scene.

" Have you ever been to France before, ma'am? " Hannah asked, perhaps noticing the sparkle of her employer's eye and the ring in her voice.

" Yes, once; I spent a week in Paris with Mr. Temperley,

and we went on afterwards to the Pyrenees. That was just before we took the Red House."

"It must have been beautiful," said Hannah. "And did you take the babies, ma'am?"

"They were neither of them in existence then," replied Mrs. Temperley. A strange fierce light passed through her eyes for a second, but Hannah did not notice it. Martha's shawl was blowing straight into her eyes, and the nurse was engaged in arranging it more comfortably.

The coast of France had become clear, some time ago; they were making the passage very quickly to-day. Soon the red roofs of Boulogne were to be distinguished, with the grey dome of the cathedral on the hill-top. Presently, the boat had arrived in the bright old town, and every detail of outline and colour was standing forth brilliantly, as if the whole scene had been just washed over with clear water and all the tints were wet.

The first impression was keen. The innumerable differences from English forms and English tones sprang to the eye. A whiff of foreign smell and a sound of foreign speech reached the passengers at about the same moment. The very houses looked unfamiliarly built, and even the letters of printed names of hotels and shops had a frivolous, spindly appearance— elegant but frail. The air was different from English air. Some *bouillon* and a slice of fowl were very acceptable at the restaurant at the station, after the business of examining the luggage was over. Hannah, evidently nourishing a sense of injury against the natives for their eccentric jargon, and against the universe for the rush and discomfort of the last quarter of an hour, was disposed to express her feelings by a marked lack of relish for her food. She regarded Hadria's hearty appetite with a disdainful expression. Martha ate bread and butter and fruit. She was to have some milk that had been brought for her, when they were *en route* again.

" *Tout le monde en voiture !* " Within five minutes, the train was puffing across the wastes of blowing sand that ran along the coast, beyond the town. The child, who had become accustomed to the noise and movement, behaved better than had been expected. She seemed to take pleasure in looking out of the window at the passing trees. Hannah was much struck with this sign of awakening intelligence. It was more than the good nurse showed herself. She scarcely condescended to glance at the panorama of French fields, French hills and streams that were rushing by. How pale and ethereal they were, these Gallic coppices and woodlands! And with what a dainty lightness the foliage spread itself to the sun, French to its graceful finger-tips! That grey old house, with high lichen-stained roof and narrow windows—where but in sunny France could one see its like?—and the little farmsteads and villages, full of indescribable charm. One felt oneself in a land of artists. There was no inharmonious, no unfitting thing anywhere. Man had wedded himself to Nature, and his works seemed to receive her seal and benediction. English landscape was beautiful, and it had a particular charm to be found nowhere else in the world; but in revenge, there was something here that England could not boast. Was it fanciful to see in the characteristics of vegetation and scenery, the origin or expression of the difference of the two races at their greatest?

"Ah, if I were only a painter!"

They were passing some fields where, in the slanting rays of the sun, peasants in blue blouses and several women were bending over their toil. It was a subject often chosen by French artists. Hadria understood why. One of the labourers stood watching the train, and she let her eyes rest on the patient figure till she was carried beyond his little world. If she could have painted that scene just as she saw it, all the sadness and mystery of the human lot would have stood forth eloquently in form and colour; these a magic harmony, not without some inner kinship with the spirit of man at its noblest.

What was he thinking, that toil-bent peasant, as the train flashed by? What tragedy or comedy was he playing on his rural stage? Hadria sat down and shut her eyes, dazzled by the complex mystery and miracle of life, and almost horrified at the overwhelming thought of the millions of these obscure human lives burning themselves out, everywhere, at every instant, like so many altar-candles to the unknown God!

"And each one of them takes himself as seriously as I take myself: perhaps more seriously. Ah, if one could but pause to smile at one's tragic moments, or still better, at one's sublime ones. But it can't be done. A remembrancer would have to be engaged, to prevent lapses into the sublime,— and how furious one would be when he nudged one, with his eternal : ' Beware !' "

It was nearly eight o'clock when the train plunged among the myriad lights of the great city. The brilliant beacon of the Eiffel Tower sat high up in the sky, like an exile star.

Gaunt and grim was the vast station, with its freezing purplish electric light. Yet even here, to Hadria's stirred imagination, there was a certain quality in the Titanic building, which removed it from the vulgarity of English utilitarian efforts of the same order.

In a fanciful mood, one might imagine a tenth circle of the Inferno, wherein those stern grey arches should loftily rise, in blind and endless sequence, limbing an abode of horror, a place of punishment for those, empty-hearted, who had lived without colour and sunshine, in voluntary abnegation, caring only for gain and success.

The long delay in the examination of the luggage, the fatigue of the journey, tended to increase the disposition to regard the echoing edifice, with its cold hollow reverberations, as a Circle of the Doomed. It was as if they passed from the realm of the Shades through the Gates of Life, when at length the cab rattled out of the courtyard of the station, and turned leftwards into the brilliant streets of Paris. It was hard to realize that all this stir and light and life had been going on night after night, for all these years, during which one had sat in the quiet drawing-room at Craddock Dene, trying wistfully, hopelessly, to grasp the solid fact of an unknown vast reality, through a record here and there. The journey was a long one to the Rue Boissy d'Anglas, but tired as she was, Hadria did not wish it shorter. Even Hannah was interested in the brilliantly lighted shops and *cafés* and the splendour of the boulevards. Now and again, the dark deserted form of a church loomed out, lonely, amidst the gaiety of Parisian street-life. Some electric lamp threw a distant gleam upon calm classic pillars, which seemed to hold aloof, with a quality of reserve rarely to be noticed in things Parisian. Hadria greeted it with a feeling of gratitude.

The great Boulevard was ablaze and swarming with life. The *cafés* were full; the gilt and mirrors and the crowds of *consommateurs* within, all visible as one passed along the street, while, under the awning outside, crowds were sitting smoking, drinking, reading the papers.

Was it really possible that only this morning, those quiet English fields had been dozing round one, those sleepy villagers spreading their slow words out, in expressing an absence of idea, over the space of time in which a Parisian conveyed a pocket philosophy?

The cabman directed his vehicle down the Rue Royale, passing the stately Madeleine, with its guardian sycamores, and out into the windy spaciousness of the Place de la Concorde.

A wondrous city! Hannah pointed out the electric light of the Eiffel Tower to her charge, and Martha put out her small hands, demanding the toy on the spot.

The festooned lights of the Champs Elysées swung themselves up, in narrowing line, till they reached the pompous arch at the summit, and among the rich trees of those Elysian fields gleamed the festive lamps of *cafés chantants*.

"*Si Madame désire encore quelque chose?*" The neat maid, in picturesque white cap and apron, stood with her hand on the door of the little bedroom, on one of the highest

storeys of the *pension.* Half of one of the long windows had
been set open, and the sounds of the rolling of vehicles over
the smooth asphalte, mingled with those of voices, were coming
up, straight and importunate, into the dainty bedroom. The
very sounds seemed nearer and clearer in this keen-edged land.
The bed stood in one corner, canopied with white and blue;
a thick carpet gave a sense of luxury and deadened the tramp
of footsteps; a marble mantel-piece was surmounted by a mirror,
and supported a handsome bronze clock and two bronze ornaments. The furniture was of solid mahogany. A nameless
French odour pervaded the atmosphere, delicate, subtle, but
unmistakeable. And out of the open window, one could
see a series of other lighted windows, all of exactly the same
tall graceful design, opening in the middle by the same device
and the same metal handle that had to be turned in order to
open or close the window. Within, the rooms obviously
modelled themselves on the one unvarying ideal. A few
figures could be seen coming and going, busy at work or
play. Above the steep roofs, a blue-black sky was alive with
brilliant stars.

"*Merci;*" Madame required nothing more.

CHAPTER XXXIII.

"... Rushes life on a race
As the clouds the clouds chase;
And we go,
And we drop like the fruits of the tree,
Even we,
Even so."

JUST at first, it was a sheer impossibility to do anything but bask and bathe in the sunny present, to spend the days in wandering incredulously through vernal Paris, over whose bursting freshness and brilliancy the white clouds seemed to be driven, with the same joy of life. The city was crammed; the inhabitants poured forth in swarms to enjoy, in true French fashion, the genial warmth and the universal awakening after the long capricious winter. It was actually hot in the sun, and fresh light clothing became a luxury, like a bath after a journey. The year had raised its siege, and there was sudden amity between man and Nature. Shrivelled man could relax the tension of resistance to cold and damp and change, and go forth into the sun with cordial *insouciance*. In many of the faces might be read this kindly amnesty, although there were some so set and fixed with past cares that not even the soft hand of a Parisian spring could smooth away the lines, or even touch the spirit.

These Hadria passed with an aching pity. Circumstance had been to them a relentless taskmaster. Perhaps they had not rubbed the magic ring of will, and summoned the obedient genius. Perhaps circumstance had forbidden them even the rag wherewith to rub—or the impulse.

Sallying forth from the *pension*, Hadria would sometimes

pause, for a moment, at the corner of the street, where it opened into the Place de la Concorde, irresolute, because of the endless variety of possible ways to turn, and places to visit. She seldom made definite plans the day before, unless it were for the pleasure of changing them. The letter of introduction to Madame Vauchelet had remained unpresented. The sense of solitude, combined for the first time with that of freedom, was too delightful to forego. One must have time to realize and appreciate the sudden calm and serenity; the sudden absence of claims and obstructions and harassing criticisms. Heavens, what a price people consented to pay for the privilege of human ties! what hard bargains were driven in the kingdom of the affections! Thieves, extortionists, usurers—and in the name of all the virtues!

"Yes, solitude has charms!" Hadria inwardly exclaimed, as she stood watching the coming and going of people, the spouting of fountains, the fluttering of big scyamore leaves in the Champs Elysées.

Unhappily, the solitude made difficulties. But meanwhile there was a large field to be explored, where these difficulties did not arise, or could be guarded against. Her sex was a troublesome obstruction. "One does not come of centuries of chattel-women for nothing!" she wrote to Algitha. Society bristled with insults, conscious and unconscious. Nor had one lived the brightest, sweetest years of one's life tethered and impounded, without feeling the consequences when the tether was cut. There were dreads, shrinkings, bewilderments, confusions to encounter; the difficulties of pilotage in unknown seas, of self-knowledge, and guidance suddenly needed in new ranges of the soul; fresh temptations, fresh possibilities to deal with; everything untested, the alphabet of worldly experience yet to learn.

But all this was felt with infinitely greater force a little later, when the period of solitude was over, and Hadria found herself in the midst of a little society whose real codes and ideas she had gropingly to learn. Unfamiliar (in any practical sense)

with life, even in her own country, she had no landmarks or
finger-posts, of any kind, in this new land. Her sentiment
had never been narrowly British, but now she realized her
nationality over-keenly; she felt herself almost grotesquely
English, and had a sense of insular clumsiness· amidst a
uprightly, dexterous people. Conscious of a thousand illusive,
but very real differences in point of view, and in nature,
between the two nations, she had a baffled impression
of walking among mysteries and novelties that she could not
grasp. She began to be painfully conscious of the effects
of the narrow life that she had led, and of the limitations that
had crippled her in a thousand ways hitherto scarcely realized.

"One begins to learn everything too late," she wrote to
Algitha. "This ought all to have been familiar long ago.
I don't know anything about the world in which I live.
I have never before caught so much as a distant glimpse of it.
And even now there are strange thick wrappings from the
past that cling tight round and hold me aloof, strive as I
may to strip off that past-made personality, and to understand,
by touch, what things are made of. I feel as if I would risk
anything in order to really know that. Why should a woman
treat herself as if she were Dresden china? She is more
or less insulted and degraded whatever happens, especially
if she obeys what our generation is pleased to call the moral
law. The more I see of life, the more hideous seems the
position that women hold in relation to the social structure,
and the more sickening the current nonsense that is talked
about us and our 'missions' and 'spheres.' It is so feeble,
so futile, to try to ornament an essentially degrading fact. It
is such insolence to talk to us—good heavens, to *us!*—about
holiness and sacredness, when men (to whom surely a sense
of humour has been denied) divide their women into two
great classes, both of whom they insult and enslave, insisting
peremptorily on the existence of each division, but treating one
class as private and the other as public property. One might
as well talk to driven cattle in the shambles about their

'sacred mission' as to women. It is an added mockery, a gratuitous piece of insolence."

Having been, from childhood, more or less at issue with her surroundings, Hadria had never fully realized their power upon her personality. But now daily a fresh recognition of her continued imprisonment, baffled her attempt to look at things with clear eyes. She struggled to get round and beyond that past-fashioned self, not merely in order to see truly, but in order to see at all. And in doing so, she ran the risk of letting go what she might have done better to hold. She felt painfully different from these people among whom she found herself. Her very trick of pondering over things sent her spinning to hopeless distances. They seemed to ponder so wholesomely little. Their intelligence was devoted to matters of the moment; they were keen and well-finished and accomplished. Hadria used to look at them in astonishment. How did these quick-witted people manage to escape the importunate inquisitive demon, the familiar spirit, who pursued her incessantly with his queries and suggestions? He would stare up from river and street and merry gardens; his haunting eyes looked mockingly out of green realms of stirring foliage, and his voice was like a sardonic echo to the happy voices of the children, laughing at their play under the flickering shadows, of mothers discussing their cares and interests, of men in blouses, at work by the water-side, or solemn, in frock-coats, with pre-occupations of business and bread-winning. The demon had his own reflections on all these seemingly ordinary matters, and so bizarre were they at times, so startling and often so terrible, that one found oneself shivering in full noontide, or smiling, or thrilled with passionate pity at "the sad, strange ways of men."

It was sweet to stretch one's cramped wings to the sun, to ruffle and spread them, as a released bird will, but it was startling to find already little stiff habits arisen, little creaks and hindrances never suspected, that made flight in the high air not quite effortless and serene.

The Past is never past; immortal as the Gods, it lives enthroned in the Present, and sets its limits and lays its
commands.

Cases have been known of a man blind from birth being
restored to sight, at mature age. For a time, the appearance of
objects was strange and incomprehensible. Their full meaning
was not conveyed to him; they remained riddles. He could not
judge the difference between near and far, between solid and
liquid; he had no experience, dating from childhood, of the
apparent smallness of distant things, of the connexion between
the impression given to the touch by solids and their effect on
the eye. He had all these things to learn. A thousand trifling
associations, of which those with normal senses are scarcely
conscious, had to be stumblingly acquired, as a child learns to
connect sound and sight, in learning to read.

Such were the changes of consciousness that Hadria found
herself going through; only realising each phase of the process
after it was over, and the previous confusion of vision had
been itself revealed, by the newly and often painfully acquired
co-ordinating skill.

But, as generally happens, in the course of passing from
ignorance to knowledge, the intermediate stage was chaotic.
Objects loomed up large and indistinct, as through a mist;
vague forms drifted by, half revealed, to melt away again;
here and there were clear outlines and solid impressions, to be
deemed trustworthy and given a place of honour; thence a
disproportion in the general conception; it being almost
beyond human power to allow sufficiently for that which is
unknown.

For some time, however, the dominant impression on
Hadria's mind was of her own gigantic ignorance. This
ignorance was far more confusing and even misleading than it
had been when its proportions were less defined. The faint
twinkle of light revealed the dusky outline, bewildering and
discouraging the imagination. Intuitive knowledge was disturbed by the incursion of scraps of disconnected experience.

This condition of mind made her an almost insoluble psychological problem. Since she was evidently a woman of pronounced character, her bewilderment and tentative attitude were not allowed for. Her actions were regarded as deliberate and cool-headed, when often they would be the outcome of sheer confusion, or chance, or perhaps of a groping experimental effort.

The first three weeks in Paris had been given up to enjoying the new conditions of existence. But now practical matters claimed consideration. The *pension* in the Rue Boissy d'Anglas was not suitable as a permanent abode. Rooms must be looked for, combining cheapness with a good situation, within easy distance of the scene of Hadria's future musical studies, and also within reach of some park or gardens for Martha's benefit.

This ideal place of abode was at last found. It cost rather more than Hadria had wished to spend on mere lodging, but otherwise it seemed perfect. It was in a quiet street between the Champs Elysées and the river. Two great thoroughfares ran, at a respectful distance, on either side, with omnibuses always passing. Hadria could be set down within a few minutes' walk of the School of Music, or, if she liked to give the time, could walk the whole way to her morning's work, through some of the most charming parts of Paris. As for Martha, she was richly provided with playgrounds. The Bois could be quickly reached, and there were always the Champs Elysées or the walk beneath the chestnuts by the river, along the Cours de la Reine and the length of the quays. Even Hannah thought the situation might do. Hadria had begun her studies at the School of Music, and found the steady work not only a profound, though somewhat stern enjoyment, but a solid backbone to her new existence, giving it cohesion and form. Recreation deserved its name, after work of this kind. Any lurking danger of too great speculative restlessness disappeared. There had been a moment when the luxurious joy of mere wandering observation and absorption, threatened to become overwhelming, and to loosen some of the rivets of the character.

But work was to the sum-total of impulse what the central weight was to one of Martha's toys : a leaden ballast that always brought the balance right again, however wildly the little tyrant might swing the creature off the perpendicular. When Hadria used to come in, pleasantly tired with her morning's occupation, and the wholesome heat of the sun, to take her simple *déjeuner* in the little apartment with Martha, a frivolous five minutes would often be spent by the two in endeavouring to overcome the rigid principles of that well-balanced plaything. But always the dead weight at its heart frustrated their attempts. Martha played the most inconsiderate pranks with its centre of gravity, but quite in vain. When a little French boy from the *étage* above was allowed to come and play with Martha, she proceeded to experiment upon *his* centre of gravity in the same way, and seemed much surprised when Jean Paul Auguste not only howled indignantly, but didn't swing up again after he was overturned. He remained supine, and had to be reinstated by Hadria and Hannah, and comforted with sweetmeats. Martha's logic received one of its first checks. She evidently made up her mind that logic was a fallacious mode of inference, and determined to abandon it for the future. These rebuffs in infancy, Hadria conjectured, might account for much !

About three weeks passed in almost pure enjoyment and peace ; and then it was discovered that the cost of living, in spite of an extremely simple diet, was such as might have provided epicurean luxuries for a family of ten. Hadria's enquiries among her acquaintances elicited cries of consternation. Obviously the landlady, who did the marketing, must be cheating on a royal scale, and there was nothing for it but to move. Hadria suggested to Madame Vauchelet, whose advice she always sought in practical matters, that perhaps the landlady might be induced to pursue her lucrative art in moderation ;

could she not put it honestly down in the bill "Peculation—so much per week?"

Madame Vauchelet was horrified. "Impossible!" she cried; one must seek another apartment. If only Hannah understood French and could do the marketing herself. But Hannah scorned the outlandish lingo, and had a poor opinion of the nation as a whole.

It was fatiguing and somewhat discouraging work to begin, all over again, the quest of rooms, especially with the difficulty about the landlady always in view, and no means of ascertaining her scale of absorption. It really seemed a pity that it could not be mentioned as an extra, like coal and lights. Then one would know what one was about. This uncertain liability, with an extremely limited income, which was likely to prove insufficient unless some addition could be made to it, was trying to the nerves.

In order to avoid too great anxiety, Hadria had to make up her mind to a less attractive suite of rooms, farther out of town, and she found it desirable to order many of the comestibles herself. Madame Vauchelet was untiring in her efforts to help and advise. She initiated Hadria into the picturesque mysteries of Parisian housekeeping. It was amusing to go to the shops and markets with this shrewd Frenchwoman, and very enlightening as to the method of living cheaply and well. Hadria began to think wistfully of a more permanent *ménage* in this entrancing capital, where there were still worlds within worlds to explore. She questioned Madame Vauchelet as to the probable cost of a *femme de ménage.* Madame quickly ran through some calculations and pronounced a sum alluringly small. Since the landlady difficulty was so serious, and made personal superintendence necessary, it seemed as if one might as well have the greater comfort and independence of this more home-like arrangement.

Madame Vauchelet recommended an excellent woman who would cook and market, and, with Hannah's help, easily do all that was necessary. After many calculations and consultations with Madame Vauchelet, Hadria finally decided to rent, for three months, a cheerful little suite of rooms near the Arc de Triomphe.

Madame Vauchelet drank a cup of tea in the little *salon* with quiet heroism, not liking to refuse Hadria's offer of the friendly beverage. But she wondered at the powerful physique of the nation that could submit to the trial daily.

Hadria was brimming over with pleasure in her new home, which breathed Paris from every pore. She had already surrounded herself with odds and ends of her own, with books and a few flowers. If only this venture turned out well, how delightful would be the next few months. Hadria did not clearly look beyond that time. To her, it seemed like a century. Her only idea as to the farther future was an abstract resolve to let nothing short of absolute compulsion persuade her to renounce her freedom, or subject herself to conditions that made the pursuit of her art impossible. How to carry out the resolve, in fact and detail, was a matter to consider when the time came. If one were to consider future difficulties as well as deal with immediate ones, into what crannies and interstices were the affairs of the moment to be crammed?

There has probably never been a human experience of even a few months of perfect happiness, of perfect satisfaction with conditions, even among the few men and women who know how to appreciate the bounty of Fate, when she is generous, and to take the sting out of minor annoyances by treating them lightly. Hadria was ready to shrug her shoulders at legions of these, so long as the main current of her purpose were not diverted. But she could not steel herself against the letters that she received from England.

Everyone was deeply injured but bravely bearing up. Her family was a stricken and sorrowing family. Being naturally heroic, it said little but thought the more. Relations whose names Hadria scarcely remembered, seemed to have waked up at the news of her departure and claimed their share of the woe. Obscure Temperleys raised astounded heads and

mourned. Henriette wrote that she was really annoyed at the
way in which everybody was talking about Hadria's conduct.
It was most uncomfortable. She hoped Hadria was able to
be happy. Hubert was ready to forgive her and to receive her
back, in spite of everything. Henriette entreated her to
return; for her own sake, for Hubert's sake, for the children's.
They were just going off to school, poor little boys. Henriette, although so happy at the Red House, was terribly
grieved at this sad misunderstanding. It seemed so strange,
so distressing. Henriette had thoroughly enjoyed looking
after dear Hubert and the sweet children. They were in
splendid health. She had been very particular about hygiene.
Hubert and she had seen a good deal of the Engletons
lately. How charming Lady Engleton was! So much tact.
She was advanced in her ideas, only she never allowed them
to be intrusive. She seemed just like everybody else. She
hated to make herself conspicuous; the very ideal of a true
lady, if one might use the much-abused word. Professor
Fortescue was reported to be still far from well. Professor
Theobald had not taken the Priory after all. It was too
large. It looked so deserted and melancholy now.

Henriette always finished her letters with an entreaty to
Hadria to return. People were talking so. They suspected
the truth; although, of course, one had hoped that the separation would be supposed to be temporary—as indeed Henriette
trusted it would prove.

Madame Bertaux, who had just returned from England to
her beloved Paris, reported to Hadria, when she called on the
latter in her new abode, that everyone was talking about the
affair with as much eagerness as if the fate of the empire had
depended on it. Madame Bertaux recommended indifference
and silence. She observed, in her sharp, good-natured, impatient way, that reforming confirmed drunkards, converting
the heathen, making saints out of sinners, or a silk purse
out of a sow's ear, would be mere child's play compared with
the task of teaching the average idiot to mind his own
business.

CHAPTER XXXIV.

THE new *ménage* went well. Therèse was a treasure, and Martha's willing slave. Expenses were kept fairly reasonable by her care and knowledge. Still it must not be forgotten that the little income needed supplementing. Hadria had been aware of this risk from the first, but had faced it, regarding it as the less perilous of the alternatives that she had to choose between. The income was small, but it was her own absolutely, and she must live on that, with such auxiliary sums as she could earn. She hoped to be able to make a little money by her compositions. The future was all vague and unknown, but one thing was at least certain: it cost money to live, and in some way or other it had to be made. She told her kind friend, Madame Vauchelet, of her plan. Madame Vauchelet consulted her musical friends. People were sympathetic, but rather vague in their advice. It was always difficult, this affair. The beginning was hard. M. Thillard, a kindly, highly-cultivated man of about sixty, who had heard Hadria play, took great interest in her talent, and busied himself on her behalf.

He said he would like to interest the great Jouffroy in this work. It had so distinct and remarkable an individuality that M. Thillard was sure Jouffroy would be enchanted with it. For himself, he held that it shewed a development of musical form and expression extremely remarkable. He could not quite understand it. There was, he knew not what, in it, of strange and powerful; a music of the North; something of bizarre, something of mysterious, even of terrible, "*une emotion épouvantable*," cried M. Thillard, working himself

314

to a climax as the theme inspired him, "There is genius in
that work, but certainly genius." Madame Vauchelet nodded
gravely at this pronouncement. It ought to be published, she
said. But this supreme recompense of genius was apparently
hard to achieve. The score was sent from publisher to
publisher : "from pillar to post," said Hadria, "if one might
venture on a phrase liable to. misconstruction on the lips
of disappointed ambition."

But at the end of a long and wearisome delay, the little
packet was returned in a tattered condition to its discouraged
author. M. Thillard made light of this. It was always thus
at first. One must have patience.

"One must live," said Hadria, "or at least such is the
prejudice under which one has been brought up."

"All will come," said M. Thillard. " You will see."

On one sunny afternoon, when Hadria had returned, thrilled
and inspired by a magnificent orchestral performance at the
Châtelet, she found Madame Vauchelet, M. Thillard, and the
great Jouffroy waiting in her *salon*. Jouffroy was small,
eccentric, fiery, with keen eager eyes, thick black hair, and
overhanging brows. M. Thillard reminded Madame Temperley
of her kind permission to present to her M. Jouffroy.
Madame Temperley was charmed and flattered by Monsieur's
visit.

It was an exciting afternoon. Madame Vauchelet was
eager to hear the opinion of the great man, and anxious for
Hadria to make a good impression.

The warm-hearted Frenchwoman, who had lost a daughter,
of whom Hadria reminded her, had been untiring in her kindness, from the first. Madame Vauchelet, in her young days,
had cherished a similar musical ambition, and Jouffroy always
asserted that she might have done great things, as a performer,
had not the cares of a family put an end to all hope of
bringing her gifts to fruition.

The piano was opened. Jouffroy played. Madame Vauchelet,
with her large veil thrown back, her black cashmere folds

falling around her, sat in the large arm-chair, a dignified and graceful figure, listening gravely. The kindly, refined face of M. Thillard beamed with enjoyment; an occasional cry of admiration escaping his lips, at some exquisite touch from the master.

The time slipped by, with bewildering rapidity.

Monsieur Thillard asked if they might be allowed to hear some of Madame's compositions—those which she had already been so amiable as to play to him.

Jouffroy settled himself to listen; his shaggy eyebrows lowering over his eyes, not in severity but in fixity of attention. Hadria trembled for a moment, as her hands touched the keys. Jouffroy gave a nod of satisfaction. If there had been no such quiver of nerves he would have doubted. So he said afterwards to M. Thillard and Madame Vauchelet.

After listening, for a time, without moving a muscle, he suddenly sat bolt upright and looked round at the player. The character of the music, always individual, had grown more marked, and at this point an effect was produced which appeared to startle the musician. He withdrew his gaze, after a moment, muttering something to himself, and resumed his former attitude, slowly and gravely nodding his head. There was a long silence after the last of the lingering, questioning notes had died away.

"Is Madame prepared for work, for hard, faithful work?"

The answer was affirmative. She was only too glad to have the chance to work.

"Has Madame inexhaustible patience?"

"In this cause—yes."

"And can she bear to be misunderstood; to be derided for departure from old rules and conventions; to have her work despised and refused, and again refused, till at last the dull ears shall be opened and all the stupid world shall run shouting to her feet?"

The colour rushed into Hadria's cheeks. "*Voila!*" exclaimed Madame Vauchelet. M. Thillard beamed with satisfaction. "Did I not tell you?"

Jouffroy clapped his friend on the back with enthusiasm. "*Il faut travailler,*" he said, "*mais travailler!*" He questioned Hadria minutely as to her course of study, approved it on the whole, suggesting alterations and additions. He asked to look through some more of her work.

"*Mon Dieu,*" he ejaculated, as his quick eye ran over page after page.

"If Madame has a character as strong as her genius, her name will one day be on the lips of all the world." He looked at her searchingly.

"I knew it!" exclaimed M. Thillard. "*Madame, je vous félicite.*"

"Ah!" cried Jouffroy, with a shake of his black shaggy head, "this is not a fate to be envied. *C'est dur!*"

"I am bewildered!" cried Hadria at last, in a voice that seemed to her to come from somewhere a long way off. The whole scene had acquired the character of a dream. The figures moved through miles of clear distance. Her impressions were chaotic. While a strange, deep confirmation of the musician's words, seemed to stir within her as if they had long been familiar, her mind entirely refused credence.

He had gone too far. Had he said a remarkable talent, but ——

Yet was it not, after all, possible? Nature scattered her gifts wildly and cruelly: cruelly, because she cared not into what cramped nooks and crannies she poured her maddening explosive: cruelly, because she hurled this fire from heaven with indiscriminate hand, to set alight one dared not guess how many chained martyrs at their stakes. Nature did not pick and choose the subjects of her wilful ministrations. She seemed to scatter at random, out of sheer *gaieté de coeur,* as Jouffroy had said, and if some golden grain chanced to be gleaming in this soul or that, what cause for astonishment? The rest might be the worst of dross. As well might the chance occur to one of Nature's children as to another. She did not bestow even one golden grain for nothing, *bien sûr;* she meant to be paid back with interest. Just one bright bead of the whole vast circlet of the truth : perhaps it was hers, but more likely that these kind friends had been misled by their sympathy.

M. Jouffroy came next day to have a long talk with Hadria about her work and her methods. He was absolutely confident of what he had said, but he was emphatic regarding the necessity for work ; steady, uninterrupted work. Everything must be subservient to the one aim. If she contemplated anything short of complete dedication to her art—well (he shrugged his shoulders), it would be better to amuse herself. There could be no half-measures with art. True, there were thousands of people who practised a little of this and a little of that, but Art would endure no such disrespect. It was the affair of a lifetime. He had known many women with great talent, but, alas ! they had not persistence. Only last year a charming, beautiful young woman, with—*mon Dieu!* —a talent that might have placed her on the topmost rank of singers, had married against the fervent entreaties of Jouffroy, and now—he shrugged his shoulders with a gesture of pitying contempt—"*elle est mère tout simplement.*" Her force had gone from herself into the plump infant, whose "*cris dechirants*" were all that now remained to the world of his mother's once magnificent voice. *Hélas !* how many brilliant careers had he not seen ruined by this fatal instinct ! Jouffroy's passion for his art had overcome the usual sentiment of the Frenchman, and even the strain of Jewish blood. He did not think a woman of genius well lost for a child. He grudged her to the fetish *la famille.* He went so far as to say that, even without the claims of genius, a woman ought to be permitted to please herself in the matter. When he heard that Madame had two children, and yet had not abandoned her ambition, he nodded gravely and significantly.

"But Madame has courage," he commented. "She must have braved much censure."

It was the first case of the kind that had come under his notice. He hoped much from it. His opinion of the sex would depend on Hadria's power of persistence. In consequence of numberless pupils who had shewn great promise, and then had satisfied themselves with "a stupid maternity," Jouffrey was inclined to regard women with contempt, not as regards their talent, which he declared was often astonishing, but as regards their persistency of character and purpose.

One could not rely on them. They had enthusiasm—Oh, but enthusiasm *à faire peur*, but presently "*un monsieur avec des moustaches seduisantes*" approaches, and then "*Phui, c'est tout fini!*" There was something of fatality in the affair. The instinct was terrible; a demoniacal possession. It was for women a veritable curse, a disease. M. Jouffroy had pronounced views on the subject. He regarded the maternal instinct as the scourge of genius. It was, for women, the devil's truncheon, his rod of empire. This "reproductive rage" held them—in spite of all their fine intuitions and astonishing ability—after all on the animal plane; cut them off from the little band of those who could break up new ground in human knowledge, and explore new heights of Art and Nature.

"I speak to you thus, Madame, not because I think little of your sex, but because I grudge them to the monster who will not spare us even one!"

Hadria worked with sufficient energy to please even Jouffroy. Her heart was in it, and her progress rapid. Everything was organized, in her life, for the one object. At the School of Music, she was in an atmosphere of work, everyone being bent on the same goal, each detail arranged to further the students in their efforts. It was like walking on a pavement after struggling uphill on loose sand; like breathing sea-breezes after inhaling a polluted atmosphere.

In old days, Hadria used to be haunted by a singular recurrent nightmare: that she was toiling up a steep mountain made of hard slippery rock, the summit always receding as she advanced. Behind her was a vast precipice down which she must fall if she lost her footing; and always, she saw hands without bodies attached to them placing stones in the path, so that they rolled down and had to be evaded at the peril of her life. And each time, after one set of stones was evaded, and she thought there would be a time of respite, another batch was set rolling, amid thin, scarcely audible laughter, which came on the storm-wind that blew precipice-wards across the mountain ; and invariably she awoke just as a final avalanche of cruel stones had sent her reeling over the hideous verge.

One is disposed to make light of the sufferings gone through in a dream, though it would trouble most of us to explain why, since the agony of mind is often as extreme as possibly could be endured in actual life. From the day of her arrival in Paris, Hadria was never again tormented with this nightmare.

Composition went on rapidly now. Soon there was a little pile of new work for M. Jouffroy's inspection. He was delighted, criticizing severely, but always encouraging to fresh efforts. As for the publishing, that was a different matter. In spite of M. Jouffroy's recommendation, publishers could not venture on anything of a character so unpopular. The music had merit, but it was eccentric. M. Jouffroy was angry. He declared that he would play something of Madame's at the next Châtelet concert. There would be opposition, but he would carry his point. And he did. But the audience received it very coldly. Although Hadria had expected such a reception, she felt a chill run through her, and a sinking of the heart. It was like a cold word that rebuffs an offer of sympathy, or an appeal for it. It sent her back into depths of loneliness, and reminded her how cut off she was from the great majority of her fellows, after all. And then Guy de Maupassant's dreadful " Solitude " came to her memory. There is no way (the hero of the sketch asserts) by which a man can break the eternal loneliness to which he is foredoomed. He cannot convey to others his real impressions or emotion, try as he may. By a series of assertions, hard to deny, the hero arrives at a terrible conclusion amounting to this : Art, affection, are in vain; we know not what we say, nor whom we love.

Jouffroy came out of the theatre, snorting and ruffled.

" But they are imbeciles, all !"

Hadria thought that perhaps *she* was the "imbecile"; it was a possibility to be counted with, but she dared not say so to the irate Jouffroy.

He was particularly angry, because the audience had confirmed his own fear that only very slowly would the quality of the music be recognized by even the more cultivated public. It had invaded fresh territory, he said, added to the range of expression, and was meanwhile a new language to casual listeners. It was rebel music, offensive to the orthodox. Hubert had always said that "it was out of the question," and he appeared to have been right.

"*Bah, ce ne sont que des moutons !*" exclaimed Jouffroy. If the work had been poorer, less original, there would not have been this trouble. Was there not some other method by which Madame could earn what was necessary, *en attendent ?*

In one of Professor Fortescue's letters, he had reminded Hadria of his eagerness to help her. Yet, what could he do? He had influence in the world of science, but Hadria could not produce anything scientific ! She bethought her of trying to write light descriptive articles, of a kind depending not so much on literary skill as on subject and epistolary freshness of touch. These she sent to the Professor, not without reluctance, knowing how overburdened he already was with work and with applications for help and advice. He approved of her idea, and advised the articles being sent the round of the magazines and papers.

Through his influence, one of the shorter articles was accepted, and Hadria felt encouraged. Her day was now very full. The new art was laborious, severely simple in character, though she studiously made her articles. Her acquaintances had multiplied very rapidly of late, and although this brought into her experience much that was pleasant and interesting, the demands of an enlarging circle swallowed an astonishing number of hours. An element of trouble had begun to come into the life that had been so full of serenity, as well as of regular and strenuous work. Hadria was already feeling the effects of anxiety and hurry. She had not come with untried powers to the fray. The reserve forces had long ago been sapped, in the early struggles, beginning in her girlhood and continuing at increasing pressure ever since. There was only enough nerve-force to enable one to live from hand to mouth. Expenditure of this force having been so often in excess of income, economy had become imperative. Yet, economy was difficult. M. Jouffroy was always spurring her to work, to throw over everything for this object; letters from England incessantly urged a very different course; friends in Paris pressed her to visit them, to accompany them hither and thither, to join musical parties, to compose little songs (some bagatelle in celebration of a birthday or wedding), to drive to the further end of the town to play to this person or that who had heard of Madame's great talent. Hadria was glad to do anything she could to express her gratitude for the kindness she had received on all hands, but, alas! there were only a certain number of hours in the day, and only a certain number of years in one's life, and art was long. Moreover, nerves were awkward things to play with.

Insidiously, treacherously, difficulties crept up. Even here, where she seemed so free, the peculiar claims that are made, by common consent, on a woman's time and strength began to weave their tiny cords around her. She took warning, and put an end to any voluntary increase of her circle, but the step had been taken a little too late. The mischief was done. To give pain or offence for the sake of an hour or two, more or less, seemed cruel and selfish, yet Hadria often longed for the privilege that every man enjoys, of quietly pursuing his work without giving either.

A disastrous sense of hurry and fatigue began to oppress her. This was becoming serious. She must make a stand.

Yet her attempts at explanation were generally taken as polite excuses for neglecting those who had been kind and cordial.

Jouffroy taxed her with looking tired. One must not be tired. One must arrange the time so as to secure ample rest and recreation after the real work was over. Women were so foolish in that way. They did everything feverishly. They imagined themselves to have inexhaustible nerves.

Hadria hinted that it was perhaps others who demanded of them what was possible only to inexhaustible nerves.

True; towards women, people behaved as idiots. How was it possible to produce one's best, if repose were lacking? Serenity was necessary for all production.

As well expect water perpetually agitated to freeze, as expect the crystals of the mind to produce themselves under the influence of incessant disturbance.

Work? Yes. Work never harmed any man or woman. It was harassment that killed. Work of the mind, of the artistic powers, that was a tonic to the whole being. But little distractions, irregular duties, worries, uncertainties— Jouffroy shook his head ominously. And not only to the artist were they fatal. It was these that drew such deep lines on the faces of women still young. It was these that destroyed ability and hope, and killed God only knew how many of His good gifts! Poverty: that could be endured with all its difficulties, if that were the one anxiety. It was never the *one* but the multitude of troubles that destroyed. Serenity there must be. A man knew that, and insisted on having it. Friends were no true friends if they robbed one of it. For him, he had a poor opinion of that which people called affection, regard. As for *l'amour*, that was the supreme egotism. The affections were simply a means to "make oneself paid." Affection! Bah! One did not offer it for nothing, *bien sûr!* It was through this insufferable pretext that one arrived at governing others. "*Comment?* Your presence can give me happiness, and you will not remain

always beside me? It is nothing to you how I suffer? To
me whom you love you refuse this small demand?" Jouffroy
opened his eyes, with a scornful glare. "It is in *that* fashion,
I promise you, that one can rule!"

"Ah, monsieur," said Hadria, "you are a keen observer.
How I wish you could live a woman's life for a short
time. You are wise now, but after *that* ——"

"Madame, I have sinned in my day, perhaps to merit
purgatorial fires; but, without false modesty, I do not think
that I have justly incurred the penalty you propose to me."

Hadria laughed. "It would be a strange piece of poetic
justice," she said, "if all the men who have sinned beyond
forgiveness in this incarnation, should be doomed to appear
in the next, as well-brought-up women."

Jouffroy smiled.

"Fancy some conquering hero reappearing in ringlets and
mittens, as one's maiden aunt."

Jouffroy grinned. "*Ce serait dur!*"

"*Ah, mon Dieu!*" cried Madame Vauchelet, "if men had
to endure in the next world that which they have made
women suffer in this—that would be an atrocious justice!"

CHAPTER XXXV.

STUBBORNLY Hadria sent her packets to the publishers;
the publishers as firmly returned them. She had two
sets flying now, like tennis balls, she wrote to Miss Du Prel:
one set across the Channel. The publishers, she feared,
played the best game, but she had the English quality of not
knowing when she was beaten. Valeria had succeeded in
finding a place for two of the articles. This was encouraging,
but funds were running alarmingly low.

The *apartement* would have either to be given up, or to
be taken on for another term, at the end of the week. A
decision must be made. Hadria was dismayed to find her
strength beginning to fail. That made the thought of the
future alarming. With health and vigour nothing seemed
impossible, but without that——

It seemed absurd that there should be so much difficulty
about earning a living. Other women had done it. Valeria
had always made light of the matter—when she had the theory
of the sovereignty of the will to support.

Another couple of articles which seemed to their creator
to possess popular qualities were sent off.

But after a weary delay, they shared the fate of their prede-
cessors. Hadria now moved into a smaller suite of rooms,
parting regretfully with Therése, and flinging herself once
more on the mercy of a landlady. This time M. Thillard
had discovered the lodging for her; a shabby, but sunny
little house, kept by a motherly woman with a reputation
for perfect honesty. Expenses were thus kept down, but
unhappily very little was coming in to meet them. It was

impossible to pull through the year at this rate. But, of course, there was daily hope of something turning up. The arrival of the post was always an exciting moment. At last Hadria wrote to ask Algitha to try and sell for her a spray of diamonds, worth about eighty pounds.

Time must be gained, at all hazards. Algitha tried everywhere, and enquired in all directions, but could not get more than five-and-twenty pounds for it. She felt anxious about her sister, and thought of coming over to Paris to see her, in order to talk over some matters that could no longer be kept out of sight.

Algitha had wished to give Hadria an opportunity for work and rest, and to avoid recurrence of worry; but it was no longer possible or fair to conceal the fact that there were troubles looming ahead, at Dunaghee. Their father had suffered several severe losses through some bank failures; and now that wretched company in which he had always had such faith appeared to be shaky, and if that were also to smash, the state of affairs would be desperate. Their father, in his optimistic fashion, still believed that the company would pull through. Of course all this anxiety was telling seriously on their mother. And, alas! she had been fretting very much about Hadria. After Algitha's misdeed, this second blow struck hard.

One must act on one's own convictions and not on those of somebody else, however beloved that other person might be, but truly the penalty of daring to take an independent line of action was almost unbearably severe. It really seemed, at times, as if there were nothing for it but to fold one's hands and do exactly as one was bid. Algitha was beginning to wonder whether her own revolt was about to be expiated by a life-long remorse!

"Ah, if mother had only not sacrificed herself for us, how infinitely grateful I should feel to her now! What sympathy there might have been between us all! If she had but given herself a chance, how she might have helped us, and what a friend she might have been to us, and we to her! But she would not."

Algitha said that her mother evidently felt Hadria's departure as a disgrace to the family. It was pathetic to hear her trying to answer people's casual questions about her, so as to conceal the facts without telling an untruth. Hadria was overwhelmed by this letter. Her first impulse was to pack up and go straight to Dunaghee. But as Algitha was there now, this seemed useless, at any rate for the present. And ought she after all to abandon her project, for which so much had been risked, so much pain inflicted? The question that she and Algitha thought they had decided long ago, began to beat again at the door of her conscience and her pity. Her reason still asserted that the suffering which people entail upon themselves, through a frustrated desire to force their own law of conduct on others, must be borne by themselves, as the penalty of their own tyrannous instinct and of their own narrow thought. It was utterly unfair to thrust that natural penalty of prejudice and of self-neglect on to the shoulders of others. Why should they be protected from the appointed punishment, by the offering of another life on the altar of their prejudice? Why should such a sacrifice be made in order to gratify their tyrannical desire to dictate? It was not fair, it was not reasonable.

Yet this conclusion of the intellect did not prevent the pain of pity and compunction, nor an inconsequent sense of guilt.

Meanwhile it would be best, perhaps, to await Algitha's arrival, when affairs might be in a less uncertain state. All decision must be postponed till then. "Try and come soon," she wrote to her sister.

To add to the anxieties of the moment, little Martha seemed to lose in energy since coming to the new abode, and Hadria began to fear that the house was not quite healthy. It was very cheap, and the landlady was honest, but if it had this serious drawback, another move, with probably another drawback, seemed to threaten. This was particularly troublesome, for who could tell how long it would be possible to remain in Paris? Hadria thought of the doctrine of the sovereignty of the will, and of all the grand and noble things that the Preposterous Society had said about it, not to mention Emerson and others—and she smiled.

However, she worked on, putting aside her anxieties, as far as was possible. She would not fail for lack of will, at any rate. But it was a hard struggle. Martha had to be very carefully watched just now.

Happily, after a few anxious days, she began to recover her fresh colour and her high spirits. The move would not be necessary, after all. Hadria had become more and more attached to the child, whose lovable qualities developed with her growth. She was becoming singularly like her unhappy mother, in feature and in colouring. ` Her eyes were large and blue and sweet, with a little touch of pathos in them that Hadria could not bear to see. It seemed almost like the after-glow of the mother's suffering.

Although adding to Hadria's anxieties, the child gave a sense of freshness and youth to the little *ménage*. She made the anxieties easier to bear.

Hadria came in, one morning, from her work, tired and full of foreboding. Hat and cloak were laid aside, and she sank into an arm-chair, lying back to lazily watch the efforts of the child to overturn the obstinate blue man, who was still the favourite plaything, perhaps because he was less amenable than the rest.

Martha looked up for sympathy. She wished to be helped in her persistent efforts to get the better of this upstart blue man with the red cap, who serenely resumed his erect position just as often as he was forced to the ground. He was a stout, healthy-looking person, inclining to *embonpoint;* bound to succeed, if only from sheer solidity of person. Hadria was drawn into the game, and the two spent a good half hour on the rug together, playing with that and other toys which Martha toddled off to the cupboard to collect. The child was in great delight. Hadria was playing with her; she liked that

better than having Jean Paul Auguste to play with. He took
her toys away and always wanted to play a different game.

The clock struck two. Hadria felt that she ought to go and
see Madame Vauchelet; it was more than a week since she had
called, and the kind old friend was always gently pained at
an absence of that length.

Then there was an article to finish, and she ought really to
write to Dunaghee and Henriette and—well the rest must
wait. Several other calls were also more than due, but it
was useless even to consider those to-day. In spite of an
oppressive sense of having much to do—perhaps *because* of
it—Hadria felt as if it were a sheer impossibility to rise from
that hearthrug. Besides, Martha would not hear of it. A
desire to rest, to idle, to float down the stream, instead of
trying always to swim against it, became overpowering. The
minutes passed away.

"The question is, Martha," Hadria said gravely, as she
proceeded to pile up a towering edifice of bricks, at the child's
command, "the question is : Are we going to stick to our plan,
or are we going to be beaten? Oh, take care, don't pull down
the fairy palace! That is a bad trick that little fingers have.
No, no, I must have my fairy palace ; I won't have it pulled
down. It is getting so fine, too ; minarets and towers, and
domes and pinnacles, all mixed beautifully. Such an architecture as you never saw ! But some day perhaps you will see
it. Those blue eyes look as if they were made for seeing it, in
the time to come."

"Pretty eyes !" said Martha with frank vanity, and then :
"Pretty house !"

"It is indeed a pretty house ; they all are. But they are so
horribly shaky. The minarets are top-heavy, I fear. That's the
fault of the makers of these bricks. They ought to make the solid
ones in proper proportion. But they can't be persuaded."

"Knock it down," said Martha, thrusting forth a mischievous
hand, which was caught in time to prevent entire destruction of
the precious edifice. Half the minarets had fallen.

"They must go up again," said Hadria. "How cruel to spoil all the work and all the beauty." But Martha laughed with the delight of easy conquest.

She watched with great interest the reconstruction, and seemed anxious that every detail should be finished and worthy her iconoclasm. Having satisfied herself that her strength would not be wasted on an incomplete object, she made a second attempt to lay the palace low. Again she was frustrated. The building had soared, by this time, to an ambitious height, and its splendour had reached the limits of the materials at command. The final pinnacle which was required to cope the structure had been mislaid. Hadria was searching for it, when Martha, seizing her chance, struck the palace a blow in its very heart, and in an instant, the whole was a wreck.

"Oh, if that is to be the way of it, why should I build?" asked Hadria.

Martha gave the command for another ornamental object which she might destroy.

"One would suppose you were a County-Council," Hadria exclaimed, "or the practical man. No, you shall have no more beauty to annihilate, little Vandal."

Martha, however, was now engaged in dissecting a doll, and presently a stream of sawdust from its chest announced that she had accomplished her dearest desire. She had found out what was inside that human effigy.

"I wish I could get at the sawdust that *I* am stuffed with," Hadria thought dreamily, as she watched the doll grow flabbier. "It is wonderful how little one does know one's own sawdust. It would be convenient to feel a little surer just now, for evidently I shall need it all very soon. And I feel somewhat like that doll, with the stream pouring out and the body getting limp."

She rose at last, and went to the window. The radiance of sun and green trees and the stir of human life; the rumble of omnibuses and the sound of wheels; the suggestion to the

imagination of the river just a little way off, and the merry
little *bateaux-mouches*—it was too much. Hadria rang for
Hannah ; asked her to take the child for a walk in the Bois,
stooped down to kiss the little upturned face, and went off.

In another ten minutes she was on board one of the steam-
boats, on her way up the river.

She had no idea whither she was going ; she would leave
that to chance. She only desired to feel the air and the sun
and have an opportunity to think. She soothed her uneasiness at the thought of Madame Vauchelet's disappointment by promising herself to call to-morrow. She sat watching
the boats and the water and the gay banks of the river with a
sense of relief, and a curious sort of fatalism, partly suggested
perhaps, by the persistent movement of the boat, and the
interminable succession of new scenes, all bubbling with
human life, full of the traces of past events. One layer of consciousness was busily engaged in thinking out the practical
considerations of the moment, another was equally busy with
the objective and picturesque world of the river side. If the
two or more threads of thought were not actually followed at
the same instant, the alternation was so rapid as not to be
perceived. What was to be done? How was the situation to
be met, if the worst came to the worst? Ah ! what far harder
contests had gone on in these dwellings that one passed by
the hundred. What lives of sordid toil had been struggled
through, in the effort to earn the privilege of continuing to
toil !

Hadria was inspired by keen curiosity concerning these
homes and gardens, and the whole panorama that opened
before her, as the little steamer puffed up the river. She
longed to penetrate below the surface and decipher the
strange palimpsest of human life. What scenes, what tragedies,
what comedies, those bright houses and demure little villas
concealed. It was not exactly consoling to remember how
small her own immediate difficulties were in comparison to
those of others, but it seemed to help her to face them. She

would not be discouraged. She had her liberty, and that had
to be paid for. Surely patience would prevail in the end.
She had learnt so much since she left home; among other
things, the habit of facing practical difficulties without that
dismay which carefully-nurtured women inevitably feel on their
first movement out of shelter. Yes, she had learnt much,
surprisingly much, in the short time. Her new knowledge
contained perhaps rather dangerous elements, for she had
begun to realize her own power, not only as an artist, but as a
woman. In this direction, had she so chosen. . . . Her
thoughts were arrested at this point, with a wrench. She felt
the temptation assail her, as of late it had been assailing her
faintly, to explore this territory.

But no, that was preposterous.

It was certainly not that she regarded herself as accountable,
in this matter, to any one but herself; it was not that she
acknowledged the suzerainty of her husband. A mere legal
claim meant nothing to her, and he knew it. But there were
moral perils of no light kind to be guarded against; the
danger such as a gambler runs, of being drawn away from the
real objects of life, of losing hold of one's main purpose, to
say nothing of the probable moral degeneration that would
result from such experiment. Yet there was no blinking the
fact that the desire had been growing in Hadria to test her
powers of attraction to the utmost, so as to discover exactly
their range and calibre. She felt rather as a boy might feel
who had come upon a cask of gunpowder, and longed to set
a match to it, just to see exactly how high it would blow off
the roof. She had kept the growing instincts at bay, being
determined that nothing avoidable should come between her
and her purpose. And then—well considering in what light
most men, in their hearts, regarded women—if one might judge
from their laws and their conduct and their literature, and the
society that they had organized—admiration from this sex was a
thing scarcely to be endured. Yet superficially, it was gratifying.

Why it should be so, was difficult to say, since it scarcely imposed upon one's very vanity. Yet it was easy enough to understand how women who had no very dominant interest in life, might come to have a thirst for masculine homage and for power over men till it became like the gambler's passion for play; and surely it had something in it of the same character.

The steamer was stopping now at St. Cloud. Yielding to an impulse, Hadria alighted at the landing-stage and walked on through the little town towards the palace.

The sun was deliciously hot; its rays struck through to the skin, and seemed to pour in life and well-being. The wayfarer stood looking up the steep green avenue, resting for a moment, before she began the ascent. At the top of the hill she paused again to look out over Paris, which lay spread far and wide beneath her, glittering and brilliant; the Eiffel Tower rising above domes and spires, in solitary inconsequence. It seemed to her as if she were looking upon the world and upon life, for the last time. A few weeks hence, would she be able to stand there and see the gay city at her feet? She plunged back along one of the converging avenues, yielding to the fascination of green alleys leading one knows not whither. Wandering on for some time, she finally drifted down hill again, towards the stately little garden near the palace. She was surprised by a hurrying step behind her, and Jouffroy's voice in her ear. She was about to greet him in her usual fashion, when he stopped her by plunging head foremost into a startling tirade—about her art, and her country, and her genius, and his despair; and finally his resolve that she should not belong to the accursed list of women who gave up their art for "*la famille.*"

The more Hadria tried to discover what had happened and what he meant, the faster he spoke and the more wildly he gesticulated.

He had seen how she was drifting away from her work and becoming entangled in little affairs of no importance, and he would not permit it. He cared not what her circumstances might be; she had a great talent that she had no right to sacrifice to

any circumstances whatever. He had come to save her. Not
finding her at her *apartement*, he had concluded that she had
taken refuge at her beloved St. Cloud. *Mon Dieu!* was he to
allow her to be taken away from her work, dragged back to
a narrow circle, crushed, broken, ruined—she who could give
such a sublime gift to her century—but it was impossible! It
would tear his heart. He would not permit it; she must
promise him not to allow herself to be persuaded to abandon
her purpose, no matter on what pretext they tried to lure her.
Hadria, in vain, enquired the cause of this sudden excitement.
Jouffroy only repeated his exhortations. Why did she not cut
herself entirely adrift from her country, her ties?

"They are to you, Madame, an oppression, a weariness,
a——"

" M. Jouffroy, I have never spoken to you about these things.
I cannot see how you are in a position to judge."

"Ah, but I know. Have I not heard *cette chère Madame
Bertaux* describe the life of an English village? And have I
not seen——?"

"Seen what?"

" *Cette dame.* I have seen her at your apartment this afternoon. Do not annihilate me, Madame; I mean not to offend
you. The lady has come from England on purpose to entrap
you; she came last night, and she stays at the Hotel du
Louvre. She spoke to me of you." Jouffroy raised his
hands to heaven. " Ha! then I understood, and I fled
hither to save you."

" Tell me, tell me quickly, Monsieur, has she fair hair and
large grey eyes. Is she tall?"

No, the lady was small, with dark hair, and brown, clever
eyes.

" A lady, elegant, well-dressed, but, ah! a woman to destroy
the soul of an artist merely by her presence. I told her that
you had decided to remain in France, to adopt it as your
country, for it was the country of your soul!"

" Good heavens!" exclaimed Hadria, unable to repress a

little burst of laughter, in spite of her disappointment and
foreboding.

" I told her that your friends would not let you go back to
England, to the land of fogs, the land of the *bourgeois*. The
lady seemed astonished, even indignant," continued Jouffroy,
waving his hands excitedly, "and she endeavoured to make
me silent, but she did not have success, I promise you. I
appealed to her. I pointed out to her your unique power. I
reminded her that such power is a gift supreme to the world,
which the world must not lose. For the making of little ones
and the care of the *ménage*, there were other women, but you
—you were a priestess in the temple of art, you were without
prejudice, without the *bourgeois* conscience, *grâce au ciel!* you
had the religion of the artist, and your worship was paid at the
shrine of Apollo. *Enfin,* I counselled this elegant lady to
return to England and to leave you in peace. Always with a
perfect politeness," added Jouffroy, panting from excess of
emotion. Hadria tried in vain to gather the object of this
sudden visit on the part of Henriette (for Henriette the
elegant lady must certainly be).

"I must return at once," she said. "I fear something must
have gone wrong at home." Jouffroy danced with fury.

"But I tell you, Madame, that she will drag you back to
your fogs; she will tell you some foolish story, she will address
herself to your pity. Your family has doubtless become ill.
Families have that habit when they desire to achieve something. Bah, it is easy to become ill when one is angry, and so
to make oneself pitied and obeyed. It is a common usage.
Madame, beware; it is for you the critical moment. One
must choose."

"It is not always a matter of choice, M. Jouffroy."

" Always," he insisted. He endeavoured to induce her to
linger, to make a decision on the spot. But Hadria hastened
on towards the river. Jouffroy followed in despair. He
ceased not to urge upon her the peril of the moment and the
need for resolute action. He promised to help her by every

means in his power, to watch over her career, to assist her in bringing her gift to maturity. Never before had he felt a faith so profound, or an interest so fervid in the genius of any woman. One had, after all, regarded them ("les femmes") as accomplished animals.

"But of whom one demands the duties of human beings and the courage of heroes," added Hadria.

"*Justement,*" cried Jouffroy. But Madame had taught him a superb truth. For her, he felt a sentiment of admiration and reverence the most profound. She had been to him a revelation. He entreated her to bestow upon him the privilege of · watching over her career. Let her only make the wise decision now, everything would arrange itself. It needed only courage.

"This is the moment for decision. Remain now among ûs, and pursue your studies with a calm mind, and I promise you—I, Jouffroy, who have the right to speak on this matter—I promise you shall have a success beyond the wildest dreams of your ambition. Madame, you do not guess your own power. I know how your genius can be saved to the world ; I know the artist's nature. Have I not had the experience of twenty years ? I know what feeds and rouses it, and I know what kills it. And this I tell you, Madame, that if you stay here, you have a stupendous future before you ; if you return to your fogs and your tea-parties— ah, then, Madame, your genius will die and your heart will be broken."

CHAPTER XXXVI.

IT was with great reluctance that Jouffroy acceded to Hadria's wish to return home alone. She watched the river banks, and the boats coming and passing, with a look of farewell in her eyes. She meant to hold out to the utmost limits of the possible, but she knew that the possible *had* limits, and she awaited judgment at the bar of destiny.

She hurried home on arriving at the quay, and found Henriette waiting for her.

"What is it? Tell me at once, if anything is wrong."

"Then you knew I was here!" exclaimed Miss Temperley.

"Yes; M. Jouffroy told me. He found me at St. Cloud. Quick, Henriette, don't keep me in suspense."

"There is nothing of immediate seriousness," Henriette replied, and her sister-in-law drew a breath of relief. Tea was brought in by Hannah, and a few questions were asked and answered. Miss Temperley having been installed in an easy chair, and her cloak and hat removed, said that her stay in Paris was uncertain as to length. It would depend on many things. Hadria rang for the tray to be taken away, after tea was over, and as Hannah closed the door, a sensation of sick apprehension overcame her, for a moment. Henriette had obviously come to Paris in order to recapture the fugitive, and meant to employ all her tact in the delicate mission. She was devoted to Hubert and the children, heart and soul, and would face anything on their behalf, including the present disagreeable task. Hadria looked at her sister-in-law with admiration. She offered homage to the prowess of the enemy.

Miss Temperley held a commanding position, fortified by

ideas and customs centuries old, and supported by allies on
every side.

It ran through Hadria's mind that it was possible to refuse
to allow the subject to be broached, and thus escape the
encounter altogether. It would save many words on both
sides. But Henriette had always been in Hubert's confidence,
and it occurred to Hadria that it might be well to define her
own position once more, since it was thus about to be directly
and frankly attacked. Moreover, Hadria began to be fired
with the spirit of battle. It was not merely for herself, but on
behalf of her sex, that she longed to repudiate the insult that
seemed to her, to be involved in Henriette's whole philosophy.

However, if the enemy shewed no signs of hostility, Hadria
resolved that she also would keep the truce.

Miss Temperley had already mentioned that Mrs. Fullerton
was now staying at the Red House, for change of air. She
had been far from well, and of course was worrying very
much over these money troubles and perils ahead, as well
as about Hadria's present action. Mrs. Fullerton had herself suggested that Henriette should go over to Paris to see
what could be done to patch up the quarrel.

"Ah!" exclaimed Hadria, and a cloud settled on her brow.
Henriette had indeed come armed *cap à pie!*

There was a significant pause. "And your mission," said
Hadria at length, "is to recapture the lost bird."

"We are considering your own good," murmured Miss
Temperley.

"If I have not always done what I ought to have done
in my life, it is not for want of guidance and advice from
others," said Hadria with a smile and a sigh.

"You are giving everyone so much pain, Hadria. Do you
never think of that?"

There was another long pause. The two women sat
opposite one another. Miss Temperley's eyes were bent on
the carpet; Hadria's on a patch of blue sky that could be
seen through a side street, opposite.

"If you would use your ability on behalf of your sex instead of against it, Henriette, women would have cause to bless you, for all time !"

"Ah ! if you did but know it, I *am* using what ability I have on their behalf," Miss Temperley replied.   "I am trying to keep them true to their noble mission.   But I did not come to discuss general questions.   I came to appeal to your best self, Hadria."

"I am ready," said Hadria.   "Only, before you start, I want you to remember clearly what took place at Dunaghee before my marriage ; for I foresee that our disagreement will chiefly hang upon your lapse of memory on that point, and upon my perhaps inconveniently distinct recollection of those events."

"I wish to lay before you certain facts and certain results of your present conduct," said Henriette.

"Very good.   I wish to lay before you certain facts and certain results of your past conduct."

"Ah ! do not let us wrangle, Hadria."

"I don't wish to wrangle, but I must keep hold of these threads that you seem always to drop.   And then there is another point : when I talked of leaving home, it was not *I* who suggested that it should be for ever."

"I know, I know," cried Henriette hastily.   "I have again and again pointed out to Hubert how wrong he was in that, and how he gave you a pretext for what you have done.   I admit it and regret it deeply.   Hubert lost his temper ; that is the fact of the matter.   He thought himself bitterly wronged by you."

"Quite so ; he felt it a bitter wrong that I should claim that liberty of action which I warned him before our marriage that I *should* claim.   He made no objection *then:* on the contrary, he professed to agree with me ; and declared that he did not care what I might think ; but now he says that in acting as I have acted, I have forfeited my position, and need not return to the Red House."

"I know.   But he spoke in great haste and anger.   He has made me his *confidante.*"

"And his ambassador ?"

Henrjette shook her head. No; she had acted entirely on her own responsibility. She could not bear to see her brother suffering. He had felt the quarrel deeply.

"On account of the stupid talk," said Hadria. "*That* will soon blow over."

"On account of the talk partly. You know his sensitiveness about anything that concerns his domestic life. He acutely feels your leaving the children, Hadria. Try to put yourself in his place. Would *you* not feel it?"

"If I were a man with two children of whom I was ex-extremely fond, I have no doubt that I should feel it very much indeed if I lost an intelligent and trustworthy superintendent, whose services assured the children's welfare, and relieved me of all anxiety on their account."

"If you are going to take this hard tone, Hadria, I fear you will never listen to reason."

"Henriette, when people look popular sentiments squarely in the face, they are always called hard, or worse. You have kept yourself thoroughly informed of our affairs. Whose parental sentiments were gratified by the advent of those children—Hubert's or mine?"

"But you are a mother."

Hadria laughed. "You play into my hands, Henriette. You tacitly acknowledge that it was not for *my* gratification that those children were brought into the world (a common story, let me observe), and then you remind me that I am a mother! Your mentor must indeed be slumbering. You are simply scathing—on my behalf! Have you come all the way from England for this?"

"You *won't* understand. I mean that motherhood has duties. You can't deny that."

"I can and I do."

Miss Temperley stared. "You will find no human being to agree with you," she said at length.

"That does not alter my opinion."

"Oh, Hadria, explain yourself! You utter paradoxes. I want to understand your point of view."

"It is simple enough. I deny that motherhood has duties except when it is absolutely free, absolutely uninfluenced by the pressure of opinion, or by any of the innumerable tyrannies that most children have now to thank for their existence."

Miss Temperley shook her head. "I don't see that any 'tyranny,' as you call it, exonerates a mother from her duty to her child."

"There we differ. Motherhood, in our present social state, is the sign and seal as well as the means and method of a woman's bondage. It forges chains of her own flesh and blood; it weaves cords of her own love and instinct. She agonizes, and the fruit of her agony is not even legally hers. Name me a position more abject! A woman with a child in her arms is, to me, the symbol of an abasement, an indignity, more complete, more disfiguring and terrible, than any form of humiliation that the world has ever seen."

"You must be mad!" exclaimed Miss Temperley. "That symbol has stood to the world for all that is sweetest and holiest."

"I know it has! So profound has been our humiliation!"

"I don't know what to say to anyone so wrong-headed and so twisted in sentiment."

Hadria smiled thoughtfully.

"While I am about it, I may as well finish this disclosure of feeling, which, again I warn you, is *not* peculiar to myself, however you may lay that flattering unction to your soul. I have seen and heard of many a saddening evidence of our sex's slavery since I came to this terrible and wonderful city: the crude, obvious buying and selling that we all shudder at; but hideous as it is, to me it is far less awful than this other respectable form of degradation that everyone glows and smirks over."

Miss Temperley clasped her hands in despair.

"I simply can't understand you. What you say is rank heresy against all that is most beautiful in human nature."

"Surely the rank heresy is to be laid at the door of those

who degrade and enslave that which they assert to be
most beautiful in human nature. But I am not speaking
to convince ; merely to shew where you cannot count upon
me for a point of attack. Try something else."

"But it is so strange, so insane, as it seems to me. Do you
mean to throw contempt on motherhood *per se ?* "

"I am not discussing motherhood *per se;* no woman has
yet been in a position to know what it is *per se,* strange as it
may appear. No woman has yet experienced it apart from
the enormous pressure of law and opinion that has, always,
formed part of its inevitable conditions. The illegal mother
is hounded by her fellows in one direction ; the legal mother
is urged and incited in another : free motherhood is unknown
amongst us. I speak of it as it is. To speak of it *per se,* for
the present, is to discuss the transcendental."

There was a moment's excited pause, and Hadria then went
on more rapidly. "You know well enough, Henriette, what
thousands of women there are to whom the birth of their
children is an intolerable burden, and a fierce misery from
which many would gladly seek escape by death. And indeed
many *do* seek escape by death. What is the use of this eternal
conspiracy of silence about that which every woman out of her
teens knows as well as she knows her own name ? "

But Henriette preferred to ignore that side of her experience.
She murmured something about the maternal instinct, and its
potency.

"I don't deny the potency of the instinct," said Hadria,
"but I do say that it is shamefully presumed upon. Strong it
obviously must be, if industrious cultivation and encourage-
ments and threats and exhortations can make it so ! All the
Past as well as all the weight of opinion and training in the
Present has been at work on it, thrusting and alluring and
coercing the woman to her man-allotted fate."

"*Nature*-allotted, if you please," said Henriette. "There
is no need for alluring or coercing."

"Why do it then ? Now, be frank, Henriette, and try not to
be offended. Would *you* feel no sense of indignity in performing

a function of this sort (however noble and so on you might think it *per se*), if you knew that it would be demanded of you as a duty, if you did not welcome it as a joy?"

" I should acknowledge it as a duty, if I did not welcome it as a joy."

" In other words, you would accept the position of a slave."

" How so ? "

" By bartering your womanhood, by using these powers of body, in return for food and shelter and social favour, or for the sake of so-called ' duty' irrespective of—perhaps in direct opposition to your feelings. How then do you differ from the slave woman who produces a progeny of young slaves, to be disposed of as shall seem good to her perhaps indulgent master? I see no essential difference."

" I see the difference between honour and ignominy," said Henriette. Hadria shook her head, sadly.

" The differences are all in detail and in circumstance. I am sorry if I offend your taste. The facts are offensive. The bewildering thing is that the facts themselves never seem to offend you ; only the mention of them."

"It would take too long to go into this subject," said Henriette. "I can only repeat that I fail to understand your extraordinary views of the holiest of human instincts."

" *That* catch-word ! And you use it rashly, Henriette, for do you not know that the deepest of all degradation comes of misusing that which is most holy?"

"A woman who does her duty is not to be accused of misusing anything," cried Miss Temperley hotly.

" Is there then no sin, no misuse of power in sending into the world swarms of fortuitous, poverty-stricken human souls, as those souls must be who are born in bondage, with the blended instincts of the slave and the master for a proud inheritance? It sounds awful I know, but truth is apt to sound awful. Motherhood, as our wisdom has appointed it, among civilized people, represents a prostitution of the reproductive powers, which precisely corresponds to that other abuse, which seems to most of us so infinitely more shocking."

Miss Temperley preferred not to reply to such a remark, and the entrance of little Martha relieved the tension of the moment. Henriette, though she bore the child a grudge, could not resist her when she came forward and put up her face to be kissed.

"She is really growing very pretty," said Henriette, in a tone which betrayed the agitation which she had been struggling to hide.

Martha ran for her doll and her blue man, and was soon busy at play, in a corner of the room, building Eiffel Towers out of stone bricks, and knocking them down again.

"I don't yet quite understand, Henriette, your object in coming to Paris." Hadria's voice had grown calmer.

"I came to make an appeal to your sense of duty and your generosity."

"Ah !"

"I came," Henriette went on, bracing herself as if for a great effort, "to remind you that when you married, you entered into a contract which you now repudiate."

Hadria started up, reddening with anger.

"I did no such thing, and you know it, Henriette. How do you *dare* to sit there and tell me that ?"

"I tell you nothing but the truth. Every woman who marries enters, by that fact, into a contract."

Miss Temperley had evidently regarded this as a strong card and played it hopefully.

Hadria was trembling with anger. She steadied her voice. "Then you actually intended to *entrap* me into this so-called contract, by leading me to suppose that it would mean nothing more between Hubert and myself than an unavoidable formality ! You tell me this to my face, and don't appear to see that you are confessing an act of deliberate treachery."

"Nonsense," cried Henriette. "There was nothing that any sane person would have objected to, in our conduct."

Hadria stood looking down scornfully on her sister-in-law. She shrugged her shoulders, as if in bewilderment.

"And yet you would have felt yourselves stained with

dishonour for the rest of your lives had you procured anything *else* on false pretences! But a woman—that is a different affair. The code of honour does not here apply, it would seem. *Any* fraud may be honourably practised on *her*, and wild is the surprise and indignation if she objects when she finds it out."

"You are perfectly mad," cried Henriette, tapping angrily with her fingers on the arm of her chair.

"What I say is true, whether I be mad or sane. What you call the 'contract' is simply a cunning contrivance for making a woman and her possible children the legal property of a man, and for enlisting her own honour and conscience to safeguard the disgraceful transaction."

"Ah," said Henriette, on the watch for her opportunity, "then you admit that her honour and conscience *are* enlisted?"

"Certainly, in the case of most women. That enlistment is a masterpiece of policy. To make a prisoner his own warder is surely no light stroke of genius. But that is exactly what I refused to be from the first, and no one could have spoken more plainly. And now you are shocked and pained and aggrieved because I won't eat my words. Yet we have talked over all this, in my room at Dunaghee, by the hour. Oh! Henriette, why did you not listen to your conscience and be honest with me?"

"Hadria, you insult me."

"Why could not Hubert choose one among the hundreds and thousands of women who would have passed under the yoke without a question, and have gladly harnessed herself to his chariot by the reins of her own conscience?"

"I would to heaven he *had!*" Henriette was goaded into replying.

Hadria laughed. Then her brow clouded with pain. "Ah, why did he not meet my frankness with an equal frankness, at the time? All this trouble would have been saved us both if *only* he had been honest."

"My dear, he was in love with you."

"And so he thought himself justified in deceiving me. There is *indeed* war to the knife between the sexes!" Hadria stood with her elbows on the back of a high arm-chair, her chin resting on her hands.

"It is not fair to use that word. I tell you that we both confidently expected that when you had more experience you would be like other women and adjust yourself sensibly to your conditions."

"I see," said Hadria, "and so it was decided that Hubert was to pretend to have no objections to my wild ideas, so as to obtain my consent, trusting to the ponderous bulk of circumstance to hold me flat and subservient when I no longer had a remedy in my power. You neither of you lack brains, at any rate." Henriette clenched her hands in the effort of self-control.

"In ninety-nine cases out of a hundred, our forecasts would have come true," she said. "I mean——"

"That is refreshingly frank," cried Hadria.

"We thought we acted for the best."

"Oh, if it comes to that, the Spanish Inquisitors doubtless thought that they were acting for the best, when they made bonfires of heretics in the market-places." Henriette bent her head and clasped the arms of the chair, tightly.

"Well, if there be any one at fault in the matter, *I* am the culprit," she said in a voice that trembled. "It was *I* who assured Hubert that experience would alter you. It was I who represented to him that though you might be impulsive, even hard at times, you could not persist in a course that would give pain, and that if you saw that any act of yours caused him to suffer, you would give it up. I was convinced that your character was good and noble *au fond*, Hadria, and I have believed it up to this moment."

Hadria drew herself together with a start, and her face darkened. "You make me regret that I ever had a good or a pitiful impulse!" she cried with passion.

She went to the window and stood leaning against the casement, with crossed arms.

Henriette turned round in her chair.

"Why do you always resist your better nature, Hadria?"

"You use it against me. It is the same with all women.

Let them beware of their 'better natures,' poor hunted fools! for that 'better nature' will be used as a dog-chain, by which they can be led, like toy-terriers, from beginning to end of what they are pleased to call their lives!"

"Oh, Hadria, Hadria!" cried Miss Temperley with deep regret in her tone.

But Hadria was only roused by the remonstrance.

"It is cunning, shallow, heartless women, who really fare best in our society; its conditions suit them. *They* have no pity, no sympathy to make a chain of; *they* don't mind stooping to conquer; *they* don't mind playing upon the weaker, baser sides of men's natures; *they* don't mind appealing, for their own ends, to the pity and generosity of others; *they* don't mind swallowing indignity and smiling abjectly, like any woman of the harem at her lord, so that they gain their object. *That* is the sort of 'woman's nature' that our conditions are busy selecting. Let us cultivate it. We live in a scientific age; the fittest survive. Let us be 'fit.'"

"Let us be womanly, let us do our duty, let us hearken to our conscience!" cried Henriette.

"Thank you! If my conscience is going to be made into a helm by which others may guide me according to their good pleasure, the sooner that helm is destroyed the better. That is the conclusion to which you drive me and the rest of us, Henriette."

"Charity demands that I do not believe what you say," said Miss Temperley.

"Oh, don't trouble to be charitable!"

Henriette heaved a deep sigh. "Hadria," she said, "are you going to allow your petty rancour about this—well, I will call it error of ours, if you like to be severe—are you going to bear malice and ruin your own life and Hubert's and the children's? Are you so unforgiving, so lacking in generosity?"

"*You* call it an error. *I* call it a treachery," returned Hadria. "Why should the results of that treachery be thrust on to *my* shoulders to bear? Why should *my* generosity be

summoned to your rescue? But I suppose you calculated
on that sub-consciously, at the time."

"*Hadria!*"

"This is a moment for plain speaking, if ever there was
one. You must have reckoned on an appeal to my generosity,
and on the utter helplessness of my position when once I was
safely entrapped. It was extremely clever and well thought
out. Do you suppose that you would have dared to act as
you did, if there had been means of redress in my hands,
after marriage?"

"If I *did* rely on your generosity, I admit my mistake,"
said Henriette bitterly.

"And now when your deed brings its natural harvest of
disaster, you and Hubert come howling, like frightened
children, to have the mischief set straight again, the consequences of your treachery averted, by *me*, of all people on
this earth!"

"You are his wife, the mother of his children."

"In heaven's name, Henriette, why do you always run into
my very jaws?"

"I don't know what you mean."

"Why do you catalogue my injuries when your point is to
deny them?"

Henriette rose with a vivid flush.

"Hadria, Hubert is one of the best men in England. I——"

"When have I disputed that?"

Hadria advanced towards Miss Temperley, and stood
looking her full in the face.

"I believe that Hubert has acted conscientiously, according
to his standard. But I detest his standard. He did not
think it wrong or treacherous to behave as he did towards
me. But it is *that very fact* that I so bitterly resent. I
could have forgiven him a sin against myself alone, which
he acknowledged to be a sin. But this is a sin against
my entire sex, which he does *not* acknowledge to be a sin.
It is the insolence that is implied in supposing it allowable for a man to trick a woman in that way, without the

smallest damage to his self-respect, that sticks so in my throat. What does it imply as regards his attitude towards all women? Ah! it is *that* which makes me feel so rancorous. And I resent Hubert's calm assumption that he had a right to judge what was best for me, and even to force me, by fraud, into following his view, leaving me afterwards to adjust myself with circumstance as best I might: to make my bitter choice between unconditional surrender, and the infliction of pain and distress, on him, on my parents, on everybody. Ah, you calculated cunningly, Henriette! I *am* a coward about giving pain, little as you may now be disposed to credit it. You have tight hold of the end of my chain."

Hadria was pacing restlessly up and down the room. Little Martha ran out with her doll, and offered it, as if with a view to chase away the perturbed look from Hadria's face. The latter stooped mechanically and took the doll, smiling her thanks, and stroking the child's fair curls tenderly. Then she recommenced her walk up and down the room, carrying the doll carefully on her arm.

"Take care of dolly," Martha recommended, and went back to her other toys.

"Yes, Henriette, you and Hubert have made your calculations cleverly. You have advocates only too eloquent in my woman's temperament. You have succeeded only too well by your fraud, through which I now stand here, with a life in fragments, bound, chafe as I may, to choose between alternative disasters for myself and for all of us. Had you two only acted straightly with me, and kindly allowed me to judge for myself, instead of treacherously insisting on judging for me, this knot of your tying which you naïvely bring me to unravel, would never have wrung the life out of me as it is doing now—nor would it have caused you and Hubert so much virtuous distress."

Hadria recommenced her restless pacing to and fro.

"But, Hadria, *do* be calm, *do* look at the matter from our point of view. I have owned my indiscretion." (Hadria gave a little scornful cry.) "Surely you are not going to throw over all allegiance to your husband on *that* account, even granting he was to blame." Hadria stopped abruptly.

"I deny that I owe allegiance to a man who so treated me. I don't deny that he had excuses. The common standards exonerate him ; but, good heavens, a sense of humour, if nothing else, ought to save him from making this grotesque claim on his victim! To preach the duties of wife and mother to *me!*" Hadria broke into a laugh. "It is inconceivably comic."

Henriette shrugged her shoulders. "I fear my sense of humour is defective. I can't see the justice of repudiating the duty of one's position, since there the position *is*, an accomplished fact not to be denied. Why not make the best of it ? "

" Henriette, you are amazing ! Supposing a wicked bigamist had persuaded a woman to go through a false marriage ceremony, and when she became aware of her real position, imagine him saying to her, with grave and virtuous mien, ' My dear, why repudiate the duties of your position, since there your position *is*, an accomplished fact not to be denied?'"

"Oh, that's preposterous," cried Henriette.

"It's preposterous and it's parallel."

"Hubert did not try to entrap you into doing what was wrong."

"We need not discuss that, for it is not the point. The point is that the position (be that right or wrong) was forced on the woman in both cases by fraud, and is then used as a pretext to exact from her the desired conduct ; what the author of the fraud euphoniously calls 'duty.'"

"You are positively insulting !" cried Henriette, rising.

By this time, Hadria had allowed the doll to slip back, and its limp body was hanging down disconsolately from her elbow, although she was clutching it, with absent-minded anxiety, to her side, in the hope of arresting its threatened fall.

"Oh, look at dolly, look, look ! " cried Martha reproach fully. Hadria seized its legs and pulled it back again, murmuring some consolatory promise to its mistress.

"It is strange how you succeed in putting me on the defensive, Henriette—I who have been wronged. A horrible wrong it is too. It has ruined my life. You will never know all that it implies, never, never, though I talk till Doomsday. Nobody will—except Professor Fortescue."

Henriette gave a horrified gesture. "I believe you are in love with that man. *That* is the cause of all this wild conduct."

Miss Temperley had lost self-control for a moment.

Hadria looked at her steadily.

"I beg your pardon. I spoke in haste, Hadria. You have your faults, but Hubert has nothing to fear from you in that respect, I am sure."

"Really?" Hadria had come forward and was standing with her left elbow on the mantel-piece, the doll still tucked under her right arm. "And you think that I would, at all hazards, respect a legal tie which no feeling consecrates?"

"I do you that justice," murmured Henriette, turning very white.

"You think that I should regard myself as so completely the property of a man whom I do not love, and who actively dislikes me, as to hold my very feelings in trust for him. Disabuse yourself of that idea, Henriette. I claim rights over myself, and I will hold myself in pawn for no man. This is no news either to you or to Hubert. Why pretend that it is?"

Henriette covered her face with her hands.

"I can but hope," she said at length, "that even now you are saying these horrible things out of mere opposition. I cannot, I simply *cannot* believe, that you would bring disgrace upon us all."

"If you chose to regard it as a disgrace that I should make so bold as to lay claim to myself, that, it seems to me, would be your own fault." Henriette sprang forward white and trembling, and clutched Hadria's arm excitedly.

"Ah! you *could* not! you *could* not! Think of your mother and father, if you will not think of your husband and children. You terrify me!"

Hadria was moved with pity at Henriette's white quivering face.

"Don't trouble," she said, more gently. "There is no thunderbolt about to fall in our discreet circle." (A hideous crash from the overturning of one of Martha's Eiffel Towers seemed to belie the words.)

Miss Temperley's clutch relaxed, and she gave a gasp of relief.

"Tell me, Hadria, that you did not mean what you said."

"I can't do that, for I meant it, every syllable."

"Promise me then at least, that before you do anything to bring misery and disgrace on us all, you will tell us of your intention, and give us a chance of putting our side of the matter before you."

"Of protecting your vested interests," said Hadria; "your right of way through my flesh and spirit."

"Of course you put it unkindly."

"I will not make promises for the future. The future is quite enough hampered with the past, without setting antici-patory traps and springes for unwary feet. But I refuse this promise merely on general principles. I am not about to distress you in that particular way, though I think you would only have yourselves to blame if I *were*."

Miss Temperley drew another deep breath, and the colour began to return to her face.

"So far, so good," she said. "Now tell me—Is there nothing that would make you accept your duties?"

"Even if I were to accept what you call my duties, it would not be in the spirit that you would desire to see. It would be in cold acknowledgment of the force of existing facts—facts which I regard as preposterous, but admit to be coercive." Henriette sank wearily into her chair.

"Do you then hold it justifiable for a woman to inflict pain on those near to her, by a conduct that she may think justifi-able in itself?"

Hadria hesitated for a moment.

" A woman is so desperately entangled, and restricted, and betrayed, by common consent, in our society, that I hold her justified in using desperate means, as one who fights for dear life. She may harden her heart—if she can."

" I am thankful to think that she very seldom *can!*" cried Henriette.

" Ah! that is our weak point! For a long time to come, we shall be overpowered by our own cage-born instincts, by our feminine conscience that has been trained so cleverly to dog the woman's footsteps, in man's interest—his detective in plain clothes!"

" Of course, if you repudiate all moral claim——" began Henriette, weakly.

" I will not insult your intelligence by considering that remark."

" Are you determined to harden yourself against every appeal?" Hadria looked at her sister-in-law, in silence.

" Why don't you answer me, Hadria?"

" Because I have just been endeavouring, evidently in vain, to explain in what light I regard appeals on this point."

" Then Hubert and the children are to be punished for what you are pleased to call his fraud—the fraud of a man in love with you, anxious to please you, to agree with you, and believing you too good and noble to allow his life to be spoilt by this girl's craze for freedom. It is inconceivable!"

" I fear that Hubert must be prepared to endure the consequences of his actions, like the rest of us. It is the custom, I know, for the sex that men call weaker, to saddle themselves with the consequences of men's deeds, but I think we should have a saner, and a juster world if the custom were discontinued."

" You have missed one of the noblest lessons of life, Hadria," cried Miss Temperley, rising to leave. " You do not understand the meaning of self-sacrifice."

" A principle that, in woman, has been desecrated by misuse," said Hadria. " There is no power, no quality, no

gift or virtue, physical or moral, that we have *not* been trained
to misuse.   Self-sacrifice stands high on the list."

Miss Temperley shrugged her shoulders, sadly and hopelessly.

"You have fortified yourself on every side.   My words only
prompt you to throw up another earthwork at the point
attacked.   I do harm instead of good.   I will leave you to
think the matter over alone."   Miss Temperley moved towards
the door.

"Ah, you are clever, Henriette!   You know well that I am
far better acquainted with the weak points of my own fortifi-
cations than you can be, who did not build them, and that
when I have done with the defence against you, I shall
commence the attack myself.   You have all the advantages on
your side.   Mine is a forlorn hope :—a handful of Greeks at
Thermopylae against all the host of the Great King.   We are
foredoomed; the little band must fall, but some day,
Henriette, when you and I shall be no more troubled with
these turbulent questions—some day, these great blundering
hosts of barbarians will be driven back, and the Greek will
conquer.   Then the realm of liberty will grow wide !"

"I begin to hate the very name !" exclaimed Henriette.

Hadria's eyes flashed, and she stood drawn up, straight and
defiant, before the mantel-piece.

"Ah! there is a fiercer Salamis and a crueller Marathon yet
to be fought, before the world will so much as guess what
freedom means.   I have no illusions now, regarding my own
chances, but I should hold it as an honour to stand and fall at
Thermopylae, with Leonidas and his Spartans."

"I believe that some day you will see things with different
eyes," said Henriette.

The doll fell with a great crash, into the fender among the
fire-irons, and there was a little burst of laughter.   Miss
Temperley passed through the door, at the same instant,
with great dignity.

CHAPTER XXXVII.

A S Hadria had foretold, she commenced the attack on herself as soon as Henriette had departed, and all night long, the stormy inner debate was kept up. Her mind never wavered, but her heart was rebellious. Hubert deserved to pay for his conduct; but if we all had to pay for our conduct to the uttermost farthing, that would be hard, if just. If Hadria assumed the burden of Hubert's debt, it would mean what M. Jouffroy had pointed out. Hubert's suffering would be only on account of offended public opinion; hers—but then her parents would suffer as well as Hubert. Round and round went the thoughts, like vast wheels, and when towards morning, she dozed off a little, the wheels were still turning in a vague, weary way, and as they turned, the life seemed to be crushed gradually out of the sleeper.

Jouffroy came to enquire whether the decision had been made. He was in a state of great excitement. He gave fervent thanks that Hadria had stood firm.

"You do not forget my words, Madame?"

"I shall never forget them, Monsieur."

Henriette discreetly forbore to say anything further on the subject of dispute. She waited, hopefully.

"Hubert has been troubled about the money that your father set apart, on your marriage, as a contribution to the household expenses," she said, one morning. "Your father did not place it all in your name."

"I know," said Hadria. "It is tied up, in some way, for the use of the family. I have a small sum only in my own control."

" Hubert is now leaving half of it to accumulate. The other half has still to go towards the expenses at the Red House. I suppose you approve ? "

"Certainly," said Hadria. "My father designed it for that purpose."

" But Hubert feared you might be running short of money, and wished to send you some; but the trustees say it is against the conditions of the trust."

"So I suppose."

" I wanted you to know about it, that is all," said Henriette. "Also, I should like to say that though Hubert does not feel that he can ask you to return to the Red House, after what has happened—he cannot risk your refusing—yet I take it on myself to tell you, that he would only be too glad if you would go back."

"Thank you, I understand."

Next morning, Henriette came with a letter in her hand

"Bad news !" Hadria exclaimed.

The letter announced the failure of the Company. It was the final blow. Dunaghee would have to be given up. Mrs. Fullerton's settlement was all that she and her husband would now have to live upon.

Hadria sat gazing at the letter, with a dazed expression. Almost before the full significance of the calamity had been realized, a telegram arrived, announcing that Mrs. Fullerton had fallen dangerously ill.

The rest of that day was spent in packing, writing notes, settling accounts, and preparing for departure.

"When—how are you going?" cried Madame Vauchelet, in dismay.

" By the night boat, by the night boat," Hadria replied hurriedly, as if the hurry of her speech would quicken her arrival in England.

The great arches of the station which had appealed to her imagination, at the moment of arrival, swept upward, hard and grey, in the callous blue light. Hadria breathed deep. Was she the same person who had arrived that night, with every nerve thrilled with hope and resolve? Ah! there had been so much to learn, and the time had been so short. Starting with her present additional experience, she could have managed so much better. But of what use to think of that? How different the homeward journey from the intoxicating outward flight, in the heyday of the spring!

What did that telegram mean? *Ill; dangerously, dangerously.* The words seemed to be repeated cruelly, insistently, by the jogging of the train and the rumble of the wheels. The anxiety gnawed on, rising at times into terror, dulling again to a steady ache. And then remorse began to fit a long-pointed fang into a sensitive spot in her heart. In vain to resist. It was securely placed. Let reason hold her peace.

A thousand fears, regrets, self-accusations, revolts, swarmed insect-like in Hadria's brain, as the train thundered through the darkness, every tumultuous sound and motion exaggerated to the consciousness, by the fact that there was no distraction of the attention by outside objects. Nothing offered itself to the sight except the strange lights and shadows of the lamp thrown on the cushions of the carriage; Henriette's figure in one corner, Hannah, with the child, in another, and the various rugs and trappings of wandering Britons. Everything was contracted, narrow. The sea-passage had the same sinister character. Hadria compared it to the crossing of the Styx in Charon's gloomy ferry-boat.

She felt a patriotic thrill on hearing the first mellow English voice pronouncing the first kindly English sentence. The simple, slow, honest quality of the English nature gave one a sense of safety. What splendid raw material to make a nation out of! But, ah, it was sometimes dull to live with! These impressions, floating vaguely in the upper currents of the mind, were simultaneous with a thousand thoughts and anxieties, and gusts of bitter fear and grief.

What would be the end of it all? This uprooting from the

old home—it wrung one's heart to think of it. Scarcely could the thought be faced. Her father, an exile from his beloved fields and hills ; her mother banished from her domain of so many years, and after all these disappointments and mortifications and sorrows ! It was piteous. Where would they live ? What would they do ?

Hadria fought with her tears. Ah ! it was hard for old people to have to start life anew, bitterly hard. This was the moment for their children to flock to their rescue, to surround them with care, with affection, with devotion ; to make them feel that at least *some*thing that could be trusted, was left to them from the wreck.

"Ah ! poor mother, poor kind father, you were very good to us all, very, very good !"

CHAPTER XXXVIII.

MRS. FULLERTON'S illness proved even more serious than the doctor had expected. She asked so incessantly for her daughters, especially Hadria, that all question of difference between her and Hubert was laid aside, by tacit consent, and the sisters took their place at their mother's bedside. The doctor said that the patient must have been suffering, for many years, from an exhausted state of the nerves and from some kind of trouble. Had she had any great disappointment or anxiety?

Hadria and Algitha glanced at one another. "Yes," said Algitha, "my mother has had a lot of troublesome children to worry and disappoint her."

"Ah!" exclaimed the doctor, nodding his head. "Well, now has come a crisis in Mrs. Fullerton's condition. This illness has been incubating for years. She must have undergone mental misery of a very acute kind, whether or not the cause may have been adequate. If her children desire to keep her among them, it will be necessary to treat her with the utmost care, and to oppose her in *nothing*. Further disappointment or chagrin, she has no longer the power to stand. There are complications. Her heart will give trouble, and all your vigilance and forbearance are called for, to avoid serious consequences. I think it right to speak frankly, for everything depends—and always hereafter will depend—on the patient's being saved as much as possible from the repetition of any former annoyance or sorrow. At best, there will be much for her to endure; I dread an uprooting of long familiar habits for any one of her age. Her life, if not her reason, are in her children's hands."

359

A time of terrible anxiety followed, for the inmates of the Red House. The doctor insisted on a trained nurse. Algitha and Hadria felt uneasy when they were away, even for a moment, from the sick-room, but the doctor reminded them of the necessity, for the patient's sake as well as their own, of keeping up their strength. He warned them that there would be a long strain upon them, and that any lack of common sense, as regards their own health, would certainly diminish the patient's chances of recovery. Nobody had his clearest judgment and his quickest observation at command, when nervously exhausted. Everything might depend on a moment's decision, a moment's swiftness of insight. The warning was not thrown away, but both sisters found the incessant precautions trying.

Every thought, every emotion was swallowed up in the one awful anxiety.

"Oh, Hadria, I feel as if this were my fault," cried Algitha, on one still, ominous night, after she had resigned her post at the bedside to the nurse, who was to fill it for a couple of hours, after which Hadria took her turn of watching.

"You? It was I," said Hadria, with trembling lips.

"Mother has never been strong," Algitha went on. "And my leaving home was the beginning of all this trouble."

"And *my* leaving home the end of it," her sister added.

Algitha was walking restlessly to and fro.

"And I went to Dunaghee so often, so often," she cried tearfully, "so that mother should not feel deserted, and you too came, and the boys when they could. But she never got over my leaving; she seemed to resent my independence, my habit of judging for myself; she hated every detail in which I differed from the girls she knew. If I had married and gone to the Antipodes, she would have been quite satisfied, but——"

"Ah, why do people need human souls for their daily food?" cried Hadria mournfully. She flung open the window of the bedroom, and looked out over the deadly stillness of the fields and the heavy darkness. "But they do need them," she said, in the same quiet, hopeless tone, "and the souls have got to be provided."

"What is the time?" asked Algitha. A clock had struck, outside. "Could it be the clock of Craddock church? The sound must have stolen down hill, through the still air."

"It struck three."

"You ought to get some sleep," cried Algitha. "Remember what the doctor said."

"I feel so nervous, so anxious. I could not sleep."

"Just for a few minutes," Algitha urged. Hadria consented at last, to go into her room, which adjoined her sister's, and lie down on the bed. The door was open between the rooms. "You must do the same," she stipulated.

There was silence for some minutes, but the silence swarmed with the ghosts of voices. The air seemed thick with shapes, and terrors, and strange warnings.

The doctor had not disguised the fact that the patient was fighting hard for life, and that it was impossible to predict the result. Everything depended on whether her strength would hold out. The weakness of the heart was an unfortunate element in the case. To save strength and give plentiful nourishment, without heightening the fever, must be the constant effort. Algitha's experience stood her in good stead. Her practical ability had been quickened and disciplined by her work. She had trained herself in nursing, among other things.

Hadria's experience was small. She had to summon her intelligence to the rescue. The Fullerton stock had never been deficient in this particular. In difficult moments, when rule and tradition had done their utmost, Hadria had often some original device to suggest, to fit the individual case, which tided them over a crisis, or avoided some threatening predicament.

"Are you sleeping?" asked Algitha, very softly.

"No," said Hadria; "I feel very uneasy to-night. I think I will go down."

"Do try to get a little rest first, Hadria; your watch is next, and you must not go to it fagged out."

"I know, but I feel full of dread. I *must* just go and see that all is right."

"Then I will come too," said Algitha.

They stole down stairs together, in the dim light of the oil lamps that were kept burning all night. The clock struck the half-hour as they passed along the landing. A strange fancy came to Hadria, that a dusky figure drifted away before her, as she advanced. It seemed as though death had receded at her approach. The old childish love for her mother had revived in all its force, during this long fight with the reaper of souls. She felt all her energies strung with the tension of battle. She fought against a dark horror that she could not face. Knowing, and realising vividly, that if her mother lived, her own dreams were ended for ever, she wrestled with desperate strength for the life that was at stake. Her father's silent wretchedness was terrible to see. He would not hear a word of doubt as to the patient's recovery. He grew angry if anyone hinted at danger. He insisted that his wife was better each day. She would soon be up and well again.

"Never well again," the doctor had confided to Hubert, "though she may possibly pull through."

Mr. Fullerton's extravagant hopefulness sent a thrill along the nerves. It was as if he had uttered the blackest forebodings. The present crisis had stirred a thousand feelings and associations, in Hadria, which had long been slumbering. She seemed to be sent back again, to the days of her childhood. The intervening years were blotted out. She realized now, with agonising vividness, the sadness of her mother's life, the long stagnation, the slow decay of disused faculties, and the ache that accompanies all processes of decay, physical or moral. Not only the strong appeal of old affection, entwined with the earliest associations, was at work, but the appeal of womanhood itself:—the grey sad story of a woman's life, bare and dumb and pathetic in

its irony and pain: the injury from without, and then the
self-injury, its direct offspring; unnecessary, yet inevitable;
the unconscious thirst for the sacrifice of others, the hungry
claims of a nature unfulfilled, the groping instinct to bring the
balance of renunciation to the level, and indemnify oneself for
the loss suffered and the spirit offered up. And that propitiation had to be made. It was as inevitable as that the doom of
Orestes should follow the original crime of the house of Atreus.
Hadria's whole thought and strength were now centred on
the effort to bring about that propitiation, in her own person.
She prepared the altar and sharpened the knife. In that subtle
and ironical fashion, her fate was steadily at work.

The sick-room was very still when the sisters entered. It
was both warm and fresh. A night-light burnt on the table,
where cups and bottles were ranged, a spirit-lamp and kettle,
and other necessaries. The night-light threw long, stealthy
shadows over the room. The fire burnt with a red glow.
The bed lay against the long wall. As the two figures
entered, there was a faint sound of quick panting, and a
moan. Hadria rushed to the bedside.

"Quick, quick, some brandy," she called. Algitha flew to
the table for the brandy, noticing with horror, as she passed,
that the nurse had fallen asleep at her post. Algitha shook
her hastily.

"Go and call Mr. Fullerton," she said sharply, "and quick,
quick." The patient was sinking. The nurse vanished.
Algitha had handed the cup of brandy to Hadria. The
sisters stood by the bedside, scarcely daring to breathe. Mr.
Fullerton entered hurriedly, with face pallid and drawn.

"What is it? Is she——?"

"No, no; I hope not. Another moment it would have
been too late, but I think we were in time."

Hadria had administered the brandy, and stood watching
breathlessly, for signs of revival. She gave one questioning
glance at Algitha. Her trust in the nurse was gone. Algitha
signed hope. The patient's breathing was easier.

"I wonder if we ought to give a little more?" Hadria whispered.

"Wait a minute. Ah! don't speak to her, father; she needs all her strength."

The ticking of the clock could be heard, in the dim light.

Algitha was holding her mother's wrist. "Stronger," she said, Hadria drew a deep sigh. "We must give food presently. No more brandy."

"She's all right again, all right again!" cried Mr. Fullerton, eagerly.

The nurse went to prepare the extract which the doctor had ordered for the patient, when quickly-digested nourishment was required. It gave immediate strength. The brandy had stimulated the sinking organs to a saving effort; the food sustained the system at the level thus achieved. The perilous moment was over

"Thank heaven!" cried Algitha, when the patient's safety was assured, and she sank back on the pillow, with a look of relief on her worn face.

"If it had not been for you, Hadria——. What's the matter? Are you ill?"

Algitha rushed forward, and the nurse dragged up a chair.

Hadria had turned deadly white, and her hand groped for support.

She drew herself together with a desperate effort, and sat down breathing quickly. "I am not going to faint," she said, reassuringly. "It was only for a moment." She gave a shudder. "What a fight it was! We were only just in time——"

A low voice came from the bed. The patient was talking in her sleep. "Tell Hadria to come home if she does not want to kill me. Tell her to come home; it is her duty. I want her."

Then, after a pause, "I have always done *my* duty,—I have sacrificed myself for the children. Why do they desert me, why do they desert me?" And then came a low moaning cry, terrible to hear. The sisters were by the bedside, in a moment. Their father stood behind them.

"We are here, mother dear; we are here watching by you," Hadria murmured, with trembling voice.

Algitha touched the thin hand, quietly. "We are with you, mother," she repeated. "Don't you know that we have been with you for a long time?"

The sick woman seemed to be soothed by the words.

"Both here, both?" she muttered vaguely. And then a smile spread over the sharpened features; she opened her eyes and looked wistfully at the two faces bending over her.

A look of happiness came into her dimmed eyes.

"My girls," she said in a dreamy voice, "my girls have come back to me—I knew they were good girls——"

Then her eyes closed, and she fell into a profound and peaceful slumber.

CHAPTER XXXIX.

" BUT, Doctor, is there no hope that with care and time, she will be able to walk again?"

"I am sorry to say, none whatever. I am only thankful that my patient has survived at all. It was little short of a miracle, and you must be thankful for that."

Mrs. Fullerton had always been an active woman, in spite of not being very robust, and a life passed on a couch had peculiar terrors for her. The nervous system had been wrecked, not by any one shock or event, but by the accumulated strains of a lifetime. The constitution was broken up, once and for all.

A cottage had been taken, as near as possible to the Red House, where the old couple were to settle for the rest of their days, within reach of their children and grandchildren. Every wish of the invalid must be respected, just or unjust. Absolute repose of mind and body was imperatively necessary, and this could only be attained for her by a complete surrender, on the part of her children, of any course of action that she seriously disapproved. The income was too limited to allow of Algitha's returning to her parents ; otherwise Mrs. Fullerton would have wished it. Algitha had now to provide for herself, as the allowance that her father had given her could not be continued. She had previously done her work for nothing, but now Mrs. Trevelyan, under whose care she had been living, offered her a paid post in a Convalescent Home in which she was interested.

"I am exceptionally fortunate," said Algitha, "for Mrs. Trevelyan has arranged most kindly, so that I can get away to see mother and father at the end of every week."

Both Mr. and Mrs. Fullerton had taken it for granted that Hadria would remain at the Red House, and that Hubert would "forgive" her, as they put it.

Circumstances seemed to take it equally for granted. Mrs. Fullerton would now depend entirely on her children for every solace and pleasure. She would require cheering, amusing, helping, in a thousand ways. Algitha was to come down each week from Saturday till Monday, and the brothers when they could. During the rest of the week, the invalid would depend on her younger daughter. Hadria's leaving home, and the rumour of a quarrel between her and Hubert, had conduced to her mother's illness, perhaps had even caused it. Mrs. Fullerton had taken it bitterly to heart. It had become obvious that Hadria would have now to remain at the Red House, for her mother's sake, and that being so, she and Hubert agreed that it was useless to discuss any other reasons for and against it. Hubert was only too glad of her return, for appearance' sake. Neither of them thought, for a moment, of what Henriette called a "reconciliation." What had passed before Hadria's departure had revealed finally, the hopelessness of such an attempt. Matters settled down heavily and with an air of finality.

If only her mother's declining years were happy and peaceful, that would be something of importance gained, but, alas! Mrs. Fullerton seemed anything but happy. Her helplessness was hard to bear, and she felt the worldly downfall, severely. All this, and the shattered state of her nerves tended to make her exacting and irritable; and as she had felt seriously aggrieved for so many years of her life, she now regarded the devotion of her children as a debt tardily paid, and the habit grew insensibly upon her of increasing her demands, as she found everyone so ready to submit to them. The possession of power had its usual effect. She knew no mercy in its use. Her daughters were made to feel that if they had been less headstrong and selfish in the past, she would have been a vigorous and active woman to this day.

Obviously, the very least they could do, was to try by all means in their power, to lighten the burden they had laid upon her. Yet Mrs. Fullerton was, by nature, unselfish. She would have gladly sacrificed herself for her children's good, as indeed she had persistently and doggedly sacrificed herself for them, during their childhood, but naturally she had her own view of what constituted their "good." It did not consist in wasting one's youth and looks among the slums of the East End, or in deserting one's home to study music and mix in a set of second-rate people, in an out-of-the-way district of Paris. As for Hadria's conduct about little Martha, Mrs. Fullerton could scarcely bring herself to speak about it. It terrified her. She thought it indicated some taint of madness in her daughter's mind. Two charming children of her own and—but Mrs. Fullerton, with a painful flush, would turn her mind from the subject. She had to believe her daughter either mad or bad, and that was terrible to her maternal pride. She could indeed scarcely believe that it had not all been a painful dream, for Hadria was now so good and dutiful, so tender and watchful; how *could* she have behaved so abominably, so crazily? Every day Hadria came to the cottage, generally with a bunch of fresh flowers to place by her mother's couch, and then all the affairs of the household were talked over and arranged, the daughter doing what was needed in the way of ordering provisions or writing notes, for the invalid could now write only with the greatest difficulty. Then Mrs. Fullerton liked to have a chat, to hear what was in the papers, what was going on in the neighbourhood, and to discuss all sorts of dreary details, over and over again. Books that Hadria would sometimes bring were generally left unread, unless they were light novels of a rigidly conventional character. Mrs. Fullerton grew so excited in her condemnation of any other kind, that it was dangerous to put them before her. In the evenings, the old couple liked to have a rubber, and often Hubert and Hadria would make up the necessary quartett; four silent human beings, who sat like

solemn children at their portentous play, while the clock on
the mantelpiece recorded the moments of their lives that they
dedicated to the mimic battle. Hours and hours were spent
in this way. But Hadria found that she could not endure
it every night, much to the surprise of her parents. The
monotony, the incessant recurrence, had a disastrous effect
on her nerves, suggesting wild and desperate impulses.

"I should go out of my mind, if I had no breaks," she said
at last, after trying it for some months. "In the interests
of future rubbers, I *must* leave off, now and then. He that
plays and runs away, will live to play another day."

Mrs. Fullerton thought it strange that Hadria could not do
even this little thing for her parents, without grumbling, but
she did not wish to make a martyr of her. They must try
and find some one else to take her place occasionally.

Sometimes Joseph Fleming would accept the post, sometimes Lord Engleton, and often Ernest or Fred, whose comparatively well-ordered minds were not sent off their balance
so easily as Hadria's. In this fashion, the time went by, and
the new state of affairs already seemed a hundred years old.
Paris was a clear, but far-off dream. An occasional letter
from Madame Vauchelet or Jouffroy, who mourned and wailed
over Hadria's surrender of her work, served to remind
her that it had once been actual and living. There still
existed a Paris far away beyond the hills, brilliant, vivid,
exquisite, inspiring, and at this very moment the people
were coming and going, the river was flowing, the little
steamers plying,—but how hard it was to realise!

The family was charmed with the position of affairs.

"It is such a mercy things have happened as they have!"
was the verdict, delivered with much wise shaking of heads.
"There can be no more mad or disgraceful behaviour on the
part of Hubert's wife, that is one comfort. She can't murder
her mother outright, though she has not been far off it!"

From the first, Hadria had understood what the future must
be. These circumstances could not be overcome by any

deed that she could bring herself to do. Even Valeria was baffled. Her theories would not quite work. Hadria looked things straight in the face. That which was strongest and most essential in her must starve; there was no help for it, and no one was directly to blame, not even herself. Fate, chance, Providence, the devil, or whatever it was, had determined against her particular impulses and her particular view of things. After all, it would have been rather strange if these powers had happened exactly to agree with her. She was not so ridiculous (she told herself) as to feel personally aggrieved, but so long as fate, chance, Providence, or the devil, gave her emotions and desires and talent and will, it was impossible not to suffer. She might fully recognise that the suffering was of absolutely no importance in the great scheme of things, but that did not make the suffering less. If it must be, it must be, and there was an end to it. Should someone gain by it, that was highly satisfactory, and more than could be said of most suffering, which exists, it would seem, only to increase and multiply after the manner of some dire disease. This was what Hadria dreaded in her own case: that the loss would not end with her. The children, Martha, everyone who came under her influence, must share in it.

Henriette irritated her by an approving sweetness of demeanour, carefully avoiding any look of triumph, or rather triumphing by that air which said: "I wouldn't crow over you for the world!"

She was evidently brimming over with satisfaction. A great peril, she felt, had been averted. The family and its reputation were saved.

"You appear to think that the eyes of Europe are riveted on the Temperley family," said Hadria; "an august race, I know, but there *are* one or two other branches of the human stock in existence."

"One *must* consider what people say," said Henriette.

Hadria's time now was filled more and more with detail, since there were two households instead of one to manage.

The new charge was particularly difficult, because she had not a free hand.

Without entirely abandoning her music, it had, perforce, to fall into abeyance. Progress was scarcely possible. But as Henriette pointed out—it gave so much pleasure to others—when Hadria avoided music that was too severely classical.

At Craddock Place, one evening, she was taken in to dinner by a callow youth, who found a fertile subject for his wit, in the follies and excesses of what he called the " new woman-hood." It was so delightful, he said, to come to the country, where women were still charming in the good old way. He knew that this new womanhood business was only a phase, don't you know, but upon his word, he was getting tired of it. Not that he had any objection to women being well educated (Hadria was glad of that), but he could *not* stand it when they went out of their sphere, and put themselves forward and tried to be emancipated, and all that sort of nonsense.

Hadria was not surprised that he could not stand it.

There had been a scathing article, the youth said, in one of the evening papers. He wondered how the "New Woman" felt after reading it ! It simply made mincemeat of her.

" Wretched creature ! " Hadria exclaimed.

The youth wished that women would really *do* something, instead of making all this fuss.

Hadria agreed that it *was* a pity they were so inactive. Could not one or two of the more favoured sex manage to inspire them with a little initiative?

The youth considered that women were, by nature, passive and reflective, not original.

Hadria thought the novelty of that idea not the least of its charms.

The youth allowed that, in her own way, and in her own sphere, woman was charming and singularly intelligent. He had no objection to her developing as much as she pleased, in proper directions. (Hadria felt really encouraged.)

But it was so absurd to pretend that women could do
work that. was peculiar to men. (Hadria agreed, with a
chuckle.) When had they written one of Shakespeare's
dramas? (When indeed? History was ominously silent on
that point.)

"Hadria, what is amusing you?" enquired her hostess,
across the table.

"Oh, well—only the discouraging fact that no woman, as
Mr. St. George convincingly points out, has ever written one
of Shakespeare's.dramas ! "

"Oh," said Lady Engleton with a broad smile, "but you
know, Mr. St. George, we really haven't had quite the same
chances, have we?"

Perhaps not quite, as far as literature went, the youth
admitted tolerantly, but there was failure in original work in
every direction. This was no blame to women; they were
not made that way, but facts *had* to be recognised. Women's
strength lay in a different domain—in the home. It was of
no use to try to fight against Nature. Look at music for
instance; one required no particular liberty to pursue *that*
art, yet where were the women-composers? If there was so
much buried talent among women, why didn't they arise and
bring out operas and oratorios?

Hadria couldn't understand it; especially as the domestic
life was arranged, one might almost say, with a special view
to promoting musical talent in the mistress of the household.
Yet where were those oratorios? She shook her head. Mr.
St. George, she thought, had clearly proved that the inherent
nature of women was passive and imitative, while that of
man, even in the least remarkable examples of the sex, was
always powerful and original to the verge of the perilous !

"I think we had better go to the drawing-room," said Lady
Engleton, discreetly. The youth twirled his moustaches
thoughtfully, as the ladies filed out.

Hadria's happiest hours were now those that she spent with
little Martha, who was growing rapidly in stature and intelli-

gence. The child's lovable nature blossomed sweetly under
the influence of Hadria's tenderness. When wearied, and sad
at heart, an hour in the Priory garden, or a saunter along the
road-side with little Martha, was like the touch of a fresh
breeze after the oppression of a heated room. Hadria's
attachment to the child had grown and grown, until it had
become almost a passion. How was the child to be saved
from the usual fate of womanhood? Hadria often felt a
thrill of terror, when the beautiful blue eyes looked out, large
and fearless, into the world that was just unfolding before
them, in its mysterious loveliness.

The little girl gave promise of beauty. Even now there
were elements that suggested a moving, attracting nature.
" At her peril," thought Hadria, "a woman moves and attracts.
If I can only save her ! "

Hadria had not seen Professor Fortescue since her return
from Paris. She felt that he, and he alone, could give her
courage, that he and he alone could save her from utter des-
pondency. If only he would come ! For the first time in her
life, she thought of writing to ask him for personal help and
advice. Before she had carried out this idea, the news came
that he was ill, that the doctor wished him to go abroad, but
that he was forced to remain in England, for another three
months, to complete some work, and to set some of his affairs
in order. Hadria, in desperation, was thinking of throwing
minor considerations to the winds, and going to see for herself
the state of affairs (it could be managed without her mother's
knowledge, and so would not endanger her health or life),
when the two boys were sent back hastily from school, where
scarlet fever had broken out. They must have caught the
infection before leaving, for they were both taken ill.

Valeria came down to Craddock Dene, for the day. She
seemed almost distraught. Hadria could see her only at
intervals. The sick children required all her attention.
Valeria wished to visit them. She had brought the poor
boys each a little gift.

" But you may take the fever," Hadria remonstrated.

Valeria gave a scornful snort.

" Are you tired of life ? "

" I ? Yes. It is absurd. I have no place in it, no tie, nothing to bind me to my fellows or my race. What do they care for a faded, fretful woman ? "

" You know how your friends care for you, Valeria. You know, for instance, what you have been in my life."

" Ah, my dear, I *don't* know ! I have a wretched longing for some strong, absorbing affection, something paramount, satisfying. I envy you your devotion to that poor little child ; you can shew it, you can express it, and you have the child's love in return. But I, who want much more than that, shall never get even that. I threw away the chance when I had it, and now I shall end my days, starving."

Hadria was silent. She felt that these words covered something more than their ostensible meaning.

" I fear Professor Fortescue is very ill," said Valeria restlessly.

Her face was flushed, and her eyes burnt.

" I fear he is," said Hadria sadly.

" If—if he were to die ——" Hadria gave a low, horrified exclamation.

" Surely there is no danger of that ! "

" Of course there is : he told me that he did not expect to recover."

Valeria was crouching before the fire, with a look of blank despair. Hadria, pale to the lips, took her hand gently and held it between her own. Valeria's eyes suddenly filled with tears. " Ah, Hadria, you will understand, you will not despise me—you will only be sorry for me—why should I not tell you ? It is eating my heart out—have you never suspected, never guessed—— ? "

Hadria, with a startled look, paused to consider, and then, stroking back the beautiful white hair with light touch, she said, " I think I have known without knowing that I knew. It wanted just these words of yours to light up the knowledge. Oh, Valeria, have you carried this burden for all these years?"

" Ever since I first met him, which was just before he met his wife. I knew, from the first, that it was hopeless. He introduced her to me shortly after his engagement. He was wrapped up in her. With him, it was once and for all. He is not the man to fall in love and out of it, over and over again. We were alike in that. With me, too, it was once for all. Oh, the irony of life!" Valeria went on with an outburst of energy, "I was doomed to doom others to similar loss; others have felt for me, in vain, what I, in vain, felt for him! I sent them all away, because I could not bring myself to endure the thought of marrying any other man, and so I pass my days alone—a waif and stray, without anything or anyone to live for."

"At least you have your work to live for, which is to live for many, instead of for one or two."

" Ah, that does not satisfy the heart."

" What *does* ?" Hadria exclaimed.

Anxiety about Professor Fortescue now made a gloomy background to the responsibilities of Hadria's present life. Valeria's occasional visits were its bright spots. She looked forward to them, with pathetic eagerness. The friendship became closer than it had ever been before, since Valeria had confided her sad secret.

"Yet, Valeria, I envy you."

" Envy me?" she repeated blankly.

" I have never known what a great passion like that means; I have never felt what you feel, and surely to live one's life with all its pettiness and pain, yet never to know its extreme experiences, is sadder than to have those experiences and suffer through them."

" Ah, yes, you are right," Valeria admitted. " I would not be without it if I could."

The thought of what she had missed was beginning to take

a hold upon Hadria. Her life was passing, passing, and the supreme gifts would never be hers. She must for ever stand outside, and be satisfied with shadows and echoes.

"Are you very miserable, Hadria?" Valeria asked, one day.

"I am benumbed a little now," Hadria replied. "That must be, if one is to go on at all. It is a provision of nature, I suppose. All that was threatening before I went to Paris, is now being fulfilled. I can scarcely realize how I could ever have had the hopefulness to make that attempt. I might have known I could not succeed, as things are. How *could* I? But I am glad of the memory. It pains me sometimes, when all the acute delight and charm return, at the call of some sound or scent, some vivid word; but I would not be without the memory and the dream—my little illusion."

"Supposing," said Valeria after a long pause, "that you could live your life over again, what would you do?"

"I don't know. It is my impression that in my life, as in the lives of most women, all roads lead to Rome. Whether one does this or that, one finds oneself in pretty much the same position at the end. It doesn't answer to rebel against the recognized condition of things, and it doesn't answer to submit. Only generally one *must*, as in my case. A choice of calamities is not always permitted."

"It is so difficult to know which is the least," said Valeria.

"I don't believe there *is* a 'least.' They are both unbearable. It is a question which best fits one's temperament, which leads soonest to resignation."

"Oh, Hadria, you would never achieve resignation!" cried Valeria.

"Oh, some day, perhaps!"

Valeria shook her head. She had no belief in Hadria's powers in that direction. Hopelessness was her nearest approach to that condition of cheerful acquiescence which, Hadria had herself said, profound faith or profound stupidity can perhaps equally inspire.

"At least," said Valeria, "you know that you are useful and helpful to those around you. You make your mother happy."

"No, my mother is not happy. My work is negative. I just manage to prevent her dying of grief. One must not be too ambitious in this stern world. One can't make people happy merely by reducing oneself, morally, to a jelly. Sometimes, by that means, one can dodge battle and murder and sudden death."

"It is terrible!" cried Valeria.

"But meanwhile one lays the seed of future calamities, to avoid which some other future woman will have to become jelly. The process always reminds me of the old practice of the Anglo-Saxon kings, who used to buy off the Danes when they threatened invasion, and so pampered the enemy whom their successors would afterwards have to buy off at a still more ruinous cost. I am buying off the Danes, Valeria."

CHAPTER XL.

" DO you know it is a year to-day, since we came to this
cottage?" exclaimed Mrs. Fullerton. "How the
time flies!"

The remark was made before the party settled to the
evening's whist.

"You are looking very much better than you did a month
after your illness, Mrs. Fullerton," said Joseph Fleming, who
was to take a hand, while Hadria played Grieg or Chopin, or
Scottish melodies to please the old people. The whist-players
enjoyed music during the game.

"Ah, I shall never be well," said Mrs. Fullerton. "One
can't recover from long worry, Mr. Fleming. Shall we cut
for partners?"

It was a quaint, low-pitched little room, filled with familiar
furniture from Dunaghee, which recalled the old place at
every turn. The game went on in silence. The cards were
dealt, taken up, shuffled, sorted, played, massed together, cut,
dealt, sorted, and so on, round and round; four grave faces
deeply engrossed in the process, while the little room was
filled with music.

Mrs. Fullerton had begun to feel slightly uneasy about
her daughter. "So much nursing has told upon her," said
everyone. The illness of the two boys had come at an unfortunate moment. She looked worn and white, and dread-
fully thin. She seemed cheerful, and at times her mood
was even merry, but she could not recover strength. At the
end of the day, she would be completely exhausted. This had
not been surprising at first, after the long strain of nursing,

378

but Mrs. Fullerton thought it was time that she began to mend. She feared that Hadria spent too many hours over her composing; she sat up at night, perhaps. What good did all this composing do? Nobody ever heard of it. Such a sad pity that she could not see the folly of persevering in the fruitless effort.

Lady Engleton was sure that Hadria saw too few people, lived too monotonous a life. Craddock Place was filled with guests just now, and Lady Engleton used her utmost persuasion to induce Hubert and Hadria to come to dinner, or to join the party, in the evening, whenever they could.

Hadria shrank from the idea. It was adding another burden to her already failing strength. To talk coherently, to be lively and make oneself agreeable, to have to think about one's dress,—it all seemed inexpressibly wearisome. But Lady Engleton was so genuinely eager to administer her cure that Hadria yielded, half in gratitude, half in order to save the effort of further resistance.

She dragged herself upstairs to dress, wishing to heaven she had refused, after all. The thought of the lights, the sound of voices, the complexity of elements and of life that she had to encounter, made her shrink into herself. She had only one evening gown suitable for the occasion. It was of some white silken stuff, with dull rich surface. A bunch of yellow roses and green leaves formed the decoration. Hubert approved of her appearance. To her own surprise she felt some new feeling creep into her, under the influence of the exquisite attire. It put her a little more in tune. At least there were beautiful and dainty things in the world. The fresh green of the rose leaves, and the full yet delicate yellow of the fragrant roses on the creamy lace, evoked a feeling akin to the emotion stirred by certain kinds of music; or, in other words, the artistic sensibility had been appealed to through colour and texture, instead of through harmony.

The drawing-room at Craddock Place was glowing with subdued candle-light. Lady Engleton's rooms carried one back to a past epoch, among the dainty fancies and art of a

more leisurely and less vulgar century. Lady Engleton
admitted nothing that had not the quality of distinction, let
it have what other quality it might. Hadria's mood, initiated
at home, received impetus at Craddock Place. It was a
luxurious mood. She desired to receive rather than to give :
to be delicately ministered to; to claim the services of
generations of artists, who had toiled with fervour to attain
that grand ease and simplicity, through faithful labour and
the benison of heaven.

Hadria had attracted many eyes as she entered the room.
Unquestionably she was looking her best to-night, in spite of
her extreme pallor. She was worthy to take her place among
the beautiful objects of art that Lady Engleton had collected
round her. She had the same quality. Hubert vaguely perceived this. He heard the idea expressed in so many words
by a voice that he knew. He looked round, and saw Professor
Theobald bending confidentially towards Joseph Fleming.

"Oh, Professor, I did not know you were to be here to-
night !"

"What has your guardian spirit been about, not to fore-
warn you?" asked the Professor.

"I am thinking of giving my guardian spirit a month's
warning," returned Hubert; "he has been extremely neglectful
of late. And how have you been getting on all this time,
Professor?"

Theobald gave some fantastic answer, and crossed the room
to Mrs. Temperley, who was by this time surrounded by a group
of acquaintances, among them Madame Bertaux, who had just
come from Paris, and had news of all Hadria's friends there.

"Mrs. Temperley, may I also ask for one passing glance
of recognition?"

Hadria turned round with a little start, and a sudden unaccountable sense of disaster.

"Professor Theobald !"

She did not look pleased to see him, and as they shook
hands, his mouth shut sharply, as it always did when his self-

love was wounded. Then, a gleam of resolve or cunning came into his face, and the next instant he was at his suavest.

"Do you know, Mrs. Temperley, I scarcely recognized you when you first came in. 'Who can this beautiful, distinguished-looking woman be?' I said to myself."

Hadria smiled maliciously.

"You think I am so much changed?

Professor Theobald began to chuckle.

"The trowel, I see, is still your weapon," she added, "but I am surprised that you have not learnt to wield the implement of sway with more dexterity, Professor."

"I am not accustomed to deal with such quick-witted ladies, Mrs. Temperley."

"You shew your hand most frankly," she answered; "it almost disarms one."

A few introductory chords sounded through the room. Hadria was sitting in front of the window, across which the pale green curtains had been drawn. Many eyes wandered towards her.

"I should like to paint you just like that," murmured Lady Engleton; "you can't imagine what a perfect bit of harmony you make, with my brocade." A cousin of Lord Engleton was at the piano. He played an old French gavotte.

"That is the finishing touch," added Lady Engleton, below her breath. "I should like to paint you and the curtains and Claude Moreton's gavotte all together."

The performance was received with enthusiasm. It deepened Hadria's mood, set her pulses dancing. She assented readily to the request of her hostess that she should play. She chose something fantastic and dainty. It had a certain remoteness from life.

"Like one of Watteau's pictures," said Claude Moreton, who was hanging over the piano. He was tall and dark, with an expression that betrayed his enthusiastic temperament. A group had collected, among them Professor Theobald. Beside him stood Marion Fenwick, the bride whose wedding had taken place at Craddock Church about eighteen months before.

It seemed as if Hadria were exercising some influence of a
magnetic quality. She was always the point of attraction,
whether she created a spell with her music, or her speech,
or her mere personality.   In her present mood, this was
peculiarly gratifying. The long divorce from initiative work
which events had compelled, the loss of nervous vigour, the
destruction of dream and hope, had all tended to throw her
back on more accessible forms of art and expression, and
suggested passive rather than active dealings with life. She
was wearied with petty responsibilities, and what she called
semi-detached duties.   It was a relief to sit down in white silk
and lace, and draw people to her simply by the cheap spell of
good looks and personal magnetism.   That she possessed
these advantages, her life in Paris had made obvious.   It was
the first time that she had been in contact with a large
number of widely differing types, and she had found that she
could appeal to them all, if she would.   Since her return to
England, anxieties and influences extremely depressing had
accustomed her to a somewhat gloomy atmosphere.   To-night
the atmosphere was light and soft, brilliant and enervating.

" This is my Capua," she said laughingly, to her hostess.

It invited every luxurious instinct to come forth and sun
itself.   Marion Fenwick's soft, sweet voice, singing Italian
songs to the accompaniment of the guitar, repeated the
invitation.

It was like a fairy gift.   Energy would be required to refuse
it.   And why, in heaven's name, if she might not have what
she really wanted, was she to be denied even the poor little
triumphs of ornamental womanhood?   Was the social order
which had frustrated her own ambitions to dominate her
conscience, and persuade her voluntarily to resign that *one*
kingdom which cannot be taken from a woman, so long as
her beauty lasts?

Why should she abdicate?   The human being was obviously
susceptible to personality beyond all other things.   And beauty
moved that absurd creature preposterously. *There*, at least,

the woman who chanced to be born with these superficial attractions, had a royal territory, so long as she could prevent her clamorous fellows from harassing and wearing those attractions away. By no direct attack could the jealous powers dethrone her. They could only do it indirectly, by appealing to the conscience which they had trained ; to the principles that they had instilled; by convincing the woman that she owed herself, as a debt, to her legal owner, to be paid in coined fragments of her being, till she should end in inevitable bankruptcy, and the legal owner himself found her a poor investment !

It would have startled that roomful of people, who expressed everything circuitously, pleasantly, without rough edges, had they read beneath Mrs. Temperley's spoken words, these unspoken thoughts.

Marion Fenwick's songs and the alluring softness of her guitar, seemed the most fitting accompaniment to the warm summer night, whose breath stirred gently the curtains by the open window, at the far end of the room.

Lady Engleton was delighted with the success of her efforts. Mrs. Temperley had not looked so brilliant, so full of life, since her mother's illness. Only yesterday, when she met her returning from the Cottage, her eyes were like those of a dying woman, and now——!

"People say ill-natured things about Mrs. Temperley," she confided to an intimate friend, "but that is because they don't understand her."

People might have been forgiven for not understanding her, as perhaps her hostess felt, noticing Hadria's animation, and the extraordinary power that she was wielding over everyone in the room, young and old. That power seemed to burn in the deep eyes, whose expression changed from moment to moment. Hadria's cheeks, for once, had a faint tinge of colour. The mysterious character of her beauty became more marked. Professor Theobald followed her, with admiring and studious gaze. Whether she had felt remorseful for her somewhat unfriendly greeting at the beginning of the evening, or from

some other cause, her manner to him had changed. It was
softer, less mocking. He perceived it instantly, and pursued
his advantage. The party still centred eagerly round the
piano. Hadria was under the influence of music; therefore
less careful and guarded than usual, more ready to sway on the
waves of emotion. And beyond all these influences, tending
in the same direction, was the underlying spirit of rebellion
against the everlasting "Thou shalt not" that met a woman at
every point, and turned her back from all paths save one. And
following that one (so ran Hadria's insurrectionary thoughts), the
obedient creature had to give up every weapon of her womanhood; every grace, every power; tramping along that crowded
highway, whereon wayworn sisters toil forward, with bandaged
eyes, and bleeding feet; and as their charm fades, in the
pursuing of their dusty pilgrimage, the shouts, and taunts, and
insults, and laughter of their taskmasters follow them, while
still they stumble on to the darkening land that awaits them,
at the journey's end : Old Age, the vestibule of Death.

Hadria's eyes gleamed strangely.

"They shall not have their way with me too easily. I can
at least give my pastors and masters a little trouble. I can
at least fight for it, losing battle though it be."

The only person who seemed to resist Hadria's influence
to-night, was Mrs. Jordan, the mother of Marion Fenwick.

"My dear madam," said Professor Theobald, bending over
the portly form of Mrs. Jordan, "a woman's first duty is to be
charming."

"Oh, that comes naturally, Professor," said Hadria, "though
it is rather for *you* than for *me* to say that. You are always
missing opportunities."

"Believe me, I will miss them no more," he said emphatically.

"Tell us *your* idea of a woman's duty, Mrs. Jordan,"
prompted Madame Bertaux maliciously. Mrs. Jordan delivered herself of various immemorial sentiments which met
the usual applause. But Madame Bertaux said brusquely

THE DAUGHTERS OF DANAUS.

385

that she thought if that sort of thing were preached at women
much longer, they would end by throwing over duty altogether,
in sheer disgust at the whole one-sided business. Mrs. Jordan
bristled, and launched herself upon a long and virtuous
sentence. Her daughter Marion looked up sharply when
Madame Bertaux spoke. Then a timid, cautious glance fell
on her mother. Marion had lost her freshness and her
exquisite ætherial quality ; otherwise there was little change in
her appearance. Hadria was struck by the way in which she
had looked at Madame Bertaux, and it occurred to her that
Marion Fenwick was probably not quite so acquiescent and
satisfied as her friends supposed. But she would not speak
out. Early training had been too strong for her.

Professor Theobald was unusually serious to-night. He
did not respond to Hadria's flippancy. He looked at her with
grave, sympathetic eyes. He seemed to intimate that he understood all that was passing in her mind, and was not balked by
sprightly appearances. There was no sign of cynicism now,
no bandying of compliments. His voice had a new ring of
sincerity. It was a mood that Hadria had noticed in him
once or twice before, and when it occurred, her sympathy
was aroused ; she felt that she had done him injustice. *This*
was evidently the real man ; his ordinary manner must be
merely the cloak that the civilized being acquires the habit of
wrapping round him, as a protection against the curiosity of
his fellows. The Professor himself expressed it almost in those
words : " It is because of the infinite variety of type and the
complexity of modern life which the individual is called
upon to encounter, that a sort of fancy dress has to be worn
by all of us, as a necessary shield to our individuality and
our privacy. We cannot go through the complex process
of adjustment to each new type that we come across,
so by common consent, we wear our domino, and respect
the unwritten laws of the great *bal masqué* that we call
society."

The conversation took more and more intimate and serious
turns. Mrs. Jordan was the only check upon it. Madame

Bertaux followed up her first heresy by others even more bold.

"Whenever one wants very particularly to have one's way about a matter," she said, "one sneaks off and gets somebody else persuaded that it is his duty to sacrifice himself for us—*c'est tout simple*—and the chances are that he meekly does it. If he doesn't, at least one has the satisfaction of making him feel a guilty wretch, and setting oneself up with a profitable grievance for life."

"To the true woman," said Mrs. Jordan, who had ruled her family with a rod of iron for thirty stern years, "there is no joy to equal that of self-sacrifice."

"Except that of exacting it," added Hadria.

"I advise everyone desirous of dominion to preach that duty, in and out of season," said Madame Bertaux. "It is seldom that the victims even howl, so well have we trained them."

"Truly I hope so!" cried Professor Theobald. "It must be most galling when their lamentations prevent one from committing one's justifiable homicide in peace and quietness. Imagine the discomfort of having a half-educated victim to deal with, who can't hold his tongue and let one perform the operation quietly and comfortably. It is enough to embitter any Christian!"

The party broke up, with many cordial expressions of pleasure, and several plans were made for immediately meeting again. Lady Engleton was delighted to see that Mrs. Temperley entered with animation, into some projects for picnics and excursions in the neighbourhood.

"Did I not tell you that all you wanted was a little lively society?" she said, with genuine warmth, as the two women stood in the hall, a little apart from the others.

Hadria's eyelids suddenly fell and reddened slightly.

"Oh, you are so kind!" she exclaimed, in a voice whose tones betrayed the presence of suppressed tears.

Lady Engleton, in astonishment, stretched out a sisterly hand, but Hadria had vanished through the open hall door into the darkness without.

CHAPTER XLI.

MRS. TEMPERLEY was much discussed at Craddock Place. Professor Theobald preserved the same grave mood whenever she was present. He only returned to his usual manner, in her absence. "Theobald has on his Mrs. Temperley manner," Claude Moreton used to say. The latter was himself among her admirers.

"I begin to be afraid that Claude is taking her too seriously," Lady Engleton remarked to her husband. He had fired up on one occasion when Professor Theobald said something flippant about Mrs. Temperley. Claude Moreton's usual calmness had caused the sudden outburst to be noticed with surprise. He hated Professor Theobald.

"What possesses you both to let that fellow come here so much?"

"The Professor? Oh, he is a very old friend, you know, and extremely clever. One has to put up with his manner."

Claude Moreton grunted. "These, at any rate, are no reasons why Mrs. Temperley should put up with his manner!"

"But, my dear Claude, as you are always pointing out, the Professor has a special manner which he keeps exclusively for her."

The special manner had already worked wonders. The Professor was to Hadria by far the most entertaining person of the party. He had always amused her, and even the first time she saw him, he had exercised a strange, unpleasant fascination over her, which had put her on the defensive, for she had disliked and distrusted him. The meetings in the Priory gardens had softened her hostility, and now she began to feel more and more that she had judged him unfairly. In those days she had a strong pre-occupying interest. He had arrived on the scene at an exciting moment, just when she was

planning out her flight to Paris. She had not considered the
Professor's character very deeply. There were far too many
other things to think of. It was simpler to avoid him. But
now everything had changed. The present moment was not
exciting ; she had no plans and projects in her head ; she
was not about to court the fate of Icarus. That fate had
already overtaken her. The waves were closing over-head ;
her wings were wet and crippled, in the blue depths. Why
not take what the gods had sent and make the most of it ?

The Professor had all sorts of strange lore, which he used,
in his conversations with Hadria, almost as a fisherman uses
his bait. If she shewed an inclination to re-join the rest of
the party, he always brought out some fresh titbit of curious
learning, and Hadria was seldom able to resist the lure.

They met often, almost of necessity. It was impossible
to feel a stranger to the Professor, in these circumstances of
frequent and informal meeting. Often when Hadria happened to be alone with him, she would become suddenly
silent, as if she no longer felt the necessity to talk or to
conceal her weariness. The Professor knew it too well ;
he saw how heavily the burden of life weighed upon her, and
how it was often almost more than she could do, to drag
through the day. She craved for excitement, no matter of
what kind, in order to help her to forget her weariness. Her
anxiety about Professor Fortescue preyed upon her. She was
restless, overwrought, with every nerve on edge, unable now
for consecutive work, even had events permitted it. She
followed the advice and took the medicines of a London
doctor, whom Mrs. Fullerton had entreated her to consult,
but she gained no ground.

"I begin to understand how it is that people take to
drinking," she said to Algitha, who used to bemoan this vice,
with its terrible results, of which she had seen so much.

"Ah! don't talk of it in that light way !" cried Algitha.
"It is the fashion to treat it airily, but if people only knew
what an awful curse it is, I think they would feel ashamed to
be 'moderate' and indifferent about it."

"I don't mean to treat it or anything that brings harm and

suffering 'moderately,'" returned Hadria. "I mean only that I can see why the vice is so common. It causes forgetfulness, and I suppose most people crave for that."

"I think, Hadria, if I may be allowed to say so, that you are finding your excitement in another direction."

"You mean that I am trying to find a substitute for the pleasures of drunkenness in those of flirtation."

"I should not like to think that you had descended to *conscious* flirtation."

Hadria looked steadily into the flames. They were in the morning-room, where towards night-fall, even in summer, a small fire usually burnt in the grate.

"When I remember what you used to think and what you used to be to us all, in the old days at Dunaghee, I feel bitterly pained at what you are doing, Hadria. You don't know where it may lead to, and besides it seems so beneath you in every way."

"Appeals to the conscience!" cried Hadria, "I knew they would begin!"

"You knew *what* would begin?"

"Appeals, exhortations to forego the sole remaining interest, opportunity, or amusement that is left one! Ah, dear Algitha, I know you mean it kindly and I admire you for speaking out, but I am not going to be cajoled in that way! I am not going to be turned back and set tramping along the stony old road, so long as I can find a pleasanter by-way to loiter in. It sounds bad I know. Our drill affects us to the last, through every fibre. My duty! By what authority do people choose for me my duty? If I can be forced to abide by their decision in the matter, let them be satisfied with their power to coerce me, but let them leave my conscience alone. It does not dance to their piping."

"But you cannot care for this sort of excitement, Hadria."

"If ·I can get nothing else―― ?"

"Even then, I can't see what you can find in it to make you willing to sink from your old ideals."

"Ideals! A woman with ideals is like a drowning creature with a millstone round its neck! I have had enough of ideals!"

"It is a sad day to me when I hear you say so, Hadria!" the sister exclaimed.

"Algitha, there is just one solitary weapon that *can't* be taken from a woman—and so it is considerately left to her. Ah, it is a dangerous toy when brandished dexterously! Sometimes it sends a man or two away howling. Our pastors and masters have a wholesome dread of the murderous thing —and what wails, and satires, and lamentations it inspires! Consult the literature of all lands and ages! Heaven-piercing! The only way of dealing with the awkward dilemma is to get the woman persuaded to be 'good,' and to lay down her weapon of her own accord, and let it rust. How many women have been so persuaded! Not I!"

"I know, and I understand how you feel; but oh, Hadria, *this* is not the way to fight, *this* will bring no good to anyone. And as for admiration, the admiration of men—why, you know it is not worth having—of this sort."

"Oh, do I not know it! It is less than worthless. But I am not seeking anything of permanent value; I am seeking excitement, and the superficial satisfaction of brandishing the weapon that everyone would be charmed to see me lay in the dust. I *won't* lay it down to please anybody. Dear me, it will soon rust of its own accord. You might as well ask some luckless warrior who stands at bay, facing overwhelming odds, to yield up his sword and leave himself defenceless. It is an insult to one's common sense."

Algitha's remonstrance seemed only to inflame her sister's mood, so she said no more. But she watched Hadria's increasingly reckless conduct, with great uneasiness.

"It really *is* exciting!" exclaimed Hadria, with a strange smile. The whole party had migrated for the day, to the hills at a distance of about ten miles from Craddock Dene. A high spot had been chosen, on the edge of woodland shade, looking out over a wide distance of plain and far-off ranges. Here, as Claude Moreton remarked, they were to spoil the landscape, by taking their luncheon.

"Or what is worse, by giving ourselves rheumatism," added Lord Engleton.

"What grumbling creatures men are!" exclaimed his wife, "and what pleasures they lose for themselves and make impossible for others, by this stupid habit of dwelling upon the disadvantages of a situation, instead of on its charms."

"We ought to dwell upon the fowl and the magnificent prospect, and ignore the avenging rheumatism," said Claude Moreton.

"Oh no, guard against it," advised Algitha, with characteristic common sense. "Sit on this waterproof, for instance."

"Ah, there you have the true philosophy!" cried Professor Theobald. "Contentment and forethought. Observe the symbol of forethought." He spread the waterproof to the wind.

"There is nothing like a contented spirit!" cried Lady Engleton.

"Who is it that says you knock a man into a ditch, and then you tell him to remain content in the position in which Providence has placed him?" asked Hadria.

"Even contentment has its dangers," said Claude Moreton, dreamily.

At the end of the meal, Hadria rose from the rug where she had been reclining, with the final assertion, that she thought the man who was knocked into the ditch and told to do his duty there, would do the best service to mankind, as well as to himself, by making a horrid clamour and trying to get out again. A group collected round her, almost immediately.

"Mrs. Fenwick, won't you give us a song!" cried Madame Bertaux. "I see you have been kind enough to bring your guitar."

Marion was enthroned upon the picnic-basket, with much pomp, and her guitar placed in her hand by Claude Moreton. Her figure, in her white gown and large straw hat, had for background the shadows of thick woods.

Professor Theobald sank down on the grass at Hadria's side. She felt that his mood was agitated. She could not be in much doubt as to its cause. The reckless *rôle* that she had been playing was bringing its result. Hadria was half alarmed, half exultant. She had a strange, vague notion of selling her life dearly, to the enemy. Only, of late, this feeling had been mixed with another, of which she was scarcely conscious. The subtle fascination which the Professor exercised over her had taken a stronger hold, far stronger than she knew.

She was sitting on a little knoll, her arm resting on her knee, and her cheek in her hand. In the exquisitely graceful attitude, was an element of self-abandonment. It seemed as if she had grown tired of guiding and directing herself, and were now commending herself to fate or fortune, to do with her as they would, or must.

Marion struck a quiet chord. Her voice was sweet and tender and full, admirably suited to the song. Every nerve in Hadria answered to her tones.

> " Oh, gather me the rose, the rose
> While yet in flower we find it ;
> For summer smiles, but summer goes,
> And winter waits behind it.
>
> " For with the dream foregone, foregone,
> The deed foreborne for ever,
> The worm regret will canker on,
> And time will turn him never."

Professor Theobald shifted his position slightly.

> " Ah, well it were to love, my love,
> And cheat of any laughter
> The fate beneath us and above,
> The dark before and after.
>
> " The myrtle and the rose, the rose,
> The sunlight and the swallow,
> The dream that comes, the dream that goes,
> The memories that follow."

The song was greeted with a vague stir among the silent audience. A little breeze gave a deep satisfied sigh, among the trees.

Several other songs followed, and then the party broke up. They were to amuse themselves as they pleased during the afternoon, and to meet on the same spot for five o'clock tea.

" I *wish* Hadria would not be so reckless ! " cried Algitha anxiously. " Have you seen her lately ? "

"When last I saw her," said Valeria, "she had strolled off with the Professor and Mr. Moreton. Mr. Fleming and Lord Engleton were following with Mrs. Fenwick."

"There is safety in numbers, at any rate, but I am distressed about her. It is all very well what she says, about not allowing her woman's sole weapon to be wrenched from her, but she can't use it in this way, safely. One can't play with human emotions without coming to grief."

"A man, at any rate, has no idea of being led an emotional dance," said Miss Du Prel.

"Hadria has, I believe, at the bottom of her heart, a lurking desire to hurt men, because they have hurt women so terribly," said Algitha.

"One can understand the impulse, but the worst of it is, that one is certain to pay back the score on the good man, and let the other go free."

Algitha shook her head, regretfully.

"Did Hadria never show this impulse before?"

"Never in my life have I seen her exercise her power so ruthlessly."

"I rather think she is wise after all," said Miss Du Prel reflectively. "She might be sorry some day never to have tasted what she is tasting now."

"But it seems to me dreadful. There is not a man who is not influenced by her in the strangest manner; even poor Joseph Fleming, who used to look up to her so. In my opinion, she is acting very wrongly."

"'He that has eaten his fill does not pity the hungry,' as the Eastern proverb puts it. Come now, Algitha, imagine yourself to be cut off from the work that supremely interests you, and thrown upon Craddock Dene without hope of respite, for the rest of your days. Don't you think you too might be tempted to try experiments with a power whose strength you had found to be almost irresistible?"

"Perhaps I should," Algitha admitted.

"I don't say she is doing right, but you must remember

that you have not the temperament that prompts to these out-
bursts. I suppose that is only to say that you are better than
Hadria, by nature. I think perhaps you are, but remember
you have had the life and the work that you chose above all
others—she has not."

"Heaven knows I don't set myself above Hadria," cried
Algitha. "I have always looked up to her. Don't you know
how painful it is when people you respect do things beneath
them?"

"Hadria will disappoint us all in some particular," said
Miss Du Prel. "She will not correspond exactly to anybody's theory or standard, not even her own. It is a defect
which gives her character a quality of the unexpected, that
has for me, infinite attraction."

Miss Du Prel had never shewn so much disposition to support Hadria's conduct as now, when disapproval was general.
She had a strong fellow-feeling for a woman who desired to
use her power, and she was half disposed to regard her
conduct as legitimate. At any rate, it was a temptation almost
beyond one's powers of resistance. If a woman might not
do this, what, in heaven's name, *might* she do? Was she not
eternally referred to her woman's influence, her woman's kingdom? Surely a day's somewhat murderous sport was allowable
in *that* realm! After all, energy, ambition, nervous force, *must*
have an outlet somewhere. Men could look after themselves.
They had no mercy on women when they lay in their power.
Why should a woman be so punctilious?

"Only the man is sure to get the best of it," she added,
bitterly. "He loses so little. It is a game where the odds
are all on one side, and the conclusion foregone."

Unexpectedly, the underwood behind the speakers was
brushed aside and Hadria appeared before them. She looked
perturbed.

"What is it? Why are you by yourself?"

"Oh, our party split up, long ago, into cliques, and we all
became so select, that, at last, we reduced each clique to one

member. Behold the very acme of selectness!" Hadria stood before them, in an attitude of hauteur.

"This sounds like evasion," said Algitha.

"And if it were, what right have you to try to force me to tell what I do not volunteer?"

"True," said her sister; "I beg your pardon."

Miss Du Prel rose. "I will leave you to yourselves," she said, walking away.

Hadria sat down and rested one elbow on the grass, looking over the sweep of the hill towards the distance. "That is almost like our old vision in the caves, Algitha; mist and distant lands—it was a false prophecy. You were talking about me when I came up, were you not?"

"Did you hear?"

"No, but I feel sure of it."

"Well, I confess it," said Algitha. "We are both very uneasy about you."

"If one never did anything all one's life to make one's friends uneasy, I wonder if one would have any fun."

Algitha shook her head anxiously.

"'Choose what you want and pay for it,' is the advice of some accredited sage," Hadria observed.

"Women have to pay so high," said Algitha.

"So much the worse, but there is such a thing as false economy."

"But seriously, Hadria, if one may speak frankly, I can't see that the game is worth the candle. You have tested your power sufficiently. What more do you want? Claude Moreton is too nice and too good a man to trifle with. And poor Joseph Fleming! That is to me beyond everything."

Hadria flushed deeply.

"I never dreamt that he—I—I never tried, never thought for a moment —— "

"Ah! that is just the danger, Hadria. Your actions entail unintended consequences. As Miss Du Prel says, 'It is always the good men whom one wounds; the others wound us.'"

Hadria was silent. "And Claude Moreton," continued Algitha presently. "He is far too deeply interested in you, far too absorbed in what you say and do. I have watched him. It is cruel."

Hadria grew fierce. "Has *he* never cruelly injured a woman? Has *he* not at least given moral support to the hideous indignities that all womanhood has to endure at men's hands? At best one can make a man suffer. But men also humiliate us, degrade us, jeer at, ridicule the miseries that they and their society entail upon us. Yet for sooth, they must be spared the discomfort of becoming a little infatuated with a woman for a time—a short time, at worst! Their feelings must be considered so tenderly!"

"But what good do you do by your present conduct?" asked Algitha, sticking persistently to the practical side of the matter.

"I am not trying to do good. I am merely refusing to obey these rules for our guidance, which are obviously drawn up to safeguard man's property and privilege. Whenever I can find a man-made precept, that will I carefully disobey; whenever the ruling powers seek to guide me through my conscience, there shall they fail!"

"You forget that in playing with the feelings of others you are placing yourself in danger, Hadria. How can you be sure that you won't yourself fall desperately in love with one of your intended victims?" Hadria's eyes sparkled.

"I wish to heaven I only could!" she exclaimed. "I would give my right hand to be in the sway of a complete undoubting, unquestioning passion that would make all suffering and all life seem worth while; some emotion to take the place of my lost art, some full and satisfying sense of union with a human soul to rescue one from the ghastly solitude of life. But I am raving like a girl. I am crying for the moon."

"Ah, take care, take care, Hadria; that is a mood in which one may mistake any twopenny-halfpenny little luminary for the impossible moon."

"I think I should be almost ready to bless the beautiful illusion," cried Hadria passionately.

CHAPTER XLII.

IN the conversation with her sister, the name which Hadria had dreaded to hear had not been mentioned. She felt as if she could not have met her sister's eyes, at that moment, had she alluded to Professor Theobald; for only five minutes before, in the wood, he had spoken to her in a way that was scarcely possible to misunderstand, though his wording was so cautious that she could not have taken offence, had she been so minded, without drawing upon herself the possible retort. "My dear lady, you have completely misunderstood me." The thought made her flush painfully. But suppose he really *had* meant what his words seemed to imply? He could intend no insult, because he despised, and knew that she despised, popular social creeds. Into what new realms was she drifting? There was something attractive to Hadria, in the idea of defying the world's laws. It was not as the dutiful property of another, but as herself, a separate and responsible individual, that she would act and feel, rightly or wrongly, as the case might be. That was a matter between herself and her conscience, not between herself and the world or her legal owner.

The Professor's ambiguous and yet startling speech had forced her to consider her position. She remembered how her instinct had always been to hold him aloof from her life, just because, as she now began to believe, there was something in him that powerfully attracted her. She had feared an attraction that appeared unjustified by the man's character. But now the fascination had begun to take a stronger grip, as the pre-occupying ideas of her life had been chased from their places. It had insensibly crept in to fill the empty throne. So long as she had cherished hope, so long as she was still struggling, this insidious half-magnetic influence had been easily resisted. Now, she was set adrift; her anchor was raised; she lay at- the wind's mercy, half-conscious of the peril and not caring.

Professor Theobald had an acute perception of the strange and confused struggle that was going on in her mind. But he had no notion of the peculiar reasons, in her case, for an effect that he knew to be far from rare among women; he did not understand the angry, corroding action of a strong artistic impulse that was incessantly baulked in full tide. The sinister, menacing voices of that tide had no meaning for him, except as expressing a *malaise* which he had met with a hundred times before. He put it down to an excess of emotional or nervous energy, in a nature whose opportunities did not offer full scope to its powers. He had grasped the general conditions, but he had not perceived the particular fact that added tenfold to the evil which exists in the more usual, and less complicated case.

He thought but little of a musical gift, having no sympathy with music; and since he had never known what it was to receive anything but help and encouragement in the exercise of his own talents, the effect upon the mind and character of such an experience as Hadria's, was beyond the range of his conceptions. He understood subtly, and misunderstood completely, at one and the same time. But to Hadria, every syllable which revealed how much he did understand, seemed to prove, by implication, that he understood the whole. It never occurred to her that he was blinder than Henriette herself, to the real centre and heart of the difficulty.

It has been said that what the human being longs for above all things, is to be understood: that he prefers it infinitely to being over-rated. Professor Theobald gave Hadria this desired sensation. His attraction for her was composed of many elements, and it was enhanced by the fact that she had now grown so used to his presence, as to cease to notice many little traits that had repelled her, at the beginning. Her critical instincts were lulled. Thus had come to pass that which is by no means an uncommon incident in human history: a toleration for and finally a strong attraction towards a nature that began by creating distrust, and even dislike.

Hadria's instinct now was to hunt up reasons for desiring the society of Professor Theobald, for the gladness that she felt at the prospect of seeing him. She wished to explain to herself how it was that he had become so prominent a figure in her life. It was surprising how rapidly and how completely he had taken a central position. Her feeling towards him, and her admiring affection for Professor Fortescue, were as different as night from day. She shrank from comparing the two emotions, because at the bottom of her heart, she felt how infinitely less fine and sound was this latter attachment, how infinitely less to be welcomed. If any one spoke disparagingly of Professor Theobald, Hadria's instinct was to stand up for him, to find ingenious reasons for his words or his conduct that threw upon him the most favourable light, and her object was as much to persuade herself as to convince her interlocutor. What the Professor had said this afternoon, had brought her to a point whence she had to review all these changes and developments of her feeling. She puzzled herself profoundly. In remembering those few words, she was conscious of a little thrill of—not joy (the word was too strong), but of something akin to it. She thought—and then laughed at herself—that it had a resemblance to the sensation that is caused to the mind by the suggestion of some new and entrancingly interesting idea—say about astronomy! And if she consulted her mere wishes in the matter, apart from all other considerations, she would explore farther in this direction. Whether curiosity or sentiment actuated her, she could not detect. It would certainly be deeply exciting to find out what her own nature really was, and still more so to gain greater insight into his. Was this heartless, cold-blooded? Or was it that she felt a lurking capacity for a feeling stronger than—or at any rate different from—any that she had hitherto felt? This was a secret that she could not discover. Hadria gave a frightened start. Was she finding herself to be bad in a way that she had never suspected? If she could but fully and completely escape from tradition, so that her judgment might be quite unhampered. Tradition seemed either to make human beings blindly submissive, or to tempt them to act out of an equally blind opposition to its canons. One could never be entirely independent. In her confusion, she longed to turn to some clear mind and sound conscience, not so much ٫or advice, as in order to test the effect upon such a mind and conscience of the whole situation.

Professor Fortescue was the only person upon whose judgment and feeling she could absolutely rely. What would he think of her? His impression would be the best possible guide, for no one opposed more strongly than he did the vulgar notion of proprietary rights between husband and wife, no one asserted more absolutely the independence of the individual. Yet Hadria could not imagine that he would be anything but profoundly sorry, if he knew the recklessness of her feeling, and the nature of her sentiment for Professor Theobald. But then he did not know how she stood; he did not know that the blue hopeful distance of life had disappeared; that even the middle-distance had been cut off, and that the sticks and stones and details of a very speckly foreground now confronted her immovably. She would like to learn how many women of her temperament, placed in her position, would stop to enquire very closely into the right and wrong of the matter, when for a moment, a little avenue seemed on the point of opening, misty and blue, leading the eye to hidden perilous distances.

And then Professor Theobald had, after all, many fine qualities. He was complex, and he had faults like the rest of us; but the more one knew him, the more one felt his kindness of heart (how good he was to little Martha), his readiness to help others, his breadth of view and his sympathy. These were not common qualities. He was a man whom one could admire, despite certain traits that made one shrink a little, at times. These moreover had disappeared of late. They were accidental rather than intrinsic. It was a matter of daily observation that people catch superficial modes of thought and speech, just as they catch accent, or as women who have given no thought to the art of dress, sometimes misrepresent themselves, by adopting, unmodified, whatever happens to be in the fashion. Hadria had a wistful desire to be able to respect Professor Theobald without reserve, to believe in him thoroughly, to think him noble in calibre and fine in fibre. She had a vague idea that emphatic statement would conduce to making all this true.

She had never met him alone since that day of the picnic, except for a few chance minutes, when he had expressed over again, rather in tone than in words, the sentiment before implied.

Algitha and Miss Du Prel were relieved to see that Hadria had, after all, taken their advice. Without making any violent or obvious change in her conduct, she had ceased to cause her friends anxiety. Something in her manner had changed. Claude Moreton felt it instantly. He spoke of leaving Craddock Place, but he lingered on. The house had begun to empty. Lady Engleton wished to have some time to herself. She was painting a new picture. But Professor Theobald remained. Joseph Fleming went away to stay with his married sister. About this time Hubert had to go abroad to attend to some business matters of a serious and tedious character, connected with a law-suit in which he was professionally interested.

From some instinct which Hadria found difficult to account for, she avoided meeting the Professor alone. Yet the whole interest of the day centred in the prospect of seeing him. If by chance, she missed him, she felt flat and dull, and found herself going over in her mind every detail of their last meeting. He had the art of making his most trifling remark interesting. Even his comments on the weather had a colour and quality of their own. Lady Engleton admired his lightness of touch.

"Did you know that our amiable Professor shews his devotion to you, by devotion to your *protégée* ?" she asked one day, when she met Hadria returning from the Priory with the two boys, whose holidays were not yet over. "I saw him coming out of the child's cottage this morning, and she shewed me the toy he had given her."

"He is very fond of her, I know," said Hadria.

"He gives her lots of things !" cried Jack, opening round and envious eyes.

"How do *you* know, sir?" enquired Lady Engleton.

"Because Mary says so," Jack returned.

Hadria was pleased at the kindness which the act seemed to indicate.

The doctor had ordered her to be in the open air as much as possible, and to take a walk every day. Sometimes she would walk with the boys, sometimes alone. In either case, the thought of Professor Theobald pursued her. She often grew wearied with it, but it could not be banished. If she saw a distant figure on the road, a little sick, excited stir of the heart, betrayed her suspicion that it might be he. She could not sincerely wish herself free from the strange infatuation, for the thought of life without it, troublesome and fatiguing though it was, seemed inexpressibly dull. It had taken the colour out of everything. It had altered the very face of nature, in her eyes. Her hope had been to escape loneliness, but with this preposterous secret, she was lonelier than she had ever been before. She could no longer make a confidante of herself. She was afraid of her own ridicule, her own blame, above all of finding herself confronted with some accusation against the Professor, some overpowering reason for thinking poorly of him. Whenever they met, she was in terror lest he should leave her no alternative. She often opened conversational channels by which he could escape his unknown peril, and she would hold her breath till it was over. She dreaded the cool-headed, ruthless critic, lurking within her own consciousness, who would hear of no ingenious explanations of words or conduct. But she would not admit to this dread—that would have been to admit everything. She had not the satisfaction of openly thinking the matter out, for the suspicion that so profoundly saddened her, must be kept scrupulously hidden. Hadria was filled with dismay when she dared to glance at the future. No wonder Valeria had warned her against playing with fire! Was it always like this when people fell in love? What a ridiculous, uncomfortable, outrageous thing it was! How destructive to common sense and sanity and everything that kept life running on reasonable lines. A poor joke at best, and oh, how stale!

*   *   *   *   *   *   *

"Shall I tell you your ruling passion, Mrs. Temperley?"

"If you can, Professor Theobald."

Before them stretched a woodland glade. The broad fronds of the bracken made bright patches of light where the sun caught them, and tall plants, such as hemlock and wild parsley, stood out, almost white against the shade; the flies and midges moving round them in the warmth. At some distance behind, the sound of voices could be heard through the windings of the wood. There were snatches of song and laughter.

"Your ruling passion is power over others."

"It has been sadly thwarted then," she answered, with a nervous laugh.

"Thwarted? Surely not. What more can you want than to touch the emotions of every one who comes across your path? It is a splendid power, and ought to be more satisfying to the possessor than a gift of any other kind."

Professor Theobald waited for her reply, but she made none.

He looked at her fixedly, eagerly. She could do nothing but walk on in silence.

"Even an actor does not impress himself so directly upon his fellows as a woman of—well, a woman like yourself. A painter, a writer, a musician, never comes in touch at all with his public. We hear his name, we admire or we decry his works, but the man or the woman who has toiled, and felt, and lived, is unknown to us. He is lost in his work."

Hadria gave a murmur of assent.

"But you, Mrs. Temperley, have a very different story to tell. It is *you*, yourself, your personality, in all its many-sided charm that we all bow to; it is *you*, not your achievements that—that we love."

Hadria cleared her throat; the words would not come. A rebellious little nerve was twitching at her eye-lid. After all, what in heaven's name was she to say? It was too foolish to pretend to misunderstand; for tone, look, manner all told the same story; yet even now there was nothing absolutely definite to reply to, and her cleverness of retort had deserted her.

"Ah! Mrs. Temperley—Hadria——" Professor Theobald had stopped short in the path, and then Hadria made some drowning effort to resist the force that she still feared. But it was in vain. She stood before him, paler even than usual, with her head held high, but eye-lids that drooped and lips that trembled. The movement of the leaves made faint quivering little shadows on her white gown, and stirred delicately over the lace at her throat. The emotion that possessed her, the mixture of joy and dismay and even terror, passed across her face, in the moment's silence. The two figures stood opposite to one another; Hadria drawing a little away, swayed slightly backward, the Professor eagerly bending forward. He was on the point of speaking, when there came floating through the wood, the sound of a woman's voice singing. The voice was swiftly recognised by them both, and the song.

Hadria's eye-lids lifted for a second, and her breathing quickened.

> "Oh, gather me the rose, the rose,
> While yet in flower we find it;
> For summer smiles, but summer goes,
> And winter waits behind it.

> "For with the dream foregone, foregone,
> The deed foreborne for ever,
> The worm regret will canker on,
> And time will turn him never."

Professor Theobald advanced a step. Hadria drew back.

> "So well it were to love, my love,
> And cheat of any laughter
> The fate beneath us and above,
> The dark before and after.

> "The myrtle and the rose, the rose,
> The sunshine and the swallow,
> The dream that comes, the dream that goes,
> The memories that follow!"

The sweet cadence died away. A bird's note took up the dropped thread of music. The Professor broke into passionate speech.

"My cause is pleaded in your own language, Hadria, Hadria; listen to it, listen. You know what is in my heart; I can't apologize for feeling it, for I have no choice; no man has where you are concerned, as you must have discovered long ago. And I do not apologize for telling you the truth, you know it does you no wrong. This is no news to you; you must have guessed it from the first. Your coldness, your rebuffs, betrayed that you did. But, ah! I have struggled long enough. I can keep silence no longer. I have thought of late that your feeling for me had changed; a thousand things have made me hope—good heavens, if you knew what that means to a man who had lost it! Ah! speak—don't look like that, Hadria,—what is there in me that you always turn from? Speak, speak!"

"Ah! life is horribly difficult!" she exclaimed. "I wish

to heaven I had never budged from the traditions in which I was educated—either that, or that everybody had discarded them. I feel one way and think another."

"Then you do love me, Hadria," he cried.

Her instinct was to deny the truth, but there seemed to her something mean in concealment, especially if she were to blame, especially if those who respected tradition, and made it their guide and rule through thick and thin, in the very teeth of reason, were right after all, as it seemed to her, at this moment, that they were. If there were evil in this strange passion, let her at least acknowledge her share in it. Let her not "assume a virtue though she had it not."

Professor Theobald was watching her face, as for a verdict of life and death.

"Oh, answer me, answer me—Yes or no, yes or no?" She had raised her eyes for a moment, about to speak ; the words were stifled at their birth, for the next instant she was in his arms. Again came the voice of the singer, nearer this time. The song was hummed softly.

> "Oh, gather me the rose, the rose,
>   While yet in flower we find it,
> For summer smiles, but summer goes,
>   And winter waits behind it."

CHAPTER XLIII.

THE need for vigilance over that hidden distrust was more peremptory now than ever. The confession once made, the die once cast, anything but complete faith and respect became intolerable. Outwardly, affairs seemed to run on very much as before. But Hadria could scarcely believe that she was living in the same world. The new fact walked before her, everywhere. She did not dare to examine it closely. She told herself that a great joy had come to her, or rather that she had taken the joy in spite of everything and everybody. She would order her affections exactly as she chose. If only she could leave Craddock Dene! Hubert and her parents considered the opinion of the public as of more importance than anything else in life ; for her mother's sake she was forced to acquiesce; otherwise there was absolutely no reason why she and Hubert should live under the same roof. It was a mere ceremony kept up on account of others. That had been acknowledged by him in so many words. And a wretched, ridiculous, irksome ceremony it was for them both.

Hadria refused now to meet Professor Theobald at the Cottage. His visits there, which had been timed to meet her, must be paid at a different hour. He remonstrated in vain. She shewed various other inconsistencies, as he called them. He used to laugh affectionately at her "glimpses of conscience," but said he cared nothing for these trifles, since he had her assurance that she loved him. How he had waited and longed for that! How hopeless, how impossible it had seemed. He professed to have fallen in love at first sight. He even declared that Hadria had done the same, though in a different way, without knowing it. Her mind had resisted and, for the time, kept her feelings in abeyance. He had watched the struggle. Her heart, he rejoiced to believe, had responded to him from the beginning. By dint of re- peating this very often, he had half convinced Hadria that it was so. She preferred to think that her feeling was of the long- standing and resistless kind.

Sometimes she had intervals of reckless happiness, when all doubts were kept at bay, and the condition of belief that she assiduously cultivated, remained with her freely. She felt no secret tug at the tether. Professor Theobald would then be at his best; grave, thoughtful, gentle, considerate, responsive to every mood.

When they met at Craddock Place and elsewhere, Hadria suffered miseries of anxiety. She was terrified lest he should do or say something in bad taste, and that she would see her own impression confirmed on the faces of others. She put it to herself that she was afraid people would not understand him as she did. The history of his past life, as he had related it to her, appealed overpoweringly to all that was womanly and protective in her nature. He was emotional by temperament, but circum- stance had doomed him to repression and solitude. This call on her sympathy did more than anything to set Hadria's mind at rest. She gave a vast sigh when that feeling of confidence became confirmed. Life, then, need no longer be ridiculous ! Hard and cruel it might be, full of lost dreams, but at least there would be something in it that was perfect. This new emotional centre offered the human *summum bonum :* release from oneself.

Hadria and the Professor met, one morning, in the gardens of the Priory. Hadria had been strolling down the yew avenue, her thoughts full of him, as usual. She reached the seat at the end where once Professor Fortescue had found her—centuries ago, it seemed to her now. How different was *this* meeting ! Professor Theobald came by the path through the thick shrubberies, behind the seat. There was a small space of grass at the back. Here he stood, bending over the seat, and though he was usually prudent, he did not even assure himself that no one was in sight, before drawing Hadria's head gently back, and stooping to kiss her on the cheek, while he imprisoned a hand in each of his. She flushed, and looked hastily down the avenue.

" I wonder what our fate would be, if anyone had been there ?" she said, with a little shudder.

" No one was there, darling." He stood leaning over the high back of the seat, looking down at his companion, with a smile.

" Do you know," he said, " I fear I shall have to go up to town to-morrow, for the day."

Hadria's face fell. She hated him to go away, even for a short time ; she could not endure her own thoughts when his influence was withdrawn. His presence wrapped her in a state of dream, a false peace which she courted.

" Oh no, no," she cried, with a childish eagerness that was entirely unlike her, " don't go."

" Do you really care so very much ?" he asked, with a deep flush of pleasure.

" Of course I do, of course." Her thoughts wandered off through strange by-ways. At times, they would pass some black cavernous entrance to unknown labyrinths, and the frightened thoughts would hurry by. Sometimes they would be led decorously along a smooth highway, pacing quietly ; sometimes they would rise to the sunlight and spread their wings, and then perhaps take sudden flight, like a flock of startled birds.

Yes, he needed sympathy, and faith, and love. He had never had anyone to believe in him before. He had met with hardness and distrust all his life. She would trust him. He had conquered, step by step, his inimical conditions. He was lonely, unused to real affection. Let her try to make up for what he had lost. Let her forget herself and her own little woes, in the effort to fill his life with all that he had been forced to forego. (An impish thought danced before her for a second—"Fine talk, but you know you love to be loved.") If her love were worth anything, that must be her impulse. Let her beware of considering her own feelings, her own wishes and fears. If she loved, let it be fully and freely, generously and without reserve. That or nothing. ("Probably it will be nothing," jeered the imp.) "Then what, in heaven's name, *is* it that I feel?" the other self seemed to cry in desperation.

"An idea has struck me," said the Professor, taking her hand and holding it closely in his, "Why should you not come up to town, say on Friday—don't start, dearest—it would be quite simple, and then for once in our lives we should stand, as it were, alone in the world, you and I, without this everlasting dread of curious eyes upon us. Alone among strangers—what bliss! We could have a day on the river, or I could take you to see—well, anything you liked—we should be free and happy. Think of it, Hadria! to be rid of this incessant need for caution, for hypocrisy. We have but one life to live; why not live it?"

"Why not live it, why not live it?" The words danced in her head, like circles of little sprites carrying alluring wreaths of roses.

"Ah, we must be careful; there is much at stake," she said.

He began to plead, eloquently and skilfully. He knew exactly what arguments would tell best with her. The imps and the other selves engaged in a free fight.

"No; I must not listen; it is too dangerous. If it were not for my mother, I should not care for anything, but as it is, I must risk nothing. I have already risked too much."

"There would be no danger," he argued. "Trust to me. I have something to lose too. It is of no use to bring the whole dead stupid weight of the world on our heads. There is no sense in lying down under a heap of rubbish, to be crushed. Let us go our way and leave other people to go theirs."

" Easier said than done."

" Oh no ; the world must be treated as one would treat a maniac who brandished a razor in one's face. Direct defiance argues folly worse than his."

"Of course, but all this subterfuge and deceit is hateful."

"Not if one considers the facts of the case. The maniac-world insists upon uniformity and obedience, especially in that department of life where uniformity is impossible. You don't suppose that it is ever *really* attained by any human being who deserves the name? Never! We all wear the livery of our master and live our own lives not the less."

"Ah, I doubt that," said Hadria. "I think the livery affects us all, right through to the bones and marrow. What young clergyman was it who told me that as soon as he put on his canonicals, he felt a different man, mind, heart, and personality?"

"Well, *your* livery has never made you, Hadria, and that is all I care for."

"Indeed, I am not so sure."

"It has not turned you out a Mrs. Jordan or a Mrs. Walker, for instance."

" To the great regret of my well-wishers."

" To the great regret of your inferiors. There is nothing that people regret so bitterly as superiority to themselves." Hadria laughed.

" I am always afraid of the gratifying argument based on the assumption of superiority ; one is apt to be brought down a peg, if ever one indulges in it."

" I can't see that much vanity is implied in claiming superiority to the common idiot of commerce," said the Professor, with a shrug.

" He is in the family," Hadria reminded him.

" The human family ; yes, confound him !" They laughed, and the Professor, after a pause, continued his pleading.

" It only needs a little courage, Hadria. My love, my dear one, don't shake your head."

He came forward and sat down on the seat beside her, bending towards her persuasively.

"Promise me to come to town on Friday, Hadria—promise me, dearest."

"But if—oh, how I hate all the duplicity that this involves! It creates wretched situations, whichever way one turns. I never realized into what a labyrinth it would lead one. I should like to speak out and be honest about it."

"And your mother?"

"Oh, I know of course——" Hadria set her teeth. "It drives me mad, all this!"

"Oh, Hadria! And you don't count *me* then?"

"Obviously I count you. But one's whole life becomes a lie."

"That is surely schoolgirl's reasoning. Strange that you should be guilty of it! Is one's life a lie because one makes so bold as to keep one's own counsel? Must one take the world into one's confidence, or stand condemned as a liar? Oh, Hadria, this is childish!"

"Yes, I am getting weak-minded, I know," she said feverishly. "I resent being forced to resort to this sort of thing when I am doing nothing wrong, according to my own belief. Why should I be forced to behave as if I *were* sinning against my conscience?"

"So you may say; that is your grievance, not your fault. But, after all, compromise is necessary in *everything*, and the best way is to make the compromise lightly and with a shrug of the shoulders, and then you find that life becomes fairly manageable and often extremely pleasant."

"Yes, I suppose you are right." Hadria was picking the petals off a buttercup one by one, and when she had destroyed one golden corolla, she attacked another.

"Fate *is* ironical!" she exclaimed. "Never in my life did I feel more essentially frank and open-hearted than I feel now."

The Professor laughed.

"My impulse is to indulge in that sort of bluff, boisterous

honesty which forms so charming a feature of our national character. Is it not disastrous?"

"It *is* a little inopportune," Theobald admitted with a chuckle.

"Oh, it is no laughing matter! It amounts to a monomania. I long to take Mrs. Walker aside and say 'Hi! look here, Mrs. Walker, I just want to mention to you——' and so on; and Mrs. Jordan inspires me with a still more fatal impulse of frankness. If only for the fun of the thing, I long to do it."

"You are quite mad, Hadria!" exclaimed the Professor, laughing.

"Oh, no," she said, "only bewildered. I want desperately to be bluff and outspoken, but I suppose I must dissemble. I long painfully to be like 'truthful James,' but I must follow in the footsteps of the sneaky little boy who came to a bad end because he told a lie. The question is: Shall my mother be sacrificed to this passionate love of truth?"

"Or shall I?" asked the Professor. "You seem to forget me. You frighten me, Hadria. To indulge in frankness just now, means to throw me over, and if you did that, I don't know how I should be able to stand it. I should cut my throat."

Hadria buried her face in her hands, as if to shut out distracting sights and sounds, so that she might think more clearly.

It seemed, at that moment, as if cutting one's throat would be the only way out of the growing difficulty.

How *could* it go on? And yet, how could she give him up? (The imp gave a fiendish chuckle.) It would be so unfair, so cruel, and what would life be without him? ("Moral development impossible!" cried the imp, with a yell of laughter.) It would be so mean to go back now—("Shocking!" exclaimed the imp.) Assuming that she ought never to have allowed this thing to happen ("Oh, fie!") because she bore another man's name (not being permitted to retain her own), ought she to throw this man over, on second and (per assumption) better thoughts, or did the false step oblige her to continue in the path she had entered?

"I seem to have got myself into one of those situations where there is *no* right," she exclaimed.

"You forget your own words: A woman in relation to society is in the position of a captive; she may justly evade the prison rules, if she can."

"So she may; only I want so desperately to wrench away the bars instead of evading the rules."

"Try to remember that you——" The Professor stopped abruptly and stood listening. They looked at one another. Hadria was deadly white. A step was advancing along the winding path through the bushes behind them: a half overgrown path, that led from a small door in the wall that ran round the park. It was the nearest route from the station to the house, and a short cut could be taken this way through the garden, to Craddock Place.

"It's all right," the Professor said in a low voice; "we were saying nothing compromising."

The step drew nearer.

"Some visitor to Craddock Place probably, who has come down by the 4.20 from town."

"Professor Fortescue!"

Hadria had sprung up, and was standing, with flushed cheeks, beside her calmer companion.

Professor Fortescue's voice broke the momentary silence. He gave a warm smile of pleasure and came forward with out-stretched hand.

"The hoped-for instant has come sooner than I thought," he cried genially.

Hadria was shocked to see him looking very ill. He said that his doctor had bullied him, at last, into deciding to go south. His arrangements for departure had been rather hastily made, and he had telegraphed this morning, to Craddock Place, to announce his coming. His luggage was following in a hand-cart, and he was taking the short cut through the Priory gardens. He had come to say good-bye to them all. Miss Du Prel, he added, had already made up her mind to go abroad, and he hoped to come across her somewhere in Italy. She had given him all news. He looked anxiously at Hadria. The flush had left her face now, and the altered lines were but too obvious.

"You ought to have change too," he said, "you are not looking well."

She laughed nervously. "Oh, I am all right."

"Let's sit down a moment, if you were not discussing anything very important——"

"Indeed, we were, my dear Fortescue," said Professor Theobald, drawing his colleague on to the seat, "and your clear head would throw much light on the philosophy of the question."

"Oh, a question of abstract philosophy," said Professor Fortescue. "Are you disagreeing?

"Not exactly. The question that turned up, in the course of discussion, was this : If a man stands in a position which is itself the result of an aggression upon his liberty and his human rights, is he in honour bound to abide by the laws which are laid down to coerce him ? "

"Obviously not," replied Professor Fortescue.

"Is he morally justified in using every means he can lay hold of to overcome the peculiar difficulties under which he has been tyrannously placed ? "

"Not merely justified, but I should say he was a poor fool if he refrained from doing so."

"That is exactly what *I* say."

"Surely Mrs. Temperley does not demur ? "

"No ; I quite agree as to the *right*. I only say that the means which the situation may make necessary are sometimes very hateful."

"Ah, that is among the cruelest of the victim's wrongs," said Professor Fortescue. "He is reduced to employ artifices that he would despise, were he a free agent. Take a crude instance : a man is overpowered by a band of brigands. Surely he is justified in deceiving those gentlemen of the road, and in telling and acting lies without scruple."

"The parallel is exact," said Theobald, with a triumphant glance at Hadria.

" Honour departs where force comes in. No man is bound in honour to his captor, though his captor will naturally try to persuade his prisoner to regard himself as so bound. And few would be our oppressions, if that persuasion did not generally succeed ! "

"The relations of women to society for instance——" began Theobald.

"Ah, exactly. The success of that device may be said to constitute the history of womanhood. Take my brigand instance and write it large, and you have the whole case in a nutshell."

" Then you would recommend rank rebellion, either by force or artifice, according as circumstances might require ? " asked Hadria.

Professor Fortescue looked round at her, half anxiously, half enquiringly.

"There are perils, remember," he warned. " The woman is, by our assumption, the brigand's captive. If she offends her brigand, he has hideous punishments to inflict. He can subject her to pain and indignity at his good pleasure. Torture and mutilation, metaphorically speaking, are possible to him. How could one deliberately counsel her to risk all that ? "

There was a long silence.

Hadria had been growing more and more restless since the arrival of the new-comer. She took no further part in the conversation. She was struggling to avoid making comparisons between her two companions. The contrast was startling. Every cadence of their voices, every gesture, proclaimed the radical difference of nature and calibre.

Hadria rose abruptly. She looked pale and perturbed.

"Don't you think we have sat here long enough?" she asked.

They both looked a little surprised, but they acquiesced at once. The three walked together down the yew avenue, and out across the lawn. Professor Fortescue recalled their past meetings among these serene retreats, and wished they could come over again.

"Nothing ever does come over again," said Hadria.

Theobald glanced at her, meaningly.

"Look here, my dear fellow," he said, grasping Professor Fortescue by the arm, and bending confidentially towards him, "I should like those meetings to repeat themselves *ad infinitum*. I have made up my mind at last. I want to take the Priory."

Hadria turned deadly pale, and stumbled slightly.

"Well, take it by all means. I should be only too glad to let it to a tenant who would look after the old place."

"We must talk it over," said Theobald.

"That won't take long, I fancy. We talked it over once before, you remember, and then you suddenly changed your mind."

"Yes; but my mind is steady now. The Priory is the place of all others that I should like to pass my days in."

"Well, I think you are wise, Theobald. The place has great charm, and you have friends here."

"Yes, indeed!" exclaimed Theobald.

Professor Fortescue looked vaguely round, as if expecting Hadria to express some neighbourly sentiment, but she said nothing. He noticed how very ill she was looking.

"Are you feeling the heat too severe?" he asked in concern. "Shall we take a rest under these trees?"

But Hadria preferred to go on and rest at home. She asked when Professor Fortescue was coming to see them at the Red House, but her tone was less open and warm than usual, in addressing him. He said that to-morrow he would walk over in the afternoon, if he might. Hadria would not allow her companions to come out of their way to accompany her home. At the Priory gate—where the griffins were grinning as derisively as ever at the ridiculous ways of men— they took their respective roads.

Some domestic catastrophe had happened at the Red House. The cook had called Mary "names," and Mary declared she must leave. Hadria shrugged her shoulders.

"Oh, well then, I suppose you must," she said wearily, and retired to her room, in a mood to be cynically amused at the tragedies that the human being manufactures for himself, lest he should not find the tragedies of birth and death and parting, and the solitude of the spirit, sufficient to occupy him during his little pilgrimage. She sat by the open window that looked out over the familiar fields, and the garden that was gay with summer flowers. The red roof of the Priory could just be caught through the trees of the park. She wished the little pilgrimage were over. A common enough wish, she commented, but surely not unreasonable.

The picture of those two men came back to her, in spite of every effort to banish it. Professor Fortescue had affected her as if he had brought with him a new atmosphere, and disastrous was the result. It seemed as if Professor Theobald had suddenly become a stranger to her, whom she criticised, whose commonness of fibre, ah me! whose coarseness, she saw as she might have seen it in some casual acquaintance. And yet she had loved this man, she had allowed him to passionately profess love for her. His companionship, in the deepest sense, had been chosen by her for life. To sit by and listen to that conversation, feeling every moment how utterly he and she were, after all, strangers to one another, how completely unbroken was the solitude that she had craved to dispel—that had been horrible. What had lain at the root of her conduct? How had she deceived herself? Was it not for the sake of mere excitement, distraction? Was it not the sensuous side of her nature that had been touched, while the rest had been posing in the foreground? But no, that was only partly true. There had been more in it than that; very much more, or she could not have deceived herself so completely. It was this craving to fill the place of her lost art,—but oh, what morbid nonsense it had all been! Why, for the first time in her life, did she feel ashamed to meet Professor Fortescue? Obviously, it was not because she thought he would disapprove of her breaking the social law. It was because she had fallen below her own standard, because she had been hypocritical with herself, played herself false, and acted contemptibly, hatefully! Professor Fortescue's mere presence had hunted out the truth from its hiding-place. He had made further self-sophistication impossible. She buried her face in her hands, in an agony of shame. She had known all along, that this had not been a profound and whole-hearted sentiment. She had known all along, of what a poor feverish nature it was; yet she had chosen to persuade herself that it was all, or nearly all, that she had dreamed of a perfect human relationship. She had tried to arrange facts in such a light as to simulate that idea. It was so paltry, so contemptible. Why could she not at least have been honest with herself, and owned to the nature of the infatuation? That, at any rate, would have been straightforward. Her self-scorn made the colour surge into her cheeks and burn painfully over neck and brow. " How little one knows oneself. Here am I, who rebel against the beliefs of others, sinning against my own. Here am I, who turn up my nose at the popular gods, deriding my own private and particular gods in their very temples! That I have done, and heaven alone knows where I should have stopped in the wild work, if this had not happened. Professor Fortescue has no need to speak. His gentleness, his charity, are as rods to scourge one!"

CHAPTER XLIV.

WHEN Professor Fortescue called at the Red House, he found that the blinds, in the drawing-room, were all half down. Hadria held the conversation to the subject of his plans. He knew her well enough to read the meaning of that quiet tone, with a subtle cadence in it, just at the end of a phrase, that went to his heart. To him it testified to an unspeakable regret.

It was difficult to define the change in her manner, but it conveyed to the visitor the impression that she had lost belief in herself, or in some one; that she had received a severe shock, and knew no longer what to trust or how to steer. She seemed to speak across some vast spiritual distance, an effect not produced by reserve or coldness, but by a wistful, acquiescent, subdued quality, expressive of uncertainty, of disorder in her conceptions of things.

" How tempting those two easy-chairs look, under the old tree on your lawn," said the Professor. " Wouldn't it be pleasant to go out ? "

Hadria hesitated for a second, and then rose. " Certainly; we will have tea there."

When they were seated under the shade taking their tea, with the canopy of walnut leaves above their heads, the Professor saw that Hadria shewed signs of serious trouble. The haggard lines, the marks of suffering, were not to be hidden in the clear light of the summer afternoon. He insensibly shifted his chair so as not to have to gaze at her when he spoke. That seemed to be a relief to her.

" Valeria is here till the day after to-morrow," she said. " She has gone for a walk, and has probably forgotten the tea-hour but I hope you will see her."

"I want to find out what her plans are. It would be pleasant to come across one another abroad. I wish you were coming too."

"Ah, so do I."

"I suppose it's impossible."

"Absolutely."

"For the mind, there is no tonic like travel," he said.

"It must be a sovereign cure for egoism."

"If anything will cure that disease." Her face saddened.

"You believe it is quite incurable?"

"If it is constitutional."

"Don't you think that sometimes people grow egoistic through having to fight incessantly for existence—I mean for individual existence?"

"It certainly is the instinct of moral self-preservation. It corresponds to the raised arm when a blow threatens."

"One has the choice between egoism and extinction."

"It almost amounts to that. Perhaps, after long experience and much suffering, the individuality may become secure, and the armour no longer necessary, but this is a bitter process. Most people become extinct, and then congratulate them-selves on self-conquest."

"Yes, I suppose so," said Hadria musingly. "How dangerous it is to congratulate oneself on anything! One never is so near to folly as then."

The Professor threw some crumbs to a chaffinch, which had flown down within a few yards of the tea-table.

"I think you are disposed, at present, to criticise yourself too mercilessly," he said in a tone that had drawn forth many a confidence. It was not to be resisted.

"No; that would be difficult."

"Your conscience may accuse you severely, but who of us escapes such accusations? Be a little charitable with your-self, as you would with others. Life, you know, is not such

an easy game to play. Beginners must make wrong moves
now and then."

There was a long pause.

"It sounds so mild when you put it like that. But I am
not a beginner. I am quite a veteran, yet I am not seasoned.
My impulses are more imperious, more blinding than I had
the least idea of." (The words hastened on.) "Life comes
and pulls one by the sleeve; stirs, prompts, bewilders, tempts
in a thousand ways; emotion rises in whirlwinds—and one
is confused, and reels and gropes and stumbles, and then
some cruel, clear day one awakes to find the print of in-
toxicated footsteps in the precincts of the sanctuary, and
recognises oneself as desecrator."

The Professor leant forward in his low chair. The chaffinch
gave a light chirp, as if to recall him to his duty. Hadria
performed it for him. The chaffinch flew off with the booty.

"There is no suffering so horrible as that which involves
remorse or self-contempt," he said, and his voice trembled.
"To have to settle down to look upon some part of one's action,
of one's moral self, with shame or scorn, is almost intolerable."

"Quite intolerable!"

"We will not extend to ourselves the forbearance due to erring
humanity. This puts us too much on a level with the rest—is
that not often the reason of our harsh self-judgments?"

"Oh, I have no doubt there is something mean and
conceited at the bottom of it!" exclaimed Hadria.

There was a step on the lawn behind them.

The Professor sprang up. He went to meet Valeria and
they came to the table together, talking. Valeria's eyes were
bright and her manner animated. Yes, she was going abroad.
It would be delightful to meet somewhere, if chance favoured
them. She thought of Italy. And at that magic name, they
fell into reminiscences of former journeyings; they talked of
towns and temples and palaces, of art, of sunshine; and
Hadria listened silently.

Once, in her girlhood, when she was scarcely sixteen,

she had gone with her parents and Algitha for a tour
in Italy. It was a short but vivid experience which had
tinged her life, leaving a memory and a longing that never
died. The movement of travel, the sense of change and
richness offered to eye and mind, remained with her always;
the vision of a strange, tumultuous, beautiful world; of exquisite Italian cities, of forests and seas; of classic plains
and snow-capped mountains; of treasures of art—the eternal
evidence of man's aloofness, on one side of him, from the
savage element in nature—and glimpses of cathedral domes
and palace walls; and villages clinging like living things to the
hill-sides, or dreaming away their drowsy days in some sunny
valley. And then the mystery that every work of man en-
shrines; the life, the thought, the need that it embodies, and
the passionate histories that it hides! It was as if the sum
and circumstance of life had mirrored itself in the memory,
once and for all. The South lured her with its languor, its
colour, its hot sun, and its splendid memories. It was exquisite pleasure and exquisite pain to listen to the anticipations
of these two, who were able to wander as they would.

"Siena?" said Valeria with a sigh, "I used to know Siena
when I was young and happy. That was where I made the
fatal mistake in my life. It is all a thing of the past now.
I might have married a good and brilliantly intellectual man,
whom I could respect and warmly admire; for whom I had
every feeling but the one that we romantic women think so
essential, and that people assure us is the first to depart."

"You regret that you held fast to your own standard?"
said Hadria.

"I regret that I could not see the wisdom of taking the
good that was offered to me, since I could not have that
which I wished. Now I have neither."

"How do you know you would have found the other good
really satisfactory!"

"I believe in the normal," said Valeria, "having devoted
my existence to an experiment of the abnormal."

"I don't think what we call the normal is, by any means, so safe as it sounds, for civilized women at any rate," observed the Professor.

Valeria shook her head, and remained silent. But her face expressed the sad thoughts left unsaid. In youth, it was all very well. One had the whole world before one, life to explore, one's powers to test. But later on, when all that seemed to promise fades away, when the dreams drift out of sight, and strenuous efforts repeated and repeated, are beaten down by the eternal obstacles; when the heart is wearied by delay, disappointment, infruition, vain toil, then this once intoxicating world becomes a place of desolation to the woman who has rebelled against the common lot. And all the old instincts awake, to haunt and torment; to demand that which reason has learnt to deny or to scorn; to burden their victims with the cruel heritage of the past; to whisper regrets and longings, and sometimes to stir to a conflict and desperation that end in madness.

"I believe I should have been happier, if I had married some commonplace worthy in early life, and been the mother of ten children," Valeria observed, aloud.

Hadria laughed. "By this time, you or the ten children would have come to some tragic end. I don't know which I would pity most."

"I don't see why I shouldn't be able to do what other women have done," cried Valeria.

"A good deal more. But think, Valeria, of ten particular constitutions to grapple with, ten sets of garments to provide, ten series of ailments to combat, ten—no, let me see, two hundred and forty teeth to take to the dentist, not to mention characters and consciences in all their developments and phases, rising, on this appalling decimal system of yours, to regions of arithmetic far beyond my range."

"You exaggerate preposterously!" cried Valeria, half annoyed, although she laughed. She had the instinctive human desire to assert her ability in the direction where of all others it was lacking.

"And think of the uprush of impulse, good and evil ; the stirring of the thought, the movements of longing and wonder, and then all the greedy selfishness of youth, with its untamed vigours and its superb hopes. What help does a child get from its parents, in the midst of this tumult, out of which silently, the future man or woman emerges—and grows, remember, according to the manner in which the world meets these generous or these baser movements of the soul ? "

"You would frighten anyone from parenthood!" cried Valeria, discontentedly.

"Admit at least, that eight, or even seven, would have satisfied you."

"Well, I don't mind foregoing the last three or four," said Valeria. "But seriously, I think that a home and so forth, is the best that life has to offer to us women. It is, perhaps, not asking much, but I believe if one goes further, one fares worse."

"We all think the toothache would be so much more bearable, if it were only in the other tooth," said the Professor.

A silence fell upon the three. Their thoughts were evidently busy.

"I feel sorry," the Professor said at last, "that this should be your testimony. It has always seemed to me ridiculous that a woman could not gratify her domestic sentiments, without being claimed by them, body and soul. But I hoped that our more developed women would show us that they could make a full and useful and interesting life for themselves, even if that particular side of existence were denied them. I thought they might forego it for the sake of other things."

"Not without regretting it."

"Yet I have met women who held different opinions."

"Probably rather inexperienced women," said Valeria.

"Young women, but——"

"Ah, young women. What do *they* know ? The element of real horror in a woman's life does not betray itself, until the moment when the sense of age approaches. Then, and not till then, she knows how much mere superficial and transitory attractions have had to do with making her life liveable and interesting. Then, and not till then, she realizes that she has unconsciously held the position of adventuress in society, getting what she could out of it, by means of personal charm ; never resting on established right, for she has none. As a wife, she acquires a sort of reflected right. One must respect her over whom Mr. So-and-So has rights of property. Well, is it not wise to take what one can get—the little glory of being the property of Mr. So-and-So ? I have scorned this opportunism all my life, and now I regret having scorned it. And I think, if you could get women to be sincere, they would tell you the same tale."

"And what do you think of the scheme of life, which almost forces upon our finest women, or tempts them to practise, this sort of opportunism ? "

" I think it is simply savage," answered Valeria.

Again a silence fell on the little group. The spoken words seemed to call up a host of words unspoken. There was to Hadria, a personal as well as a general significance in each sentence, that made her listen breathlessly for the next.

" How would you define a good woman ? " she asked.

"Precisely as I would define a good man," replied the Professor.

"Oh, I think we ask more of the woman," said Valeria.

" We do indeed ! " cried Hadria, with a laugh.

"One may find people with a fussy conscience, a nervous fear of wrong-doing, who are without intelligence and imagination, but you never meet the noblest, and serenest, and largest examples of goodness without these attributes," said the Professor.

"This is not the current view of goodness in women," said Hadria.

"Naturally. The less intelligence and imagination the better, if our current morality is to hold its own. We want our women to accept its dogmas without question. We tell them how to be good, and if they don't choose to be good in that way, we call them bad. Nothing could be simpler."

"I believe," said Hadria, "that the women who are called good have much to do with the making of those that are called bad. The two kinds are substance and shadow. We shall never get out of the difficulty till they frankly shake hands, and admit that they are all playing the same game."

"Oh, they will never do that," exclaimed Valeria, laughing and shaking her head. "What madness!"

"Why not? The thing is so obvious. They are like the two sides of a piece of embroidery : one all smooth and fair, the other rough and ugly, showing the tag ends and the fastenings. But since the embroidery is insisted on, I can't see that it is of any moral consequence on which side of the canvas one happens to be."

"It is chiefly a matter of luck," said the Professor.

A long shadow fell across Hadria as she spoke, blotting out the little flicker of the sunlight that shone through the stirring leaves. Professor Theobald had crept up softly across the lawn, and as the chairs were turned towards the flower-borders, he had approached unobserved.

Hadria gave so violent a start when she heard his voice, that Professor Fortescue looked at her anxiously. He thought her nerves must be seriously out of order. The feverish manner of her greeting to the new-comer, confirmed his fear. Professor Theobald apologized for intruding. He had given up his intention of going up to town to-day. He meant to put it off till next week. He could not miss Fortescue's visit. One could not tell when one might see him again.

And Professor Theobald led the conversation airily on ; talking fluently, and at times brilliantly, but always with that indefinable touch of something ignoble, something coarse, that now filled Hadria with unspeakable dismay. She was terrified lest the other two should go, and he should remain. And yet she ought to speak frankly to him. His conversation was full of little under-meanings, intended for her only to understand ; his look, his manner to her made her actually hate him. Yet she felt the utter inconsequence and injustice of her attitude.

He had not changed. There was nothing new in him. The change was in herself. Professor Fortescue had awakened her. But, of course, he was one in ten thousand. It was not fair to make the comparison by which Professor Theobald suffered so pitiably. At that moment, as if Fate had intended to prove to her how badly Professor Theobald really stood comparison with any thoroughly well-bred man, even if infinitely beneath him intellectually, Joseph Fleming happened to call. He was his old self again, simple, friendly, contented. Theobald was in one of his self-satisfied moods. Perhaps he enjoyed the triumph of his position in regard to Hadria. At any rate, he seemed to pounce on the new-comer as a foil to his own brilliancy. Joseph had no talent to oppose to it, but he had a simple dignity, the offspring of a kind and generous nature, which made Professor Theobald's conduct towards him appear contemptible. Professor Fortescue shifted uncomfortably in his chair. Hadria tried to change the topic; the flush deepening in her cheeks. Professor Fortescue attempted to come to her aid. Joseph Fleming laughed good-naturedly.

They sat late into the evening. Theobald could not find an excuse to outstay his colleague, since they were both guests at the same house.

"I must see you alone some time to-morrow," he managed to whisper. There was no time for a reply.

"I shall go and rest before dinner," said Valeria.

Hadria went into the house by the open window of the drawing-room. She sank back on the sofa; a blackness came before her eyes.

"No, no, I won't, I *won't*. Let me learn not to let things overpower me, in future."

When Valeria entered, dressed for dinner, she found Hadria, deadly pale, standing against the sofa, whose arm she was grasping with both hands, as if for dear life. Valeria rushed forward.

"Good heavens, Hadria! are you going to faint?"

"No," said Hadria, "I am not going to faint, if there is such a thing as human will."

CHAPTER XLV.

THE morning had passed as usual, but household arrangements at the Cottage had required much adjustment, one of the maids being ill. She had been sent away for a rest, and the difficulty was to find another. Mary went from the Red House as substitute, in the mean time, and the Red House became disorganised.

"You look distracted with these little worries, Hadria. I should have said that some desperate crisis was hanging over you, instead of merely a domestic disturbance." Valeria was established on the lawn, with a book.

"I am going to seek serenity in the churchyard," explained Hadria.

"But I thought Professor Theobald said something about calling."

"I leave you to entertain him, if he comes," Hadria returned, and hastened away. She stopped at Martha's cottage for the child. Ah! What would become of her if it were not for Martha? The two sauntered together along the Craddock road.

All night long, Hadria had been trying to decide when and how to speak to Professor Theobald. Should she send for him? Should she write to him? Should she trust to chance for an opportunity of speaking? But, no, she could not endure to see him again in the presence of others, before she had spoken! Yesterday's experience had been too terrible. She had brought pencil and paper with her, in order to be able to write to him, if she decided on that course. There were plenty of retired nooks under the shade of the yew-trees in

the churchyard, where one could write. The thick hedges
made it perfectly secluded, and at this hour, it was always
solitary. Little Martha was gathering wild-flowers in the
hedges. She used to pluck them to lay on her mother's grave.
She had but a vague idea of that unknown mother, but
Hadria had tried to make the dead woman live again, in the
child's mind, as a gentle and tender image. The little offering
was made each time that they took their walk in the direction
of Craddock. The grave looked fresh and sweet in the
summer sunshine, with the ivy creeping up the tomb-stone
and half obliterating the name. A rose-tree that Hadria and
Martha had planted together, was laden with rich red blooms.

The two figures stood, hand in hand, by the grave. The
child stooped to place her little tribute of flowers at the head
of the green mound. Neither of them noticed a tall figure
at the wicket gate. He stood outside, looking up the path,
absolutely motionless. Martha let go Hadria's hand, and ran
off after a gorgeous butterfly that had fluttered over the head-
stone : a symbol of the soul; fragile, beautiful, helpless thing
that any rough hand may crush and ruin. Hadria turned to
watch the graceful, joyous movement of the child, and her
delight in the beauty of the rich brown wings, with their
enamelled spots of sapphire.

"Hadria!"

She gave a little gasping cry, and turned sharply. Professor
Theobald looked at her with an intent, triumphant expression. She stood before him, for the moment, as if
paralysed. It was by no means the first time that this look
had crossed his face, but she had been blind, and had not
fully understood it. He interpreted her cry and her paleness,
as signs of the fullness of his power over her. This pleased
him immeasurably. His self-love basked and purred. He
felt that his moment of triumph had come. Contrasting this
meeting with the last occasion when they had stood together
beside this grave, had he not ground for self-applause? He
remembered so well that unpleasant episode. It was Hadria

who stood *then* in the more powerful position. He had actually feared to meet her eye. He remembered how bitterly she had spoken, of her passion for revenge, of the relentless feud between man and woman. They had discussed the question of vengeance; he had pointed out its futility, and Hadria had set her teeth and desired it none the less. Lady Engleton had reminded her of a woman's helplessness if she places herself in opposition to a man, for whom all things are ordered in the society that he governs; her only chance of striking a telling blow being through his passions. If he were in love with her, *then* there might be some hope of making him wince. And Hadria, with a fierce swiftness had accepted the condition, with a mixture of confidence in her own power of rousing emotion, if she willed, and of scorn for the creature who could be appealed to through his passions, but not through his sense of justice. That she might herself be in that vulnerable condition, had not appeared to strike her as possible. It was a challenge that he could not but accept. She attracted him irresistibly. From the first moment of meeting, he had felt her power, and recognized, at the same time, the strange spirit of enmity that she seemed to feel towards him, and to arouse in him against her. He felt the savage in him awake, the desire of mere conquest. Long had he waited and watched, and at last he had seen her flush and tremble at his approach; and as if to make his victory more complete and insolent, it was at *this* grave that she was to confess herself ready to lose the world for his sake! Yes; and she should understand the position of affairs to the full, and consent nevertheless!

Her adoption of the child had added to his triumph. He could not think of it without a sense of something humourous in the relation of events. If ever Fate was ironical, this was the occasion! He felt so sure of Hadria to-day, that he was swayed by an overpowering temptation to reveal to her the almost comic situation. It appealed to his sense of the absurd, and to the savagery that lurked, like a beast of prey, at the

foundation of his nature. Her evident emotion when he
arrived yesterday afternoon and all through his visit, her
agitation to-day, at the mere sound of his voice, assured him
that his hold over her was secure. He must be a fool indeed
if he could not keep it, in spite of revelations. To offer
himself to her threatened vengeance of his own accord, and to
see her turned away disarmed, because she loved him; that
would be the climax of his victory!

There was something of their old antagonism, in the attitude
in which they stood facing one another by the side of the grave,
looking straight into one another's eyes. The sound of the
child's happy laughter floated back to them across the spot
where its mother lay at rest. Whether Theobald's intense
consciousness of the situation had, in some way, affected
Hadria, or whether his expression had given a clue, it would
be difficult to say, but suddenly, as a whiff of scent invades the
senses, she became aware of a new and horrible fact which had
wandered into her mind, she knew not how; and she took a
step backwards, as if stunned, breathing shortly and quickly.
Again he interpreted this as a sign of intense feeling.

" Hadria," he said bending towards her, " you do love me?"
He did not wait for her answer, so confident did he feel.
" You love me for myself, not for my virtues or qualities, for
I have but few of those, alas!" She tried to speak, but he
interrupted her. " I want to make a confession to you. I can
never forget what you said that day of Marion Fenwick's
wedding, at the side of this very grave; you said that you
wanted to take vengeance on the man who had brought such
misery to this poor woman. You threatened—at least, it
amounted to a threat—to make him fall in love with you, if
ever you should meet him, and to render him miserable
through his passion. I loved you and I trembled, but I
thought to myself, ' What if I could make her return my
love? Where would the vengeance be *then?*'"

Hadria had remained, for a second, perfectly still, and then
turned abruptly away.

"I knew it would be a shock to you. I did not dare to tell you before. Think what depended on it for me. Had I told you at that moment, I knew all hope for me would be at an end. But now, it seems to me my duty to tell you. If you wish for vengeance still, here I am at your mercy—take it." He stretched out his arms and stood waiting before her. But she was silent. He was not surprised. Such a revelation, at such a moment, must, of necessity, stun her.

"Hadria, pronounce my fate. Do you wish for vengeance still? You have only to take it, if you do. Only for heaven's sake, don't keep me in suspense. Tell me your decision."

Still silence.

"Do you want to take revenge on me now?" he repeated.

"No;" she said abruptly, "of what use would it be? No, no, wait, wait a moment. I want no vengeance. It is useless for women to try to fight against men; they can only *hate* them!"

The Professor started, as if he had been struck.

They stood looking at one another.

"In heaven's name, what is the meaning of this? Am I to be hated for a sin committed years ago, and long since repented? Have you no breadth of sympathy, no tolerance for erring humanity? Am I never to be forgiven? Oh, Hadria, Hadria, this is more than I can bear!"

She was standing very still and very calm. Her tones were clear and deliberate.

"If vengeance is futile, so is forgiveness. It undoes no wrong. It is not a question of forgiveness or of vengeance. I think, after all, if I were to attempt the impossible by trying to avenge women whom men have injured, I should begin with the wives. In this case " (she turned to the grave), "the tragedy is more obvious, but I believe the everyday tragedy of the docile wife and mother is even more profound."

"You speak as coldly, as bitterly, as if you regarded me as

your worst enemy—I who love you." He came forward a
step, and she drew back hurriedly.

"All that is over. I too have a confession to make."

"Good heavens, what is it? Are you not what I thought
you? Have you some history, some stain—? Don't for pity's
sake tell me that!"

Hadria looked at him, with a cold miserable smile. "That
is really amusing!" she cried; "I should not hold myself
responsible to you, for my past, in any case. My confession
relates to the present. I came up here with this pencil
and paper, half resolved to write to you—I wanted to tell
you that—that I find—I find my feelings towards you have
changed——"

He gave a hoarse, inarticulate cry, and turned sharply
round. His hands went up to his head. Then he veered
suddenly, and went fiercely up to her.

"Then you *are* in earnest? You *do* hate me! for a sin
dead and buried? Good God! could one have believed
it? Because I was honest with you, where another man
would have kept the matter dark, I am to be thrown over
without a word, without a chance. Lord, and this is what
a woman calls love!"

He broke into a laugh that sounded ghastly and cruel, in
the serene calm of the churchyard. The laugh seemed to get
the better of him. He had lost self-control. He put his
hands on his hips and went on laughing harshly, yet sometimes with a real mirth, as if by that means only could he
express the fierce emotions that had been roused in him.
Mortified and furious as he was, he derived genuine and
cynical amusement from the incident.

"And the devotion that we have professed—think of it!
and the union of souls—ha, ha, ha! and the common interests
and the deep sympathy—it is screaming! Almost worth the
price I pay, for the sake of the rattling good joke! And by
this grave! Great heavens, how humorous is destiny!"
He leant his arms on the tombstone and laughed on softly,

his big form shaking, his strange sinister face appearing over the stone, irradiated with merriment. In the dusk, among the graves, the grinning face looked like that of some mocking demon, some gargoyle come to life, to cast a spell of evil over the place.

"Ah, me, life has its comic moments!" His eyes were streaming. "I fear I must seem to you flippant, but you will admit the ludicrous side of the situation. I am none the less ready to cut my throat—ha, ha, ha! Admit, my dear Hadria—Mrs. Temperley—that it appeals also to *your* sense of humour. A common sense of humour, you know, was one of our bonds of union. What more appropriate than that we should part with shaking sides? Oh, Lord! oh, Lord! what am I to do? One can't live on a good joke for ever."

He grasped his head in his hands; then suddenly, he broke out into another paroxysm. "The feminine nature always the same, always, always; infinitely charming and infinitely volatile. Delicious, and oh how instructive!"

He slowly recovered calmness, and remained leaning on the gravestone.

"May I ask when this little change began to occur!" he asked presently.

"If you will ask in a less insolent fashion."

He drew himself up from his leaning attitude, and repeated the question, in different words.

Hadria answered it, briefly.

"Oh, I see," he said, the savage gleam coming back to his eyes. "The change in your feelings began when Fortescue appeared?"

Hadria flushed.

"It was when he appeared that I became definitely aware of that which I had been struggling with all my might and main to hide from myself, for a long time."

"And that was—— ?"

"That there was something in you that made me—well, why should I not say it?—that made me shrink."

He set his lips.

"You have not mentioned the mysterious something."

"An element that I have been conscious of from the first day I saw you."

"Something that *I* had, and Fortescue had *not*, it would seem."

"Yes."

"And so, on account of this diaphanous, indescribable, exquisite something, I am to be calmly thrown over; calmly told to go about my business!" He began to walk up and down the pathway, with feverish steps, talking rapidly, and representing Hadria's conduct in different lights, each one making it appear more absurd and more unjust than the last.

"I have no defence to make," she said, "I know I have behaved contemptibly; self-deception is no excuse. I can explain but not justify myself. I wanted to escape from my eternal self; I was tired of fighting and always in vain. I wanted to throw myself into the life and hopes of somebody else, somebody who *had* some chance of a real and effective existence. Then other elements of attraction and temptation came; your own memory will tell how many there were. You knew so well how to surround me with these. Everything conspired to tempt me. It seemed as if, in you, I had found a refuge from myself. You have no little power over the emotions, as you are aware. My feeling has been genuine, heaven knows! but, always, always, through it all, I have been aware of this element that repels me; and I have distrusted you."

"I knew you distrusted me," he said gloomily.

"It is useless to say I bitterly regret it all. Naturally, I regret it far more bitterly than you can do. And if my conduct towards you rankles in your heart, you can remember that I have to contend with what is far worse than any sense of being badly treated : the sense of having treated someone badly."

He walked up and down, with bent head and furrowed brows. He looked like some restless wild animal pacing its cage. Intense mortification gave him a strange, malicious expression. He seemed to be casting about for a means of returning the stunning blow that he had received, just at the moment of expected triumph.

" Damn ! " he exclaimed with sudden vehemence, and stood still, looking down into Hadria's face, with cruel, glittering eyes.

He glanced furtively around. There was no one in sight. Even little Martha was making mud-pies by the church door. The thick yew trees shut in the churchyard from the village. There was not a sound, far or near, to break the sense of seclusion.

"And you mean to tell me we are to part ? You mean to tell me that this is your final decision ? "

She bowed her head. With a sudden strong movement, he flung his arms round her and clasped her in an embrace, as fierce and revengeful as the sweep of the wind which sends great trees crashing to the ground, and ships to the bottom of the sea.

" You don't love me ? " he enquired.

"Let me go, let me go—coward—madman ! "

" You don't love me ? " he repeated.

" I *hate* you—let me go ! "

" If this is the last time——"

" I wish I could *kill* you ! "

" Ah, that is the sort of woman I like ! "

" You make me know what it is to feel like a murderess ! "

" And to look like one, by heaven ! "

She wrenched herself away, with a furious effort.

"Coward ! " she cried. " I did right to mistrust you ! "

Little Martha ran up and offered her a wild heartsease which she had found on one of the graves. Hadria, trembling and white, stooped instinctively to take the flower, and as she did so, the whole significance of the afternoon's revelation broke over her, with fresh intensity. His child !

He stood watching her, with malice in his eyes.

"Come, come, Martha, let us go, let us go," she cried, feverishly.

He moved backwards along the path, as they advanced.

"I have to thank you for bestowing a mother's care on my poor child. You can suppose what a joy the thought has been to me all along."

Hadria flushed.

"You need not thank me," she answered. "As you know, I did it first for her mother's sake, and out of hatred to you, unknown as you then were to me. Now I will do it for her own sake, and out of hatred to you, bitterer than ever."

She stooped to take the child's hand.

"You are most kind, but I could not think of troubling you any longer. I think of taking the little one myself. She will be a comfort to me, and will cheer my lonely home. And besides you see, duty, Mrs. Temperley, duty——"

Hadria caught her breath, and stopped short.

"You are going to take her away from me? You are going to revenge yourself like that?"

"You have made me feel my responsibilities towards my child, as I fear I did not feel them before. I am powerless, of course, to make up for the evil I have done her, but I can make some reparation. I can take her to live with me; I can give her care and attention, I can give her a good education. I have made up my mind."

Hadria stood before him, white as the gravestone.

"You said that vengeance was futile. So it is. Leave the child to me. She shall—she shall want for nothing. Only leave her to me."

"Duty must be our first consideration," he answered suavely.

"I can give her all she needs. Leave her to me."

But the Professor shook his head.

"How do I know you have told me the truth?" Hadria exclaimed, with a flash of fury.

"Do you mean to dispute it?" he asked.

She was silent.

"I think you would find that a mistaken policy," he said, watching her face.

"I don't believe you can take her away!" cried Hadria. "I am acting for her mother, and her mother, not having made herself into your legal property, *has* some legal right to her own child. I don't believe you can make me give her up."

The Professor looked at her calmly.

"I think you will find that the law has infinite respect for a father's holiest feelings. Would you have it interfere with his awakening aspirations to do his duty towards his child? What a dreadful thought! And then, I think you have some special views on the education of the little one which I cannot entirely approve. After all, a woman has probably to be a wife and mother, on the good old terms that have served the world for a fair number of centuries, when one comes to consider it: it is a pity to allow her to grow up without those dogmas and sentiments that may help to make the position tolerable, if not always satisfactory, to her. Though, as a philosopher, one may see the absurdity of popular prejudices, yet as a practical man, one feels the inexpediency of disturbing the ideas upon which the system depends, and thus adding to the number of malcontents. All very well for those who think things out for themselves; but the education of a girl should be on the old lines, believe me. You will not believe me, I know, so I think it better, for this as well as for other reasons, to take my daughter under my own care. I am extremely sorry that you should have had all this trouble and responsibility for nothing. And I am grieved that your educational idea should be so frustrated, but what am I to do? My duty is obvious!"

"I regret that you did not become a devotee to duty, either a little sooner or a little later," Hadria returned. "For the present, I suppose Martha will remain with Hannah, until your conscience decides what course you will take, and until I see whether you can carry out your threat."

"Certainly, certainly! I don't wish to give you any unnecessary pain."

"You are consideration itself." Hadria stooped to take the child's hand. The little fingers nestled confidingly in her palm.

"Will you say good-bye, Martha?" asked the Professor, stooping to kiss her. Martha drew away, and struck her father a sturdy blow on the face. She had apparently a vague idea that he had been unkind to her protectress, and that he was an enemy.

"Oh, cruel, cruel! What if I don't bring her any more toys?" Martha threatened tears.

"Will you allow us to pass?" said Hadria. The Professor stood aside, and the two went, hand in hand, down the narrow path, and through the wicket gate out of the churchyard. Hadria carried still the drooping yellow heartsease that the little girl had given her.

CHAPTER XLVI.

PROFESSOR THEOBALD made his confession to Lady Engleton on that same night, when he also announced that he found it suddenly necessary to return to town.

It was some time before she recovered from her astonishment and horror. He told his story quietly, and without an effort to excuse himself.

"Of course, though I can't exonerate you, Professor, I blame her more than you," she said finally, "for her standard in the matter was so different from your's—you being a man."

The Professor suppressed a smile. It always seemed strange to him that a woman should be harder on her own sex than on his, but he had no intention of discouraging this lack of *esprit de corps ;* it had its obvious conveniences.

"Did she confess everything to her aunt after her return from Portsmouth?" asked Lady Engleton.

"Yes ; I have that letter now."

"In which your name is mentioned?"

"In which my name is mentioned. I sent money to the girl, but she returned it. She said that she hated me, and would not touch it. So I gave the money to the aunt, and told her to send it on, in her own name, to Ellen, for the child's support. Of course I made secrecy a condition. So as a matter of fact, I have acknowledged the child, though not publicly, and I have contributed to its support from its birth."

"But I thought Mrs. Temperley had been supporting it !" cried Lady Engleton.

"Nevertheless I have continued to send the money to the aunt. If Mrs. Temperley chose to take charge of the child,

I certainly had nothing to complain of. And I could not openly contribute without declaring myself."

" Dear me, it is all very strange ! What would Hadria say if she knew ? "

" She does know."

" What, all along ? "

" No, since yesterday."

" And how does she take it ? "

" She is bitter against me. It is only natural, especially as I told her that I wanted to have the child under my own care."

" Ah, that will be a blow to her. She was wrapped up in the little girl."

Professor Theobald pointed out the difficulties that must begin to crop up, as she grew older. The child could not have the same advantages, in her present circumstances, as the Professor would be able to give her. Lady Engleton admitted that this was true.

" Then may I count on you to plead my cause with Mrs. Temperley ? "

" If Hadria believes that it is for the child's good, she will not stand in the way."

" Unless ———. You remember that idea of vengeance that she used to have ? "

" Oh, she would not let vengeance interfere with the child's welfare ! "

" I hope not. You see I don't want to adopt strong measures. The law is always odious."

" The law ! " Lady Engleton looked startled. " Are you sure that the law would give you the custody of the child ? "

" Sure of the law ? My dear lady, one might as well be sure of a woman—pardon me ; you know that I regard this quality of infinite flexibility as one of the supreme charms of your sex. I can't say that I feel it to be the supreme charm of the law. Mrs. Temperley claims to have her authority through the mother, because she has the written consent of the aunt to the adoption, but I think this is rather stretching a point."

" I fear it is, since the poor mother was dead at the time."

" I can prove everything I have said to the satisfaction of anybody," continued Theobald, " I think my claim to take charge of my child is well established, and you will admit the wish is not unreasonable."

" It does you great credit, but, oh dear, it will be hard for Mrs. Temperley."

" I fear it will. I am most grieved, but what am I to do ? I must consider the best interests of the child."

" Doubtless, but you are a trifle late, Professor, in thinking of that."

" Would you prefer it to be never than late ? "

" Heaven forbid ! "

" Then I may rely on you to explain the position of affairs to Mrs. Temperley? You will understand that it is a painful subject between us."

Lady Engleton readily promised. She called at the Red House immediately after Professor Theobald's departure. The interview was long.

" Then I have not spoken in vain, dear Hadria ? " said Lady Engleton, in her most sympathetic tone. Hadria was very pale.

" On the contrary, you have spoken to convince."

" I knew that you would do nothing to stand in the way of the child."

Hadria was silent.

" I am very sorry about it. You were so devoted to the little girl, and it does seem terribly hard that she should be taken away from you."

" It was my last chance," Hadria muttered, half audibly.

" Then I suppose you will not attempt to resist ? "

" No," said Hadria.

" He thinks of leaving Martha with you for another month."

" Really? It has not struck him that perhaps I may not

keep her for another month. Now that it is once established
that Martha is to be regarded as under *his* guardianship and
authority, and that my jurisdiction ceases, he must take her at
once. I will certainly not act for *him* in that matter. Since
you are in his confidence, would you kindly tell him that? "

Lady Engleton looked surprised. "Certainly; I suppose he
and his sister will look after the child."

" I shall send Martha up with Hannah."

" It will astonish him."

" Does he really think I am going to act as his deputy? "

" He thought you would be glad to have Martha as long as
possible."

" As the child of Ellen Jervis, yes—not as his child."

" I don't see that it matters much, myself," said Lady
Engleton, "however, I will let him know."

" By telegram, please, because Martha will be sent to-
morrow."

" What breathless haste ! "

" Why delay? Hannah will be there—she knows everything
about her charge ; and if she is only allowed to stay——"

" He told me he meant to keep her."

" I am thankful for that ! "

By this time, the story had flown through the village; nothing
else was talked of. The excitement was intense. Gossip ran
high in hall and cottage. Professor Fortescue alone could not
be drawn into the discussion. Lady Engleton took him aside
and asked what he really thought about it. All he would say
was that the whole affair was deeply tragic. He had no
knowledge of the circumstances and feelings involved, and his
judgment must therefore be useless. It seemed more practical
to try to help one's fellows to resist sin, than to shriek at
convicted sinners.

His departure had been fixed for the following morning.

" So you and poor little Martha will go up together by the
afternoon train, I suppose," said Lady Engleton.

Hadria spent the rest of the day at Martha's cottage.

There were many preparations to make. Hannah was bustling about, her eyes red with weeping. She was heart-broken. She declared that she could never live with "that bad man." But Hadria persuaded her, for Martha's sake, to remain. And Hannah, with another burst of tears, gave an assurance which amounted to a pledge, that she would take a situation with the Father of Evil himself, rather than desert the blessed child.

"I wonder if Martha realizes at all what is going to happen," said Hadria sadly, as she stood watching the little girl playing with her toys. Martha was talking volubly to the blue man. He still clung to a precarious existence (though he was seriously chipped and faded since the Paris days), and had as determined a centre of gravity as ever.

"I don't think she understands, ma'am," said Hannah. "I kep' on tellin' her, and once she cried and said she did not want to go, but she soon forgot it."

Hadria remained till it was time to dress for dinner. Professor Fortescue had promised to dine with her and Valeria on this last evening. Little Martha had been put early to bed, in order that she might have a long rest before the morrow's journey. The golden curls lay like strands of silk on the pillow, the bright eyes were closed in healthful slumber. The child lay, the very image of fresh and pure and sweet human life, with no thought and no dread of the uncertain future that loomed before her. Hannah had gone upstairs to pack her own belongings. The little window was open, as usual, letting the caressing air wander in, as sweet and fresh as the little body and soul to which it had ministered from the beginning.

The busy, loud-ticking clock was working on with cheerful unconcern, as if this were just like every other day whose passing moments it had registered. The hands were pointing towards seven, and the dinner hour was half-past seven. Hadria stood looking down at the sleeping child, her hands resting on the low rail of the cot. There was a desolate look in her eyes, and something more terrible still, almost beyond definition. It was like the last white glow of some vast fire that has been extinguished.

Suddenly—as something that gives way by the run, after a long resistance—she dropped upon her knees beside the cot with a slight cry, and broke into a silent storm of sobs, deep and suppressed. The stillness of the room was unbroken, and one could hear the loud tick-tack of the little clock telling off the seconds with business-like exactness.

CHAPTER LVII.

THE evening was sultry. Although the windows of the dining-room were wide open, not a breath of air came in from the garden. A dull, muggy atmosphere brooded sullenly among the masses of the evergreens, and in the thick summer foliage of the old walnut tree on the lawn.

" How oppressive it is ! " Valeria exclaimed.

She had been asked to allow a niece of Madame Bertaux, who was to join some friends in Italy, to make the journey under her escort, and the date of her departure was therefore fixed. She had decided to return to town on the morrow, to make her preparations.

Valeria declared impulsively that she would stay at home, after all. She could not bear to leave Hadria for so many lonely months.

" Oh, no, no," cried Hadria in dismay, " don't let me begin *already* to impoverish other lives ! "

Valeria remonstrated but Hadria persisted.

" At least I have learnt *that* lesson," she said. " I should have been a fool if I hadn't, for my life has been a sermon on the text."

Professor Fortescue gave a little frown, as he often did when some painful idea passed through his mind.

" It is happening everywhere," said Hadria, "the poor, sterile lives exhaust the strong and full ones. I will not be one of those vampire souls, at least not while I have my senses about me."

Again, the little frown of pain contracted the Professor's brow.

447

The dusk had invaded the dinner table, but they had not thought of candles. They went straight out to the still garden. Valeria had a fan, with which she vainly tried to overcome the expression of the atmosphere. She was very low-spirited. Hadria looked ill and exhausted. Little Martha's name was not mentioned. It was too sore a subject.

"I can't bear the idea of leaving you, Hadria, especially when you talk like that. I wish, *how* I wish, that some way could be found out of this labyrinth. Is this sort of thing to be the end of all the grand new hopes and efforts of women? Is all our force to be killed and overwhelmed in this absurd way?"

"Ah, no, not all, in heaven's name!"

"But if women won't repudiate, in practice, the claims that they hold to be unjust, in theory, how can they hope to escape? We may talk to all eternity, if we don't act."

Hadria shrugged her shoulders.

"Your reasoning is indisputable, but what can one do? There *are* cases——in short, some things are impossible!"

Valeria was silent. "I have thought, at times, that you might make a better stand," she said at last, clinging still to her theory of the sovereignty of the will.

Hadria did not reply.

The Professor shook his head.

"You know my present conditions," said Hadria, after a silence. "I can't overcome them. But perhaps some one else in my place might overcome them. I confess I don't see how. Do you?"

Valeria hesitated. She made some vague statement about strength of character, and holding on through storm and stress to one's purpose; had not this been the history of all lives worth living?

Hadria agreed, but pressed the practical question. And that Valeria could not answer. She could not bring herself to say that the doctor's warnings ought to be disregarded by Hadria, at the risk of her mother's life. It was not merely a risk, but a practical certainty that any further shock or trouble would be fatal. Valeria was tongue-tied.

"Now do you see why I feel so terrified when anyone proposes to narrow down his existence, even in the smallest particular, for my sake?" asked Hadria. "It is because I see what awful power a human being may acquire of ravaging and of ruling other lives, and I don't want to acquire that power. I see that the tyranny may be perfectly well-intentioned, and indeed scarcely to be called tyranny, for it is but half conscious, yet only the more irresistible for that."

"It is one's own fault if one submits to *conscious* tyranny," the Professor put in, "and I think tyrant and victim are then much on a par."

"A mere *demand* can be resisted," Hadria added; "it is *grief*, real grief, however unreasonable, that brings people to their knees. But, oh, may the day hasten, when people shall cease to grieve when others claim their freedom ! "

Valeria smiled. "I don't think you are in much danger of grudging liberty to your neighbours, Hadria; so you need not be so frightened of becoming a vampire, as I think you call it."

" Not *now*, but how can one tell what the result of years and years of monotonous existence may be, or the effect of example ? How did it happen that my mother came to feel aggrieved if her daughters claimed some right of choice in the ordering of their lives ? I suppose it is because *her* mother felt aggrieved if *she* ventured to call her soul her own."

Valeria laughed.

" But it is true," said Hadria. "Very few of us, if any, are in the least original as regards our sorrowing. We follow the fashion. We are not so presumptuous as to decide for ourselves what shall afflict us."

"Or what shall transport us with joy," added Valeria, with a shrug.

"Still less perhaps. Tradition says 'Weep, this is the moment,' or 'Rejoice, the hour has come,' and we chant our

dirge or kindle our bonfires accordingly. Why, it means a
little martyrdom to the occasional sinner who selects his own
occasion for sorrow or for joy."

Valeria laughed at the notion of Hadria's being under
the dictatorship of tradition, or of anything else, as to her
emotions.

But Hadria held that everybody was more or less subject
to the thraldom. And the thraldom increased as the mind
and the experience narrowed. And as the narrowing process
progressed, she said, the exhausting or vampire quality grew
and grew.

"I have seen it, I have seen it! Those who have been
starved in life, levy a sort of tax on the plenty of others, in
the instinctive effort to replenish their own empty treasure-
house. Only that is impossible. One can gain no riches in
that fashion. One can only reduce one's victim to a beggary
like one's own."

Valeria was perturbed.

"The more I see of life, the more bitter a thing it seems to
be a woman! And one of the discouraging features of it is,
that women are so ready to oppress each other!"

"Because they have themselves suffered oppression," said
the Professor. "It is a law that we cannot evade; if we are
injured, we pay back the injury, whether we will or not, upon
our neighbours. If we are blessed, we bless, but if we are
cursed, we curse."

"These moral laws, or laws of nature, or whatever one
likes to call them, seem to be stern as death!" exclaimed
Valeria. "I suppose we are all inheriting the curse that has
been laid upon our mothers through so many ages."

"We are not free from the shades of our grandmothers,"
said Hadria, "only I hope a little (when I have not been to
the Vicarage for some time) that we may be less of a
hindrance and an obsession to our granddaughters than our
grandmothers have been to us."

"Ah! that way lies hope!" cried the Professor.

"I wish, I *wish* I could believe!" Valeria exclaimed.

"But I was born ten years too early for the faith of this generation."

"It is you who have helped to give this generation its faith," said Hadria.

"But have you real hope and real faith, in your heart of hearts? Tell me, Hadria."

Hadria looked startled.

"Ah! I knew it. Women *don't* really believe that the cloud will lift. If they really believed what they profess, they would prove it. They would not submit and resign themselves. Oh, why don't you shew what a woman can do, Hadria?"

Hadria gave a faint smile.

She did not speak for some time, and when she did, her words seemed to have no direct reference to Valeria's question.

"I believe that there are thousands and thousands of women whose lives have run on parallel lines with mine."

She recalled a strange and grotesque vision, or waking-dream, that she had dreamt a few nights before: of a vast abyss, black and silent, which had to be filled up to the top with the bodies of women, hurled down to the depths of the pit of darkness, in order that the survivors might, at last, walk over in safety. Human bodies take but little room, and the abyss seemed to swallow them, as some greedy animal its prey. But Hadria knew, in her dream, that some day it would have claimed its last victim, and the surface would be level and solid, so that people would come and go, scarcely remembering that beneath their feet was once a chasm into which throbbing lives had to descend, to darkness and a living death.

Valeria looked anxious and ill at ease. She watched Hadria's face.

She was longing to urge her to leave Craddock Dene, but was deterred by the knowledge of the uselessness of such advice. Hadria could not take it.

"I chafe against these situations!" cried Valeria. "I am

so unused, in my own life, to such tethers and limitations. They would drive me crazy !"

"Oh," Hadria exclaimed, with an amused smile, "this is a new cry !"

"I don't care," said Valeria discontentedly. "I never supposed that one *could* be tied hand and foot, in this way. I should never stand it. It is intolerable !"

"These are what you have frequently commended to me as 'home ties,'" said Hadria.

"Oh, but it is impossible !"

"You attack the family !" cried the Professor.

"If the family makes itself ridiculous——?"

The Professor and Hadria laughed. Valeria was growing excited.

"The natural instinct of man to get his fun at his neighbour's expense meets with wholesome rebuffs in the outer world," said the Professor, "but in the family it has its chance. That's why the family is so popular."

Valeria, with her wonted capriciousness, veered round in defence of the institution that she had been just jeering at.

"Well, after all, it is the order of Nature to have one's fun at the expense of someone, and I don't believe we shall ever be able to practise any other principle, I mean on a national scale, however much we may progress."

"Oh, but we shan't progress unless we *do*," said the Professor.

"You are always paradoxical."

"There is no paradox here. I am just as certain as I am of my own existence, that real, solid, permanent progress is impossible to any people until they recognise, as a mere truism, that whatever is gained by cruelty, be it towards the humblest thing alive, is not gain, but the worst of loss."

"Oh, you always go too far !" cried Valeria.

"I don't admit that in a horror of cruelty, it is possible to go too far," the Professor replied. "Cruelty is the one unpardonable sin." He passed his hand across his brow, with a weary gesture, as if the pressure of misery and tumult and anguish in the world, were more than he could bear.

"You won't give up your music, Hadria," Valeria said, at the end of a long cogitation.

"It is a forlorn sort of pursuit," Hadria answered, with a whimsical smile, "but I will do all I can." Valeria seemed relieved.

"And you will not give up hope?"

"Hope? Of what?"

"Oh, of—of——. What an absurd question!"

Hadria smiled. "It is better to face facts, I think, than to shroud them away. After all, it is only by the rarest chance that character and conditions happen to suit each other so well that the powers can be developed. They are generally crushed. One more or less——." Hadria gave a shrug.

The Professor broke in, abruptly.

"It is exactly the one more or less that sends the balance up or down, that decides the fate of men and nations. An individual often counts more than a generation. If that were not so, nothing would be possible, and hope would be insane."

"Perhaps it is!" said Hadria beneath her breath.

The Professor had risen. He heard the last words, but made no remonstrance. Yet there was a something in his expression that gave comfort.

"I fear I shall have to be going back," he said, looking at his watch. As he spoke, the first notes of a nightingale stole out of the shrubbery. Voices were hushed, and the three stood listening spellbound, to the wonderful impassioned song. Hadria marvelled at its strange serenity, despite the passion, and speculated vaguely as to the possibility of a paradox of the same kind in the soul of a human being. Passion and serenity? Had not the Professor combined these apparent contradictions?

There was ecstasy so supreme in the bird's note that it had become calm again, like great heat that affects the senses, as with frost, or a flooded river that runs swift and smooth for very fulness.

Presently, a second nightingale began to answer from a distant tree, and the garden was filled with the wild music. One or two stars had already twinkled out.

" I ought really to be going," said the Professor.

But he lingered still. His eyes wandered anxiously to Hadria's white face. He said good-night to Valeria, and then he and Hadria walked to the gate together.

"You will come back and see us at Craddock Dene soon after you return, won't you ? " she said wistfully.

"Of course I will. And I hope that meanwhile, you will set to work to get strong and well. All your leisure ought to be devoted to that object, for the present. I should be so delighted to hear from you now and again, when you have a spare moment and the spirit moves you. I will write and tell you how I fare, if I may. If, at any time, I can be of service to you, don't forget how great a pleasure it would be to me to render it. I hope if ever I come back to England——"

"When you come back," Hadria corrected, hastily.

——"that we may meet oftener."

" Indeed, that will be something to look forward to ! "

They exchanged the hearty, lingering handshake of trusty friendship and deep affection. The last words, the last good wishes, were spoken, the last wistful effort was made of two human souls to bid each other be of good cheer, and to bring to one another comfort and hope. Hadria leant on the gate, a lonely figure in the dim star-light, watching the form that had already become shadowy, retreating along the road and gradually losing itself in the darkness.

CHAPTER XLVIII.

AUTUMN had come round again. Craddock Dene had calmed down after the exciting event of the summer. Martha's little cottage was now standing empty, the virginia creeper trailing wildly, in thick festoons and dangling sprays over the porch and creeping up round the windows, even threatening to cover them with a ruddy screen, since now the bright little face no longer looked out of the latticed panes, and the cottage was given over to dust and spiders.

Mrs. Temperley was often seen by the villagers passing along the road towards Craddock. She would sometimes pause at the cottage, to gather a few of the flowers that still came up in the tiny garden. It was said that she gathered them to lay on Ellen Jervis's grave.

"Dear, dear, she do take on about that child!" Dodge used to say, as she passed up the street of Craddock. And Mrs. Gullick, good soul, would shake her head and express her sympathy, in spite of not "holding" with Mrs. Temperley's "ways."

Her poorer neighbours understood far more than the others could understand, how sorely she was grieving about the child. Because she said nothing on the subject, it was generally supposed that she had ceased to care. After all, it was an act of charity that she had undertaken, on an impulse, and it was quite as well that she should be relieved of the responsibility.

Hannah used to write regularly, to let her know how Martha was. Professor Theobald had directed Hannah to do this. The nurse had to admit that he was very good and very devoted to the child. She throve in her new home, and seemed perfectly happy.

455

Hadria was now delivered over to the tender mercies of her own thoughts. Her memories burnt, as corrosive acids, in her brain. She could find no shadow of protection from her own contempt. There was not one nook or cranny into which that ruthless self-knowledge could not throw its cruel glare. In the hours of darkness, in the haunted hours of the early morning, she and her memories played horrible games with one another. She was hunted, they the hunters. There was no thought on which she could rest, no consoling remembrance. She often wished that she had followed her frequent impulse to tell Miss Du Prel the whole wretched story. But she could not force herself to touch the subject through the painful medium of speech. Valeria knew that Hadria was capable of any outward law-breaking, but she would never be prepared for the breaking of her own inner law, the real canon on which she had always laid so much stress. And then she had shrunk from the idea of betraying a secret not solely her own. If she told the story, Valeria would certainly guess the name. She felt a still greater longing that Professor Fortescue should know the facts; he would be able to help her to face it all, and to take the memory into her life and let its pain eat out what was base and evil in her soul. He would give her hope; his experience, his extraordinary sympathy, would enable him to understand it all, better than she did herself. If he would look at this miserable episode unflinchingly, and still hold out his hand to her, as she knew he would, and still believe in her, then she might believe still in herself, in her power of rising after this lost illusion, this shock of self-detection, and of going on again, sadder, and perhaps stronger; but if he thought that since she was capable of a real treason against her gods, that she was radically unsound at heart, and a mass of sophistication, then— Hadria buried her face in the pillow. She went through so often now, these paroxysms of agony. Do what she would, look where she might, she saw no relief. She was afraid to trust herself. She was afraid to accept her own suggestions of comfort, if ever a ray of it came to her, lest it should be but another form of self-deception, another proof of moral instability. In her eternal tossing to and fro, in mental anguish, the despairing idea often assailed her : that after all, it did not matter what she did or thought. She was but an atom of the vast whole, a drop in the ocean of human life.

She had no end or motive in anything. She could go on doing what had to be done to the last, glad if she might bring a little pleasure in so acting, but beyond that, what was there to consider? The wounds to her vanity and her pride ached a little, at times, but the infinitely deeper hurt of disillusion overwhelmed the lesser feeling. She was too profoundly sad to care for that trivial mortification.

Sometimes, Professor Fortescue used to write to Hadria, and she looked forward to these letters as to nothing else. She heard from Valeria also, who had met the Professor at Siena. She said he did not look as well as she had hoped to find him. She could not see that he had gained at all, since leaving England. He was cheerful, and enjoying sunny Italy as much as his strength would allow. Valeria was shocked to notice how very weak he was. He had a look in his face that she could not bear to see. If he did not improve soon, she thought of trying to persuade him to return home to see his doctor again. When one was ill, home was the best place after all.

"You and Professor Fortescue," she said, in closing her letter, "are the two people I love in the world. You are all that I have in life to cling to. Write to me, dearest Hadria, for I am very anxious and wretched."

The affairs of life and death mix themselves incongruously enough, in this confused world. The next news that stirred the repose of Craddock Dene, was that of Algitha's engagement to Wilfrid Burton. In spite of his socialistic views, Mrs. Fullerton was satisfied with the marriage, because Wilfrid Burton was well-connected and had good expectations. The mother had feared that Algitha would never marry at all, and she not only raised no objection, but seemed relieved. Wilfrid Burton had come down to stay at the Red House, during one of Algitha's holidays, and it was then that the betrothal had taken place. The marriage promised to be happy, for the couple were deeply attached and had interests in common. They intended to continue to work on the same lines after they were married. Both parents were favourably impressed by the son-in-law elect, and the Cottage became the scene of exciting arguments on the subject of socialism. Mr. Fullerton insisted on holding Wilfrid Burton responsible for every sort of theory that had ever been attributed not merely to socialists, but to communists, anarchists, collectivists, nihilists, and the rest ; and nothing would persuade him that the young man was not guilty of all these contradictory enormities of thought. Wilfrid's personality, however, overcame every prejudice against him, on this account, after the first meeting.

Joseph Fleming, among others, congratulated Algitha heartily on her engagement.

"I can see you are very happy," he said naïvely. She laughed and coloured.

"Indeed I ought to be. Life is gloriously worth living, when it is lived in the presence of good and generous souls."

"I wish *I* had married," said Joseph pensively.

"It is not too late to mend," suggested Algitha.

"How reckless you are !" exclaimed her sister. "How can you recommend marriage in the abstract? You happen to have met just the right person, but Mr. Fleming hasn't, it would seem."

"If one person can be so fortunate, so can another," said Algitha.

"Why tempt Providence? Rather bear the ills you have——"

"I am surprised to hear you take a gloomy view of anything, Mrs. Temperley," said Joseph ; "I always thought you so cheerful. You say funnier things than any lady I have ever met, except an Irish girl who used to sing comic songs."

Both sisters laughed.

"How do you know that, in the intervals of her comic songs, that girl has not a gloomy disposition?" asked Hadria.

"Oh no, you can see that she is without a care in the world; she is like Miss Fullerton, always full of good cheer and kindness."

"Had she also slums to cheer her up?" asked Hadria.

"No, not at all. She never does anything in particular."

"I am surprised that she is cheerful then," said Algitha. "It won't last."

"It is her slums that keep my sister in such good spirits," said Hadria.

"Really! Well, if you are fond of that sort of thing, Mrs. Temperley, there are some nasty enough places at the lower end of Craddock——"

"Oh, it isn't that one clings to slums for slums' sake," cried Hadria laughing.

"I am afraid they are already overrun with visitors," Joseph added. "There are so many Miss Walkers."

It was not long after this conversation, that Craddock Dene was thrilled by another piece of matrimonial news. Joseph Fleming was announced to be engaged to the Irish girl who sang comic songs. She was staying with Mrs. Jordan at the time. And the Irish girl, whose name was Kathleen O'Halloran, came and sang her comic songs to Craddock Dene, while Joseph sat and beamed in pride and happiness, and the audience rippled with laughter.

Kathleen was very pretty and very fascinating, with her merry, kind-hearted ways, and she became extremely popular with her future neighbours.

Little changes had taken place in the village, through death or marriage or departure. Dodge had laid to rest many victims of influenza, which visited the neighbourhood with great severity. Among the slain, poor Dodge had to number his own wife. The old man was broken down with his loss. He loved to talk over her illness and death with Hadria, whose presence seemed to comfort him more than anything else, as he assured her, in his quaint dialect.

Sometimes, returning through the Craddock Woods, Hadria would pass through the churchyard on her way home, after her walk, and there she would come upon Dodge patiently at work upon some new grave, the sound of his pickaxe breaking the autumn silence, ominously. His head was more bent than of yore, and his hair was whiter. His old face would brighten up when he heard Hadria's footstep, and he would pause, a moment or two, for a gossip. The conversation generally turned upon his old "missus," who was buried under a yew tree, near the wicket gate. Then he would ask after Hadria's belongings ; about her father and mother, about Hubert, and the boys. Mr. Fullerton had made the gravedigger's acquaintance, and won his hearty regard by many a chat and many a little kindness. Dodge had never ceased to regret that Martha had been taken away from Craddock. The place seemed as if it had gone to sleep, he said. Things weren't as they used to be.

Hadria would often go to see the old man, trying to cheer him and minister to his growing ailments. His shrewdness was remarkable. Mr. Fullerton quoted Dodge as an authority on matters of practical philosophy, and the old gravedigger became a sort of oracle at the Cottage. Wilfrid Burton complained that he was incessantly confronted with some saying of Dodge, and from this there was no appeal.

The news from Italy was still far from reassuring. Valeria was terribly anxious. But she felt thankful, she said, to be with the invalid and able to look after him. The doctors would not hear of his returning to England at the approach of winter. It would be sheer suicide. He must go further south. Valeria had met some old friends, among them Madame Bertaux, and they had decided to go on together, perhaps to Naples or Sorrento. Her friends had all fallen in love with the Professor, as every one did. They were a great help and comfort to her. If it were not for the terrible foreboding, Valeria said she would be perfectly happy. The Professor's presence seemed to change the very atmosphere. He spoke often about Hadria, and over and over again asked Valeria to watch over her and help her. And he spoke often about his wife. Valeria confessed that, at one time, she used to be horribly and shamefully jealous of this wife, whom he worshipped so faithfully, but now that feeling had left her. She was thankful for the great privilege of his friendship. A new tone had come over Valeria's letters, of late; the desperate, almost bitter element had passed away, and something approaching serenity had taken its place.

No one, she said, could be in the Professor's presence every day, and remain exactly the same as before. She saw his potent, silent influence upon every creature who crossed his path. He came and went among his fellows, quietly, beneficently, and each was the better for having met him, more or less, according to the fineness and sensitiveness of the nature.

"My love for him," said Valeria, "used at one time to be a great trouble to me. It made me restless and unhappy. Now I am glad of it, and though there must be an element of pain in a hopeless love, yet I hold myself fortunate to have cherished it."

Hadria received this letter from the postman when she was coming out of Dodge's cottage.

It threw her into a conflict of strong and painful feeling: foreboding, heart-sickness, a longing so strong to see her friends that it seemed as if she must pack up instantly and go to them, and through it all, a sense of loneliness that was almost unbearable. How she envied Valeria! To love with her whole heart, without a shadow of doubt; to have that element of warmth in her life which could never fail her, like sunshine to the earth. Among the cruelest elements of Hadria's experience had been that emptying of her heart; the rebuff to the need for love, the conviction that she was to go through life without its supreme emotion. Professor Theobald had thrown away what might have been a master-passion.

The outlook was so blank and cold, so unutterably lonely! She looked back to the days at Dunaghee, as if several lifetimes had passed between her and them. What illusions they had all harboured in those strange old days!

"Do you remember our famous discussion on Emerson in the garret?" she said to Algitha.

"Do I? It is one of the episodes of our youth that stands out most distinctly."

"And how about Emerson's doctrine? *Are* we the makers of our circumstances? *Does* our fate 'fit us like a glove?'"

Algitha looked thoughtful. "I doubt it," she said.

"Yet you have brilliantly done what you meant to do."

"My own experience does not overshadow my judgment entirely, I hope," said Algitha. "I have seen too much of a certain tragic side of life to be able to lay down a law of that sort. I can't believe, for instance, that among all those millions in the East End, not *one* man or woman, for all these ages, was born with great capacities, which better conditions might have allowed to come to fruition. I think you were right, after all. It is a matter of relation."

The autumn was unusually fine, and the colours sumptuous beyond description. The vast old trees that grew so tall and strong, in the genial English soil, burnt away their summer life in a grand conflagration.

Hubert had successfully carried the day with regard to the important case which had taken him abroad, and had now returned to Craddock Dene. Henriette came to stay at the Red House.

She followed her brother, one day, into the smoking-room, and there, with much tact and circumlocution, gave him to understand that she thought Hadria was becoming more sensible; that she was growing more like other people, less opinionated, wiser, and better in every way.

"Hadria was always very sweet, of course," said Henriette, "but she had the faults of her qualities, as we all have. You have had your trials, dear Hubert, but I rejoice to believe that

Hadria will give you little further cause for pain or regret."
Hubert made no reply. He placed the tips of his fingers
together and looked into the fire.

"I think that the companionship of Lady Engleton has
been of great service to Hadria," he observed, after a long
pause.

"Unquestionably," assented Henriette. "She has had an
enormous influence upon her. She has taught Hadria to see
that one may hold one's own ideas quietly, without flying in
everybody's face. Lady Engleton is a pronounced agnostic,
yet she never misses a Sunday at Craddock Church, and I
am glad to see that Hadria is following her example. It must
be a great satisfaction to you, Hubert. People used to talk
unpleasantly about Hadria's extremely irregular attendance. It
is such a mistake to offend people's ideas, in a small place
like this."

"That is what I told Hadria," said Hubert, "and her mother
has been speaking seriously to her on the subject. Hadria
made no opposition, rather to my surprise. She said that she
would go as regularly as our dining-room clock, if it gave us
all so much satisfaction."

"How charming!" cried Henriette benevolently, "and
how characteristic!"

As Hadria sank in faith and hope, she rose in the opinion
of her neighbours. She was never nearer to universal un-
belief than now, when the orthodox began to smile upon her.

Life presented itself to her as a mere welter of confused
forces. If goodness, or aspiration, or any godlike thing arose,
for a moment—like some shipwrecked soul with hands out-
stretched above the waves—swiftly it sank again submerged,
leaving only a faint ripple on the surface, soon overswept and
obliterated.

She could detect no light on the face of the troubled
waters. Looking around her at other lives, she saw the story
written in different characters, but always the same; hope,
struggle, failure. The pathos of old age wrung her heart;

the sorrows of the poor, the lonely, the illusions of the seeker after wealth, the utter vanity of the objects of men's pursuit, and the end of it all !

"I wonder what is the secret of success, Hadria?"

"Speaking generally, I should say to have a petty aim."

"Then if one succeeds after a long struggle," said Algitha pensively.

"One finds it, I doubt not, the dismalest of failures."

A great cloud of darkness seemed to have descended over the earth. Hadria felt cut off even from Nature. The splendours of the autumn appeared at a vast distance from her. They belonged to another world. She could not get near them. Mother earth had deserted her child.

A superficial apathy was creeping over her, below which burnt a slow fire of pain. But the greater the apathy, which expressed itself outwardly in a sort of cheerful readiness to take things as they came, the more delighted everybody appeared to be with the repentant sinner. Her associates seemed to desire earnestly that she should go to church, as they did, in her best bonnet——and why not? She would get a best bonnet, as ridiculous as they pleased, and let Mr. Walker do his worst. What did it matter? Who was the better or the worse for what she thought or how she acted? What mattered it, whether she were consistent or not? What mattered it if she seemed, by her actions, to proclaim her belief in dogmas that meant nothing to her, except as interesting products of the human mind? She had not enough faith to make it worth while to stand alone.

Lord Engleton said he thought it right to go to church regularly, for the sake of setting an example to the masses, a sentiment which always used to afford Hadria more amusement than many intentional witticisms.

She went often to the later service, when the autumn twilight lay heavy and sad upon the churchyard, and the peace of evening stole in through the windows of the church. Then, as the sublime poetry of psalmist or prophet rolled through the Norman arches, or the notes of the organ stole out of the shadowed chancel, a spirit of repose would creep into the heart of the listener, and the tired thoughts would take a more rhythmic march. She felt nearer to her fellows, at such moments, than at any other. Her heart went out to them, in wistful sympathy. They seemed to be standing together then, one and all, at the threshold of the great Mystery, and though they might be parted ever so widely by circumstance, temperament, mental endowment, manner of thought, yet after all, they were brethren and fellow sufferers; they shared the weakness, the longing, the struggle of life; they all had affections, ambitions, heart-breakings, sins, and victories; the differences were slight and transient, in the presence of the vast unknown, the Ultimate Reality for which they were all groping in the darkness. This sense of brotherhood was strongest with regard to the poorer members of the congregation : the labourers with their toil-stained hands and bent heads, the wives, the weary mothers, their faces seamed with the ceaseless strain of child-bearing, and hard work, and care and worry. In their prematurely ageing faces, in their furrowed brows, Hadria could trace the marks of Life's bare and ruthless hand, which had pressed so heavily on those whose task it had been to bestow the terrible gift. Here the burden had crushed soul and flesh ; here that insensate spirit of Life had worked its will, gratified its rage to produce and reproduce, it mattered not what in the semblance of the human, so long only as that wretched semblance repeated itself, and repeated itself again, *ad nauseam,* while it destroyed the creatures which it used for its wild purpose——

And the same savage story was written, once more, on the faces of the better dressed women : worry, weariness, apathy, strain ; these were marked unmistakeably, after the first freshness of youth had been driven away, and the features began to take the mould of the habitual thoughts and the habitual impressions.

And on these faces, there was a certain pettiness and cold-ness not observable on those of the poorer women.

Often, when one of the neighbours called and found Hadria alone, some chance word of womanly sympathy would touch a spring, and then a sad, narrow little story of trouble and difficulty would be poured out; a revelation of the bewildered, toiling, futile existences that were being passed beneath a smooth appearance; of the heart-ache and heroism and mis-placed sacrifice, of the ruined lives that a little common sense and common kindness might have saved; the unending pain and trouble about matters entirely trivial, entirely absurd; the ceaseless travail to bring forth new elements of trouble for those who must inherit the deeds of to-day; the burdened existences agonizing to give birth to new existences, equally burdened, which in their turn, were to repeat the ceaseless oblation to the gods of Life.

"Futile?" said Lady Engleton. "I think women are generally fools, *entre nous;* that is why they so often fill their lives with sound and fury, accomplishing nothing."

Hadria felt that this was a description of her own life, as well as that of most of her neighbours.

"I can understand so well how it is that women become conventional," she said, apparently without direct reference to the last remark, "it is so useless to take the trouble to act on one's own initiative. It annoys everybody frightfully, and it accomplishes nothing, as you say."

"My dear Hadria, you alarm me!" cried Lady Engleton, laughing. "You must really be very ill indeed, if you have come to this conclusion!"

In looking over some old papers and books, one afternoon, Hadria came upon the little composition called *Futility*, which a mood had called forth at Dunaghee, years ago. She had almost forgotten about it, and in trying it over, she found that it was like trying over the work of some other person.

It expressed with great exactness the feelings that over-whelmed her now, whenever she let her imagination dwell upon the lives of women, of whatever class and whatever kind. Futility! The mournful composition, with its strange modern character, its suggestion of striving and confusion and pain, expressed as only music could express, the yearning and the sadness that burden so many a woman's heart to-day.

She knew that the music was good, and that now she could compose music infinitely better. The sharpness of longing for her lost art cut through her. She half turned from the piano and then went back, as a moth to the flame.

How was this eternal tumult to be stilled? Facts were definite and clear, there was no room for doubt or for hope. These facts then had to be dealt with. How did other women deal with them? Not so much better than she did, after all, as it appeared when one was allowed to see beneath the amiable surface of their lives. They were all spinning round and round, in a dizzy little circle, all whirling and toiling and troubling, to no purpose.

Even Lady Engleton, who appeared so bright and satisfied, had her secret misery which spoilt her life. She had beauty, talent, wealth, everything to make existence pleasant and satisfactory, but she had allowed externals and unessentials to encroach upon it, to govern her actions, to usurp the place of her best powers, to creep into her motives, till there was little germ and heart of reality left, and she was beginning to feel starved and aimless in the midst of what might have been plenty. Lady Engleton had turned to her neighbour at the Red House in an instinctive search for sympathy, as the more genuine side of her nature began to cry out against the emptiness of her graceful and ornate existence. Hadria was startled by the revelation. Hubert had always held up Lady Engleton as a model of virtue and wisdom, and perfect contentment. Yet she too, it turned out, for all her smiles and her cheerfulness, was busy and weary with futilities. She too, like the fifty daughters of Danaus, was condemned to the idiot's labour of eternally drawing water in sieves from fathomless wells.

CHAPTER XLIX.

ALGITHA'S marriage took place almost immediately. There was no reason for delay. She stayed at the Cottage, and was married at Craddock Church, on one of the loveliest mornings of the year, as the villagers noticed with satisfaction. Both sisters had become favourites in the neighbourhood among the poorer people, and the inhabitants mustered to see the wedding.

It was only for her mother's sake that Algitha had consented to a conventional ceremony. She said that she and Wilfrid both hated the whole barbaric show. They submitted only because there was no help for it. Algitha's mother would have broken her heart if they had been bound merely by the legal tie, as she and Wilfrid desired.

"Indeed, the only tie that we respect is that of our love and faith. If that failed, we should scorn to hold one another in unwilling bondage. We are not entirely without self-respect."

The couple were to take a tour in Italy, where they hoped to meet Valeria and Professor Fortescue. Joseph Fleming was married, almost at the same time, to his merry Irish girl.

The winter came suddenly. Some terrific gales had robbed the trees of their lingering yellow leaves, and the bare branches already shewed their exquisite tracery against the sky. Heavy rain followed, and the river was swollen, and there were floods that made the whole country damp, and rank, and terribly depressing. Mrs. Fullerton felt the influence of the weather, and complained of neuralgia and other ailments. She needed watching very carefully, and plenty of cheerful companionship. This was hard to supply. In struggling

468

to belie her feelings, day after day, Hadria feared, at times, that she would break down disastrously. She was frightened at the strange haunting ideas that came to her, the dread and nameless horror that began to prey upon her, try as she would to protect herself from these nerve-torments, which she could trace so clearly to their causes. If only, instead of making one half insane and stupid, the strain of grief would but kill one outright, and be done with it !

Old Dodge was a good friend to Hadria, at this time. He saw that something was seriously wrong, and he managed to convey his affectionate concern in a thousand little kindly ways that brought comfort to her loneliness, and often filled her eyes with sudden tears. Nor was he the only friend she had in the village, whose sympathy was given in generous measure. Hadria had been able to be of use, at the time of the disastrous epidemic which had carried off so many of the population, and since then had been admitted to more intimate relationship with the people ; learning their troubles and their joys, their anxieties, and the strange pathos of their lives. She learnt, at this time, the quality of English kindness and English sympathy, which Valeria used to say was equalled nowhere in the world.

Before the end of the winter, Algitha and her husband returned.

" I 'm real glad, mum, that I be," said Dodge, " to think as you has your sister with you again. There ain't nobody like one's kith and kin, wen things isn't quite as they should be, as one may say. Miss Fullerton—which I means Mrs. Burton —is sure to do you a sight o' good, bless 'er."

Dodge was right. Algitha's healthy nature, strengthened by happiness and success, was of infinite help to Hadria, in her efforts to shake off the symptoms that had made her frightened of herself. She did not know what tricks exhausted nerves might play upon her, or what tortures they had in store for her.

Algitha's judgments were inclined to be definite and clear-cut to the point of hardness. She did not know the meaning of over-wrought nerves, nor the difficulties of a nature more imaginative than her own. She had found her will-power sufficient to meet all the emergencies of her life, and she was disposed to feel a little contemptuous, especially of late, at a persistent condition of difficulty and confusion. Her impulse was to attack such a condition and bring it to order, by force of will. The active temperament is almost bound to mis-understand the imaginative or artistic spirit and its difficulties. A real *cul de sac* was to Algitha almost unthinkable. There *must* be some means of finding one's way out.

Hadria's present attitude amazed and irritated her. She objected to her regular church-going, as dishonest. Was she not, for the sake of peace and quietness, professing that which she did not believe? And how was it that she was growing more into favour with the Jordans and Walkers and all the narrow, wooden-headed people? Surely an ominous sign.

After the long self-suppression, the long playing of a fatiguing rôle, Hadria felt an unspeakable relief in Algitha's presence. To her, at least, she need not assume a false cheerfulness.

Algitha noticed, with anxiety, the change that was coming over her sister, the spirit of tired acquiescence, the insidious creeping in of a slightly cynical view of things, in place of the brave, believing, imaginative outlook that she had once held towards life. This cynicism was more or less superficial however, as Algitha found when they had a long and intimate conversation, one evening in Hadria's room, by her fire; but it was painful to Algitha to hear the hopeless tones of her sister's voice, now that she was speaking simply and sincerely, without bitterness, but without what is usually called resignation.

"No; I don't think it is all for the best," said Hadria. "I think, as far as my influence goes, it is all for the worst. What fatal argument my life will give to those who are seeking reasons to hold our sex in the old bondage! My struggles, my failure, will add to the staggering weight that we all stumble under. I have hindered more—that is the bitter thing—by having tried and failed, than if I had never tried at all. Mrs. Walker, Mrs. Gordon herself, has given less arguments to the oppressors than I."

" But why ? But how ? " cried Algitha incredulously.

" Because no one can point to *them*, as they will to me, and say, 'See, what a ghastly failure ! See how feeble after all, are these pretentious women of the new order, who begin by denying the sufficiency of the life assigned them, by common consent, and end by failing in that and in the other which they aspire to. What has become of all the talent and all the theories and resolves ?' And so the next girl who dares to have ambitions, and dares to scorn the *rôle* of adventuress that society allots to her, will have the harder fate because of my attempt. Now nothing in the whole world," cried Hadria, her voice losing the even tones in which she had been speaking, " nothing in the whole world will ever persuade me that *that* is all for the best ! "

" I never said it was, but when a thing has to be, why not make the best of it ? "

" And so persuade people that all is well, when all is not well ! That 's exactly what women always do and always have done, and plume themselves upon it. And so this ridiculous farce is kept up, because these wretched women go smiling about the world, hugging their stupid resignation to their hearts, and pampering up their sickly virtue, at the expense of their sex. Hang their virtue ! "

Algitha laughed.

" It *is* somewhat self-regarding certainly, in spite of the incessant renunciation and sacrifice."

" Oh, self-sacrifice in a woman, is always her easiest course. It is the nearest approach to luxury that society allows her," cried Hadria, irascibly.

" It is most refreshing to hear you exaggerate, once more, with the old vigour," her sister cried.

" If I have a foible, it is under-statement," returned Hadria, with a half-smile.

"Then I think you haven't a foible," said Algitha.

"That I am ready to admit; but seriously, women seem bent on proving that you may treat them as you like, but they will 'never desert Mr. Micawber.'"

Algitha 'smiled.

"They are so mortally afraid of getting off the line and doing what might not be quite right.   They take such a morbid interest in their own characters.   They are so particular about their souls.   The female soul is such a delicate creation —like a bonnet.   Look at a woman trimming and poking at her bonnet—that's exactly how she goes on with her soul."

Algitha laughed and shrugged her shoulders.

"It has trained her in a sort of heroism, at any rate," she said.

"Heroism! talk of Spartan boys, they are not in it!   A woman will endure martyrdom with the expression of a seraph, —an extremely aggravating seraph.   She looks after her soul as if it were the ultimate fact of the universe.   She will trim and preen that ridiculous soul, though the heavens fall and the rest of her sex perish."

"Come now, I think there are exceptions."

"A few, but very few.   It is a point of honour, a sacred canon.   Women will go on patiently drawing water in sieves, and pretend they are usefully employed because it tires them!"

"They believe it," said Algitha.

"Perhaps so.   But it's very silly."

"It is really well meant.   It is a submission to the supposed will of heaven."

"A poor compliment to Heaven!"   Hadria exclaimed.

"Well, it is not, of course, your conception nor mine of the will of heaven, but it is their's."

Hadria shrugged her shoulders.   "I wish women would think a little less of Heaven in the abstract, and a little more of one another, in the concrete."

"Nobody has ever taught them to think of one another; on the contrary, they have always been trained to think of

men, and of Heaven, and their souls. That training accounts
for their attitude towards their own sex."

"I suppose so. A spirit of sisterhood among women
would have sadly upset the social scheme, as it has been
hitherto conceived. Indeed the social scheme has made
such a spirit well-nigh impossible."

"A conquering race, if it is wise, governs its subjects
largely through their internecine squabbles and jealousies.
But what if they combine——?"

"Ah!" Hadria drew a deep sigh. "I wish the moment of
sisterhood were a little nearer."

"Heaven hasten it!" cried Algitha.

"Perhaps it is nearer than we imagine. Women are quick
learners, when they begin. But, oh, it is hard sometimes
to make them begin. They are so annoyingly abject; so
painfully diffident. It is their pride to be humble. The
virtuous worm won't even turn!"

"Poor worm! It sometimes permits itself the relief of
verbal expression!" observed Algitha.

Hadria laughed. "There are smiling, villainous worms, who
deny themselves even *that!*"

After a long silence, Algitha taking the poker in her hand
and altering the position of some of the coals, asked what
Hadria meant to do in the future; how she was going to
"turn," if that was her intention.

"Oh, I cannot even turn!" replied Hadria. "Necessity
knows no law. The one thing I won't do, is to be virtuously
resigned. And I won't 'make the best of it.'"

Algitha laughed. "I am relieved to hear so wrong-
headed a sentiment from you. It sounds more like your
old self."

"I won't be called wrong-headed on this account," said
Hadria. "If my life is to bear testimony to the truth, its
refrain ought to be, 'This is wrong, this is futile, this is cruel,
this is damnable.' I shall warn every young woman I come
across, to beware, as she grows older, and has people in her

clutches, not to express her affection by making unlimited demands on the beloved objects, nor by turning the world into a prison-house for those whom she honours with her devotion. The hope of the future lies in the rising generation. You can't alter those who have matured in the old ideas. It is for us to warn. I *won't* pretend to think that things are all right, when I know they are not all right. That would be mean. What is called making the best of it, would testify all the wrong way. My life, instead of being a warning, would be a sort of a trap. Let me at least play the humble rôle of scarecrow. I am in excellent condition for it," she added, grasping her thin wrist.

Algitha shook her head anxiously.

"I fear," she said, "that the moral that most people will draw will be: 'Follow in the path of Mrs. Gordon, however distasteful it may seem to you, and whatever temptations you feel towards a more independent life. If you don't, you will come to grief.'"

"Then you think it would be better to be 'resigned,' and look after one's own soul?"

"Heaven knows what would be better!" Algitha exclaimed. "But one thing is certain, you ought to look after your body, for the present at any rate."

CHAPTER L.

HADRIA had found the autumn saddening, and the winter tempt her to morbid thoughts, but the coming of spring made her desperate. It would not allow her to be passive, it would not permit her emotions to lie prone and exhausted. Everything was waking, and she must wake too, to the bitterest regret and the keenest longings of which she was capable.

She had tried to avoid everything that would arouse these futile emotions; she had attempted to organise her life on new lines, persisting in her attitude of non-surrender, but winning, as far as she was able, the rest that, at present, could only be achieved by means of a sort of inward apathy. It was an instinctive effort of self-preservation. She was like a fierce fire, over which ashes have been heaped to keep down the flames, and check its ardour. She had to eat her heart out in dullness, to avoid its flaming out in madness. But the spring came and carried her away on its torrent. She might as well have tried to resist an avalanche. She thought that she had given up all serious thought of music; the surrender was necessary, and she had judged it folly to tempt herself by further dallying with it. It was too strong for her. And the despair that it awoke seemed to break up her whole existence, and render her unfit for her daily task. But now she found that, once more, she had underrated the strength of her own impulses. For some time she resisted, but one day, the sun shone out strong and genial, the budding trees spread their branches to the warm air, a blackbird warbled ecstatically from among the Priory shrubberies, and Hadria passed into the garden of the Griffins.

The caretaker smiled, when she saw who stood on the doorstep.

"Why ma'am, I thought you was never coming again to play on the piano; I *have* missed it, that I have. It makes the old place seem that cheerful—I can almost fancy it's my poor young mistress come back again. She used to sit and play on that piano, by the hour together."

"I am glad you have enjoyed it," said Hadria gently. The blinds were pulled up in the drawing-room, the piano was uncovered, the windows thrown open to the terrace.

"You haven't had much time for playing since your mamma has been ill," the woman continued, dusting the keys and setting up the music-rest.

"To-day my mother has a visitor; Mrs. Joseph Fleming is spending the afternoon with her," said Hadria.

"To be sure, ma'am, to be sure, a nice young lady, and so cheerful," said the good woman, bustling off to wind up the tall old clock with the wise-looking face, that had been allowed to run down since Hadria's last visit. "Seems more cheerful like," observed the caretaker, as the steady tick-tack began to sound through the quiet room.

"And have you fed my birds regularly, Mrs. Williams?" asked Hadria, taking off her hat and standing at the open window looking out to the terrace.

"Yes indeed, ma'am, every day, just as you used to do when you came yourself. And they has got so tame; they almost eats out of my hand."

"And my robin? I hope he has not deserted us."

"Oh, no, he comes right into the room sometimes and hops about, just as he did that afternoon, the last time you was here! I think it's the same bird, for he likes to perch on that table and pick up the crumbs."

"Poor little soul! If you will give me a scrap of bread, Mrs. Williams——"

The caretaker left the room, and returned with a thick slice, which Hadria crumbled and scattered on the window-sill, as she stepped out to the terrace.

The calm old mansion with its delicate outlines, its dreamy exquisite stateliness, spoke of rest and sweet serenity. The place had the melancholy but also the repose of greatness. It was rich in all that lies nearest to the heart of that mysterious, dual-faced divinity that we call beauty, compounded of sorrow and delight.

Ah! if only its owner could come and take up his abode here. If only he would get well! Hadria's thoughts wandered backwards to that wonderful evening, when she had played to him and Algitha, and they had all watched the sunset afterwards, from the terrace. How long was it since she had touched the piano in this old drawing-room? Never since she returned from Paris. Even her own piano at home had been almost equally silent. She believed that she had not only quite abandoned hope with regard to music, but that she had prepared herself to face the inevitable decay of power, the inevitable proofs of her loss, as time went on. But so far, she had only had proofs that she could do astonishingly much if she had the chance.

To-day, for the first time, the final ordeal had to be gone through. And her imagination had never conceived its horror. She was to be taken at her word. The neglected gift was beginning to show signs of decay and enfeeblement. It had given fair warning for many a year, by the persistent appeal that it made, the persistent pain that it caused; but the famine had told upon it at last. It was dying. As this fact insinuated itself into the consciousness, in the teeth of a wild effort to deny it, despair flamed up, fierce and violent. She regretted that she had not thrown up everything long ago, rather than endure this lingering death; she cursed her hesitation, she cursed her fate, her training, her circumstances, she cursed herself. Whatever there was to curse, she cursed. What hideous nonsense to imagine herself ready to face this last insult of fate! She was like a martyr, who invites the stake and the faggot, and knows what he has undertaken only when the flames begin to curl about his feet. She had offered up her power, her imperious creative instinct, to the Lares and Penates; those greedy little godlets whom there was no appeasing while an inch of one remained that they could tear to pieces. She clenched her hands, in agony. The whole being recoiled now, at the eleventh hour, as a fierce wild creature that one tries to bury alive. She looked back along the line of the past and saw, with too clear eyes, the whole insidious process, so stealthy that she had hardly detected it, at the time. She remembered those afternoons at the Priory, when the restless, ill-trained power would assert itself, free for the moment, from the fetters and the dismemberment that awaited it in ordinary life. But like a creature accustomed to the yoke, she had found it increasingly difficult to use the moments of opportunity when they came. The force of daily usage, the necessary bending of thoughts in certain habitual direc-tions, had assisted the crippling process, and though the power still lay there, stiffer than of yore, yet the preliminary movements and readjustments used up time and strength, and then gradually, with the perpetual repetition of adverse habits, the whole process became slower, harder, crueler.

"Good heavens! are *all* doors going to be shut against me?"

It was more than she could bear! And yet it must be borne—unless—no, there was no "unless." It was of no use to coquet with thoughts of suicide. She had thought all that out long ago, and had sought, at more than one crisis of desperate misery, for refuge from the horror and the insults of life. But there were always others to be considered. She could not strike them so terrible a blow. Retreat was ruthlessly cut off. Nothing remained but the endurance of a conscious slow decay; nothing but increasing loss and feebleness, as the surly years went by. They were going, going, these years of life, slipping away with their spoils. Youth was departing, everything was vanishing; her very self, bit by bit, slowly but surely, till the House of Life would grow narrow and shrunken to the sight, the roof descend. The gruesome old story of the imprisoned prince flashed into her mind ; the wretched captive, young and life-loving, who used to wake up, each morning, to find that of the original seven windows of his dungeon, one had disappeared, while the walls had advanced a foot, and to-morrow yet another foot, till at length the last window had closed up, and the walls shrank together and crushed him to death.

"I can't, I *can't* endure it ! "

Hadria had leaned forward against the key-board, which gave forth a loud crash of discordant notes, strangely expressive of the fall and failure of her spirit.

She remained thus motionless, while the airs wandered in from the garden, and a broad ray of sunlight showed the strange incessant gyrations of the dust atoms, that happened to lie within the revealing brightness. The silence was perfect.

Hadria raised her head at last, and her eyes wandered out to the sweet old garden, decked in the miraculous hues of spring. The unutterable loveliness brought, for a second, a strange, inconsequent sense of peace; it seemed like a promise and a message from an unknown god.

But after that momentary and inexplicable experience, the babble of thought went on as before. The old dream mounted again heavenwards, like a cloud at sunset; wild fancies fashioned themselves in the brain. And then, in fantastic images, Hadria seemed to see a panorama of her own life and the general life pass before her, in all their incongruity and confusion. The great mass of that life showed itself as prose, because the significance of things had not been grasped or suspected ; but here and there, the veil was pierced —by some suffering soul, by some poet's vision—and the darkness of our daily, pompous, careworn, ridiculous little existence made painfully visible.

"It is all absurd, all futile ! " (so moved the procession of the thoughts); "and meanwhile the steady pulse of life beats on, not pausing while we battle out our days, not waiting while we decide how we shall live. We are possessed by a sentiment, an ideal, a religion; old Time makes no comment, but moves quietly on; we fling the thing aside as tawdry, insufficient; the ideal is tarnished, experience of the world converts us—and still unmoved, he paces on. We are off on another chase; another conception of things possesses us; and still the beat of his footstep sounds in our ears, above the tumult. We think and aspire and dream, and meanwhile the fires grow cold upon the hearth, the daily cares and common needs plead eloquently for our undivided service; the stupendous movement of Existence goes on unceasingly, at our doors; thousands struggling for gold and fame and mere bread, and resorting to infamous devices to obtain them; the great commercial currents flow and flow, according to their mystic laws; the price of stocks goes up, goes down, and with them, the life and fate of thousands; the inconsequent bells ring out from Craddock Church, and the people congregate; the grave of the schoolmistress sleeps in the sunshine, and the sound of the bells streams over it—meaning no irony—to lose itself in the quiet of the hills; rust and dust collect in one's house, in one's soul; and this and that, and that and this,—like the pendulum of the old time-piece, with its solemn tick—dock the moments of one's life, with each its dull little claim and its tough little tether, and lead one decorously to the gateway of Eternity."

There was a flutter of wings, in the room. A robin hopped in at the window and perched daintily on the table-ledge, its delicate claws outlined against the whiteness of the dust-sheet, its head inquisitively on one side, as if it were asking the reason of the musician's unusual silence. Suddenly, the little creature fluffed out its feathers, drew itself together, and warbled forth a rich ecstatic song, that seemed to be deliberately addressed to its human companion. Hadria raised her bowed head. Up welled the swift unaccustomed tears, while the robin, with increasing enthusiasm, continued his song. His theme, doubtless, was of the flicker of sun-lit shrubberies, the warmth of summer, the glory of spring, the sweetness of the revolving seasons. For cure of heart-ache, he suggested the pleasantness of garden nooks, and the repose that lingers about a dew-sprinkled lawn. All these things were warmly commended to the human being whose song of life had ceased.

"But they break my heart, little singer, they break my heart!"

The robin lifted up its head and warbled more rapturously than ever.

The tears were falling fast now, and silently. The thoughts ran on and on. "I know it all, I know it all, and my heart is broken—and it is my own fault—and it does not matter—the world is full of broken hearts—and it does not matter, it does not matter. But, oh, if the pain might stop, if the pain might stop! The robin sings now, because the spring is here; but it is not always spring. And some day—perhaps not this winter, but some day—the dear little brown body will agonize — it will die alone, in the horrible great universe; one thinks little of a robin, but it agonizes all the same when its time comes; it agonizes all the same."

The thoughts were drowned, for a moment, in a flood of terrible, unbearable pity for all the sorrow of the world.

The robin seemed to think that he had a mission to cheer his companion, for he warbled merrily on. And beside him, the dust-motes danced the wildest of dances, in the shaft of sunshine.

"It is very lovely, it is very lovely—the world is a miracle, but it is all like a taunt, it is like an insult, this glory of the world. I am born a woman, and to be born a woman is to be exquisitely sensitive to insult and to live under it always, always. I wish that I were as marble to the magic of Life, I wish that I cared for nothing and felt nothing. I pray only that the dream and the longing may be killed, and killed quickly!"

In the silence, the bird's note sounded clear and tender. The dance of the dust-motes, like the great dance of Life itself, went on without ceasing.

The robin seemed to insist on a brighter view of things. He urged his companion to take comfort. Had the spring not come?

"But you do not understand, you do not understand, little soul that sings—the spring is torturing me and taunting me. If only it would kill me!"

The robin fluffed out his feathers, and began again to impart his sweet philosophy. Hadria was shedding the first unchecked tears that she had shed since her earliest childhood. And then, for the second time to-day, that strange unexplained peace stole into her heart. Reason came quickly and drove it away with a sneer, and the horror and the darkness closed round again.

"If I might only die, if I might only die!"

But the little bird sang on.

CHAPTER LI.

"QUITE hopeless!"

Joseph Fleming repeated the words incredulously.

"Yes," said Lady Engleton, "it is the terrible truth."

The Professor had been growing worse, and at length, his state became so alarming that he decided to return to England. Miss Du Prel and an old friend whom she had met abroad, accompanied him.

"I understand they are all at the Priory," said Joseph.

"Yes; Miss Du Prel telegraphed to Mrs. Temperley, and Mrs. Temperley and I put our heads together and arranged matters as well as we could in the emergency, so that the Professor's wish might be gratified. He desired to return to the Priory, where his boyhood was spent."

"And is there really no hope?"

"None at all, the doctor says."

"Dear me, dear me!" cried Joseph. "And is he not expected to live through the summer?"

"The summer! ah no, Mr. Fleming, he is not expected to live many days."

"Dear me, dear me!" was all that Joseph could say. Then after a pause, he added, "I fear Mrs. Temperley will feel it very much. They were such old friends."

"Oh! poor woman, she is heart-broken."

*　　*　　*　　*　　*　　*

The Professor lingered longer than the doctor had expected. He was very weak, and could not bear the fatigue of seeing many people. But he was perfectly cheerful, and when feeling

483

a little better at times, he would laugh and joke in his old kindly way, and seemed to enjoy the fragment of life that still remained to him.

"I am so glad I have seen the spring again," he said, "and that I am here, in the old home."

He liked to have the window thrown wide open, when the day was warm. Then his bed would be wheeled closer to it, so that the sunshine often lay across it, and the scent of the flowering shrubs and the odour of growth, as he called it, floated in upon him. He looked out into a world of exquisite greenery and of serene sky. The room was above the drawing-room, and if the drawing-room windows were open, he could hear Hadria playing. He often used to ask for music.

The request would come generally after an exhausting turn of pain, when he could not bear the fatigue of seeing people.

"I can't tell you what pleasure and comfort your music is to me," he used to say, again and again. "It has been so ever since I knew you. When I think of the thousands of poor devils who have to end their lives in some wretched, lonely, sordid fashion, after hardships and struggles and very little hope, I can't help feeling that I am fortunate indeed, now and all through my life. I have grumbled at times, and there have been sharp experiences—few escape those—but take it all round, I have had my share of good things."

He had one great satisfaction: that he had discovered, before the end of his days, the means which he had so long been seeking, of saving the death-agony of animals that are killed for food. Some day perhaps, he said, men might cease to be numbered among the beasts of prey, but till then, at least their victims might be spared as much pain as possible. He had overcome the difficulty of expense, which had always been the main obstacle to a practical solution of the problem. Henceforth there was no need for any creature to suffer, in dying for man's use. If people only knew and realized how much needless agony is inflicted on these helpless creatures, in order to supply the daily demands of a vast flesh-eating population, they would feel that, as a matter of fact, he had been doing the human race a good turn as well as their more friendless fellow-beings. It was impossible to imagine that men and women would not suffer at the thought of causing suffering to the helpless, if once they realized that suffering clearly. Men and women were not devils! Theobald had always laughed at him for this part of his work, but he felt now, at the close of his life, that he could dwell upon that effort with more pleasure than on any other, although others had won him far more applause, and this had often brought him contempt. If only he could be sure that the discovery would not be wasted.

"It shall be our business to see that it is not," said Valeria, in a voice tremulous with unshed tears.

The Professor heaved a sigh of relief, at this assurance.

"My earlier work is safe ; what I have done in other directions, is already a part of human knowledge and resource, but this is just the sort of thing that might be so easily lost and forgotten. These sufferings are hidden, and when people do not see a wrong, they do not think of it ; make them think, make them think !"

A week had gone by since the Professor's arrival at the Priory. He was in great pain, but had intervals of respite. He liked, in those intervals, to see his friends. They could scarcely believe that he was dying, for he still seemed so full of interest in the affairs of life, and spoke of the future as if he would be there to see it. One of the most distressing interviews was with Mr. Fullerton, who could not be persuaded that the invalid had but a short time to live. The old man believed that death meant, beyond all question, annihilation of the personality, and had absolutely no hope of meeting again.

"Don't be too sure, old friend," said the Professor ; "don't be too sure of anything, in this mysterious universe."

The weather kept warm and genial, and this was favourable to his lingering among them a little longer. But his suffering, at times, was so great that they could scarcely wish for this delay. Hadria used always to play to him during some part of the afternoon. The robin had become a constant visitor, and had found its way to the window of the sick-room, where crumbs had been scattered on the sill. The Professor took great pleasure in watching the little creature. Sometimes it would come into the room and hop on to a chair or table, coquetting from perch to perch, and looking at the invalid, with bright inquisitive eyes. The crumbs were put out at a certain hour each morning, and the bird had acquired the habit of arriving almost to the moment. If, by chance, the crumbs had been forgotten, the robin would flutter ostentatiously before the window, to remind his friends of their neglected duty.

During the last few days, Hadria had fancied that the Professor had divined Valeria's secret, or that she had betrayed it.

There was a peculiar, reverent tenderness in his manner towards her, that was even more marked than usual.

"Can't we save him? can't we save him, Hadria?" she used to cry piteously, when they were alone. "Surely, surely there is some hope. Science makes such professions; why doesn't it do something?"

"Ah, don't torture yourself with false hope, dear Valeria."

"The world is monstrous, life is unbearable," exclaimed Valeria, with a despairing break in her voice.

But one afternoon, she came out of the sick-room with a less distraught expression on her worn face, though her eyes shewed traces of tears.

The dying man used to speak often about his wife to Hadria. This had been her room, and he almost fancied her presence about him.

"Do you know," he said, "I have found, of late, that many of my old fixed ideas have been insidiously modifying. So many things that I used to regard as preposterous have been borne in upon me, in a singular fashion, as by no means so out of the question. I have had one or two strange experiences and now a hope—I might say a faith—has settled upon me of an undying element in our personality. I feel that we shall meet again those we have loved here — some time or another."

"What a sting that would take from the agony of parting," cried Hadria.

"And, after all, is it less rational to suppose that there is some survival of the Self, and that the wild, confused earthly experience is an element of a spiritual evolutionary process, than to suppose that the whole universe is chaotic and meaningless? For what we call mind exists, and it must be contained in the sum-total of existence, or how could it arise out of it? Therefore, some reasonable scheme appears more likely than a reasonless one. And then there is that other big fact that stares us in the face and puts one's fears to shame : human goodness."

Hadria's rebellious memory recalled the fact of human cruelty and wickedness to set against the goodness, but she was silent.

"What earthly business has such a thing as goodness or pity to appear in a fortuitous, mindless, soulless universe? Where does it come from? What is its origin? Whence sprang the laws that gave it birth?"

"It gives more argument to faith than any thing I know," she said, "even if there had been but one good man or woman since the world began."

"Ah, yes ; the pity and tenderness that lie in the heart of man, even of the worst, if only they can be appealed to before they die, may teach us to hope all things."

There was a long silence. Through the open window, they could hear the soft cooing of the wood-pigeons. Among the big trees behind the house, there was a populous rookery, noisy now with the squeaky voices of the young birds, and the deeper cawing of the parent rooks.

"I have been for many years without one gleam of hope,"

said the Professor slowly. "It is only lately that some of
my obstinate preconceptions have begun to yield to other
suggestions and other thoughts, which have opened up a
thousand possibilities and a thousand hopes. And I have not
been false to my reason in this change; I have but followed
it more fearlessly and more faithfully."

"I have sometimes thought," said Hadria, "that when we
seem to cling most desperately to our reason, we are really
·refusing to accept its guidance into unfamiliar regions. We
confuse the familiar with the reasonable."

"Exactly. And I want you to be on your guard against
that intellectual foible, which I believe has held me back
in a region of sadness and solitude that I need not have
lingered in, but for that."

There was a great commotion in the rookery, and presently
a flock of rooks swept across the window, in loud controversy,
and away over the garden in a circle, and then up and up till
they were a grey little patch of changing shape, in the blue of
the sky.

The dying man followed them with his eyes. He had
watched such streaming companies start forth from the old
rookery, ever since his boyhood. The memories of that time,
and of the importunate thoughts that had haunted him then,
at the opening of life, returned to him now.

He had accomplished a fraction of what he had set out to
attempt, with such high hopes. His dream of personal happiness had failed; many an illusion had been lost, many a
bitterly-regretted deed had saddened him, many an error had
revenged itself upon him. He drew a deep sigh.

"And if the scheme of the universe be a reasonable one,"
he said half dreamily, "then one can account better for the
lives that never fulfil themselves; the apparent failure that
saddens one, in such numberless instances, especially among
women. For in that case, the failure is only apparent, however
cruel and however great. If the effort has been sincere, and
the thought bent upon the best that could be conceived by

the particular soul, then that effort and that thought must play their part in the upward movement of the race. I cannot believe otherwise."

Hadria's head was bent. Her lips moved, as if in an effort to speak, but no sound came.

"To believe that all the better and more generous hopes of our kind are to be lost and ineffectual, that genius is finally wasted, and goodness an exotic to be trampled under foot in the blind movements of Nature—that requires more power of faith than I can muster. Once believe that thought is the main factor, the motive force of the universe, then everything settles into its place, and we have room for hope; indeed it insists upon admission; it falls into the shadow of our life like that blessed ray of sunlight."

It lay across the bed, in a bright streak.

"The hope leads me far. My training has been all against it, but it comes to me with greater and greater force. It makes me feel that presently, when we have bid one another farewell, it will not be for ever. We shall meet again, dear Hadria, believe me." She was struggling with her tears, and could answer nothing.

"I wish so much that I could leave this hope, as a legacy to you. I wish I could leave it to Valeria. Take care of her, won't you? She is very solitary and very sad."

"I will, I will," Hadria murmured.

"Do not turn away from the light of rational hope, if any path should open up that leads that way. And help her to do the same. When you think of me, let it be happily and with comfort."

Hadria was silently weeping.

"And hold fast to your own colours. Don't take sides, above all, with the powers that have oppressed you. They are terrible powers, and yet people won't admit their strength, and so they are left unopposed. It is worse than folly to underrate the forces of the enemy. It is always worse than folly to deny facts in order to support a theory. Exhort people to face and conquer them.   You can help more than you dream, even as things stand.   I cannot tell you what you have done for me, dear Hadria."   (He held out his hand to her.) "And the helpless, human and animal—how they wring one's heart !   Do not forget them ;   be to them a knight-errant. You have suffered enough yourself, to know well how to bind their wounds."   The speaker paused, for a moment, to battle with a paroxysm of pain.

"There is so much anguish," he said presently, "so much intolerable anguish, even when things seem smoothest.   The human spirit craves for so much, and generally it gets so little.   The world is full of tragedy ; and sympathy, a little common sympathy, can do so much to soften the worst of grief.   It is for the lack of that, that people despair and go down.   I commend them to you."

*   *   *   *   *   *

The figure lay motionless, as if asleep.   The expression was one of utter peace.   It seemed as if all the love and tenderness, all the breadth and beauty of the soul that had passed away, were shining out of the quieted face, from which all trace of suffering had vanished.   The look of desolation that used, at times, to come into it, had entirely gone.

Hadria and Valeria stood together, by the bedside.   At the foot of the bed was a glass vase, holding a spray of wild cherry blossom; Hadria had brought it, to the invalid's delight, the day before.   There were other offerings of fresh flowers ; a mass of azaleas from Lady Engleton ; bunches of daffodils that Valeria had gathered in the meadows ; and old Dodge had sent a handful of brown and yellow wallflower, from his garden.   The blind had been raised a few inches, so as to let in the sunlight and the sweet air.   It was a glorious morning. The few last hot days had brought everything out, with a rush. The boughs of the trees, that the Professor had loved so to watch during his illness, were swaying gently in the breeze, just as they had done when his eyes had been open to see them. The wood-pigeons were cooing, the young rooks cawing shrilly in the rookery. Valeria seemed to be stunned. She stood gazing at the peaceful face, with a look of stony grief.

" I *can't* understand it ! " she exclaimed at last, with a wild gesture, " I *can't* believe he will never speak to me again ! It's a horrible dream—oh, but too horrible—ah, why can't I die as well as he ? " She threw herself on her knees, shaken with sobs, silent and passionate. Hadria did not attempt to remonstrate or soothe her. She turned away, as a flood of bitter grief swept over her, so that she felt as one drowning.

Some minutes passed before Valeria rose from her knees, looking haggard and desolate. Hadria went towards her hastily.

" What's that ? " cried Valeria with a nervous start and a scared glance towards the window.

"The robin ! " said Hadria, and the tears started to her eyes.

The bird had hopped in at his usual hour, in a friendly fashion. He picked up a few stray crumbs that had been left on the sill from yesterday, and then, in little capricious flights from stage to stage, finally arrived at the rail of the bed, and stood looking from side to side, with black, bright eyes, at the motionless figure. Hitherto it had been accustomed to a welcome. Why this strange silence? The robin hopped round on the rail, polished his beak meditatively, fluffed out his feathers, and then, raising his head, sang a tender requiem.

THE END.

AFTERWORD

And in one way the untilled field is a piece of good
fortune for the Women Writers of the future—the
women who (among other things) are going to fulfill, at
last, the ancient Euripidean prophecy of a day when the
old bards' stories—

"Of frail brides and faithless shall be
shrivelled as with fire . . .
And woman, yea, woman, shall be terrible in
story.
The tales, too, meseemeth, shall be other
than of yore
For a fear there is that cometh out of woman
and her glory
And the hard hating voices shall encompass
her no more."

—Elizabeth Robins, *Way Stations* (1910)

I

IN AUGUST 1888, a thirty-four-year-old woman almost
unknown to the reading public[1] wrote an article of sixteen pages in the *Westminster Review* that sent Victorian
England into yet another uproar and got the nineties
going a little early. It was quietly titled "Marriage," and
in a voice that could not be dismissed—a plain-spoken,
pithy, scathing, learned, and authoritative voice, a voice
perfectly calibrated for its audiences—it argued that for
women marriage was "a vexatious failure."[2] A storm
broke.

The *Westminster Review,* of course, was John Chap-

man's radical quarterly, whose impeccable credentials
dated from its early relationship with John Stuart Mill.
From such a quarter might well emerge a level female
voice that would compare women to dogs chained up
for life, to caged prisoners who slowly die of starvation
in the public square watched by the curious. But Mona
Caird went farther than expected. Linking women's contemporary inferiority to the Reformation, she called
Luther "a thick-skinned, coarse-fibred monk" ("Marriage,"p. 191); on religion's role in subduing women, she
commented dryly, "To drive a hard bargain, and to ser-
monize one's victims at the same time, is a feat distinctly
of the Philistine order" ("Marriage," p. 191). Merely in
passing, she dropped shocking assertions: that chastity
"has virtually no connection with the woman's own nature" ("Marriage," p. 193), being a derivative of male
jealousy related to purchase-marriage; that it is "folly to
inveigh against mercenary marriages [as long as] there is
no reasonable alternative" ("Marriage," p. 195); and that
the entire social system in England amounted to "legal-
ized injustice" ("Marriage," p. 200).

Still, even if the article caused a stir among the literate,
well-off readers of quarterlies, how many others would
pay any attention? But then the *Daily Telegraph* picked
up the pace of the scandal by opening a letters column
provocatively titled "Is Marriage a Failure?", and it maintained the brouhaha by publishing responses daily until
it had received some 27,000 letters and the Whitechapel
murders of "Jack the Ripper" turned its attention to sen-
sational rather than symbolic slaughters of women.[3]
Shortly, however, a collection of these letters appeared,
presenting an allegedly representative sample of them
(although omitting Caird's original article). She had
signed herself "Mona Caird," but as "Mrs. Caird" (for it
appeared she was married herself) she was for a while
probably the best-known and certainly the most decried
feminist in England.

But why do we always privilege the conservatives and their easy shock? A feminist point of view might argue not only that Caird's article got the nineties going early, but also that the nineties were preeminently, despite the persistence of other, flashier labels, a decade of change for women. Perhaps, considering the energies expended in that decade, the incredible expansion of discourse about women *by women*, the revolutionary changes in fiction that occurred, and the long-term effects of that expansion, the nineties might be regarded as another symbolic starting point of the wider modern movement whose spread is still in the process of becoming worldwide and all-inclusive.[4]

To be sure, turning a hot light on the mystique of marriage was not new. Regarding marriage sociologically, anthropologically, and philosophically had been done before by (among others) the writers listed in Caird's footnotes. What was new was that this fierce interrogation of the "respectable institution" was being enabled by the *Daily Telegraph*, which could not cut off the deep chords it struck merely by pulling the column. Women who didn't go to see Ibsen's plays or buy the literary journals or George Gissing's *Odd Women*, who didn't think of themselves as culturally advanced, could be caught up in *this* debate. Feminism, which had been the province of intellectuals and activists drawn by causes like the Married Women's Property Acts (1870, 1884) and the repeal of the Contagious Diseases Acts (1886), suddenly became a body of opinions about what women felt and suffered and wanted—opinions to which every woman could personally and emotionally contribute, whatever her age or class or marital status. Caird, who thought strategically about disseminating her feminist discontent to women who held traditional opinions, must have been exhilarated to see self-described "barmaids" and "shop-girls" and older women at home involved in the debate.[5]

* * *

Beginning in 1883, when Caird published her first novel at the age of twenty-nine, she poured most of her formidable writing energies into the feminist movement, first as a novelist and then as a polemical essayist and then as both in turn. "Marriage" was the word—the system—she chose to deconstruct. In the system that enforced female dependency and made marriage a market she located the main obstacles that women encountered when they aspired to change their lot. Caird wanted women to have equal rights and freedom for self-development, for designing their lives according to their own wishes and talents—"for it is diversity in every possible aspect which inspires and creates."[6]

In the Greek myth she alluded to in the title of her best novel, the fifty daughters of Danaus had been married *en masse*.[7] Caird saw more clearly than most people how systematic society was in programming all women mindlessly to undertake the one adult career path that connoted female "success": marriage and child-rearing. Without divorce, it was a life sentence. (Forty-nine of Danaus's daughters slaughtered their husbands on their wedding night to get free.) The Home was commonly known as woman's "Sphere," implying that she should be submissive to its demands—responsible for all the work in it. Most of that work Caird saw mainly via the punishment given the fifty daughters, as "the idiot's labour of eternally drawing water in sieves from fathomless wells."[8] Married working-class women were equally responsible for the Home, but without help: responsible for children, for parents, for all domestic service. All married women were responsible for sexual services to the master of the local institution. All were intended to breed without remission, "condemned to one function for the best years of life, and that function an extremely painful and exhausting one."[9] Most insulting of all, they were trained to praise their condition of servitude using

a male language of "holy" sphere and "sacred" mission.[10]
Caird made the inequities/iniquities of the system exceptionally vivid—far more vivid than Mill had done in his
scrupulously reasoned essay on *The Subjection of Women*
in 1869.[11] Clearly what this author valued were *women's*
points of view: their subjectivity and their subjection.

We are only now beginning to understand deeply the
degree to which marriage was made to seem cotermi-
nous with the entire adult female life course. Believing
this required people to be oblivious to many facts, among
them the fact that since the 1830s England had contained more women than men. As H. G. Wells's Ann
Veronica argued in 1909, "There's twenty-one and a half
million women to twenty million men. Suppose our
proper place is a shrine. Still, that leaves a million shrines
short."[12] There were "superfluous" or "odd" women who
could not marry; most would have to find work in the
marketplace, or, as feminists and socialists called it, "the
sweating system." One way or the other, women's economic dependence, Caird argued, "eternally stands in
the way of any improvement, as regards their legal and
social status, and . . . often obliges them to submit to a
thousand wrongs and indignities which could not otherwise be placed upon them" (*MM,* p. 165). Caird "saw
the emancipation of women in essentially vocational and
professional terms . . . [She] was the first woman in the
late Victorian era to push this contention to the point
of notoriety."[13]

Caird had observed in all classes that the figures in
the shrines were actually *male.* She wanted to jar domestic life, dismantle the shrines, and make women want to
leap out of the Sphere. She argued for divorce and birth
control (in veiled but clear terms); for education, career
and job opportunities; for a mother's stipend; for legal,
sexual, economic and personal freedom in relation to
men. She believed that all women, both the "successes"
and the "failures," were degraded by the Procrustean

ideology of marriage. When marriage was independently judged from a woman's point of view and found decidedly wanting, "eternal" values shivered. Caird had stated on the first page of her first article that these values were in no way "eternal." She made plain as dishcloths notions whose revolutionary implications we still haven't come to the end of—that women's roles have always been socially constructed, that we can't know yet what woman's "nature" truly is, that maybe women have many "natures," all worthy of fulfillment.

The Daughters of Danaus (1894) is the fiction in which she most enduringly combined her feminism and her remarkable literary skills. She was exactly forty and in full control of her powers. In 1897 she collected her polemical articles as *The Morality of Marriage*. Even some of her critics admitted she was "a brilliant writer."[14] Looking back, her friend Elizabeth Sharp believed that "these brave articles . . . and the novels written by the same pen, have been potent in altering the attitude of the public mind in its approach to and examination of such questions, in making private discussion possible."[15] Ellis Ethelmer, another contemporary progressive, called her "an unwearying pioneer of humanity."[16] A reviewer in the feminist monthly *Shafts* called *The Daughters of Danaus* "one of the best books the century has produced."[17] *Shafts* devoted parts of four issues to reviewing and quoting extensively from the novel: awed by what she called "one of those great developments of human thought," Margaret Shurmer Sibthorp said about it, "This work in every line of it is a grand battle for new life for woman. Each page is worth a long study" (*Shafts*, p. 41). She prophesied that it "will grow in favor and be more fully understood with each passing year" (*Shafts*, p. 40) and concluded, "There hath not yet appeared such a book as this, nor one which will so powerfully sway the future of women" (*Shafts*, p. 56).

Mainstream reviewers made sure that couldn't happen Sibthorp reports that nearly all the London dailie and many leading Scottish, English, and Irish papers treated *The Daughters of Danaus* with anger and contempt. It was blamed for the woman's revolt, and one reviewer augured that it would end the revolt. Both the blame and the augury were wrong. Caird never got even as much attention as other New-Woman novelists received. But her voice—unmistakably that of a New Woman, even before the term had been coined[18]—must have shaken and awakened or spoken directly and sympathetically to many. Even Harry Quilter, the editor of that biased collection of *Daily Telegraph* letters on the non-failure of marriage, whose intent was to tidy up the battleground, could not entirely suppress women's agreement with Caird, and their gratitude. Whatever made him include Edith Maxwell's letter? It gave the game away. "Women are afraid to speak for themselves and their rights. Mrs. Caird has made a beginning . . . every woman, especially the unhappily married, should bless her and call her friend."[19]

II

"Not all literature above a century old should perish. It would simply be that books *not reprinted* for a century would vanish."

—Leslie Stephen[20]

With The Feminist Press's republication of *The Daughters of Danaus* not much short of 100 years after its original appearance, it is now possible to follow Edith Maxwell's injunction. When I first discovered the novel via Elizabeth Chapman's tantalizing quotations from it in her 1897 volume, *Marriage Questions in Modern Fiction*, I thought Caird was too good to be believed. *The Daughters of Danaus* is not only an aesthetic achievement and an important addition to the canon of women's fiction, but also a major feminist novel written in English in the

nineteenth century. Caird is a foremother we needed to
find or invent—a missing voice of radical feminism in
fiction.

I had read the canonical women-centered texts of the
period: Ibsen's *A Doll's House* (1879; performed in London 1889), Olive Schreiner's *Story of an African Farm*
(1883), Gissing's *The Odd Women* (1893), Kate Chopin's
The Awakening (1899). Later, placing Caird's achievements more squarely in their contexts, I read Americans
like Elizabeth Stuart Phelps and Sara Orne Jewett, who
preceded her, and then the others who were writing
along with her in England in the nineties—sometimes
thought of as *the* decade of the New Woman—when, out
of a burst of simultaneous feminist inspiration, the public was hit by a barrage of magazine articles by women,
George Egerton's *Keynotes* (1893) and *Discords* (1894),
Sarah Grand's *The Heavenly Twins* (1893), Grant Allen's
The Woman Who Did (1895), and Caird's *The Daughters of
Danaus.* If we begin the decade early, we can start it with
Caird's own *The Wing of Azrael* (1889) and Grand's *Ideala*
(1888), which Caird quoted as soon as it appeared. To
understand her importance fully one should also read
the writers who followed her in describing other women
artists; these protagonists have problems related to the
culture's view of their gender, but unlike Hadria, the
heroine of *The Daughters of Danaus,* they are able to have
successful careers. Such protagonists include Mary Austin's heroine in *A Woman of Genius* (1912), Willa Cather's
in *Song of the Lark* (1915), and May Sinclair's in *Mary
Olivier* (1919).[21] In short, Caird belongs to that world of
forward-looking writers, mainly novelists and journalists,
who were creating and validating the image of the New
Woman by describing their own many versions of female
possibility and the world in which the New Woman might
(or might not) enact herself. Every reader unfamiliar with
this group of literary revolutionaries will want to know
some of them. Caird does not merely join this company;

through the interlocking inventions of *The Daughters of Danaus* she seems to me to loom in different ways over its variously distinguished and interesting members.

Most of their novels now stand as period pieces. We read them as studies in social history or as inadvertent psychological self-revelations—with more or less pleasure, depending upon the writer's skills. In its main lines, however, *The Daughters of Danaus* will be read now—with pleasure—by people who can empathize in almost every way with Hadria's young-adult predicament, her post-marital complexities, and her thwarted talents.

To some extent this is an accident of our own historical moment. We have finally returned to a level of feminist consciousness at which it seems possible for a young woman to anticipate that it may *not* be in her best interest to marry. Or at which it seems plausible for two progressive young people to make a deal about the conditions under which they plan to live once married. And at which a woman who finds she hates the agreement may have a lot of language available to understand it with, but not—depending upon her circumstances—a lot of options. To some degree the novel seems real because marriage did not disappear, as some theorists—but not Caird—thought it might. Nor did enough New Men and Women appear for marriage to improve itself out of recognition. There are still men around like Hubert Temperly who make promises they cannot understand or keep. There are still Henriettes braying that women shouldn't agitate for change, because "when, at some future time, wider privileges should have been conquered by the exertions of someone else, then the really nice woman could saunter in and enjoy the booty" (*DD*, p. 124). There are still mothers like Mrs. Fullerton trying to socialize their daughters into submissiveness, and parents who expect more self-sacrifice from daughters than from sons. For all women, how to reconcile family responsibilities with their work remains a problem. And

talented women still find special, gendered obstacles to
their careers. So the novel's sociological analysis and psychological insights speak to our own situation. Caird's
boldest ideas have become our general convictions, and
her language is still—to an amazing degree—our language.

The other half of the astonishing relevance of *The
Daughters of Danaus* lies, then, precisely in Caird's unfet-
tered intellect operating to fictionalize unrecognized
facts about women's adult lives. She manages to avoid
most of the conventional fictional traps of 1894, which
means she gets points for realism that others—even other
feminists—lose. Although the novel suffers toward the
end from some sentimentality, it is never sentimental
toward the conventional items. Caird is unsentimental
not only about marriage but about children; there probably have never been harsher remarks made about the
way children are used to keep women in line. She doesn't
villainize Herbert; more unexpectedly yet, she makes him
negligible. Caird makes Hadria's marriage a simple case
of incompatibility, itself an ingenious invention antici-
pating no-fault divorce. She is free of Victorian religi-
osity, which to my taste spoils Schreiner's novel, and of
other forms of nineties' spiritualism: she doesn't think
women are closer to God than are men, or want to prom-
ulgate a female Savior. She is not morbid; in fact, she's
consistently, helpfully, blessedly sane. These qualities
mark a *mentalité* akin to our own.

She fleshes out common situations that others skip
over. How many English writers had described the period after the wedding at all? Some—like Henry James
in *The Portrait of a Lady* (1880)—couldn't let go of the
"sacredness" of the marital bond. Others—George Eliot
in *Middlemarch*—suggested that a second marriage would
cure all.[22] New-Woman novelists, specializing in disaster,
depicted the pitfalls of marriage as syphilis, alcoholism,
desertion. Caird, for her part, steps *over the threshold* with

sensible militancy. Here finally is an exposé of the end-less distractions of ordinary domestic life and the wear-ing down of a strong woman's will and constitution by family demands. In her hands this is a heroic subject. Phelps's 1877 *The Story of Avis* (about a painter who falls away from her art after marriage) is comparable but rel-atively lifeless, and Phelps wriggled out of her situation by killing off Avis's inconvenient husband. Ibsen had gotten Nora married, discontented, and out the door. Caird's novel implies that he'd done it too quickly: he had missed painful stages in her development and slighted such a woman's bravery. Most of all, with a cau-tion she taught herself over her years as a working nov-elist, she avoids the deepest trap in the culture, the (male-invented, realist) stereotype of female decline, which led other novelists like Schreiner and Chopin to slaugh-ter their brave women rebels at the end of the story. Led by her own sense of women's dangers and their resist-ances, Caird invented a new heroine with her own thrill-ing tone of voice, and constructed a plot poised to avoid a woman's standard fictional fates—either marital fulfill-ment or extra-marital sexuality, despair, and death. Now we have *The Daughters of Danaus* as a bridge between the narrowly marriage-focused fictions of the nineteenth century and the more open-ended midlife novels that came thirty years later, such as D. H. Lawrence's *St. Mawr* and Virginia Woolf's *Mrs. Dalloway.*

III
A Heroine's Tongue

Perhaps Hadria's speech is the most remarkable quality of the novel—Caird's most invigorating gift to the reader. Hadria dancing a wild, uncanny reel and declaring vig-orously, "Emerson never was a girl!" (*DD,* p. 14)—these two forms of energy introduce the heroine whom Caird meant to make exceptional. (New Women and new girls—even the intellectual and artistic ones—always have a free stride, a tomboy's habit of liking exercise, a love of country air and country walks.[23]) To mark Hadria's forceful and articulate character, a reader can start by observing what happens *on the page* after her statement of Emerson's gender limitations. What impresses me is not so much the content of her argument (that women have a harder time using their greatness than do men), although the argument is striking enough, since such beliefs make possible Woolf's much later creation of Judith Shakespeare in *A Room of One's Own*. What is impressive is this girl's persistence. Hadria continues to speak her mind about women's conflicts despite the opposition of two brothers and a sister; she answers every objection they raise; and her speeches, instead of dwindling, get longer and more rhetorical.

This is not merely a woman-centered novel—it's centered on a woman who comes on stage indignant and gets to be by turns sarcastic, cunning, militant, and exalted, as well as sympathetic, loyal, dispirited, cynical, conscience-stricken, and despairing. Most of all, she is resistant. "It gives me a keen, fierce pleasure to know that for all their training and constraining and incitement and starvation, I have not developed masses of treacly instinct . . ." (*DD*, p. 210).

How few big-voiced women there are before her in English fiction. By pathetic contrast, I think of Maggie Tulliver in *The Mill on the Floss*, psychologically unable to counter her brother's cruel, unjust descriptions of her, and sobbing instead. From the moment that Hadria objects to Emerson, we know that Caird has passed beyond the silent women, and also the soft-voiced, graceful, careful-spoken or innately sweet heroines favored even by many feminist novelists, like Phelps's Avis and Dr. Zay in the novels named after them, and Grand's Evadne in *The Heavenly Twins*. Their function, of course, was to make the New Woman assimilable.

After the establishment of the New Woman in fiction, the time came when the feminist heroine was *supposed* to be capable of incisive, decisive speech. (But Shaw, taking advantage of this permission in 1898, gave his Candida only one set speech, and no real opposition.[24]) And before Caird, how few get verbal power of any kind. We admire the resisters, whose speeches when pushed to the wall fire our blood and awaken opposition in us: Jane Eyre standing up to St. John Rivers, or Miriam Rooth in James's *The Tragic Muse* telling Sherringham the terms under which she might marry him, or here, Hadria advocating revenge toward Ellen Jarvis's seducer in his very presence (*DD*, p. 265). On a psychological continuum with political implications, Jane Eyre represents a moment of anger, the first emotion the oppressed feel when they realize they are being manipulated against their own best interest. In the next moment, ideally, the anger gets put to work on the offensive, redescribing the world on the basis of analysis and principles and in the hope of effecting change.

This is the moment in which, at least in this novel, Caird was most free, most inventive, and most effective. *The Daughters of Danaus* still has much to teach us about flexing the rhetoric of assertion in fiction. To create a character who can articulate an ideology rather than fumbling toward personal expression, and yet sound not like an editorial, but rather like an individual necessarily pressed into radical thoughts by a constraining situation—English and American writers have not, on the whole, been comfortable creating even *male* characters who function this way. Shaw could do that for the same reason that Caird could: they weren't still in the process of convincing themselves of what they believed. And therefore they had figured out how to state it more startlingly than others in the collective that had helped them think it. Shaw had listened hard to feminists on the marriage issue. *The Quintessence of Ibsensism* (1891) sounds like

Caird's "Marriage" essays, and later Shavian characters often sound something like Hadria, whose radical consciousness flows into speech spontaneously under the varied impulses of the moment. Like Trefusis in *An Unsocial Socialist,* Hadria speaks promptly and strikingly. But she's not posing or quoting her author; nor is she always at the same even pitch of determination. She's an unfixed character who doesn't always know what she'll do next.

One doesn't tire of Hadria. Her talk remains a compendium of effective reactions to simple-minded, obstinate sexism—paradoxes with pain in them, metaphors wearing a grimace. Are women naturally mothers? Women become motherly as an "acquired trick" (*DD,* p. 23). Is egoism the opposite of self-sacrifice? She changes the opposition. "Don't you think people grow egoistic through having to fight incessantly for existence—I mean for individual existence? . . . One has the choice between egoism and extinction" (*DD,* p. 421). The allegedly loving family "cannibalizes" its members. Hadria's long contention with Henriette, who represents the woman's Sphere, is likely to teach us the degree to which we are still imbued with ideas about natural maternal feeling. (Children—"little ambassadors of the established and expected" [*DD,* p. 187]—can still be set up in that portable shrine.)

In their self-reflectiveness and doubling back, the thoughts given Hadria often anticipate Lawrence. People who admire the wedding scene early on in *Women in Love* should put beside it Caird's view, some twenty-five years earlier, of the wedding service and the sexual initiation, lying, and secrecy that will follow the bride's intuitions. "She gave a start and a shiver as she stepped out into the brilliant day, turning with a half-scared look to the crowd of faces. It seemed almost as if she were seeking help in a blind, bewildered fashion" (*DD,* p. 249).

For a novel whose heroine slowly loses her resilience

in circumstances that become progressively gloomier, the tone begins cheerful and free of pain and long remains steady and under control. "Discontent was certainly the initiator of all movement; but there was a kind of sullen discontent that stagnated and ate inwards, like a disease," Hadria reminds herself (*DD*, p. 194). The fresh air of intellectual discovery and unimpeded assertion governs most of the book; and even as her situation worsens, Hadria (in contrast to Hardy's Sue Bridehead) never recants her feminism. When brother Fred early on repeats the threat of the next century, that "girls who have ideas like yours will never get any fellow to marry them," "laughter loud and long greeted this announcement" (*DD*, p. 27). Some of the siblings' early laughter has potentially ironic echoes in retrospect. They laugh at the idea of Hadria as "the family consolation" (*DD*, p. 30), and that is precisely the role her sister Algitha's absence and her mother's illness push her into. But if the girls' youthful good humor in tossing intellectual bombs turns out to be ignorant, the reader's first and durable impression must still be that more freedoms can be taken with dangerous ideas and words than she might have thought.

After her marriage, Hadria becomes bitter but no less candid. When she falters, Caird reintroduces Algitha, a foil who can be stronger than Hadria because she has less imagination. And then Fortescue, a character George Eliot would have admired, and Jouffroy, the loyal mentor and curmudgeon, who utters truths Hadria can't. It's as if Caird rescues the reader as well as Hadria. There are limits to Hadria's voice: eventually one notices that Caird never turns it against Hadria's husband or her mother directly. Women of more or less the same age dominate the conversations, as if the social movement consisted of advanced women (encouraged by a few supportive men) educating other women as fast as they can. In any case, most of the novel—even after Hadria is forced to come back from Paris—constitutes a long course in overhearing revolution, and revolution is made to feel brave rather than reckless.

In the nineties, many New-Woman plots showed a woman acting in what for fiction were uncustomary ways: having a baby out of wedlock (in Allen's *The Woman Who Did*), refusing to sleep with her husband when she discovers that he's promiscuous (in Grand's *The Heavenly Twins;* she infers that he's syphilitic), going off to live in a women's community (in Egerton's *The Wheel of God,* 1898). Hadria's going to Paris without a great fuss, but with a sufficiency of obliging preparation, is another model of liberating action, arguably more plausible than some others, at least for middle-class women with access to private schools and maids.

But I want to suggest that for many of the oppressed, hearing a new, unfaltering tone of voice is even more useful. For one thing, it's available to all women, married or unmarried, with maids or without them. It's a form of knowledge that can become, more drastically, a form of power. It encourages and provides a model for any woman's own next step in the process of putting resistance into speech. For those who think that deference and appeal can be their only weapons, hearing a woman speak out can be a thrilling occasion. For those who continue to do their own speaking out but have not found many congenial fictional sisters doing so, Hadria may be a treasure: a woman with a steady, flexible, self-assertive voice that her author identifies with and refuses to ironize or punish.

IV
The Avoidance of Suicide

> "Don't take sides, above all, with the powers that have oppressed you."
> —*The Daughters of Danaus,* p. 489

Having created a big, independent female voice, Caird's second major innovation and legacy to the history of fiction was not to kill it at the end of the story.

The temptation to martyr Hadria must have been great. Caird was deeply, consciously, interested in writing feminist tragedy. She believed that the *normal* life of women was potentially tragic—painful, wrenching, unnatural, and full of suffering. "The history of woman from the time of the general establishment of the rule of man is tragic in the extreme."[25] Some feminists treated submissive women as the class enemy; Caird thought it unfair to expect more from average women than the heroism they were already exhibiting in daily life. "In the face of prejudices so illiberal as those which had grown up around the family, one had, it seemed, to choose between unconditional submission and piteous tragedy," according to a character looking for a way out at the end of Caird's 1915 novel, *The Stones of Sacrifice* (p. 427). She had sympathy for the plight of the self-sacrificing woman—even though she believed that such a woman reinforced the family members' laziness, sadism, and injustice, while not ultimately protecting herself. "And [yet] submission, even in naturally conforming natures . . . did not always suffice to avoid a tragic issue" (*SS*, p. 437).

As for the fate of the remarkable women who were actively pushing against social conventions and millennial beliefs in what Caird saw as a dangerous transition period, that to her was tragic in the more classic and dramatic sense. It was a grand *agon*, with tremendous powers on both sides and a catastrophe in the making. It was "the tragedy that threatens all spirits who are pointing towards the new order, while the old is still working out its unexhausted impetus" (*DD*, p. 112). Abetting a woman who wants to "move things an inch" is "to egg you on to the Fifth Act of your tragedy" (*SS*, p. 269). Her design in *The Daughters of Danaus*, she wrote in one of her few extant letters, was to create "a situation which arrives at its tragic climax in the case which I have presented of a woman with great power and large heart placed face to face with the forces of tradition and prejudice, fully conscious of what awaits her."[26] What Hadria suffers mainly at the end is not the loss of a lover, a friend, and a daughter-figure, but the primary loss, of her own potential self: the power to develop, to shape a future.

Most important in Caird's understanding of tragedy was her conviction that women had an internal enemy—that they themselves internalized society's dictates. "Conscience," too, was for Caird an artificial, coercive creation; so were "remorse" and most of the other alleged "instincts." In the history of the fictional demolition of the ideal of feminine self-sacrifice, *The Daughters of Danaus* takes its troubled, honorable place. A woman like Hadria—"the most essentially mutinous and erratic of the whole brood" (*DD*, p. 168)—although convinced that her mother's continued life will entail for her something like moral death, still finds herself fulfilling obligations she cannot help but feel. " 'You are chained by the most inflexible of all chains... your own compunction" (*DD*, p. 242); "the little threads that hampered her spontaneity ... were made of heartstrings" (*DD*, p. 268). Caird constructed the gap between the female generations as wide as any feminist has, perhaps, but then she gave Hadria, the victim in the youth generation, startling insight into "the grey sad story of [an older] woman's life, bare and dumb and pathetic in its irony and pain: the injury from without, and then the self-injury, its direct offspring...." (*DD*, pp. 362–63). When Claudia in *The Stones of Sacrifice* charges her cousin with fatalism, Helena Duncan's answer reverberates:

> "Helena, when I think of you living in this appalling solitude of spirit for all these years by sheer strength of will and courage, I feel that there's no fatality except that which we make for ourselves."
>
> "And what fatality could be more fatal?" (*SS*, p. 410)

The philosopher Foster, in *The Wing of Azrael* (1889), gloomily explains what then seemed to Caird the intrinsic limits to any individual's freedom. "Our freedom *can* only exist, if at all, in a certain very modified degree. We are conscious of an ability to *choose,* but our choice is, after all, an affair of temperament, and our temperament a matter of inherited inclinations, and so forth, modified from infancy by outward conditions."[27] Part of a woman's fatalism comes from being trained to foresee "shipwreck and disaster" if she tries to change her condition. When Viola Sedley Dendraith, in *The Wing of Azrael,* makes this self-dooming prophecy, a loving man anxiously warns her, "That is a dangerous fancy . . . it will make you yield to circumstances instead of erecting your own will into a circumstance dominating all the rest" (*WA* III, 87).

The finer her sensibility, the more a woman trapped herself. Caird described Hadria in a letter to a German scholar written soon after the publication of *The Daughters of Danaus,* as

> a woman, exceptional in her power and insight, whose life is spent in a long and bitter contest with the conditions common to all women, but which bear upon her [more than upon her] sisters, since in all directions she sees and feels and thinks more than they do.
>
> She fails in the end because these great traditional forces have the art of turning her own powers against herself, pressing conscience and pity into the service.
>
> Had she been less developed intellectually, with a smaller heart, she might have had a nearer approach to success at the expense of certain sides of her nature and those the best. (Foerster, p. 53. In English in the original.)

It was to heighten the agon that Caird gave Hadria feminist resistances. For the same reason, she endowed her with remarkable talent and feeling for music. With all its other claims to attention, *The Daughters of Danaus*

is probably also the first English novel whose center of
consciousness is a woman artist, the first female *Kunstler-
roman*.[28] Hadria's talent is worked into the novel in intri-
cate, organic, insistent ways. If she had not fallen into a
sensuous trance at the dance, she would probably never
have agreed to marry Hubert. If it were not for her com-
positional ability—we know it's avant-garde because
Hubert dislikes its cacophony—she would not have upset tradition by leaving her family to go to Paris for training and mentorship. The fact that she no longer has
scope for her brilliant career darkens the other hardships of her return. Yet those inclined to cavil at the
"exceptionality" of Caird's heroine might want to remember in this connection Caird's belief that *all* women
(and all people oppressed by poverty[29]) were likely to
have neglected talents or other suppressed individuating
characteristics; she draws no sharp romantic line between "the Artist" and the rest.

Caird had, moreover, already succumbed to the allure
of one kind of "tragedy" five years earlier, in *The Wing
of Azrael*. At the end of her tether, which her husband is
holding sadistically short, Viola stabs him to death, refuses escape, and throws herself off a cliff. *The Wing of
Azrael* is a feminist Gothic. If anything could justify—
require—Gothic trappings and spouse-murder, this picture of an entire family tormenting a sensitive woman
would fill the bill. Viola is forced by her impecunious
parents to marry a man determined to govern not merely
her body and her behavior but her emotions as well. The
castle-keep, the endless sea, the dark rain, the deep drop,
the tiny dagger she sometimes wears in her hair, are all
aspects of her inner condition. Dendraith talks on and
on insultingly, until any woman in the world would stab
him, and then he curses her as he's dying. Her choice,
such as it is, had seemed to be between murdering him
or killing herself. She recalls women who had done themselves in. "Perhaps they were wrong, but Viola's heart

leapt up in sympathy towards them. They were her true sisters" (*WA* III, p. 181). Pushing her message of explosive inner need, but also punishing Viola for the murder, Caird's plot kills the criminalized woman as well as the male villain. If it anticipates the plots of martyrdom that some critics have objected to as stereotypical in New-Woman fiction written somewhat later, it also provides some revenge. It was not Caird's own experience that came to be transmuted into the oddities of *The Wing of Azrael*, but her angry, stymied reasoning about the general helplessness of women. This was "piteous tragedy."

In relishing Caird's brave decision to let Hadria live, we should recall the powerful influence of the European fictional tradition that kills women (and sometimes babies). The existence of *The Daughters of Danaus* forces us to rethink that tradition, meaning not only such works as Rousseau's *Julie* (1761), Goethe's *Elective Affinities* (1812), Flaubert's *Madame Bovary* (1857), and Tolstoy's *Anna Karenina* (1877), but also Eliot's *Mill on the Floss* (1860), Schreiner's *Story of an African Farm* (1883), and some later feminist novels in which women die. At some level, such deaths accept the culture's determination that marriage be the only successful life course for adult women. The authors' "acceptance" operates at that subterranean level at which alternative fates for transgressive women cannot be imagined, except for death. Caird moved out of this bipolar situation by imagining unhappy survival.

It's an inconclusive, open ending. No outcome is suggested for Hadria's musical career, her marital relations, her maternal cares, her filial burdens. If the approach of the ending makes us want to cry out, "Hadria, show us what a woman can do!", it also teaches us to value high-minded failure, failure that is completely unwilled and extraneous to the will. The ending produces terrible losses: Fortescue's death in particular can be read as the disappearance of humane optimism and male sympathy. On the other hand, the Professor's trust in Hadria's moral stature survives; Valeria is beside her, Algitha not far away. Not everything has been substracted, and she lives to make decisions another day.

What changed between 1889 and 1894? Mona Caird in her relation to fiction, first. It's possible that the traditional closure which stands behind the ending of *The Wing of Azrael,* exemplified especially by Lyndall's death in Schreiner's novel, closed off certain avenues for Caird. She was forced to recognize how her own views were evolving. It might be possible "to reveal the unrecognized tragedy of womanhood" without having the female protagonist kill herself: it might be done so as "to reveal indirectly the dim pathways of redemption and hope" (Foerster, p. 54). Caird didn't think women were so entirely masochistic—she makes Hadria strong and prudent and self-regarding enough to resist running off with a man unworthy of her, for example, although she makes her deeply enough attracted to him to want to. Caird's dislike of children was abstract, not fearful enough to make her kill their fictional surrogates. She had always hated "the primitive ideas of sacrifice and punishment."[30] What is likeliest is that she had developed a principled resistance to killing her heroines. We might read back into this decision her 1905 criticism of novels that show the " 'pray-knock-me-down-and-trample-upon-me' instinct in full bloom and vigor" ("The Duel of the Sexes," p. 111). Her charge against *The Dark Lantern,* a novel by Elizabeth Robins (who had been an early Ibsen actress and was to become a few years later the first president of the Women Writers' Suffrage League), is that "the writer betrays sympathy with the submission of the heroine" ("The Duel of the Sexes," p. 110). The idea that plots coerce women via "punishment" was in the air.[31] As a novelist, how might Caird have understood the words of final advice that she put in the Professor's mouth on his deathbed? Killing a heroine might have come to seem like another way of siding submissively with the enemy powers that want to oppress her.

What changed between 1889 and 1894? England, more than Caird. In 1891, 1892, 1893, that outburst of pro-feminist writings made it look as if England were likely to catch up with her, fast. Temperamentally, as the early essays show, she was already an energetic rationalist; she was joky when other people were solemn, frank when they were hypocritical; she was cutting. She was well armored. Her instinct was to teach resistance, not defeat. (Even Viola in *The Wing of Azrael* makes astonishingly brave announcements to her husband.) She knew how to fight depression, the wrong kind of discontent, and "slow suicide" (*DD*, p. 114). In 1894 she let herself contrive fiction that was more like herself in these respects.

Her ideals didn't change. She had careened into journalism because she believed in the possibility of progress—personal, social, political. Like all reformers, she loved the future. *"Belief in the power of man to choose his direction of change*: this is the creed of the future, and it will soon come to be the distinctive mark of the essentially modern thinker" (*MM*, p. 116; emphasis in original). But her optimism grew as more women were heard from. It began to seem to her as if numbers of women—manipulated, dispossessed, emotionally starved; trained to piety, obedience, ignorance, and self-distrust—could change. "It is the women of the race who are now presenting the remedial 'ideas' which taste so bitter to their generation. . . . The result, in the long run, promises to be . . . a social revolution, reaching in its results almost beyond the region of prophecy" (*MM*, p. 137). She had always believed that "It is human *conditions*, not human nature, which constitute the difficulty."[32]

As far as marriage was concerned, even before the *Daily Telegraph* opened its pages to national consciousness-raising, she had believed in the possibility of "the day when men and women shall be comrades and fellow workers as well" ("Marriage," p. 201). "Such an ideal may be held by the few, spreading gradually to the many, long before legal freedom is attained or even attempted" (*MM*, pp. 146–7). In 1889, the few had seemed too few. For normative diffusion to work, the Old Woman needed to become a New Woman, and the New Woman required a New Man. In 1889 Caird thought the Man would be ready sooner than the Woman. *The Wing of Azrael* had provided the man— "genial, ready to help, quick to foresee and avoid what might wound another's feelings; daring, nevertheless, in the expression of unpopular opinion to the last extreme" (*WA* I, 81)—but put him out of the heroine's enfeebled grasp. That was the tragic situation. In *The Wing of Azrael*, the New Man had wondered "whether, after all, it would not have been wiser to leave Viola with her convictions undisturbed. It seems a hopeless task to free her from them so entirely that she would be ready for action" (*WA* III, 67). The woman's movement cheered Caird. In 1905 she declared about it, "A strong and growing sentiment is a big sociological fact" ("The Duel of the Sexes," p. 117). Now if a woman changed her convictions, she would have some support in her actions and more options for action.

Over the years, as the ideal spread, the general level of female well-being seemed elevated. In *The Stones of Sacrifice* (1915), judging once again the chances of young marriageable women for happiness, Caird expresses an optimism that slides in places toward complacency: "heaven was, in fact, a very attainable state," says one of the lucky feminist brides. "All that one needed was a really fine human type" (*SS*, p. 438). Caird foresaw not just friendly respect between men and women, but also—amazingly, for a woman who had done much to invent and justify the female generation gap—accommodation between the generations. She had come to feel how unfair it was to blame "the daughter's disaster, if not on the woman herself, then on her nearest female relative" (*SS*, p. 449). There would be less hatred and anger in all intimate relationships. Claudia augurs that in the future "the torture of well-meaning human beings by one another would have become a tragedy of the past as surely as cannibalism or witch-baiting have been banished from the life of today" (*SS*, p. 438). Something rather blithe, indeed, permits Caird to write, "Life was a huge scientific experiment. We were all just *trying things*" (*SS*, p. 439). In midlife, she had lived herself away from tragedy.

Fortunately *The Daughters of Danaus* was written at a median, the perfect point along her private trajectory between nineteenth-century fictional fatalism regarding the lot of the high-average woman, and early twentieth-century optimism. It represents that moment, for one writer, at which the swing just perceptibly starts its upward climb. The tension between the two attitudes assures space for treating Hadria's situation with deep seriousness and emotional deference. But it assures also that Hadria will survive her accumulated losses. Even more important, for the reader: by deciding against dooming her heroine to death, the novelist is spared from having to think through and demonstrate in detail how a strong woman's spirit can be broken to make a tragic ending plausible.

Keeping this side of the multifaceted *Daughters of Danaus* in view, perhaps those of us who, as teachers and thinkers, use a category called "the feminist novel" may now want to "start" it, as it were, at a new point. Because of the weight of precedent in historical thinking, the problems posed by nineteenth century novels linking women and suicide (or accidental death) have dogged writers and critics all through the twentieth. It has been too easy for women to end their fictions with premature deaths. Although some theorists have shown the conventionality of the ending, others continue to

feature female suicide. When we start a course or an
argument with this traditional plot, we may find ourselves caught in death and failure: explaining, justify-
ing, exculpating, accusing. The feminist novel as a
category slides perilously close to its male forebears and
then must be rhetorically wrenched away from them.
Now we can use *The Daughters of Danaus* to tell another
story, of a countertradition that privileges not martyrdom but endurance.

V

Vita

Alice Mona Alison married in Christ Church, Pad-
dington (London) on December 19, 1877 at the age of
twenty-three—young for that era. She was already deeply
interested in all questions relating to women. An Englishwoman, born at Ryde in the Isle of Wight, she married
a Scot named James Alexander Caird who was eight years
older than she. They had only one child, a boy she called
Alister James, born on March 22, 1884[33]—facts which
suggest that she used one of the birth control proce-
dures she advocated. About the quality of her own marriage she wrote nothing, and there is only one brief comment on it, from a young woman who knew her in
London in the late eighties well enough to come to one
of her large parties, but not well enough to ask her directly the question that everyone wanted to know. Was
the so-called "anti-marriage" woman happily married?
Young Katherine Tynan thought she must have been,
because James was so inoffensive. "Her own [marriage],
I am sure, was happy enough. Her husband was a most
unassertive person, who was present at his wife's parties,
but was unrecognised by nine out of ten people as their
host." Tynan's explanation for the polemical novels and
essays was that Mona had suffered sympathetically

through someone's—possibly a sister's—"unfortunate marriage."[34] Mona was, however, an only daughter.[35]

Already, in asking this question of inevitable interest to Caird's readers, we discover that hers is one of those many women's lives that, not having been preserved at the time, come to us as shards, few and fragmented. There is no autobiography, no journal, no biography. So little is known about her that even a short life story is more of an archeological reconstruction than usual.

My own construction—based on the novels and scattered indications elsewhere—is that Caird managed to write for herself what felt like a surprising safe-at-last story, in which she survived a Victorian childhood and the shock of matrimony to achieve success in her work, deep rewarding friendship, a wide circle of interesting acquaintances, and a good marriage. There are elements in the portrait of Viola Sedley as a child in *The Wing of Azrael* that sound—if we subtract the Gothic details—rather like the successful portrait a woman of thirty might draw of herself if she felt that she had escaped from childhood without carrying too many burdens of the past. Viola is a solitary, shy, self-denying person. She's an incipient atheist, "disturbed by the stories of holy treachery and slaughter" in the Hebrew Bible (*WA* I, p. 53). "Music being one of her passions," her hour's practice a day gives her the only privacy she can count on as well as a vigorous physical outlet (*WA* I, p. 58). Viola is educated at home by her mother, who gives her lessons in history, geography and arithmetic. Of Caird's childhood, factually, we know only that she started writing early and practiced many genres.

She was born on May 24, 1854—not in 1858, as other accounts mistakenly report. Her mother was nineteen when Mona was born; her father at forty-one was twenty-two years older than his wife. In Mona's biographical entries, John Alison, a Scot, is listed as an engineer who invented the upright steam boiler, but standard histories of technology do not mention him. He was also a landed proprietor who lived off his dividends. Her mother, Matilda Ann Jane Hector, was born in Schleswig-Holstein, into the kind of well-to-do family in which china and furniture are passed down in the female line from generation to generation. No one records anything else about this crucial figure, unfortunately. In midlife the Alisons lived in London—in Lancaster Gate, Kensington—with an establishment of five servants, including a cook (or housekeeper), a ladies' maid, and a footman.

Marriage brought Mona into a prominent Scottish family. James called himself a "farmer," but he had 1,782 acres. James's father was a well-known agronomist, knighted for his work, a large landowner with property along the southwest coast of Scotland, at Cassencary, on the Cree near Creetown. Her husband's mother was a Henryson, descended from the medieval poet.

The development of her fictions suggests that she started married life unprepared and angry. Sexuality seems to have come as a disagreeable surprise, and even worse—in retrospect—were the constraints of domestic togetherness. But she recovered enough to generalize from her experience. James did not prevent her from having a career, and at the height of her notoriety he appeared in full public view with her, letting her enjoy its social consequence. As early as 1888 she was writing on "ideal marriage" as well as on the inadequacies that were built into the system as a system. The modern relationship that she brings about at the end of *The Pathway of the Gods* (her sixth work of fiction, 1898) and those she describes in *The Stones of Sacrifice* (1915) and *The Great Wave* (1931, her last) are likely to have been modelled on her own. The trajectory I intuit took time, but by 1915 it was, as we have seen, so complete that the tone of her fiction about marriage had become complacent. To be sure, she was sixty-one and had been married almost forty years. James died in 1921.

The woman who wrote *The Stones of Sacrifice* had de-cided that a happy marriage was a solution to many of life's difficulties. Alpin and Claudia are "preposterously happy" (*SS*, p. 379) in their "individualistic marriage" (*SS*, p. 383). They have achieved the separate, parallel lives that Caird thought of as the prerequisite for friend-ship and intimacy. They have scandalized "the County" by having separate sets of friends and separate quarters on either side of a big livingroom which functions as their joint and social space. In the same novel, a grim relationship between a former rake and his wife is saved when Claudia arranges for the wife to take a six-month trip to the Continent with the children. It is certainly true that Caird took vacations away from her husband; she went to the Carpathian Alps with her close friend, Elizabeth Sharp, in 1889, and to Rome with the Sharps in the winter of 1890–91. Elizabeth spoke of these trips as necessary for her friend's health, but Mona is just as likely to have seen them as useful to the health of the marriage.

Mona's marriage to James allowed her to travel, liter-ally and imaginatively, between London and Cassencary. She spent more time in England than in Scotland during the period for which there are any records: before her son's birth either with her parents at Lancaster Gate, or in a Caird house in Northbrook, Micheldever (near Win-chester). Later they lived in Hampstead, which was con-sidered high and healthy and country-like, first in Leyland Arkwright Road and later in a townhouse in Goldhurst Terrace. They still had access to the Micheld-ever residence. Later yet she moved to St. John's Wood (where she died).

Her London world was full of literary and artistic peo-ple. To make it so, she had in Hampstead the help of close friends like Elizabeth and William Sharp, whom she had known before her marriage. William was a poet who, in 1894—reflecting a kind of gender envy not un-

natural in that crowd and in that year—started writing
under a female pseudonym. Elizabeth, to whom Mona
dedicated *The Wing of Azrael,* encouraged her feminism,
shared her interests in music, and herself translated
Heine and produced *Women's Voices: An Anthology of the
Most Characteristic Poems by English, Scotch and Irish Women*
(1887) and *Women Poets of the Victorian Era* (1891). William Sharp's success preceded that of the women, so that
at first it was the couple who introduced Mona to "everybody"—Pater, Rossetti, J. A. Symonds, Dr. Garnett.
The Sharps called their Hampstead house, two minutes'
walk away from hers, Wescam, after their three names:
William, Elizabeth, Mona; the two couples attended one
another's parties. Another couple figured in this close-
knit set. The woman who inspired William Sharp to write
as a woman was Mona's cousin by marriage, Edith Win-
gate Rinder, wife of Frank Rinder and mother of Mona's
goddaughter, Esther Mona.

In the eighties, Mona had some connection with the
Men and Women's Club, which meant that she knew Olive Schreiner; Emma Brooke, author of *The Superfluous
Woman;* Karl Pearson, then a socialist, the leader of the
group, and himself the author of a historically oriented
critique of marriage; and Annie Besant in her feminist
phase. Caird didn't join the Club: one historian says she
was refused admission,[36] but she can't have let herself
long to belong. From her point of view, the Club was too
much interested in sexual liberation, both theoretically
and in practice; moreover, discourse was dominated by
men. Viscerally, Caird would have disliked the atmosphere. (Readers of *The Daughters of Danaus* may think of
the girls and boys in the Preposterous Club as an anti-
dote and corrective to the particular tone represented
by the London group.) She did join the most advanced
and the most egalitarian feminist club in London, the
Pioneer.[37]

After her first novel, published when she was twenty-nine, her second appeared in 1887, her third in 1889. A collection of stories, *A Romance of the Moors*, was published in 1891. *The Daughters of Danaus* came next. She also used these prolific years to read omnivorously—in sociology, history, ethnology, economics, philosophy, feminist thought; at some point she started reading in science. She gave herself the equivalent of an undergraduate and a graduate education; she seems to have known exactly what it was she wanted to know. She possessed "a clear and searching intellect, backed by a remarkably retentive memory."[38]

Her own renown in journalism and fiction brought other contacts among editors and younger writers (both poets and novelists), socialists, and people who liked literature. At the party in 1889 that Katherine Tynan attended were the editor of *Literature*, H. D. Traill; the artist Sydney Hall; and Emily Hickey, a poet and the founder of the Browning Society. Mona knew other progressive women writers: Mathilde Blind, who had translated the ambitious, pathetic diary of Marie Bashkirtseff in 1890; Dinah Maria Craik, the author of several novels gently advocating reforms; Augusta Webster. The Hampstead parties were an education in themselves. Caird became known as a hostess; she made many friends. "As friend she was true as steel," some friend reciprocated in the Glasgow *Herald* when she died. She could be funny; and in argument (there must have been many arguments, even in these sets) she remained "gracious and responsive" (*Herald*). She had a zestful laugh.

Our only description of "Mrs. Caird" comes from the spring after the *Daily Telegraph* inquiry, when she was "one of the sensations of that year."

> She was a very agreeable surprise to those who met her. She was a pretty young woman, with a look of honest sunburn about her, and very true, gentle brown eyes, and she dressed charmingly. That year we were all wear-

ing streamers to our hats, and I have a vivid memory of
her green ribbons, going well with the browns of her
face and eyes and hair (Tynan, p. 341).

The photograph reproduced on the back cover of this
edition was published in 1899, accompanying her satirical
tour-de-force, "Does Marriage Hinder a Woman's Self-
development?" Where other writers, including the for-
midably credentialled Sarah Grand, hedged and privatized
when answering the question, Mona zipped into a dev-
astating two-page description of gender discrimination
as practiced in a world where being *female* was the chief
superiority, written very disconsolately indeed from
the points of view first of a house-husband forced into
unrelieved domesticity, and then of a brother whose scientific bent is denied for the sake of his less talented
sister. (This is reprinted here in an appendix.) The photograph published in *The Ladies' Realm* shows a woman
who could be described as pretty, demure, and fashionable. To me she has the thoughtful look of a person who
prefers solitude to the camera's eye. She is rather less
formally posed than the other, titled women who appear
in the journal; she is unsmiling, and by holding lilies she
displays "aesthetic" rather than more "society" tendencies, in the code of the day. Even though we can't see the
honest sunburn and the strong legs that went with it, that
photograph reads and is intended to read "difference."

Marriage brought her more deeply into Scottish life,
both the aristocratic life of the Henryson Cairds and the
rural and seafaring life of their neighbors, with its various accompaniments of religious denial, pagan superstition, gypsy caravans, black magic, mountain walks and
the sounding sea. These material and spiritual phenom-
ena of Dumfries and Galloway fill the cracks of *The Stones
of Sacrifice*. The mansion at Cassencary plays an important role in many of her novels and in one pot-boiling
short story, "For Love or Money." In reality, the mansion

had a tower and two distinguished libraries lined with old calf-covered books going back to the time of the poet Henryson in the fourteenth century. One of these librar- ies had served Walter Scott as a setting for his own fic- tion; when Caird died in 1932 it was still a landmark building and a tourist attraction. (It has since fallen into disrepair and been sold, but Mona's great-grandson is restoring a building on the property as an inn.) In her novels Caird Gothicized it, beetled it over the ocean, moated it. She clearly loved the hilly, wooded, beautiful, warm (by Scottish standards), country setting. Giving it to Hadria as a rather idyllic childhood backdrop seems to me a kind of affectionate taking of possession of the place, as if it had been where she herself would have liked to grow up. But a Scottish manor also serves as a setting for stifling conversations.

Moving into Scottish circles also gave her a boost up the ladder of anthropologically-oriented feminism. Scot- land was in advance of England in many ways. A higher percentage of women were literate. In public schools girls and boys were educated together. In the very year Mona married, Scotland passed a Married Women's Property Act, and St. Andrew's instituted a certificate, "Literate in Arts," that women could work towards.[39] No one could overlook "the striking difference between the marriage laws of two nations so nearly connected."[40] Civil mar- riage was possible. Scottish divorce law "reverses the ec- clesiastical law, and makes marriage dissoluble for both sexes and all classes."[41] When Caird set off her first blast in the *Westminster Review,* the Lords had recently estab- lished that a Scottish divorce was valid in England.

On the other hand, it's likely that the ingrained hunting and military traditions of Scottish gentlemen affected her life in more painful and durable ways. *The Stones of Sacri- fice* suggests how appalling, as an anti-vivisectionist, she found the annual animal carnage. Her only son, Alister, joined the Army; he survived World War I and his mother, and had become a major by the time of her death. A son of his, Murray Alister Cooper James, also joined the Army and retired as a captain. He resided at the Coach House at Cassencary, and died in the summer of 1988. When he sold Cassencary and the library (separately), he saved for himself only two or three of his grandmother's works.

Caird was a prolific writer from 1883 on through the late nineties, and continued writing until the year before she died. She moved easily between fiction and non-fiction. Her essays on marriage thread through her thirties and forties, along with the six fictional works she wrote before the turn of the century. During those years she wrote many times on animal rights in general and against vivisection; she was the president of the Independent Anti-Vivisection League, whose members included Besant and Shaw. She wrote a travel book, *The Romantic Cities of Provence* (1906), which was published in New York as well as in London. The marriage essays had been reprinted in America, and in 1906 she must still have been well known. She delivered the 1913 Presidential address to the Personal Rights Association, a civil-liberties advocacy group.

Her versatility as a writer need not suggest fragmentation. On the contrary, she was essentially unified and consistent; her expanding interests, too, derive from a core. In her travel book she was still a feminist. In her novels she found unobtrusive ways to appeal for animals: we recall that one of Hadria's typical domestic crises occurs because there is no butcher's meat. (Animal rights' advocates often appealed to women by arguing that domestic life could be simplified by having meals that were lighter and less focused on meat than the usual Victorian dinners.) Later, she argued in fiction against the dangers of fascism. The core derived psychologically (probably from Caird's childhood) from what Hadria calls "the awful power . . . of ravaging and of ruling other lives, and I don't want to acquire the power" (*DD*, p. 449). On the one hand, the core contained a great fear of hierarchy, unequal power relations, and the brutality of the strong, whether on the part of individual men, the state toward its subjects, or nations toward one another. This was matched, or overmatched, by a great tenderness toward those she identified as the oppressed and sacrificed: primarily women and animals. The core, then, was emotional, but was always distanced by rationality. Over time, that distance widened.

After the turn of the century, she wrote more infrequently, presumably only when the topics seemed urgent. Most of the qualities for which one admires her as a thinker are still in evidence. She is still a dissident, a *raisonneur*, a believer in progress, a moralist capable of weighing conflicting claims and giving judgment. In 1908 she weighed in on the fraught subject of "Punishment for Crimes Against Women and Children": despite the crimes, she opposed "savage forms of reprisal" that would continue the cycle of violence.[42] When the suffragist movement moved into the street, she didn't join the women who broke windows, went to jail, and were involuntarily fed through pipes during their hunger strikes, but she defended them.[43] As a practical matter the decision not to join the militants put her out of the advance guard of the women's movement. Socialism too might have warmed the noli-me-tangere side of her individualism, but she moved away from it on the ground (expressed in *The Stones of Sacrifice*) that it was linked with pseudo-scientific social Darwinists liable to turn fascistic and kill "criminals" and "degenerates." A few years later, in Mussolini's Italy, this might have seemed prescient; in England in 1915, where the socialists were a beleaguered minority, it was simply odd. Her connection with Karl Pearson, former socialist turned eugenicist, may explain it.[44] Going against the current right after the war began in 1915, as she had in the nineties—but this time, if possible, against an even more irrational current—she argued in "The Role of Brute Force in Human Destiny" that force would inevitably become less idealized; that international agencies would be formed to contain it. A year before she died, in her last novel (*The Great Wave,* 1931), she worried about the use that might be made in wartime of a scientific discovery that produced unending energy from a minute particle. The gentle scientist who discovers this procedure uses it to power a robot that vacuums.

Something is missing from this late work, however— the connectedness that had compacted the early prose and launched it with such perfect aim. Perhaps she had lost some sense of audience and solidarity, the sense that so many writers (men as well as women) possessed in the nineties, that together they were rocking a whole system and risking having hard fragments rained down on their own heads.

This is a reader's version of her later life. It need not coincide with what I have imagined as her own personal narrative, that story of serenity achieved in good part through writing. One can imagine Caird in her fifties and sixties and early seventies—she died February 4, 1932—unperturbed by her loss of notoriety and superior status in the avant-garde, surrounded by appreciative friends and relatives, living in beautiful surroundings, traveling, playing the piano, reading, arguing about the League of Nations. As the hostess of Cassencary, she was seen as "chivalrous, dignified, picturesque," as an admirer writing in the Glasgow *Herald* put it. A reader's summation can be detached from this biographical picture and uninfluenced by it, and tends to be brusque and tendentious and exclusive. To this reader, *The Morality of Marriage* remains a remarkable document about the social construction of gender and inequality, by one of the best minds of that revolutionary time. And *The Daughters of Danaus* survives as a novel that deserves to be read and admired and turned into the stuff we call self.

Margaret Morganroth Gullette

Notes

Two generous researchers provided this essay with some of its most interesting new documentation. They are Vanessa Webster, in London, and Maggie Sinclair, in Edinburgh. For editing advice I am extremely grateful to Jerome Buckley, Lee-Ann Einert, Mary Anne Ferguson, David Gullette, Seth Koven, and Carolyn Williams. I am also grateful to Matina Horner for a grant from the President's Discretionary Fund (Radcliffe).

1. At that time she had published two novels: *Whom Nature Leadeth* (1883), under a male pseudonym, "G. Noel Hatton," and *One That Wins* (1887), "by the author of *Whom Nature Leadeth.*" After 1888, everything else appeared under the name Mona Caird. She may have published earlier than 1883, but that was the first work she acknowledged.

2. Mona Caird, "Marriage," *Westminster Review* 130, #2 (August 1888), p. 197. Further page references to "Marriage" will appear in the text.

3. Judith R. Walkowitz elaborates on the relationship between "West End gender relations" and "the carnage of the East End" in "Science, Feminism and Romance: The Men and Women's Club 1885–1889," *History Workshop* 21 (Spring 1986), pp. 55–56.

4. When "feminism" begins is a contested point, and wanting to date its onset usually reveals a polemical purpose. Since the entire nineteenth century in Britain, as in America and on the Continent, can be seen as a series of losses and victories in the struggle to improve women's situation, any decision about periodization will emphasize some aspect at the expense of others. I am emphasizing an era when more women began to feel their own resistance and recognize that of others to the existing order, and when more women began to believe in their right to manage their own private lives.

5. The conservatism of such women can be gauged, in part, by the advice given in the ladies' magazines that some of them read. "As a general rule, the lower the class of readership, the more home-centred a magazine's contents tended to be." See Cynthia White, *Women's Magazines 1693–1968* (London: Michael Joseph, 1970), p. 82. See also pp. 74–75, 82–91.

6. Mona Caird, "The Role of Brute Force in Human Destiny," *Quest* VII (1915), p. 44.

7. Aeschylus's *The Suppliants* is the first and only extant play in a trilogy about the daughters; the trilogy apparently carried their story up to the murders. The punishment they allegedly received in the afterlife is a later accretion to the myth.

8. Mona Caird, *The Daughters of Danaus* (London: Bliss, Sands, 1894), p. 467. Future page references to *DD* will appear in the text.

9. Mona Caird, *The Morality of Marriage and Other Essays on the Status and Destiny of Women* (London: George Redway, 1897), p. 174. Future page references to *MM* will appear in the text.

10. Mona Caird, *The Stones of Sacrifice* (London: Simpkin, Marshall, 1915), p. 343. Future page references to *SS* will appear in the text.

11. Mill's essay, and the rights argument in general, were indispensable. See also Annie Besant's *Marriage: As It Is, As It Was and As It Should Be (1879)*. They made inequality seem unjust; Caird made it seem mean and ridiculous.

12. H. G. Wells, *Ann Veronica* (London: Dent, 1971), p. 103. Caird knew Augusta Webster, who wrote as early as 1879, "The dearth of husbands was known as a statistical discovery, but it was not recognized as a practical fact with direct bearing on the everyday life of the everyday world." *A Housewife's Opinions* (London: Macmillan, 1879), p. 239. The numerical disproportion between men and women worsened in the decade 1900–1910. See White, *Women's Magazines,* p. 81. Caird saw clearly many of the direct bearings. "Every woman under the conditions of our social order is willy-nilly the business rival of every other woman. . . . This fact has tended to destroy or to prevent the development of all *esprit de corps* among women."

"The Lot of Women," *Westminster Review* 174 no. 1 (July 1910), p. 58.

13. William L. O'Neill, *Divorce in the Progressive Era* (New Haven: Yale University Press, 1967), p. 127.

14. Mary Gilliland Husband, reviewing *The Morality of Marriage* in *International Journal of Ethics* (October 1898), p. 132.

15. Elizabeth A. Sharp, *William Sharp (Fiona Macleod): A Memoir* (London: William Heinemann, 1910), p. 142.

16. Ellis Ethelmer, "Feminism," *Westminster Review* 149 (January 1898), p. 61.

17. Anon., Review of *The Morality of Marriage, Shafts* (February and March 1898), p. 24. The references that follow in the text are all to Margaret Shurmer Sibthorp's "Reviews" of *The Daughters of Danaus* in *Shafts* in the spring of 1895.

18. For definitions and discussions of the "New Woman," see especially (the bibliography is large and growing) Leone Scanlon, "The New Woman in the Literature of 1883–1909," *University of Michigan Papers in Women's Studies* 2 no. 2 (1976), pp. 133–58, and Gail Cunningham, *The New Woman and the Victorian Novel* (London: Macmillan, 1978). *The Daughters of Danaus* has been read by few literary critics. Cunningham devotes a few pages to it; Laura Stempel Mumford's thesis of 1984, "Virile Mothers, Militant Sisters: British Feminist Theory and Novels," contains a chapter with some consideration of the novel; Elaine Showalter mentions Caird briefly in *A Literature of Their Own* (Princeton: Princeton University Press, 1977), pp. 32, 188.

19. Harry Quilter, ed., *Is Marriage a Failure?* (1888; rpt. New York: Garland, 1984), p. 22. Clementina Black, intending to criticize Caird during the height of the controversy, found herself writing, "and I will go so far with Mrs. Caird as to admit that the prevailing fault is a tendency to domineer, to tyrannise, to enforce a surrender more or less complete of the wife's will and individuality." *Fortnightly Review* 53 (April 1890), p. 591. The shifts occasioned by a radical debate can often be most accurately gauged by the concessions that the more conservative find themselves making.

20. Quoted in Henry Duff Traill, *The New Fiction and Other Essays on Literary Subjects* (London: Hurst and Blackett, 1897), p. 38. Emphasis added.

21. David Rubenstein discusses other less well-known feminist novelists in *Before the Suffragettes: Women's Emancipation in the 1890s* (Brighton [England]: Harvester, 1986), pp. 27–32.

22. "Second-Chance Novels" and other eighteenth- and nineteenth-century plots that construct the life course past marriage are discussed in my forthcoming book, *Midlife Fictions.*

23. Carolyn Forrey talks about the way the tomboy leads to the New Woman in Sarah Orne Jewett's *A Country Doctor* (1884) and Louisa May Alcott's *Jo's Boys* (1886). "The New Woman Revisited," *Women's Studies* II, #1 (1974), p. 43. Linda Huf describes "the artist-heroine" created by women novelists as "stalwart, spirited and fearless," in *A Portrait of the Artist as a Young Woman* (New York: Ungar, 1983), p. 4.

24. Caird would not have approved of Candida's condescending infantilization of her husband. She felt that women had too much at stake to want to hold back male development. See "Marriage," pp. 200–1, for one of many discussions of joint male-female development.

25. "The Emancipation of the Family," *North American Review* 150, #6 (June 1890), p. 702.

26. Ernst Foerster, *Die Frauenfrage in den Romanen Englisher Schriftstellerinen der Gegenwart* (Marburg, 1907), p. 53. Future page references to Foerster will appear in the text. Foerster prints Caird's letter in English, as it was sent to Wilhelm Viëtor in the nineties.

27. *The Wing of Azrael* (London: Trübner, 1889), I, p. 78. Future page references to *WA* will appear in the text.

28. The first in any language is Mme. de Stael's *Corinne.* Many American writers aside from Elizabeth Stuart Phelps had written novels about women who become artists or doctors. Henry James's *The Tragic Muse* (1890) describes the development and brilliant success of an actress, but the main plot (and the problems usually associated with women, like rigid family expectations) are given to a man. I would include doctor-novels (Howells and Jewett as well as Phelps wrote one) in the same feminist category as artist-novels: what they have in common is that all of them want to construct a woman led by powerful inner forces to abandon the universal female life. The most

thorough account of early "Medical Women in Fiction" may still be Sophia Jex-Blake's article of that title in *The Nineteenth Century* 33, #192 (February 1893), pp. 261–72.

29. See, in Mona Caird, "The Duel of the Sexes," *Fortnightly* 84 (July 1905), p. 112, the passage beginning, "Why do we never hear of a genius arising among the slum-population of our great cities . . . ?" Future page references to "The Duel of the Sexes" will appear in the text.

30. Mona Caird, "A Ridiculous God," *Monthly Review* XXV, #74 (November 1906), p. 46.

31. By 1909, Edith Searle Grossman, writing in the *Westminster Review*, could say, "Misogyny is curiously mixed with a growing sense of fair play to women. . . . And even in our fleshly fiction the woman sinner does not receive the monstrously disproportionate share of punishment dealt out to her formerly." "The New Sex Psychology," *Westminster Review* (November 1909), p. 510.

32. Mona Caird, "The Greater Community," *Fortnightly Review* 110 (November 1918), p. 743.

33. According to the widow of Mona's grandson, Alister James died in 1950.

34. Katherine Tynan [Hinkson], *Twenty-five Years: Reminiscences* (New York: Kevin-Adair Co., 1913), p. 342. Future page references to Tynan will appear in the text.

35. Victor Plarr is one of those who describes her as "only daughter"; it's unclear whether she was an only child as well. *Men and Women of the Time: A Dictionary of Contemporaries*, 15th edition (London: George Routledge and Sons, 1899), p. 166.

36. Walkowitz says she was "refused admission" (*History Workshop*, p. 54).

37. The Pioneer was famous for its debates, its desire to attract professional women of lower income, and its general dedication to the advancement of women. See Evelyn Wills, "Ladies' Clubs in London," *The Ladies' Realm* V (1899), pp. 312–313.

38. Obituary, Glasgow *Herald*, February 5, 1932. Future page references to the *Herald* will appear in the text.

39. Rosalind K. Marshall, *Virgins and Viragos: A History of*

Women in Scotland from 1080 to 1980 (Chicago: Academy Chicago, 1983), p. 302.

40. H. A. Smith, "A Survey of the Laws of Marriage and Divorce," in Quilter, p. 272.

41. Caroline Norton, quoted in Helsinger et al., *The Woman Question: Society and Literature in Britain and America 1837–1883* (New York: Garland, 1983), Vol. II, p. 25.

42. Mona Caird, "Punishment for Crimes against Women and Children," *Westminster Review* 169 (May 1908), p. 553.

43. Mona Caird, "Militant Tactics and Woman's Suffrage," *Westminster Review* 170 (November 1908), pp. 525–30.

44. "Pearson's response to the Woman Question was marked by the same proto-eugenicist tendencies," according to Walkowitz (*History Workshop,* p. 39).

APPENDIX

"Does Marriage Hinder a Woman's Self-development?"

In 1899, The Ladies' Realm *asked several well-known women to write on the set topic, "Does Marriage Hinder a Woman's Self-development?" We reprint Mona Caird's ingenious response.*

PERHAPS it might throw some light on the question whether marriage interferes with a woman's self-development and career, if we were to ask ourselves honestly how a man would fare in the position, say, of his own wife.

We will take a mild case, so as to avoid all risk of exaggeration.

Our hero's wife is very kind to him. Many of his friends have far sadder tales to tell. Mrs. Brown is fond of her home and family. She pats the children on the head when they come down to dessert, and plies them with chocolate creams, much to the detriment of their health; but it amuses Mrs. Brown. Mr. Brown superintends the bilious attacks, which the lady attributes to other causes. As she never finds fault with the children, and generally remonstrates with their father, in a good-natured way, when *he* does so, they are devoted to the indulgent parent, and are inclined to regard the other as second-rate.

Meal-times are often trying in this household, for Sophia is very particular about her food; sometimes she sends it out with a rude message to the cook. Not that John objects to this. He wishes she would do it oftener, for the cook gets used to Mr. Brown's second-hand version of his wife's language. He simply cannot bring himself to hint at Mrs. Brown's robust objurgations. She *can* express herself when it comes to a question of her creature comforts!

John's faded cheeks, the hollow lines under the eyes, and hair out of curl, speak of the struggle for existence as it penetrates to the fireside. If Sophia but knew what it meant to keep going the multitudinous details and departments of a household! Her idea of adding housemaids and pageboys whenever there is a jolt in the machinery has landed them in expensive disasters, time out of mind. And then, it hopelessly cuts off all margin of income for every other purpose. It is all rather discouraging for the hero of this petty, yet gigantic tussle, for he works, so to speak, in a hostile camp, with no sympathy from his entirely unconscious spouse, whom popular sentiment nevertheless regards as the gallant protector of his manly weakness.

If incessant vigilance, tact, firmness, foresight, initiative, courage and judgment—in short, all the qualities required for governing a kingdom, and more—have made things go smoothly, the wife takes it as a matter of course; if they go wrong, she naturally lays the blame on the husband. In the same way, if the children are a credit to their parents, that is only as it should be. But if they are naughty, and fretful, and stupid, and untidy, is it not clear that there must be some serious flaw in the system which could produce such results in the offspring of Mrs. Brown? What word in the English language is too severe to describe the man who neglects to watch with sufficient vigilance over his children's health and moral training, who fails to see that his little boys' sailor-suits and knickerbockers are in good repair, that their boot-lace ends do not fly out from their ankles at every step, that their hair is not like a hearth-brush, that they do not come down to dinner every day with dirty hands?

To every true man, the cares of fatherhood and home are sacred and all-sufficing. He realises, as he looks around at his little ones, that they are his crown and recompense.

John often finds that *his* crown-and-recompense gives him a racking headache by war-whoops and stampedes of infinite variety, and there are moments when he wonders in dismay if he is really a true man! He has had the privilege of rearing and training five small crowns and recompenses, and he feels that he could face the future if further privilege, of this sort, were denied him. Not but that he is devoted to his family. Nobody who understands the sacrifices he has made for them could doubt that. Only, he feels that those parts of his nature which are said to distinguish the human from the animal kingdom, are getting rather effaced.

He remembers the days before his marriage, when he was so bold, in his ignorant youth, as to cherish a passion for scientific research. He even went so far as to make a chemical laboratory of the family box-room, till attention was drawn to the circumstance by a series of terrific explosions, which shaved off his eyebrows, blackened his scientific countenance, and caused him to be turned out, neck and crop, with his crucibles, and a sermon on the duty that lay nearest him,—which resolved itself into that of paying innumerable afternoon calls with his father and brothers, on acquaintances selected—as he declared in his haste—for their phenomenal stupidity. His father pointed out how selfish it was for a young fellow to indulge his own little fads and fancies, when he might make himself useful in a nice manly way, at home.

When, a year later, the scapegrace Josephine, who had caused infinite trouble and expense to all belonging to her, showed a languid interest in chemistry, a spare room was at once fitted up for her, and an extraordinary wealth of crucibles provided by her delighted parents; and when explosions and smells pervaded the house, her father, with a proud smile, would exclaim: "What genius and enthusiasm that dear girl does display!" Josephine afterwards became a distinguished professor, with an awestruck family, and a husband who made it his chief duty and privilege to save her from all worry and interruption in her valuable work.

John, who knows in his heart of hearts that he could have walked round Josephine, in the old days, now speaks with manly pride of his sister, the Professor. His own bent, however, has always been so painfully strong that he even yet tries to snatch spare moments for his researches; but the strain in so many directions has broken down his health. People always told him that a man's constitution was not fitted for severe brain-work. He supposes it is true.

During those odd moments, he made a discovery that seemed to him of value, and he told Sophia about it, in a mood of scientific enthusiasm. But she burst out laughing, and said he would really be setting the Thames on fire if he didn't take care.

"Perhaps you will excuse my remarking, my dear, that I think you might be more usefully, not to say becomingly employed, in attending to your children and your household duties, than in dealing with explosive substances in the back dining-room."

And Sophia tossed off her glass of port in such an unanswerable manner, that John felt as if a defensive reply would be almost of the nature of a sacrilege. So he remained silent, feeling vaguely guilty. And as Johnny took measles just then, and it ran through the house, there was no chance of completing his work, or of making it of public value.

Curiously enough, a little later, Josephine made the very same discovery—only rather less perfect—and every one said, with acclamation, that science had been revolutionised by a discovery before which that of gravitation paled.

John still hoped, after twenty years of experience, that presently, by some different arrangement, some better management on his part, he would achieve leisure and mental repose to do the work that his heart was in; but that time never came.

No doubt John was not infallible, and made mistakes in dealing with his various problems: do the best of us achieve consummate wisdom? No doubt, if he had followed the advice that we could all have supplied him with, in such large quantities, he might have done rather more than he did. But the question is: Did his marriage interfere with his self-development and career, and would many other Johns, in his circumstances, have succeeded much better?

The Feminist Press at The City University of New York offers alternatives in education and in literature. Founded in 1970, this non-profit, tax-exempt educational and publishing organization works to eliminate sexual stereotypes in books and schools and to provide literature with a broad vision of human potential. The publishing program includes reprints of important works by women, feminist biographies of women, and nonsexist children's books. Curricular materials, bibliographies, directories, and a quarterly journal provide information and support for students and teachers of women's studies. Through publications and projects, The Feminist Press contributes to the rediscovery of the history of women and the emergence of a more humane society.

New and Forthcoming Books

Always a Sister: The Feminism of Lillian D. Wald, a biography by Doris Groshen Daniels. $24.95 cloth.

Bamboo Shoots after the Rain: Contemporary Stories by Women Writers of Taiwan, 1945–1985, edited by Anne C. Carver and Sung-sheng Yvonne Chang. $29.95 cloth, $12.95 paper.

A Brighter Coming Day: A Frances Ellen Watkins Harper Reader, edited by Frances Smith Foster. $29.95 cloth, $13.95 paper.

The Daughters of Danaus, a novel by Mona Caird. Afterword by Margaret Morganroth Gullette. $29.95 cloth, $11.95 paper.

The End of This Day's Business, a novel by Katharine Burdekin. Afterword by Daphne Patai. $24.95 cloth, $8.95 paper.

Families in Flux (formerly *Household and Kin*), by Amy Swerdlow, Renate Bridenthal, Joan Kelly, and Phyllis Vine. $9.95 paper.

How I Wrote Jubilee *and Other Essays on Life and Literature,* by Margaret Walker. Edited by Maryemma Graham. $29.95 cloth, $9.95 paper.

Lillian D. Wald: Progressive Activist, a sourcebook edited by Clare Coss. $7.95 paper.

Lone Voyagers: Academic Women in Coeducational Institutions, 1870–1937, edited by Geraldine J. Clifford. $29.95 cloth, $12.95 paper.

Not So Quiet: Stepdaughters of War, a novel by Helen Zenna Smith. Afterword by Jane Marcus. $26.95 cloth, $9.95 paper.

Seeds: Supporting Women's Work in the Third World, edited by Ann Leonard. Introduction by Adrienne Germain. Afterwords by Marguerite Berger, Vina Mazumdar, Kathleen Staudt, and Aminita Traore. $29.95 cloth, $12.95 paper.

Sister Gin, a novel by June Arnold. Afterword by Jane Marcus. $8.95 paper.

These Modern Women: Autobiographical Essays from the Twenties, edited, and with a revised introduction by Elaine Showalter. $8.95 paper.

Truth Tales: Contemporary Stories by Women Writers of India, selected by Kali for Women. Introduction by Meena Alexander. $22.95 cloth, $8.95 paper.

We That Were Young, a novel by Irene Rathbone. Introduction by Lynn Knight. Afterword by Jane Marcus. $29.95 cloth, $10.95 paper.

What Did Miss Darrington See? An Anthology of Feminist Supernatural Fiction, edited by Jessica Amanda Salmonson. Introduction by Rosemary Jackson. $29.95 cloth, $10.95 paper.

Women Composers: The Lost Tradition Found, by Diane Peacock Jezic. $29.95 cloth, $12.95 paper.

For a free, complete backlist catalog, write to The Feminist Press at The City University of New York, 311 East 94 Street, New York, NY 10128. Send book orders to The Talman Company, Inc., 150 Fifth Avenue, New York, NY 10011. Please include $1.75 postage and handling for one book, $.75 for each additional.